VAMPIRE

OUTLAW

The Immortal Knight Chronicles Book 2

Richard of Ashbury
and the invasion of England
May 1216 to September 1217

DAN DAVIS

For information contact :
dandaviswrites@outlook.com

ISBN: 9781521827376
First Edition: July 2017

For HEMA researchers, instructors, students and aficionados all over the world.

ONE ~ ARCHER HUNT

WHEN YOU WANT TO ATTACK A HALL and kill those inside, it is best to do it in the hours before dawn. Your victims will be sleeping at their deepest and will be easy prey. I have carried out such attacks myself on many a dark night over the centuries.

One late spring night in 1216 it was my own hall that was attacked. It was I that slept inside when William's blood drinking monsters came to burn my home to the ground. My home was the manor house of Ashbury in Derbyshire, England. I was still the lord there but I would not be for very much longer.

"Richard," Jocelyn said. He shook me awake. "Richard, wake up, you drunken sod."

"Get off me," I said to the man-shaped shadow above me. My head pounded. My throat was full of wine-flavoured bile. I had been sleeping heavily, dead to the world.

"We are attacked," Jocelyn cried. "Arm yourself before they force their way inside."

It was dark but for Jocelyn's lamp, held high by his head. The shadows it cast on his face made him look older than his thirty-one years.

I rolled from my bed and pulled myself upright on his arm. "Out of my way."

Usually, I slept naked but I had fallen into bed without fully undressing the night before so I wore a long shirt and hose. I staggered to my swords. Always, I have kept at least one near me when I slept. Keep your weapons within reach at all times, or else why even keep them? I grabbed the best blade from the stand in the corner and the familiar feel of a hilt against my palm brought me to my senses.

A man was shouting outside. A sharp thud echoed through the building. Then another. It was coming from the ground floor, just below my bedchamber.

"What is happening?" I growled at Jocelyn as I pushed my bare feet into a pair of shoes. "What is that fellow yelling about?"

"Sounds as though he is urging us to wake up," Jocelyn said. "And the banging noise, I assume, means they are attempting to break down the hall door."

I grunted. I had made sure that the main door into my hall was reinforced with iron bands and heavy timbers. "They are welcome to try. What of Emma?" I asked him.

"I checked on her. She said her door is barred and she had armed herself behind it." Jocelyn shrugged. "What she is armed with, I can only imagine. A stern word, perhaps."

"Where is Anselm?" I asked as I pushed by Jocelyn. He was not tall but he was as broad at the shoulder as an ox.

He stomped after me out of my chamber and through what was called the solar, or the day room, that led to the stairs down into the hall below. Two other doors led off the solar, Jocelyn's bedchamber and his sister Emma's bedchamber. Both very small rooms but I could never have afforded to build anything larger.

"Stay in your chamber, Emma," I shouted as we stomped through.

She shouted something I did not hear but no doubt it was very witty.

Jocelyn answered my earlier question. "Anselm is carrying our shields to the hall." He spoke French, as we did when talking amongst ourselves.

"Good man," I said, meaning his squire.

Two more thuds in quick succession resounded on the timbers downstairs.

The shouting man outside the hall fell silent. Yet the massive thudding continued as I clattered down the stairway into the rear of the hall. A dozen of my servants waited down there in the parlour, gathered together like frightened geese. All but two were men. Some faces were young, most were old. They smelled of stale smoke and the shivering-sweat stink of fresh fear.

"Do not be concerned," I said to the servants in English as I descended the stairs. "It sounds as though we have a few drunken robbers attempting a raid." I looked at each face in turn. "We must suppose that they do not know who is the lord here. If they know this is the manor house of Sir Richard of Ashbury then they are desperate outlaws indeed, are they not?"

I was never particularly gifted when it came to levity. A few of them chuckled but they were nervous. Everyone in Ashbury remembered the attack on the manor house twenty-five years earlier when the lord, his family and almost all the servants had been slaughtered in the night by William de Ferrers and his knights. The lord back then had been my brother Henry. My half-brother, as I had discovered, although no one in Ashbury knew I was a bastard. So they feared the Ashbury family curse had returned. A few of the people before me had lost family of their own in that same attack.

A huge blow from the fellows pounding and hacking on the door shook the timbers again. A couple of servants jumped, startled at the sound. They had been woken from where they slept in the hall, were shivering in thin shifts and undergarments under their cloaks or blankets. Most were ashen-faced in the candlelight.

Yet, Old Cuthbert, my faithful, sour-faced steward, clutched a splitting axe to his chest and had his ancient iron helm jammed down upon his narrow head. Others had grabbed their spears. Those without true weapons had their daggers in their hands, even the women who clutched tight to their husbands.

"Look at you all," I said. "You brave souls would strike terror into any man who broke in here. I could almost pity them. Perhaps we should pray for them, what do you say?"

The pounding continued. There was a crack as one of the door timbers split.

Jocelyn pushed past me and through the servants and strode into the hall, calling to his squire, Anselm.

4

"They must be hungry indeed to attempt such an attack as this," I said to my servants, speaking lightly. "We must ensure we give them a proper welcome. Cuthbert, see that the hearth fire is started. Light plenty of lamps and candles and have them placed throughout the hall, especially by the door. Do so as quickly as you can and then wait together at the back of the hall where I can see you all."

"Yes, my lord," Old Cuthbert said and turned to the others, his weasel face pinched with concern. "Right then, you heard the lord. Let's prepare for visitors." He snapped out orders like a veteran commander so I left him to it and followed Jocelyn into the darkness of my hall.

At the far end was Jocelyn's squire, Anselm, who was sixteen years' old and full to the brim with a powerful sense of duty. Anselm held a lamp aloft, casting a faint ring of yellow light about him and Jocelyn.

"Your shield," Jocelyn said and generously held it for me while I threaded my arm into the strap. It was kite-shaped, with a flat top. Jocelyn favoured the old fashioned sort with the longer, tapered shape, like a beech leaf to better protect his left leg when on horseback.

"Shall I bring your hauberks, my lords?" Anselm asked, his eyes wide in the torchlight. The lad was, strictly speaking, Sir Jocelyn's squire alone but the boy was performing double duty. I decided I had to hurry up and accept a new squire. It was not fair on Anselm to look after two knights.

The door thudded and cracked again. There were angry voices outside, beyond the door. Likely, it was no more than two or three men, I thought. I could hear no other voices through the timber walls to either side of the hall.

The axe blade on the other side squeaked as it was wiggled from the cleft it had gouged into my door.

"We have plenty of time to put on our hauberks, Richard," Jocelyn said, seeing my hesitation. "They would need an army with a battering ram to break down that ridiculous door."

My servants busied themselves behind me, whispering to each other as they lit lamps and tallow candles. Few of them understood French well enough to know what Jocelyn was saying.

"No need for us to be armoured," I said, loudly and in English for my servant's benefit. "It is no more than a handful of desperate peasants. We could deal with them in our underwear."

Jocelyn looked unconvinced. Of course, he was quite right. I was being an arrogant fool, as usual.

The door shuddered again. The reinforced frame shook.

"He's strong," I said, appreciatively.

Jocelyn grunted. "Still take them forever to get through it. What are we going to do with ourselves until then?"

It was light enough in the hall to see by. My servants gathered at the back of the hall by the top table, as far from the door as possible.

"Do not be absurd, man," I said to Jocelyn. "I am not allowing them to damage that door any more than they already have. Do you know how much that timber cost me? I had to send Cuthbert all the way to Nottingham to buy the iron for the hinges. We shall open it and let them in."

"I understand your reasoning with regards to preserving the

door," Jocelyn said. "But you have no knowledge of what is on the other side of it. You yourself have said to me that knowledge of your enemy should be the first place that you strike."

"I have never uttered anything as absurd as that. Go on, Jocelyn, stand by the door and be ready to lift the bar," I said and drew my sword. I swung it in arcs to loosen my arm. "I should have taken a piss," I said.

Jocelyn shook his head. "I have not seen you this happy since Normandy."

"Men are breaking into my home," I said. "I am not happy."

He snorted and went to the door, leaving his squire standing by my side.

"What should I do, my lord?" Jocelyn's squire Anselm asked.

"You know your duty," Jocelyn said from the shaking door.

I glanced at the boy. His eyes shone in the candlelight. He was brave and strong but I remembered well what it was like to be young. "Stand by Jocelyn's side, with your sword and shield held ready. Remember your training. Anselm, have I ever told you that you are as fine a squire as I have ever known?"

There was just enough light to see his face flush. "No, sir."

"You'll do well. "

"Yes, sir."

The door cracked again, shaking under the power of the blow.

"He is not tiring, is he," Jocelyn said and he spat on his hands and rubbed them on his tunic. His sword was sheathed and hanging from his belt and he slung his shield on his back by the shoulder strap.

"If it goes against us and we fall," I added to Anselm. "You run to the Lady Emma's bedchamber and defend her door against intruders. Understand?"

"I shall defend her with my life, my lord," Anselm said, swallowing hard.

"Good lad."

I nodded to Jocelyn. He waited until the centre of the door resounded once more from a blow and he lifted the locking beam out of its iron hooks. It was a heavy thing, thick enough for a castle keep, but Jocelyn was strong and he pulled it up and tossed it aside, it bouncing and rolling to a stop.

Jocelyn yanked the door open wide.

When that door opened, I expected to find two or three starving peasants, shivering in the night air. I expected the largest of them to be holding a woodman's axe. I would see them cast in the lamplight from my hall and hopefully they would be blinded by it. My intention was to charge into the men there and knock them senseless. I was hoping that they would not give up without, at least, having a go at me. Depending on how well they fought, I would either knock them senseless or spill their guts onto my doorstep.

So I was not afraid.

And despite all that, I lifted up my shield.

It was a reflex. It was the most natural thing in the world. I had trained for years to hold my shield high and head low at the beginning of combat. It was as natural as taking a deep breath before plunging into a cold lake.

And a lucky thing it was, too.

An arrow shot through the door before it was halfway open.

It thudded into the top of my shield, sheering off to the side but hitting with power enough to knock the rim back to strike me upon the forehead.

It hurt.

I kicked myself for not taking the time to dress for war. Why would I not take the time to put on a helmet or a mail coif or even an arming doublet? Sheer arrogance. My anger boiled up and I stepped forward to murder that bastard bloody peasant archer.

A man charged through the door, two-handed axe raised over his head. He came right at me, screaming a wordless challenge. His hair and beard were wild, matted and filthy. The fellow was soaked, his dark green clothes heavy with rain.

For a big, heavy man he was faster than he had any right to be.

I let him come to me. He swung the axe at an angle, down and round at my head in a wide arc. Instead of taking such a wild, log-splitting blow upon my shield, I stepped back. His axe whooshed past my face leaving him overbalanced, his mouth snarled up behind his beard. I braced and smashed the side of his body with my shield.

With my incredible strength, a thump like that would knock most men down, sprawling, dazed, and weeping. Instead, with that huge hairy madman, it was like bashing a stone wall. He rocked back, shook his head like a bull and swung again.

His hand speed was fast. But he was swinging for power, not for swiftness. His strike came from down low, up toward my balls but he assumed that I would stand and wait for the blow to fall, as if I were a tree trunk or a hall door.

I stepped forward and drove the point of my sword through his chest, punching through his clothes, skin and flesh up the crosspiece, which I punched into him and bore him down. My blade was as sharp as the devil's tongue and I yanked the steel out of his body without catching on ribs or cloth, before the point touched the floor. Blood gushed and bubbled out of his chest, front and back. I had managed to run him through the heart, or close enough. The smell of that fresh blood was delicious. I wanted to bury my face in the body, to close my mouth about the frothing wound and drink it down. Instead, I resisted and came to my senses.

To shouting and the clash of arms.

A second man drove Jocelyn back away from the doorway, snarling and smacking against his shield with a huge blade. Jocelyn was trying to turn the attacker, stepping sideways as he retreated.

Anselm shuffled away in a guard position to give his master room to fight. My servants shouted encouragement and screamed in terror behind me.

Another arrow flashed from the darkness beyond the open doorway.

I raised my shield and the thing thudded hard through the layered wood and leather. The whole arrowhead, barbs and all, punched through. The wicked point on it stopped an inch from my eyeball.

I peered over the rim.

Two bowmen lurked outside in the dark, ten yards beyond the doorway on the path. Little more than shadows in the shade.

"I'll gut you bastards," I roared, shaking my sword and shield like a madman. I strode toward them.

The archers fled. They flitted like black-grey birds and ran. I reached the doorway in time to see them swarming up and over the ten-foot high gateway like rats. Then they were gone.

They moved with a speed and manner the like of which I had not seen for more than twenty years and a thousand miles.

Full with the blood lust, I ran back inside to the remaining attacker. That man hacked at Jocelyn's shield with the widest falchion I had ever seen. It was a cross between a sword and a meat cleaver.

"Out of the way, Anselm," I shouted at the squire, who should have been running the attacker through instead of standing back from him.

Despite his attempts at clever footwork, Jocelyn had cornered himself. His shield was being chopped to pieces by the huge blade that the man smashed down over and over with an animal ferocity. His shield all but gone, Jocelyn was parrying with his blade.

"Now you die," I said to the man as I came within range of a strike.

He spun like a whip and his blade slashed at me, roaring in anger with his reeking, rotten mouth. I was expecting it, wanted it, but he was faster than any man I had fought in years. Faster even than the axemen I had felled. The blade cut the air over my head but he was hugely overextended and before he could recover, I straightened to smash the pommel of my sword into the top of his head. It cracked his skull in and his legs buckled.

Still, he fell no further than to one knee, resting his weight upon his falchion. It was a blow that would have felled a horse and yet the fellow struggled to his feet.

William de Ferrers' men, those he had fed with his own blood, had been able to resist such a strike.

Jocelyn pushed forward and bashed what was left of the shield into the man's back. He staggered forward, slammed into the wall beside the doorway, breaking off a whole section of the painted plaster I had done a couple of years before. The man slumped and dropped his falchion by his side. His eyes glazed over and a trickle of shining dark blood ran down his cheek from the crack I had made in his skull.

Jocelyn, his face twisted in anger, stalked forward to finish the stranger off.

"Wait," I commanded.

Jocelyn half-turned to me. "He is mine to kill."

"Yes but I wish to know who he is," I said, fighting the urge to crack Jocelyn on the skull for speaking to me with such disrespect.

"He's a bloody madman, is who he is," Jocelyn said, his eyes wide. "Do you see what he has done to my shield, Richard?"

I was laughing when the man leapt to his feet and charged me, screaming like a demon.

"Christ!" Jocelyn shouted and jumped back out of the way.

I checked the man's rush, the arrow stuck in my shield snapping against his body. He rebounded from me and I pushed him back down against the wall in a shower of plaster. The damage to the wall was particularly infuriating because I had spent money I did not have in order to brighten up my hall in an effort to keep Emma happy.

So I stamped on his knee, hard and all he did was growl at me so I smashed his nose with my fist, crunching the bone and splitting the skin apart. His head rocked back and he settled down, finally, clutching his destroyed face and whimpering.

He was younger than I had first thought. His green clothes were dirty but not ragged and had barely been mended, suggesting they were new. He wore a cap dyed the same shade of green. Like his friend, he was sopping wet from the night's rain.

"You are a keen fellow," I said. "Who are you?"

He snarled and started to rise so I stabbed my sword through his knee and ground the point against the bones inside. He screamed like an animal. And he smelled like one, too.

"He moves as quickly as you do," Jocelyn said, sounding offended. "Or almost."

The man thrashed around and cursed, his voice hoarse from screaming. He was smearing his blood all over my wall and floor.

"Go and see to the door," I said to Jocelyn. "There was a third and fourth man. Archers, both. They ran."

"I am sure they did," Jocelyn said and ran to the door. His squire followed and together they shut it and came back to me.

"Watch him closely," I said to Jocelyn and turned to my servants. "It is over for now. The sun will be up soon enough. There are at least two more of these fellows but I doubt they will return. Cuthbert, I shall ride out for those archers this morning. Have the horses readied. My grey courser. Bert the Bone, wake up your bloody useless dogs. We shall all need food. God bless your brave souls. Worry not about this man here, nor the filthy fellow over there. I shall deal with them both. Now, be about your day."

They busied themselves with excited whispers and I turned my attention to my prisoner.

The man was jammed up against the wall, half propped up and half lying to one side. He leaned on one elbow and his other hand clutched his ruined knee. I had no doubt he would walk with a limp for the rest of his life. His head was bleeding and his nose smashed. A stream of blood welled from his head and ran down his face and neck onto his chest. The blood from his leg leaked onto the floor. It smelled wonderful, almost masking the foulness of his skin and hair.

"I am Sir Richard of Ashbury," I said to the man speaking English. "I am lord of the manor. I should take you to the sheriff, I suppose but I think that instead I shall kill you."

In truth, I had no intention to kill him. My blood lust was fading. His speed and power intrigued me, as it reminded me of the men I had fought many years before, in Palestine. Instead, I was attempting to unsettle him.

He laughed. A gurgling, hacking laugh that shook his body.

"I cannot die," the man said, his manner of speech that of a commoner. His voice was a growl like gravel grinding on steel. "I will live forever in Eden. By the power of the Green Lord's blood in this life. I die and I live again. I cannot die. You can do nothing to me, nothing."

Jocelyn bristled. "He is truly a madman," he said and stopped when he turned to me. "What is it?"

His words were echoes of the mad ravings of the followers of

14

William de Ferrers twenty-five years before, in the Holy Land. The talk of a Green Lord was new but it was the same madness.

"Richard?" Jocelyn said, prompting me. I shook my head.

Could it be, I wondered, that William had returned to England? It was the sort of attack he liked to make. If so, why send merely a few men to attack me? I was almost offended that he would send so few, and those few barely competent. If it was indeed William, surely he would have known they would fail.

Jocelyn sighed at my prolonged silence and sank to his knees before the man. The hall behind me grew lighter as the hearth fire grew to flame and the servants busied themselves lighting more tallow candles.

"Did you not hear?" Jocelyn said. "Are your ears stoppered with mud? A lord has commanded you to speak your name. From where have you come? Why did you attack us so? You know that we are knights, do you not? You could never have defeated us."

The man stared at Jocelyn. His eyes ran, behind his smashed nose, a small smile on his bloody lips. He chuckled, like a saw catching on a knot of wood.

"Do not think feigning madness will save you," Jocelyn said. "Madness or not, you shall be tried and the court will certainly condemn you to death. Do you understand that? Do you? But perhaps you can do right by God. Perhaps the court will treat you with sympathy if you were merely doing as commanded. Did your lord send you here? Who is he? Is he one of the rebels? Which of the rebel barons is your master?"

The man's eyes were wild and full of joy. His bloody smile spread slowly wider across his face. The man licked his lips.

"Jocelyn," I said, starting a warning.

Jocelyn half turned to me and the man darted forward, quick as a cat and yanked Jocelyn's dagger from his belt.

Startled, Jocelyn fell back and scrambled away. I moved forward, ready to stop the man in green from stabbing Jocelyn.

Instead, the man plunged the dagger into his own eye, up to the hilt.

He was laughing as he died.

We all fell silent as the body slumped sideways to the floor. It lay still, but for a jerking foot.

"What in the name of God?" Jocelyn cried.

The hall crackled with the sound of the growing hearth fire. My servants froze in the middle of whatever task they were doing. Anselm's face, behind me, was white.

"He murdered himself," Jocelyn said.

"I saw."

Anselm cleared his throat. "Why would he do such a thing, lord?"

I looked back at the body of the other attacker. It may have been my imagination or the flickering of the firelight but I thought perhaps the dead man's body moved. A leg jigging. Bodies did that sometimes and yet I wanted to be certain.

Jocelyn spoke to Anselm. "He was a madman," he said. "Moon touched."

"We will carry both men into the yard," I said to Jocelyn and Anselm. "We three. We shall take their heads and toss the corpses into a pit by the pig sty." They both stared at me as if I was mad. I cuffed at my mouth. The smell of the blood was making me salivate. "And then we shall eat while our horses are prepared. We have a pair of archers to catch."

With those archers, I had two more chances to discover if my old enemy had truly returned to England.

If so, I would torture from them the truth of what William de Ferrers' intentions were.

And where, precisely, I could find him.

∞

"But why did we take off their heads?" Jocelyn asked as we mounted our horses in the courtyard in front of the house.

It was an unpleasant business and I had taken their heads by lamplight out beyond the workshops by the middens. I did not truly expect them to rise up from their deaths but I could not be sure. If they were William's men, and I thought it likely, then they would have a bellyful of his blood. His blood made them strong, fast and quick to heal. I doubted the blood could heal them from such terrible wounds but it was not worth the risk.

So, to be safe, I hacked their heads from their bodies before tumbling them into a shallow grave. After that, we three men-at-arms had dressed in our mail hauberks and carried our helms and undamaged shields. It was light enough to see by, the sun brightening the damp world from over the wooded horizon.

"Sometimes a man can seem dead but get to his feet again," I said. "I did not wish to take any chances while we pursue these archers."

"Surely they were dead," Jocelyn said. "Did you think they

were witches?"

"Perhaps," I said, not meeting his eye.

Jocelyn looked at me suspiciously. He might not have said it but he must already have suspected what they were. When he was a little lad, William and his followers took him. I had saved Jocelyn and his sister Emma before William could drain the children of their blood. Even then, I had barely rescued them from a terrible inferno that had engulfed their wooden cage, started by William so that he could escape while I saved the prisoners.

We never spoke of what happened in that cavern, what the siblings had seen. Emma was far too young at the time to remember anything of it at all. I was sure, though, that Jocelyn must have remembered me bathing in a bath of blood, drinking it down and curing myself of terrible burns in mere moments.

But it had happened twenty-five years before and Jocelyn was a man in the prime of his life so if he wanted to pretend ignorance then I was willing to let him.

We rode through the gate and out into the dawn, scattering chickens. The air was damp, but spring-damp, a smell of succulent young leaves and the whiff of blossom here and there in the grey-purple light. The manor house and outbuildings at Ashbury were surrounded by a timber wall and deep ditch but they were meant to deter petty thieves, keep animals from crossing the boundary either way. Properly manned, it could also have formed a sturdy barrier against an armed attack.

Mostly, I had built it as a way of announcing my return to the ancestral home after ten years in the Holy Land. My intention was to bring the villagers and servants together in a sort of festival of digging and log splitting. That had been fifteen years ago and the wall was sagging in places. I did not have the money to rebuild yet it remained an adequate defence.

But without a guard posted, a ten-foot timber wall would never keep out a determined man.

There were footprints in the mud that Anselm claimed to be able to interpret as the tracks left by two men running. It seemed as though the archers had run east along the track toward the smaller of my woods near to the village. That track and the wood came out on the roads toward Derby and, beyond, Nottingham.

I wished I had more men with which to cover more ground but times were hard and all I had was the ancient hunting dogs and their more ancient kennel master riding one of my sway-backed old nags.

Though it was not raining, the world was sodden. Water dropped from every leaf and the grass drenched with fresh rainwater. The sun struggled to shine through the wet blanket clouds hanging over us. But it was light enough to hunt.

We rode along the track toward the wood. It was a lane, really, with dense hazel hedgerows both sides and the hedge on the northern side growing thicker until it became the Ashbury high wood. The air was clear, refreshed. Even wet, an early summer morning in England was a lovely thing. I felt good to have killed a man again. I looked forward to catching the archers. I looked forward to them telling me where their master hid.

"They could be miles away," Jocelyn protested again. "In any direction."

"Not according to your squire," I pointed out.

Jocelyn scoffed at Anselm's tracking and hunting abilities. The lad was ranging ahead so could not take offence. The dogs bounded ahead of us, excited to be outside but useless at tracking the archers. It was simply too wet for them to sniff the men out.

"You should have those dogs killed," Jocelyn said. "They're far too old. Half of them are mad and the other half are blind. All of them are as stupid as Bert the Bone."

Bert was the kennel master and nothing Jocelyn said was entirely incorrect.

"We shall find them," I said, loudly, because a lord must appear confident even when he is not.

Anselm rode back along the track. He rode very well for a lad of sixteen, nothing flashy about his style at all.

"A smear of mud, my lords," he said, grinning. "Up ahead where the wood begins beside the lane."

Off the side of the track, he showed us where the ground had been disturbed by something. Perhaps a man slipping, dragging a swathe of long grass up leaving the wet earth bared below. It was right by a gap in the hazel and alder, leading into the blackness of the wood proper. A mixed wood of hazel, ash and oak with elder everywhere in the understorey. A couple of great elms poked above the canopy in the centre. The leaves were heavy, dripping and subdued. The air felt dense and close. Even the birds were keeping close counsel.

"We cannot ride through there," Jocelyn said. He loved sitting atop his horse, a fine bay courser that I had bought for him, and fairly detested walking.

The dogs were so far up ahead they were almost out of sight and playing with each other and the kennel master Bert berated them.

"If you find a scent," I shouted to Bert the Bone. "Blow the horn."

He raised a skeletal hand in acknowledgement and I dismounted.

"How did those dogs miss this?" Jocelyn said, nodding down at the disturbed ground. "I told you they are useless. You should invest in a new pack. I heard Ralph's brother Walter has a pregnant bitch. Good dogs, his lot, you should see them track a deer."

"That would break old Bert's heart," I pointed out.

"He's even more useless than his dogs," Jocelyn said.

"Says you who won't even get off his horse," I said. "Come now."

We tethered our horses and went forward into the darkness on foot with our shields raised, me, Jocelyn and Anselm. A bowman was worth little without his bow, whether he used a crossbow or a war bow. But a single arrow could fell a knight, no matter how brave and skilled he was. Something that King Richard found to his cost so many years before when he blundered into the range of the crossbow that killed him. I intended to keep my shield up.

Anselm went first and we followed. The morning wind rustled the leaves in the canopy above, shedding a steady pattering of rain down on us. My shield, helm and everything else caught on branches and budding twigs and the drenched leaves soaked my mail hauberk. Anselm and my servants would be busy scouring the rust off everything. I decided again that I needed to find a new squire.

"The branches are broken here," Anselm said, over his shoulder. "Someone pushed through this bush, not long ago."

"You fancy yourself a tracker, Anselm?" I asked, keeping my voice low. "I know that hunting appeals to you."

"Yes, my lord," he said, whispering. "My father loves to take deer."

"Surprised he has leisure time," I said.

"How can you even see anything?" Jocelyn muttered behind me in the darkness.

"Spread out," I said to them both. "Leave space between us. Together we make too tempting a target."

It was yet black as night under the dripping trees and I imagined an archer taking aim at me from the shadows. It smelled powerfully of mushroom and mould under the canopy. We pushed on through the woodland toward the fields beyond, my shoes sinking into the soft woodland floor with each step. I was slowly realising we had no chance of finding men, creeping through at a careful walking pace.

Ahead, a group of rooks chattered in their high nests. They began cawing wildly, jostling and flapping in the branches. A few swooped through the trunks before us, like apparitions. Their cawing set off more birds, the noise spreading through the wood in every direction.

"Our archers have scared them," I said, meaning the rooks. "They sound rather far ahead, would you not say? We must hurry."

"They will be running for their lives," Jocelyn said. "And they will be unarmoured. We will never catch them like this. We should get back on our horses and ride around. We could get in front of them by midday."

"You are probably right," I admitted. While I knew I could out-pace and out-distance any mortal man even in my armour, I also knew my men could not. "Anselm, what do you think?"

"Me?" The lad spluttered, looking down. "I do not know, my lord."

"Ah," I said. "So you disagree? Come on, speak up, boy. And keep going. That way."

We kept moving forward and Anselm spoke without looking round at us. "It is simply that following a trail is the best way to find a man who does not want to be found. My father says a man can go to ground in an acre of woodland and it would take a dozen men a week to find him."

"He does, does he?" Jocelyn said. "I take it that your father likes to exaggerate. Or perhaps you do."

"No, sir," Anselm said, ducking the water-laden leaves of a wild stand of hawthorn. "He also says you can flush a man out if you frighten him enough. You and your men can thrash the bushes, curse his name and list the things you will do to his family if he does not give himself up."

"Your father is the most honourable knight in Christendom," Jocelyn whispered, snapping branches aside with his shield. "He would never say such a thing."

"But he did," Anselm blurted. "He won his fortune taking

hundreds of knights in tournaments. Many of them fled the field and had to be hunted down."

"Keep your voices down," I hissed at them.

Jocelyn grumbled. "These robbers are hardly tournament knights."

"Nevertheless," I said. "I agree with Anselm. Or, rather, I trust his father's advice in this, as in all things. We should push on a while, follow this trail. Follow our frightened little birds."

The trees got larger in the centre of the wood. Many were still coppiced but more were single trunk oaks, scraggly-topped elms and a few beech that spread their leaves so well that little grew beneath them. The under layer thinned out and the going became easier. Still, we were all soaked from brushing against sodden leaves and branches and the dripping from the trees above.

"If these bowmen are fleeing," Jocelyn said, stomping through the wet litter behind me. "Surely catching them matters not? Their friends have received their earthly justice and will no doubt be suffering their eternal one today. Why not let these men go?"

"It is a lord's duty to protect those sworn to him," I said over my shoulder to Jocelyn. "If we do not capture these men, the folk of Ashbury will be nervous for weeks. And what if they raid the village? Or the Priory? This is our duty. Remember that when you have your own lands."

Jocelyn scoffed. "The chance of such a thing would be very fine indeed."

Anselm stopped by a small clearing and peered at the trampled grass.

I lifted my shield up higher. "What is it?" I asked, standing behind him.

"Deer, perhaps," the squire said. "Or men."

"Watch for arrows," I said. "Keep your shields high."

Anselm walked around the edges of the clearing, poking at the ground with his toes, looking out for what supposed trackers like Bert called sign. There were a couple of badger or deer tracks leading out of the clearing but I would not have known a man's trail if I had laid eyes on it. That sort of thing was beyond me so I left Anselm to it.

"Did you not wonder why those men were so fast?" I asked Jocelyn. "So strong?"

Jocelyn stared at me. "You are imagining things."

"You were very young," I said to him. "Perhaps you do not remember how William's blood drinking monsters were in Palestine but—"

"I remember everything." Jocelyn stared at me, his eyes wild.

"Of course," I said, as gently as I could. "Yet when was the last time you were bested by a single man?"

Anselm, across the clearing, glanced back at us. He knew little about our past. I gestured at him to keep looking.

"I was not bested," Jocelyn said. "I defended, knowing that he would tire."

I said nothing.

"Perhaps we should return?" Jocelyn said. "We have no hope of finding the peasant bastards."

"It may be best if you go to the manor house," I said and a thought struck me. Had we been lured away intentionally? I should have left one good man at home. "Yes. Yes, go. Guard your sister while Anselm and I push on for a while. That is if you do not mind lending me your squire?"

Jocelyn agreed and turned to head back when Anselm hissed a warning from up ahead.

We all dropped lower, crouching behind our shields.

"What is it?" I whispered as I crept up beside him.

"Ahead," Anselm said, peering low through the trees. "Man lying in wait for us."

I followed his outstretched finger. Water patted down all around, dripping and dripping.

A dark mass lay in the shadows beneath a cluster of young oak.

The scent of blood was in the air.

"He lays in wait," I said. "But not for us."

I stood, drew my sword and approached the dead body, listening for movement. The others stalked behind me.

"Keep your shields raised high," I said as we came near.

One of the bowmen lay upon his back. He wore the same kind of dyed green tunic, cloak and green hood as the attackers who had died in my hall. A bow lay nearby, his arrow bag squashed under him, the arrow shafts poking out into the mud. The dead fellow in green staring up at the branches with one open eye.

The other eye had been obliterated by an arrow. The shaft stuck straight out of the socket. The goose feather fletching shone white in the gloom.

"I suppose they had a disagreement," Jocelyn observed.

"Perhaps the killer did not want his fellow caught and questioned," I said. "Protecting his master, as your beast with the falchion did in the hall."

"Why did they go for the eyes?" Jocelyn asked, pointing at the man's lack of armour. "Surely that is a needlessly difficult shot to make?"

"It is a sure way into the head," I said. "When a man has a belly full of William's blood then he can recover from blows that would fell a mortal man. But I found that a blade to the brain is a reliable way to kill them."

Jocelyn shook his head. His doubts were understandable. "At least there is one archer left for us to take. I suppose there is no need for me to return to the manor."

"Indeed," I said, looking through the trees. "Stay vigilant. He could be watching us now."

"Forgive me, my lord," Anselm said. He had gone further ahead and stood looking down at his feet. I was about to berate him for lowering his shield but he kept speaking. "There are tracks of two men leading away from here."

"You cannot possibly know that from tracks in the leaf litter." Jocelyn sighed and stomped over to his squire. "It is too dark beneath these trees to make out anything."

"Here, right here," Anselm said. "One footprint here, with another laid over it, distorting it."

"It belongs to the same man," Jocelyn said. "Retracing his steps. Or it belongs to the dead one and he was dragged back here after he was shot. Yes, that is it."

Anselm opened his mouth to protest and I was about to say that it did not matter either way when the uproar started.

Through the trees, up ahead. Men yelling.

I ran, pushing past them both with a clatter of shields. They followed on my heels.

At the edge of the woodland, the coppiced trees ended abruptly. Beyond, strips of fields ran away uphill, a sea of bright green shoots, wet and shining in the morning light. We had come out in the upper village field.

Halfway up it, two men fought in the furrows.

One was on his back, scrabbling away from the man standing over him. The one on his back in the dirt was gangly, young, and skinny limbed, like a spider. He wore a dark brown tunic, covered with mud, his hood pulled off to reveal his blonde hair.

The man over him was stocky, older, dressed all in green and held a long dagger high over his head. He was wavering, swaying and shaking his head as if to clear it.

He also had three arrows driven deep into his chest. Blood soaked his green tunic.

Any remaining doubt that I was dealing with William's men was immediately gone.

I ran up the hill, shaking my arm from the strap and tossing my shield aside. Though I wore a thick gambeson under a heavy hauberk, I ran as if I was naked. My sword in my right hand, I pumped my legs to close as much of the distance as I could before they noticed me. I was faster than I remembered and immediately outpaced Jocelyn, even though he was fifteen years younger.

I shot up that hillside like an arrow from a bow, the damp earth flying out beneath my heels, trampling the shoots of wheat and rye.

The stocky man turned as I was almost upon him and his mouth gaped open just in time for my fist, closed around the hilt of my sword, to crash into his jaw. The impact jarred my hand up to the elbow. It shattered his teeth and knocked him into the furrows.

He groaned and rolled over, trying to get away but by so doing he bent, snapped and pushed the arrow shafts further through his flesh.

I stalked after him.

I heard Jocelyn and Anselm behind me seizing the youth.

The man I had struck coughed out a few teeth and spat them out with a mass of blood and sputum onto the new shoots of spring. He fumbled next to himself for his dropped dagger but I stabbed my sword point through his wrist and placed my foot on the back of his neck.

"You do not get to murder yourself," I growled. "You will tell me about William."

I reached down and rolled him over, thrilled to be able to discover where my enemy was hiding.

Unfortunately, however, the man in green died. His breath bubbled as his mouth worked, opening and closing, forming words with no breath. His eyes rolled back. I slapped his face but there was no life there. The man was drenched in blood. Tunic through to surcoat and down to his stockings. The earth was pooling here and there with it. The delicious aroma filled my nose, my head. It was dizzying. The arrows, I supposed, had finally finished him. Drained him of blood.

I turned about in time to see Jocelyn strike the side of the young man's hooded head with the back of his mailed hand, the skull resounding with a sickening thud. The lad fell, senseless and

Jocelyn stepped forward to finish him.

"Do not kill him," I shouted.

"He struck me," Jocelyn objected. "This peasant struck me."

Jocelyn's jaw was bright red.

Anselm stood staring at the scene. His eyes wide but I was pleased to see that they were unwavering. The squire started hunting around again, looking at the tracks and he moved away, looking for something.

"These are no ordinary peasants. We take that one back to Ashbury," I said, sheathing my blade and staring at Jocelyn and Anselm, both breathing heavily from the short chase and fight. "We shall bind him tightly. And you shall treat him gently, the both of you, no matter what he does. He is the last one alive. This lad could lead me to William. Jocelyn, watch him while I deal with this skewered one."

"Here is a bow, my lord," Anselm said, trudging a few paces back to us through the furrows with a huge bow held aloft in one hand, with a quiver and a few arrows over his shoulder. All were muddy.

As I took the head off the dead man, a horn sounded nearby, from the wood at the bottom of the hill.

My dogs howled from the trees and came bounding from the shadows, through the brush and up the hill toward us, mud kicking up in a shower of soil.

Bert the Bone, the kennel master, rode behind on his nag. Soaking wet, covered with leaves from following his dogs through the wood and a huge grin on his scrawny old face.

"They found a scent, my lord," he shouted, as his dogs sniffed and howled at the body, their tales wagging. "There is a body in the woods. He's got an arrow right through his eye, he has."

"Keep them away from the blood. Do not let them drink the stuff or who knows what they will become," I roared, startling Bert from his idiotic joy. He had no idea why I was afraid. Perhaps the blood of William's men would have no effect on animals but it was not worth taking the risk. "And keep them away from the prisoner. We ride for Ashbury. I have questions for this boy."

TWO ~ AMBUSHED

"WHO ARE YOU?" I asked as the young man opened his eyes. I spoke English, as the lad was clearly a commoner.

Jocelyn had not cracked the side of his skull apart but the lad had a lump above his temple the size of a goose egg. The young fellow's eyes were unfocused and he blinked and peered about.

When I pulled off his dirty, brown hood, the blonde hair beneath was long, tangled and filthy. He reeked of old sweat and mushrooms.

I had ordered him sat upon a high stool and bound to a thick post in the scutching workshop. It was late morning and plenty of light came from the open door and open window. Poultry scratched and clucked in the yard beyond the door.

I would not have one of William's beasts in my house. Not least because I planned to bleed him dry. Nor did I want to frighten the servants with what I was going to do to the boy. Though no doubt they would hear his screams from across the yard and inside the house. I could not bleed a man in the stables and frighten the horses. Thus, I decided that the workshops were the best place to flay this man.

"Where am I?" he asked, blinking and mumbling.

"Look at me," I said to him and slapped his face.

His blue eyes flashed with anger as they focused on mine.

"Yes, here I am," I said. "You are mine now, boy. You will tell me what I want to know."

The eyes flicked to Jocelyn and Anselm standing behind me. I slapped his cheek again.

"Look to me," I said. "No man here will save you."

There was murder in his eyes.

"Must Anselm be here for this?" Jocelyn asked.

I kept my eyes on the boy as I answered. "Yes," I said. "Anselm, you do not mind seeing a murderer's blood spilled, do you?"

"No, my lord," said Anselm.

I saw the flicker of fear I wanted to see. "Of course, if this scrawny streak of piss answers my questions then no one will see any more blood this day. Murderer or not."

"I am no murderer," the young man said, speaking with passion.

His voice betrayed his status. A commoner, of course, though he spoke clearly and with confidence. Often, I found that a villager I had treated kindly for ten years would still mumble and stare at the floor when he addresses me.

"Not a murderer?" I said. "Are you claiming that you did you not kill your two friends back there?"

He looked confused for a moment. "They were no friends of

mine."

"Yet you did shoot your arrows into them, did you not?"

He stuck out his chin. "Is it murder when the men you kill are murderers themselves?" he asked.

"Yes," Jocelyn said. "Of course, you fool."

The lad shot him an angry look. "Then it should not be so."

Jocelyn scoffed. "The arrogance of this serf."

"I am no serf," the boy said, straining at his bonds. "And it is you who is arrogant."

I thumped him hard with the back of my hand.

"Do not speak thus to a knight," I said. He glared at me, both cheeks now bright red, and I was certain he would have tried to kill me were he not restrained. "What is your name?"

He looked at me and said nothing.

I drew my dagger, slowly and I held it front of his face. "Do you see how sharp the blade is? I do not use this one for eating or for common tasks. I keep it honed so that it slips through flesh like butter. What is your name, lad?"

His eyes fixed on the point of the blade as I twisted and turned it for him so that it caught the light.

"Is it worth losing your finger," I said. "To keep your name?"

"Swein," he blurted. "My name's Swein."

"What is your real name, boy?" Jocelyn said. He had been raised in the Holy Land and had come to England as a grown man so he spoke English somewhat awkwardly.

"It's Swein," he said, gritting his teeth, still looking at the blade.

"You lie," Jocelyn said.

34

"It matters not what his real name is," I said. "Swein, then. Tell me, where is your master, William?"

"Who?" he asked, as if genuinely confused.

I flipped the dagger over in my hand, holding the blade and rapped the hilt against his nose.

Swein jerked back, crying out, coughing as his eyes ran and blood streamed from his nostrils and down his throat. He leaned forward as far as his bindings would allow, blood dripping onto the earth floor, drip dripping and spattering amongst the dusty remains of last year's chaff. It was bright and shining upon his lips.

I wanted to drink it from his face and found myself leaning forward, breathing in the hot metallic scent of it.

I denied the desire, pushed it away. It was unworthy of me. Base, corrupt.

"Do you see, Anselm," I said over my shoulder, "how a small blow to the nose can be so terribly disorienting? Such little damage caused and yet the distress it affects is remarkable."

"Yes, my lord." Anselm was a dutiful squire.

"Now, Swein," I said. "I shall ask you again and this time, please ensure you answer truthfully."

"No," Swein coughed. "I have no master. I know no William."

"If that is true then who do you truly serve?" Jocelyn said.

"I am a free man," Swein said, sitting up straight as he could with his arms tied behind his back. "As was my father."

"But you have a lord," I said. "Who is he? What village are you from? Where in England were you born?"

Swein spat blood on the floor. Jocelyn bristled but I waited.

"Yorkshire," Swein admitted. "I was born in Yorkshire. We lived just north of Sherwood. Me and my dad."

"How did you come to leave your shire?" I asked.

"Is it not obvious?" Jocelyn said. "The boy is an outlaw."

I examined Swein's face and knew it to be true. The youth looked back at me, steadily, defiant. I should have slapped him again or, at least, threatened him but my heart was no longer on the road I had set it upon.

"Yes," I said. "You were outlawed. You fled Yorkshire and went to another county. In some way, you came to serve a new lord. A powerful man. A man who can bestow great gifts upon those that follow him. He may not go by the name William but you know the man I mean."

"No. You are wrong. I do not serve him," Swein said, straining at his bonds. "I would never serve such evil."

My heart raced. Whether he served William or not, he knew of him.

The lad could lead me to him.

"Why were you with those others?" I asked. "The ones who attacked my home, who you fought in the village field?"

"I was not with them," Swein said, watching me closely. "I followed them."

"Why?" I asked.

"To kill them," he said.

"A murderer," Jocelyn said. "He admits it before witnesses."

"Quiet, Jocelyn," I snapped. "Go on, Swein. Why did you think you could kill four men, alone?"

Swein nodded at me and took a deep breath.

"They were six when they set out," he said, smiling. "After I shot the first one, they got careful. And they were quick, quicker than any man has a right to be. But they were all six of them from towns. Me, though? I'm from the wood."

"I knew it," Jocelyn said. "An outlaw."

I ignored him and Swein continued.

"They hunted me but they never found me. I followed their trail in the day, stalked them and watched from afar when they rested. Like the first, I waited until he come away from the others. Arrow through his head just in front of his ear. Went in one side and poked right out the other. So I reckon, anyway. Don't rightly know what they thought had happened. They just drank his blood and moved on.

"But when I took the second of them, they knew then that I was hunting them. They kept watch. They were ready to chase me, baiting me, so I waited. Then last night, it was raining, so I crept up close, waiting for one to go piss so I could send a shaft right through his eye. The rain weren't too loud and I got close enough to hear them talking, arguing."

He hesitated, aware no doubt he was talking too much himself.

"Tell it all, Swein, tell all and tell it right now," I urged him on. "No point to holding on to anything. Only the whole truth will help you now."

"This were just outside your house," Swein said. "Outside your wooden walls, in a meadow."

"Why did they argue?" I asked.

"Two of them were saying they were supposed to burn your

house down in the night and burn all the other buildings. They were supposed to start fires outside the doors and throw brands into the thatch but it was raining so those two they wanted to wait. The other two said their strength was wearing off every day and they should attack anyway, burn down the house from the inside after they killed everyone who mattered."

"No need to ask who won the argument," Jocelyn quipped.

"They got over the walls like they were nothing. Almost jumped right over the gateway. And what could I do about it by then? A wall between me and them and my bowstrings, even my spares, were wet through because I slipped when crossing the river down by the crossroads. I did not know what to do. So I thought I should warn you. I climbed the wall myself and while they were trying to find a way in, I tossed stones at your house and cried out warnings."

"That was you shouting," I said. "In the night. I remember. I thought it was them, jeering and mocking us, meaning to frighten us."

"I did shout. Then I ran and waited. I hoped you would finish them all off. They were afraid of you, even the ones who said they were not. When the two outside ran, I followed until it dried and I got one of them. The other man chased me. He was moving too fast for me to hit his head so I shot into his torso while he charged me. Three arrows in the chest and he did not even slow. He would have killed me for certain if you had not arrived and killed him for me."

"Your arrows killed him eventually," I said, shaking my head. "Not I. I wanted him alive."

A smile grew under his bloody nose.

"So you killed four out of six men," I said. "Six of William's monsters. Men filled with the power of William's blood. Men who were stronger and faster than most knights."

"If what he says is the truth," Jocelyn said.

"Indeed."

"It is the truth," Swein shot back, his blue eyes reflecting the bright sunlight of the doorway behind me.

"But why?" I asked. "Why would you do this?"

Swein opened his mouth and thought better of whatever it was he had been about to say. "Because they deserved it."

"Do you know where their leader is?" I asked. "The man of evil you mentioned."

Swein nodded. "I followed them to here from there."

"Well, where is it?" I grabbed his shoulder. "Out with it, for the love of God."

"Sherwood," Swein said. "The man of great evil is in Sherwood."

"Anselm," I said and stood up. "Untie this man."

Jocelyn started behind me. "Surely, you do not believe this pack of lies?"

"I do."

"His story is preposterous," Jocelyn said.

"We shall clean him up and bring him to dinner. I shall have Cuthbert find him an old shirt and tunic of mine. They will hang slack upon him but he is almost of a height with me, do you not think?"

"Richard," Jocelyn said, his tone grave. "You cannot invite this man into the hall to eat with us."

I considered Jocelyn to be a dear friend and he was, along with his sister, the closest thing to a real family that I had in the world. But I was also his lord.

"It is my hall," I said, fixing him with my best stare. "And I say who dines within."

Swein looked between Jocelyn and me with wonder, fear and amusement in his eyes. Anselm untied the many knots securing Swein to the post.

"What are you smirking at?" I said to Swein and leaned in once more. Close enough to breathe in the scent of blood drying on his nose and lips. I held the point of the dagger to his face. "If you do anything to make me suspicious of you, if you make any sudden movements or touch anything that I have not given you leave to touch, then you will be the next man who gets a dagger to the eye. Do you understand?"

He paused for a moment and nodded.

"Good," I said. "Because I am famished."

∞

"Emma, may I introduce Swein," I said as I escorted the freshly scrubbed young man into my hall and to the top table. The servants had the hall trestle tables set up and ale and food were being served. Dinner, held at midday, was both the first and the main meal of the day. So it was hearty and could take up much of the day itself. I had known many a dinner to become daylong drinking sessions, depending on the company.

Emma broke off speaking to my steward Old Cuthbert, turned and smiled at Swein as if he was an old friend.

"A pleasure to meet you, Swein," she said, "I am told that we have you to thank for saving our lives last night."

"Lady Emma is Jocelyn's sister," I said to the skinny young fellow.

Like most men, Swein was flustered by her beauty and stood to gape at her like the commoner he was. Emma wore a simple but long, pale green tunic with unfashionably short sleeves. Her hair was styled simply but it shone golden, even in the dimness of the hall.

I nudged Swein with my elbow. "Speak a greeting, you simple-minded young fool," I said.

Swein, I guessed, had lived as a farmer or worked in the woods his whole life, even before fleeing justice and living as an outlaw. His life had no doubt been rough, green, and small. No doubt, he knew every soul in every village for ten miles around and not a single thing about the world beyond.

Emma was a creature from another world. She and Jocelyn had grown up in the Holy Land in a wealthy, noble family after both their parents died. I had abandoned them there, truth be told, when they were very young. But they had received an upbringing that was proper to their station. Emma had been married and widowed by the time she and Jocelyn found me again in Derbyshire. She was around ten years older than Swein, perhaps pushing twice as old, but it seemed to me that the years had only enhanced her beauty.

"Morning, my lady," Swein mumbled and bobbed his head.

"Sheer poetry," I said.

Emma laughed. "Come and sit with us," she said.

Jocelyn stomped by and took his customary seat next to my empty chair. Anselm moved to sit beside him. Emma sat in the chair to my left and invited a stunned Swein to the stool next to hers. The lad had murdered two men, almost been killed himself, was then captured, bound and threatened with flaying just that morning. Yet now we treated him like an honoured guest. He kept looking about at the servants laying food and drink before us as if fearing it was all a trick.

In truth, I was not especially afraid of him. He could shoot a bow, no doubt about it but he was barely into his manhood, I guessed, and willowy as a girl. And I mostly believed his story. I wanted more of it but he was too nervous. I wanted him to feel safe and to begin to trust me.

And if he attempted to flee or to harm anyone in my house then I would take off his hands and torture the whole tale out of him.

"What do you intend to do now, Richard?" Emma asked, pouring ale into Swein's cup. While my servants made Swein presentable, Jocelyn had told his sister everything that had occurred that morning.

Jocelyn spoke up before I could answer. "Turn the lad over to the sheriff and be done with him." He took a slurp of his ale.

Swein's head shot up. "I ain't done nothing, my lord," he said. "Nothing that weren't their due."

Jocelyn paused with his cup half to his lips and stared at the lad in shock.

"Speak like that again," I said to Swein, "and I shall cut out your tongue."

"Richard," Emma said, offended. "Cut out your own instead. This is not a tavern."

I caught Jocelyn smirking. "And you can wipe that idiot smile from your face," I said to him, feeling like a disrespected father to bickering children. "Do not leap down the man's throat every time that he opens it and do not disagree with me. I know your feelings. You have made yourself perfectly clear on this matter. Stuff your mouth up with bread, won't you? Why, in God's name, can I not have peace in my hall?"

"A lord himself sets the example for his household to follow," Emma said, cutting bread for Swein.

I rubbed my face.

Jocelyn and Emma had never respected me. I was their last resort, their last port of call in their travels from the Holy Land to their ancestral seat. I knew they were with me because they had nowhere else to go in the whole world. That was fine by me. I loved them both and without them, I would have no one. So I put up with their disrespect. And they knew it well.

"Those who attacked us were certainly William de Ferrer's men," I said to Emma, as gently as I could, for William had murdered her mother. "It was in their manner."

She nodded. "By that you mean they fought with that ferocity particular to William's devils?"

"Indeed, and there is more. William sent them. Swein here says he followed the attackers from the Forest of Sherwood," I said, looking beyond her at the young man shoving cheese into his mouth straight from the platter, not offering any to Emma's plate. "And that is where their master lies. I shall have the full tale from Swein on the way."

"On the way?" Jocelyn said, coughing out his ale. "You do not mean to travel to Sherwood?"

"William is there."

"That monster is most likely long dead," Jocelyn said. "Those men were strong, I grant you but enough ale can drive a man into a killing frenzy, we have both seen it on the battlefield. You desire William to be so close because you want to kill him yourself. And that has you seeing things that are not true and trusting the word of a peasant outlaw and confessed murderer. William is dead, I tell you. Leave it. You cannot know different."

"Dead he most certainly is," I said. "But that has not stopped him from sending men to burn us in our sleep. I am sure. It must be William. It was in the way they moved. Although he is not using his own name, I am certain it is him. The way those men spoke. They were filled with his madness, with the way William twists men's minds. He has come home. Come home to England, bringing murder and madness with him. I know, yes, I know."

"This is not suitable talk for the table," Emma said, her face pale.

The servants were listening very closely. It was so quiet in my hall that I could hear a blackbird trilling in the courtyard.

"You are quite right," I said to her. "Let us eat. We have preparations to make. I will leave in the morning. And Jocelyn, Anselm and Swein will accompany me."

44

"In God's name, you do not mean to ride us into Sherwood looking for a dead man?" Jocelyn said.

"Firstly, we will ride for Nottingham," I said. "To see the sheriff."

∞

"Please, lord," Swein said quietly. "Do not take me to the sheriff."

We stood in the stable yard, in the murk before dawn the next day. My grooms preparing our horses and my servants organising our supplies and equipment. Jocelyn and Anselm were with us, seeing to their own horses. Anselm was across the yard whispering sweet words to his sorrel rouncey, a well-tempered beast with good stamina and a charge that would embarrass no one.

I wondered what I could do to bind Swein to me. Whether I should attempt to frighten and bully him into compliance or to be kind and welcoming.

"I am not taking you to the sheriff," I said. "I am going to see the sheriff, a man who is my friend. You are merely coming with me so that you may help me find William. Your great evil in Sherwood."

Swein looked me in the eye and lowered his voice. "You cannot hold me captive," he said. "I am free to leave. I am not wanted in this shire."

My instinct was to punch his teeth down his throat and choke him but I controlled myself. Perhaps he saw my thoughts reflected in my eyes, as he took a step back.

I grabbed his upper arm. He twisted away. For such a skinny young fellow, he was immensely strong. But my grip was iron.

"You go nowhere but where I say," I said. Swein looked about for help but my men paid us no mind. "You are outlawed in at least one county. You appear to be friendless. And no man who is not mine knows you ever were here. What is to stop me from burying you with the men you killed, out beyond the rubbish heap?"

"The king's justice?" Swein said, holding my gaze. "Or God's?"

I laughed at that. "I have seen little of either. Listen to me. Does the sheriff know your face?" I released his arm.

"One of his bailiffs does." Swein rubbed his arm. "A great giant of a man, a nasty piece of work."

"So, a single man. I doubt we shall see him and if we do, I shall swear that you have served me for years. And Swein is not your true name?"

He looked sullen.

"Well, Swein you shall be from now on," I said. "Tell me, for what crime were you summoned?"

He scuffed his boot on the ground. "A crime far outweighed by the punishment."

"Do you want me to beat it out of you?" I asked. "I would rather not do so. If you tell me true, no matter the answer, I shall not take you to justice nor allow you to be taken while you serve me. Not even if it were murder or homicide."

He plainly did not believe me. But what choice had I allowed him? "I took a deer."

"Ah," I said. "In Sherwood?"

"My father were outlawed in Yorkshire when I was a boy. Few years back. We went to Nottinghamshire, my dad's brother died, left his land to us. Sherwood was a good place. But the foresters are proper bastards. My dad bought a few pigs and herded them back to our little wood. But to get there he had to go through Sherwood, he had to. No other way. The forester found him, said he was feeding his pigs on the king's acorns. Then they said our land was in the king's forest and that we hadn't permission to dig a ditch around the boundary. They charged him and fined him so much that we lost everything. Then, last winter I took a deer. We were starving. They caught me. Said that as I were sixteen years old I would be tried as a man. I ran into the wood."

I understood why he had run instead of face a trial. A friendless man had no chance against the warden, verderers and foresters.

The penalty for taking a deer in the king's forest was death.

In 1216, nearly a third of the land in England was under the law of the forest. When people say forest today, they mean to say a large wood. But back then, a forest was an area of land where the king himself had legal control over the management and distribution of all resources within the borders of the afforested land. Mainly, the kings claimed land for themselves as a means of generating wealth for themselves and also to create lands for hunting. A forest could be wooded but also had heathland, farmland and villages within. Sherwood had all of the above but was one of the few forests in England that remained almost entirely dense woodland. That wood was some of the finest hunting land in the country and contained thousands of deer and boar, the hunting of which was the exclusive right of the king and his foresters. The shire wood of Nottingham contained a half dozen deer parks and a couple of remote hunting lodges maintained by lords that existed for the king to hunt in.

"So that was where you found William?"

"He ain't called William," Swein said, shaking his head. "They call him the Green Knight. They call him the Lord of Eden. Some folk say his name is Sir Robert. I never saw him. Saw his men, though. They're stronger than you would believe. Faster than you can see. They rounded everyone up. My father fought them. They killed him and I ran. Some of the men who attacked your hall? They was there. The rest are back in Sherwood. I'll go back and kill as many as I can before they catch me."

I looked closely at him. If he was telling the truth, it meant he was a remarkable young man.

"Your arrows took William's men in the eyes," I said. "You must be a fine archer."

"Finest in all England, lord," Swein said, his eyes shining.

Jocelyn snorted. "So says every other peasant in England."

"It is the truth," Swein said to me without even glancing at Jocelyn, who mounted, eager to be off. There was little he loved more than riding.

"What other weapons can you use?" I asked.

"My fists?"

I made a decision.

"Swear service to me," I said.

"You what?" Swein said, looking left and right. "Lord."

"I need a squire."

48

"Richard," Jocelyn said from atop his sleek courser. "You cannot mean to take this peasant as a squire."

"A page, then," I said. "Does it matter what we call him?"

"He is a man grown," Jocelyn almost wailed. "He is as common as the dirt under his nails. You would make a mockery of the position, whatever you call it.

"It is not as though I mean to make him a knight," I said. "Someone needs to replace Geoffrey. I was happy enough without while we were at home. We can look for more men in Nottingham but with the country the way it is, I may need someone to help me."

"It takes years to train a squire," Jocelyn said.

"We will not teach him to fight," I pointed out. "I do not want him as a cup-bearer at my table. I do not want him to recite poetry and play the harp. All he needs to do is carry a spare shield, clean my armour and pass me a waterskin when I ask. Hardly a task beyond a man such as this one."

"May I carry my bow, lord?" Swein asked.

"A bow is not a typical squire's weapon," I said, wondering how it would look. "Yet you shall be no typical squire. But let no man in Nottingham see you with it or there will be questions to answer. We wish to be asking them, not answering. Do you understand?"

"Do you have it, lord?"

"It will be brought with us, yes," I said. "I even had the bow cords dried out because I have seen the power of your bow and your remarkable ability with it. Yet, I cannot hand you a weapon unless I know that I may trust you with it. If you swear to be my squire, then you shall have my trust and you shall have your bow."

"What if I do not want to be your squire, lord?" Swein asked.

"How dare you," Jocelyn cried. "It is the greatest honour you should ever have, you rotten little turd."

"Jocelyn," I said. He turned his courser away, mumbling about having nothing to do with it. "If you do not swear to be my man, Swein, then I will never be able to trust you. If I cannot trust you then I have no use for you. I will have to hand you over to the sheriff."

"If you do that you may as well kill me yourself," he said, shaking with the injustice of it. "My lord."

"You have no family, now. And you have no friends."

"I did have," he said.

"But now you are alone."

"What if I do not want a master?" Swein looked down. "What if I like living in the wood, answering to no one?"

I was pleased that he was reluctant to swear to me. It showed that he would take his oath seriously, not swear one day and run the next. Although, anything was possible.

"Every man has a master," I said. "All that living outside the law means is that any man who is not can have power over you. Can kill you on sight. But when you serve me, you shall have food in your belly and usually a roof over your head. You will learn much that you could not learn any other way."

He scraped at the ground with his shoe. "How long would I be bound by this oath?"

"Until I release you from it," I said. "And I will do so when I find and kill William. Or if I am myself killed."

"What must I do?" Swein said, sighing. "There is a ceremony?"

"There is," I said. "But we must make haste."

And, I did not add, you are too low born to warrant it.

"Kneel. Hold out your hands to me as if in prayer. I will take them, you will repeat my words back to me and mean them in your heart. For the men here will bear witness and God will know the truth in you. Now, speak thusly. I promise on my faith that I will in the future be faithful to my lord Sir Richard of Ashbury, never cause him harm and will observe my homage to him completely against all persons in good faith and without deceit."

The lad did so swear, I clapped him on the back and saw to my horse.

"My lord," Swein said. "May you grant to me my bow now?"

"Gladly."

A servant brought the unstrung bow stave, quiver and arrows, all of which Swein snatched.

The lad caressed the thing like a lover, checking it all over for damage. He licked his thumb to wipe off some stain or other.

When all was ready, I gave the servants my final commands and told Anselm to ride out. Jocelyn was by then through the gate and ranging away, gloomy and irate.

"Lord," Swein said, looking anxiously at the packhorses and remounts as Anselm swung onto his fine young rouncey. "I know not how to ride." Swein's cheeks coloured.

I laughed at his ignorance. "Nor shall you learn," I said. "You will walk. As befits your station. We will not ride quickly, merely fifteen or twenty miles a day or so. Now, follow Anselm. Carry these bags."

Swein was relieved and angry at the same time.

When all was ready, I kissed Emma at the gate.

"We shall not be far," I said. "I shall miss you."

"I will not miss you," she said, smiling. "I may finally get your house in order with you out of it."

"It is your house as much as it is mine," I said. "More so. I would have been ruined many times over without you, as you well know. Bar the gate and the doors each night long before dark. The men know their duty and someone or other will be on watch every night. Every labourer able to fight will sleep in the hall and take turns upon the walls. The door is repaired so thoroughly that it is stronger than ever. I would not leave if I thought I left you unsafe."

"Do not go hard on that boy Swein," Emma said. "He is a bright young man. I know why you took him into your service but with the right kind of guidance, he could serve you well."

"He'll never be tamed, that one," I said. "It is only a matter of when he breaks his oath and whether he commits a grave crime or simply flees. Oh, do not glare at me so, I know his station is not of his making but he is an outlaw, I will not have him."

"At least, promise me that you will look after Jocelyn," Emma said. "He is in one of his black moods again."

"And do I not know it," I said. "He needs a battle."

"He needs a wife," she said. "As do you."

"As you need a husband, girl," I shot back, for the hundredth time.

She hesitated. "I know that you do not wish to hear it," she said. "But I will pray that you let God back into your life. You stop yourself from feeling anything that has hurt you but you are also denying yourself any joy from life or from God's love. It is not God's will that you continue to deny your soul his love."

I ground my teeth and took a breath before answering. "I will feel joy again when I bring justice to William de Ferrers."

"God be with you, Richard," Emma said, disappointed in me, somehow. "I hope you find that which you seek."

"I shall find it," I said, swinging into my saddle. "Find it, and then stick its head upon a spike."

∞

It was a day's slow ride from Ashbury to Derby. From there it was one road straight to Nottingham. A simple, two-day journey. But before we reached our destination, we were ambushed.

That first day, Swein was battling within himself, wondering if he had made a mistake when he had sworn himself to me. He trudged silently, bent under the loads he carried and the decision he had made.

I wanted to question him about William but I let him be, walking beside the horses, his bow stave resting upon his shoulder.

Jocelyn ranged ahead, watching for trouble.

In 1216, England was at war with itself. King John, the youngest and favourite son of old King Henry had ruled the country for the seventeen years since Richard the Lionheart had died. John had faced enormous problems from the start of his reign, losing his family's vast possessions in France one after the other. He had spent years mounting unsuccessful campaigns to regain those lands, beggaring the country with taxes and fines.

Tired of being divested of their money for over a decade, the rebel barons had finally taken up arms against King John. England was a country up in arms. One lord after another had declared for one side or the other and everywhere there were armed knights, men-at-arms, their squires, mercenaries and locally levied commoners assembling here and there to defend or attack one castle or another. Men-at-arms were what we called anyone who fought in full armour, usually on horseback. All knights were men-at-arms but not all men-at-arms were knights. They could be squires or mercenaries or freemen and burgesses who could afford the equipment to so arm themselves.

In fact, every man in England would be armed and armoured in the appropriate fashion unless he had good reason to do otherwise. Arming yourself to the fullest extent allowable by your station was not just desirable, or honourable, it was carefully prescribed in law.

But the road to Derby was familiar and well travelled and I felt safe. Anselm stayed beside me, leading the packhorses with his well-behaved rouncey.

"I do not wish to add to your burdens," I said to Anselm as we rode. The day was cold and blustery but winter felt over and it was dry. "Since Geoffrey left us you have been squiring for two knights. You are already overworked. Even squiring for Jocelyn without the help of a page or two is too much for one squire."

"No, my lord," Anselm said, his cheeks flushed pink with the cold.

"I grew up with many knights and many squires," I said. "It was hard work, I remember it well. I wish I could afford to keep more men. With things the way they are in England, I do not know when this will change."

"I understand, my lord," Anselm said.

"I know you do," I said. "And that is why I will ask even more of you. You must show Swein how to pass for a squire."

Anselm and Swein shot looks at each other, one looking down and one looking up.

"I know this task is not possible, even with a year of work," I said and held up a hand to forestall Swein's protests. "I say this not as a slight to you but because it is true for any man. It takes years to make a knight. Any knight. I was seven when I started my training. How old are you, Swein?"

He did not want to tell me but he did. "Sixteen years old, my lord."

"The same age as Anselm," I said. "How long have you been learning to squire, Anselm?"

"Nine years."

"How long from now before you can become a knight?"

"Another five years."

"You will never be a knight," I said to Swein. "I do not try to make you one. But you will listen to Anselm. He knows everything that you must learn. You must keep rust from my armour and weapons. You must carry them and prepare them for me, should I need them. You will fetch me food and water, on the road, at inns, in battle. You will stand watch at night. You will rise early to build a fire. You will do all that is asked of you, without complaint."

"A servant, then," Swein said, his voice full of bitterness.

"Yes," I said. "That is what a squire is. You think these tasks beneath you?"

He looked away.

"I did these things. Jocelyn did these things. I also served as a cupbearer and server at banquets, bringing drunken lords their wine. I emptied nightsoil buckets and dug pits for my lords to shit in. Anselm scrubs our armour with vinegar and sand, scouring his hands raw. You never get the stench off your hands, I know. You think service is beneath you? Anselm, who is your noble father?"

"William Marshal, the Earl of Pembroke."

Swein's mouth dropped open and his step faltered. He looked upon Anselm with amazement. "I have heard of that man."

I laughed aloud. "Have you, indeed?"

"I am merely a fifth son," Anselm said, undermining my point.

"Nevertheless," I said. "His father is the most famous, most celebrated knight in Christendom. Anselm, would you dig me a pit to shit into, if I asked it."

"You have asked it," Anselm said, smiling. "I do it gladly."

"So," I said to Swein. "You will learn everything Anselm teaches you."

"I already know how to shit in a hole," Swein said.

∞

Overnight we stayed at Darley Abbey, sleeping upon the floor of the hospital. Darley Abbey had been one of the many houses partly founded by Robert de Ferrers, the great lord who had sired me. William de Ferrers was his son and heir, whereas I had not known about my true parentage until I had confronted William in Palestine. Our special blood came from our father but if the old man had known any secrets of our bloodline, it had died with him. William had poisoned our father and then cut off his head when he later rose from the dead.

Darley Abbey had many benefactors in the years since but it was no great religious house. The hospital was small but it was ours alone. There were so few travellers at that time. Most folks stayed in their parish and went no further than the nearest market but there were always travelling folk, tradesmen and ambitious men going from place to place. But not in 1216.

It suited me. I had not travelled without servants for many years. Doing many simple things for myself on that journey was almost refreshing. It would have reminded me of the lonely travels of my youth were it not for the constant bickering between my sworn men, who were all children whether grown men or not.

From the Abbey outside Derby, we had one more day's ride to Nottingham Castle. The road was quiet. We saw hardly a man walking and none riding. The war had frightened many into staying at home or, at least, staying away from the main routes. The brothers in the abbey had warned us about folk preying upon travellers outside of the towns.

"It is sad that England is such a dangerous place that her people go about in fear," Jocelyn said. He spoke in French, as we usually did but I knew he was purposely excluding Swein.

"Jocelyn grew to knighthood in the Holy Land," I said to Swein in English. "He claims that the roads there are so safe that a woman can travel without an escort, with gold in both hands, from Antioch to Acre and remain unmolested."

"I said no such thing," Jocelyn said.

"Not sober, anyway," I said to Swein, who grinned. "Listen, all of you. Monks are terrified of the world. They shut themselves away because they are cowards. Monks impart nothing but fear because that is all they have to give. Never was there a monk in all the world who did not warn travellers of the dangers of the roads. They seek to frighten you into giving alms. Monks and priests are peddlers of fear. A war in the land is good fortune for every religious house, order, monk, deacon and bishop."

"Do not listen to this man, Anselm," Jocelyn said. "He is making a jest."

Perhaps Jocelyn was warning me not to say anything that may get back to Anselm's mighty father. If so, it was probably good advice.

"Sherwood stretches north many miles from Nottingham, does it not?" I said to Swein, wondering how I would search so large a place.

"It's a right big place, alright."

"Then you had better lead me to where William hides."

We rode for a while up and down the hills. The land was coming into full bloom. White blossom lining the hedgerows.

"Are there outlaws in these parts?" I asked, looking at a dark band of trees on the horizon.

"There are outlaws everywhere, lord."

Ten miles from Derby, the road passed through a sizable wood, at least, a couple of miles long. It looked to be full of sturdy oak and uncounted coppiced ash beneath.

"May I hunt, lord?" Swein asked, holding up his unstrung bow.

"We do not have time to wait while you amuse yourself," I said. "We must reach Nottingham before nightfall."

"I'll run ahead through the wood alongside the road," he said. "I move quickly. I may find us a deer or a boar."

Jocelyn laughed from his belly, startling his horse. "You'd be lucky to find a dormouse in these woods."

"I must practice my bow," Swein said, attempting another angle in his argument.

I looked down at him. "Go, then, if you must. But you must find us at the other side of the wood, upon the road. We will wait for you until midday."

He nodded his thanks and ran to the south, crashing through the undergrowth, and vanished into the gloom.

Jocelyn stared at me. "And that is the last you shall see of him."

"Possibly," I said. "He has told me enough to make a start."

In truth, I felt wounded by his betrayal. I had offered him the chance to squire for me. Knights from the best families in England offered me their sons that they may learn from me the skill in battle that had made me famous. And the filthy commoner had betrayed his oath almost as soon as it was uttered.

"I will have to find another squire," I said to Jocelyn. "When we get to Nottingham, I am sure there will be some lads or grown men who would leap into the arms of my employment."

"A squire for you and some general servants," Jocelyn said, whom I kept armed and equipped at my own expense. I loved him like a son and he loved to spend my money.

The robber's ambush was sprung was when we were about halfway through the wood.

Jocelyn, riding ahead of Anselm and me as usual, came galloping back to us from beyond a bend in the road. He cared greatly for horses, his own mounts he loved, and would never sweat them unnecessarily.

"A line of brush has been dragged across the road," he said. "Less than half a mile away."

I looked around into the shadows of the wood to either side. The wind rustled the young leaves above. It was not possible to see more than a few yards through the dense coppiced ash poles stretching away.

"Surely, robbers would not attack two knights and a squire?" I looked to Anselm for confirmation, as if he would know.

"It was a hard winter," Jocelyn said, shrugging. "And the hungry peasants grow bold."

"Perhaps the brush has been there a while," I said to him while drawing my own sword. "Perhaps the men are already far away with their spoils."

"The travellers in front of us this morning must have passed through the wood," Jocelyn said. "This trap was laid for us. They are out there. No doubt they are heading back to us here through the trees."

"Get our shields," I said to Anselm.

The good lad was already moving, sliding from his saddle to go for the packhorses behind when the first arrows came flitting in.

The first I saw cut the air where Anselm had been sitting. The second I felt as it smashed into my shoulder, hard enough to throw me from my horse.

I smashed into the road and knocked the wind from my chest.

A broken arrow shaft stuck out sideways from my upper arm. I must have snapped it as I fell.

Someone was shouting. Jocelyn.

My dear grey courser bolted. As always, my sword was still in my hand.

"Run for the trees," Jocelyn cried.

It was good advice. If surrounded, choose a place, attack it with all your might and break free of the encirclement. More arrows thumped in. I was exposed, vulnerable. I rolled to my feet and staggered toward the trees after Jocelyn and Anselm.

Without my hauberk, I felt naked. An arrow slashed through a bush next to me and clattered into a coppiced stand of hazel.

There were men there. The robbers had driven us from one side of the road into the arms of their fellows, who came screaming out of the trees with spears and axes.

The pain in my shoulder vanished. Three men converged on me, their faces contorted with the rage of battle, the first thrusting a long spear underarm, up toward my belly. The man on my left was big-boned but thin. He attacked with an old sword that he swung at my head as though he were splitting a log, his yellow teeth bared, spraying spittle into his beard. To my right, a young fellow screamed a wordless, high cry and thrust at my legs with his staff, hoping to trip me or smash a knee.

All my life, I had been either fighting or training to fight. I was always strong, quick, and skilful. Ever since I was first killed in the Holy Land, my physical abilities had been even greater. The men rushing me were full of desperate rage, fully committed to killing. My left arm was numbed and practically useless. I was unarmoured. But bringing death to my enemies was my purpose in life.

I flicked the spearhead aside with my blade and stepped inside the thrust, the point sliding past me and I thrust my sword through his guts, stepping close enough to him to smell his sour breath. I pushed him away off my blade. As I did so, I sliced the leading edge across his body, spilling the thick ropes of his guts out into the leaf litter, leaving a trail of offal as he went reeling away. The stink of blood and hot shit filled the air. The swordsman was following up his missed swing, grunting with the strain of changing direction when his weight was all in the blow itself. I twisted and ripped my point through his throat. He let go of his sword and clutched his destroyed throat, staring at me as he staggered backward. His mouth was a black hole. Blood sprayed from it and his neck as I turned on the boy with the quarterstaff, who was backing away shouting something in a confused scream. I ran him through the heart and his blood pulsed out as he fell back, dying. He put his hands over his chest as if he could hold in the blood. His face turned white. In the moment before his eyes closed, he knew he was about to die.

Jocelyn and Anselm had been fighting other men. The memory of it, the awareness of their combat nearby while I had been fighting my own battle, came back to me.

Those men they had fought were dead, too, a pair of them lying in a swathe of bright green nettles. Blood spattered the young leaves. Jocelyn and Anselm stood together, breathing heavily. Their swords were bloodied. Neither my knight nor his squire appeared to be injured.

The bowmen on the other side of the road had fled or were hiding, no doubt horrified by the swift deaths of their friends.

"The boy was begging for his life," Jocelyn said stepping behind me. "When you ran him through."

"He was?" Dark blood flowed from his chest, soaking his plain tunic.

"Look how young he was. Not more than twelve or thirteen, perhaps."

The smell of the blood was overwhelming. My mouth watered.

"You are wounded," Jocelyn said, pointing at the arrow sticking from the top of my arm.

"Cut it out," I said. "Anselm? Are you well?"

The young squire was staring at the blood on his sword, his eyes wild when they turned to me. "Lord? Yes, lord." He gulped.

"Did you kill your first man?" I asked him. The two dead men in the nettles where Anselm stood had their heads slashed and bashed in.

"I am not certain," he said, voice shaking and looking to

Jocelyn, who shrugged. I understood. Most men are confused by battle and they say it quickly fades from memory.

"Anselm fought very well," Jocelyn said. "He kept his head, parried, moved in the proper fashion. Just as we have trained. Yes, he did very well."

"Well done, lad. We shall discuss every detail later over ale and wine," I said. "Firstly, you must catch the horses before their fellows take them away. Jocelyn will help you after he removes this arrow."

Jocelyn took his dagger, sliced away my clothes and held the point against the flesh where it was drawn in, around the broken shaft. "Perhaps we should wait until we can get you to Nottingham. There will be monks there. If you are blessed, perhaps even a barber."

"Cut it out, you coward," I said. "Be quick about it."

Jocelyn licked his lips and hesitated. "The monks—" he started.

"For the love of God," I cried. "Go. Assist Anselm with the horses. Those bowmen will marshal their courage soon enough."

Relief flooded his features. "Are you sure you can manage yourself?" he asked. "You will make a mess of your arm."

"I will heal," I said, staring at the blood still welling from the dead boy's chest. "When you catch the horses, clear the brush that closed the path. I shall come and find you there."

Jocelyn followed my eyes. I caught his look of disgust and horror before he turned away and hurried down the road.

I took my dagger and wiped the blade upon my surcoat. My left hand I placed upon a sturdy trunk and twisted my shoulder so I could see the entry place of the arrow. Likely, it would be headed with the barbed broadhead type. I would have to cut away much flesh, slicing down to the bone, in order to free the path that the barbs must take. Without knowing how the arrow was oriented, I did not know where to cut the line. So I started in along the shaft, pushing the point of my dagger against the skin. It depressed a long way before the skin gave way with a sudden, wet pop. The pain speared through me and I was worried because it hurt and yet that was the least of it. I recalled that I had experienced much worse, many times over. Steeling myself, I sawed down, slicing through the flesh. Blood welled out, hot and fragrant. I was thirsty. The pain burned and sweat pricked out all over my body. I glanced around, checking no man was near. The wood was quiet, even starting to fill with birds flying back. Crows cawed overhead, drawn by the scent of fresh death and a pair of pigeons clattered away from them.

Blood had obscured the wound. My water and wine were on the horses so I had to continue by feel alone. I sawed down until the tip of my dagger was tapping against both the bone and the point of the arrowhead. The tip was lodged in the bone itself. I paused while I vomited a little then felt around with the dagger to find the orientation of the barbs. I sawed my way back out, above them. Blood flowed freely and I dropped my dagger twice as my hand was slippery with it. When I felt I had enough flesh cut away, I wiped my hand upon my surcoat, gripped the shaft and pulled. Agony shot through me. It was as though I could feel every bone in my body.

I cursed myself for my weakness, ground my teeth and yanked

the thing out with a cry loud enough to terrify even the crows. The blood gushed out while I held on to the tree for a long moment. I knew I was not yet done. I peered closely at the arrowhead. The point had bent, compressed from hitting my bone but otherwise seemed whole. Anything not of your body that remains inside a wound would encourage corruption. I had seen it many times in others. I thrust my fingers inside and felt around. There was a scrap of my linen shirtsleeve inside that I had mistaken for a long blood clot. When I was close to certain, I sat for a moment.

Anselm and Jocelyn would be waiting. Other travellers would be along the road soon. I walked passed the bodies of the three I had killed. Already, the death smell was overwhelming.

The crows had returned and a brave few stood upon the earth, watching me.

The bearded man, so full of fury in life, looked at peace but for his ruined throat. His eyes were still open though one eye was white and the other red. I stepped around the trail of quivering, gelatinous guts joined to the spearman and knelt by the boy I had stabbed in the heart. I tried to avoid looking at his face. His blood was drying up and his body growing cold.

I had to hurry. I looked out along the road. No one was around. I slit the boy's dirty clothes and exposed the wound. He stank but I had to have blood if my arm was to heal. And I needed my arm to kill William.

I dug out a few clots from the wound, sank my lips to it and sucked in the blood. It had been so long since I had tasted it. The blood from inside him was yet warm and that warmth spread through me until it burned with a wondrous heat. Like hot sunlight on a cold day. Like cold water from a spring after a hot day. I drank until my belly was heavy with it and then I drank some more.

A noise. I looked up, my hearing improved by the magic of the blood. A figure moved in the trees on the other side of the road, knew it was spotted and fled, slipping through the wood. The man moved with skill, making barely a rustle or snapping a twig. But the blood allowed me to hear him crashing away like a boar.

I wiped myself down, collected my sword and followed the road.

At the edge of the wood, with our horses, Jocelyn and Anselm waited.

And beside them, his bow at his side, stood Swein.

THREE ~ THE LADY MARIAN

"THE LAD LOOKS TERRIFIED," JOCELYN SAID to me in French as we rode the final miles to Nottingham.

We were well on our guard, dressed for war in mail with our shields slung and helms at hand. The shadows grew long before us along the road. Every few yards there was another blossoming bush in the hedgerow perfuming the evening air. I prayed that no enemy lurked beyond them.

He was speaking of Swein, who had shocked Jocelyn by returning to us after all. Swein walked beside Anselm's rouncey, a way behind us, with his head lowered and his face unseen inside his hood.

"He saw me," I said, keeping my eyes on the hedgerows.

I doubted we would be ambushed again. There were people about on the road, heading to Nottingham from the countryside.

Most walking, a few driving a cow or a sheep and one with a tired old pony pulling a cart loaded with shit-stinking chicken crates. They all gave us space, taking off their caps and staring at us going about so armed. Knights were one thing. Knights armoured for war meant trouble and the sight of us no doubt made them fear war would follow. My shoulder had fully healed, the blood doing its work in moments. Yet, I would not be caught out again. Let the peasants fear.

"He saw you?" Jocelyn asked. "You do not mean he saw you drinking?"

"At the end, he was in the trees." I kept my voice low, though I thought Swein would likely not understand French. "I suspect he believed he was well hidden."

"You saw that it was him?"

"It must have been him," I said.

Jocelyn shook his head. "If it was, why ever would he have returned?"

I looked at Jocelyn. "You saw me drink, once, when you were a boy. Yet you returned."

"That is different." His mouth wrinkled up as if tasting something foul.

"It is," I allowed. "Well, whatever his reason, he is here now."

Jocelyn looked over his shoulder. "Have you considered that he led us there? That he disappeared at precisely the right moment? That he was one of the archers? It may have been him that shot you."

"Of course I considered it," I said, irritated that he thought me so foolish. "Yet the fletching on the arrows that were shot at us was grey."

"So?"

"Swein's are white," I said.

Jocelyn pursed his lips. "Perhaps he borrowed his friend's arrows."

"Perhaps. But if he had been a part of it," I said, "why did he come back?"

Jocelyn thought for a while. "Could he be William's man after all?"

I considered it. "Could be."

"What are you going to do about it?" Jocelyn said.

"I do not know," I admitted. "Watch my back?"

We arrived with the sun low in the sky and the air growing cool. Nottingham was a thriving place. It was not a market day, nor a holy day nor a Sunday and yet it was busier even than Derby. The castle sat high on a natural sandstone cliff edge on the southwestern corner of town, covering the approach road. The town arced along the northern side of a bend in the wide, meandering River Trent.

While we found rooms, I sent Anselm up to the castle to ask if the sheriff would see me and if so, when I could call upon him. We handed the horses to the grooms at the stable, along with dire warnings should they not be properly cared for.

Swein was nervous, peering out of the stable into the street. "I should not be here."

"You are unlikely to see the bailiffs, are you not?" I lowered my voice. "Even if they claim to know you, I shall state you have served me for two years. Swein is not the name they know you by, so do not concern yourself. If anyone tries to take you from me I shall bash his bloody skull."

Swein attempted a smile but his face was white as bleached bone. I was sure he had seen me, he was afraid of me and yet he stood bravely before me. His will was strong, even back then when he was so young.

Anselm returned.

"Sir Richard," Anselm said. "They told me that the sheriff wants to see you immediately." Anselm was good enough to speak in English, which we rarely did when alone. He spoke thusly so that Swein would understand what was being said. I resolved to do the same and speak in English whenever my new squire was in hearing.

"The sheriff wants to see me tonight? Not the morning? Very well, you all eat and drink and I shall be back later."

Jocelyn offered to send Anselm to serve me, as befitted my station or even to come with me himself but I wanted them to rest. I needed them all to be strong for the fight against William.

The castle at Nottingham was a fine, neat place, built atop an imposing sandstone cliff with the River Leen running at the base. Not a huge river and not a large castle but a formidable place to assault none the less.

After waiting at the gate for what seemed to be a long time, I was escorted through the outer gate, the bailey and inner wall into the castle keep and the Great Hall.

The sheriff's men were drinking at the tables in the gloom. A couple of well-dressed knights sat at the top table. There were no women, other than a couple of servants moving about. It was quiet. The men's eyes followed me as I was led through.

The sheriff was not there.

He was up a flight of stairs at the end of the hall, sitting at a table in his solar, attended by two clerks and a priest. They were gathered about the table behind stacked rolls of parchment and scratching away at a fresh section when I was introduced.

The sheriff, Roger de Lacy, looked up from his work and stared at me, confused for a moment. He started and lurched to his feet.

"By God," he said, pushing his clerks aside and coming around the table. "By God, Richard, can that truly be you?" He peered at my face, narrowing his eyes.

I had been expecting a reaction of some kind, because of my complete lack of ageing. I had no way to explain it. How could I say that I had been killed and resurrected by unknown means at the age of twenty-two?

"Roger, I am so pleased to see you again," I said.

He had greyed and filled out. He was bulky underneath his superbly rich cloth and his belly stretched his tunic tight. His face was deeply lined and his eyes were tired and sagging. But the young man I had known many years ago was still there and he had aged better than most men. Especially one who was never active in the martial sense. Roger de Lacy was an enormously able administrator and a wily politician but he had rarely taken up arms. As a local representative of the king, his position as sheriff had infested him personally with the unpopularity of King John.

"Richard, I do not understand this," Roger said, stepping slowly toward me, peering at my face. "Do my eyes deceive me?

You have not aged a day. How long has it been?"

"I am told that I have retained my youthful aspect."

"Retained your youthful aspect?" Roger grabbed a lamp from his desk and held it close to my face. I blinked at the light. "You still look like a twenty-year-old boy. Ten years ago, I could forgive it but now we are almost fifty. What sorcery is this?"

"What can I say?" I said, pushing the lamp away from my face. "I have been blessed. No doubt the years will catch up with me all of a sudden. Now, tell me, Roger, how do you yourself fare?"

He shook his head, put the lamp down and took my arm. "I am beset on all sides by madmen," he said, fervently. "And that was why I was as delighted as I was surprised to hear you had come to my gate. Take a stool, come on. Will you take a drink? Of course you will. I have some very fine stuff, the finest. Come, take your seat, take a drink."

I took both, gladly. The power of the blood was fading.

"Beset by madmen, you said?" I asked, glancing at the young priest, who was not introduced.

A servant came in the small side door, poured for us and retired without a word.

"You come to me dressed for war," he said, looking me up and down and I was suddenly aware of my stench. "Is there news I must know? Do you have word for me from your lord? I must say, I am astonished Hugh has finally allowed you to leave your lands."

"The archbishop did not grant me leave," I said. "I came of my own volition. I have no news of the war, nor knowledge of it. Indeed, I was hoping that you could inform me."

"I am honoured," he said, waving his clerks away. The priest lurked but Roger shot him a look and he also backed out. "So you came simply to discuss the war?"

I took a drink. "This wine is wonderful."

He snorted. "It costs a fortune. How I wish the king had not lost Gascony. I heard you were there?"

"I am sure that you did."

Roger laughed. "I never believed what they said about you." He looked at me closely again. "Not until you walked through that door. Is this why the archbishop keeps you locked away? Because of your disgusting eternal youth?"

"I am sure he has his reasons. But whatever they truly are, it is beyond me. You must see him more than I do."

"He is almost always with the king," the sheriff said, clearing his throat. "Or in York. Or seeing to his own lands, which continue to be acquired, here and there. On occasion, he has honoured me with his presence on his way to or from York. So, Richard. If he has not let you off your leash, why are you here?"

"I hear there is trouble in Sherwood."

He nodded without meeting my eye, drinking. "There is always trouble in Sherwood."

"Oh?" I said. "There is no new figure arrived in the shire, no outlaw leader?"

He looked up sharply. "I do not remember you as a man who dances around your meaning. What do you know, Richard?"

"A tinker came to my hall. He had come from somewhere up north and he said there were murders happening in Sherwood. A new leader, uniting the outlaws and robbers."

"These people are always banding together for a time. Leaders never last long."

"Is there a reason you are ignoring my question, Roger?"

He sighed and stood up, crossing to his narrow window. Night had fallen outside. "I am not certain you should become involved in this. In fact, I know that you should not."

"What is it?"

He turned to face me.

"I first heard about this fellow the summer before last. Some of the men living in the forest fled. A handful fell into our hands. They all told the same story. A new man living deep in the green wood at some special place. None of them could agree on where in the wood it was but they all said he was a knight. A nobleman. Nonsense, of course. They all claim to be some disposed, wronged hero when they are in fact a burglar from Bodmin. Nevertheless, whoever he was he was scaring men that I would have placed money on being beyond fear. I sent my best bailiff, John, to Mansfield to find out if there was any truth to the rumours. He was to go from there into the centre of the woodland." Roger paused to look out the window again.

"And?" My heart thudded against my chest.

"My chief bailiff never returned, nor the men I sent with him. John the Bailiff was a good man. Not kind, not at all, but he was sharp and I relied upon him. He had his ear to the ground, despite his head being so far above it. But they disappeared. Then the bodies of villagers and outlaws starting washing up dead in the fall rains. Washing up against Cunigsworth Ford. Others were found in the Rivers Meden, the Maun and in Rainworth Water. A dozen, all told. Men and women both, even a child. Killed from being savaged about the neck."

I gripped the table as sweat broke out all over my body. My muscles tensed, I resisted the urge to leap up and throw over the table.

Roger nodded at my expression. "Yes, like you, I too thought of the massacre of Ashbury Manor."

I took a slow breath. "Why did I not hear of this?"

"The forester and his deputies claimed it was all the work of a wolf or a bear. The wounds were well washed by the waters and the skin was clearly torn, not cut. And the bodies were bloated and many corrupted so it was simple enough to claim it was thus. Most of all, the victims were largely outlawed folk so no one other than their families was concerned by the deaths. God knows, the king and his court had enough to concern themselves with. But the people around here were afraid. Praise God, it went quiet over winter and I prayed that was the end of it. I even began to believe it had been wolves or some sort of enraged bear.

"Last year I had to go to the king, down to Windsor. It was a rather unpleasant summer. The barons forced the king to sign their ludicrous document. When I returned to Nottingham, I found my men had kept to the castle and the town, fearing to venture into the wood. The forester was drowning in drink, sitting on his behind and doing nothing but fining and harassing those who live outside the woodland but still inside the boundary of the legally afforested area. Nothing would get that man into the trees again, he said."

"Was he just afraid?" I asked. "Or had someone bribed him?"

"Is the fear not enough?" Roger asked. "In the short time I was away down south, the Knight of the Greenwood had tightened his grip. All the villages and farms in and around the wood were paying their tithes to this king of the outlaws. All were calling him the Green Knight or the Knight of the Green or some such nonsense. And the warden was collecting no fees. No forest courts were held. The foresters were out there giving the money to this leader, as were the agisters. The verderers were scared witless. The woodwards and the rest had disappeared. Everything was going to this outlaw leader."

The king's forest warden and his deputies the foresters set up forest courts and made inspections of forest lands. They were, therefore, the Crown's least popular servants as they received forest income, levied fines for violations of forest law and extorted every penny. Permission was required before forest land could be cleared and cultivated and the Crown received rent in perpetuity for that land. The right to pasture animals was controlled and would be withdrawn by the foresters, in the king's name, for the slightest offense. Of course, they might just look the other way if you paid them what they asked for. If an individual offender could not be identified in the forest courts, the forester would gleefully impose the required fine on the entire family, village or community.

It was not just the warden and his deputies who made up the forest bureaucracy. Each forest had verderers who reported to the king rather than the warden. They were elected locally, often held the post for life and did little other than rake in money so the posts were coveted, fought over and as corrupted as Judas. The agisters collected the fees from everyone who had permission to keep cattle and pigs in the forest and they creamed money off the top.

The king granted deer parks, chases and warrens to his barons and those lords employed woodwards, warreners, reeves and beadles in private offices all over the forest, each the master of his specific domain.

There was barely any oversight by the king's justicar and the officials were as corrupt, exploitative and self-interested as it was possible to be. No commoner who lived in a forest wished to be under forest law. But such is the way of things. A forester's rampant corruption was inevitable and unavoidable. They lived to line their own pockets. An appointment to most of the posts meant you would be set for life.

Which is why it made no sense that they had given up all that. No sense at all, unless the Green Knight was someone of astonishing power. Someone who could terrify all those officials. It was a wonder the great lords of the land had not done something about it.

"By God," I said. "But what about the Church? The priests in the villages. They would not stand for this. Does the archbishop know about this?"

"I wrote to him," Roger said. "More than once. He finally said that he had written to his men and that I was overreacting. The local deacon was not concerned. The Prior and monks at Newstead Priory claimed to be perfectly happy with their situation."

"I do not understand," I said. "The Church was unconcerned with the loss of their local authority?"

"No, indeed," Roger said. "Now I believe that the monks, the priests, all of them had been frightened or bought into silence. But this green fellow is most certainly stealing from the poorest and the wealthiest in Sherwood and taking it all for himself."

With every word the sheriff spoke, I was more certain that the Knight of the Greenwood was William de Ferrers. There was no longer a modicum of doubt in my mind. Who else could terrify an entire shire into compliance without raising alarm in the outside world? It was remarkable.

"Did the archbishop offer nothing in the way of help?" I asked. "He has the ear of the king, after all."

"King John is negotiating with the Pope and Philip the King of France and, therefore, has no time for your petty local issues. So our wise archbishop wrote to me. He finished with something that I shall attempt to quote to you verbatim. I suggest you keep your own counsel in this matter, he wrote, and if you cannot then the king will have to take an interest in your existing position for the Crown."

"I do not understand," I said. "He thought that you were at fault?"

Roger chuckled and took his seat back at the table. He drank down a cup of the Gascony wine. "All England knows you are a terror on the battlefield, Richard. But you will never make a courtier."

"No, thank God. Tell me his meaning, then."

"It was a threat. Be silent about the events in Sherwood or I shall remove you from your position."

"He has the king's ear to such an extent?"

Roger shrugged. "Hugh is the Archbishop of York. He and the Archbishop of Canterbury vie for influence. The Marshal, of course, remains the most powerful loyal baron and I know that the great man struggles to resist the ambition of both archbishops." He broke off. "I heard the Marshal's son was your squire?"

"Anselm, his least important son. A good lad. He is Jocelyn de Sherbourne's squire."

"So you retain a following of sorts," the sheriff said, "despite being held back by the archbishop."

"Jocelyn and our squires are all I can afford to keep," I admitted. "And if the price of everything goes up much further I shall have to sell my horses, send Anselm back to his father and call myself a beggar."

"Of course, of course, times are hard indeed, very hard," Roger said, as if he had ever known anything close to privation. "I wonder, though. Do you think you could attract more men? Perhaps if you had the coin to pay them?"

"My reputation cannot be so tarnished that hungry men would not take my coin," I said. "What are you asking me?"

He rubbed his eyes, sighing. "Last year I commissioned a knight to scour the wood clean of this infestation. A man named Sir Geoffrey of Norton."

"But I know this man," I said. "He fought beside me on the walls of Acre when we were young. A solid knight. Somewhat headstrong but he had the strength to justify it. He had a marvellous voice. I think he was injured at Arsuf and returned home."

"Indeed? Well, he was not so young when I found him. I paid him and two knights, a half dozen squires, and twenty bowmen to go into the wood."

"He is dead?"

Roger sighed. "It was his intention to catch the outlaws in the villages and homes of their families over winter. They rode into the wood to roust out the outlaws and force them to give up their master or, at least, the camp and to burn it. Bring the man out of hiding."

"A good plan."

The sheriff shook his head. "Three days after they left here, two surviving bowmen dragged themselves to the Priory before succumbing to their wounds. The Knight of the Greenwood, the Green Knight or his men ambushed Sir Geoffrey. There was a great slaughter. I had hoped to receive a ransom for the man but it has been four months and we have had no word. I hesitate to conclude that the worst has happened and so I hold out hope for his survival. It is likely that they are holding him until they need his ransom. But whatever the truth of it, his commission was a failure."

"And you want me to take his place," I stated. "To finish what Sir Geoffrey began to do."

"As soon as they told me you were at my gate, I knew that God had answered my prayers. But with times being as they are, I am afraid that I have no money. I can hire few men. One or two perhaps, if they are desperate enough. You shall have a commission and a warrant to arrest or slay the Green Knight but I do not know how you would accomplish this task. It is too much to ask, I know."

"Roger," I said, leaning forward. "Surely if you know me at all then you know it is a task I had assigned myself before ever I came to see you," I said. "It is a task I would carry out without your commission, without even your leave. For the Green Knight must surely be William de Ferrers and I am sworn to end his days with the edge of my sword."

He looked at me for a long time, judging me, perhaps or deciding whether to tell me something. Before he did so, his brows knitted together and he glanced at the main door to his chamber.

The sheriff coughed and said loudly, "Shall we descend to the hall for a little food? I am utterly famished, are you not?"

He spoke as men do when they wished their servants to attend to them, instead of calling for them directly, so I expected the door to the corridor to open. The sheriff looked nervous.

When no servant entered, on a whim I jumped to my feet, stepped to the door and yanked it wide open. It was an instinct that had served me well before and would continue to serve me for centuries. I half imagined that Roger had betrayed me and that armed men were about to burst in through that door and slit my throat.

Instead, a young woman stood there, caught leaning forward at the waist listening at the gap between door and frame. Huge eyes stared up at me. Her lips formed a plump circle of surprise.

I believe my own expression would have been rather similar.

"Marian!" Roger shouldered me aside. "What are you doing, girl? Lurking about in the corridor?"

She stood up straight, closed her mouth and stared at Roger with loathing.

The girl was extremely beautiful. Startlingly so. Her eyes were clear, her hair shining and dark and her skin was perfect.

"Lurking?" she shot back at him. She thrust her chin up and set her shoulders back, straining her dress against her chest. She may have been young but she was no girl and my loins stirred for the first time in many moons. "How can I do anything other than lurk in this God-forsaken place?"

Roger looked shocked. Hurt, even. "Marian..." he mumbled.

She stared at him for a moment longer, her cheeks flushed. The girl scoffed at his hesitation. With a final glance up at me, she spun on her heel and strode off, clattering down the stairs.

The sheriff stared after her, frozen to the spot.

I cleared my throat. "Your daughter?" I asked him.

"No," he said, his face turning dark. "Come, let us eat."

∞

Later, we sat full of meat and ale, his men drinking at the tables in the hall. But it was not a joyous hall to drink in. The food was poor, little more than onions, meat, and bread in various combinations. At least it was plentiful.

The subdued atmosphere I had noticed among those men while walking through the hall earlier now made sense. They had lost Sherwood to murder and sedition. They did not understand what was happening but they knew enough of their enemy to be afraid and that fear had kept them in the castle for months. They were ashamed.

We talked of the war. Which barons were where and what each was doing, what the king's plans likely were in fighting them. Lots of rumour, plenty of martial opinion offered though little of any value. My hauberk felt like a hundredweight on my shoulders. My gambeson underneath was stifling. It was foolish of me to wear it indoors and yet I could not rid myself of the feeling that I was at war and at risk, even inside that fine castle.

After a while, Roger's head was nodding. He had drunk an astonishing amount of ale before calling for wine. His misery was profound and I suspected that the cause of it was more than the presence of the Green Knight nearby.

"The girl," I said. "Roger, listen. You called her Marian. Who is she?"

Roger was rather unfocused but the mention of her name woke him up. "That girl," he said, grimacing. "That damned girl. She is the daughter of Sir Geoffrey of Norton."

"What is she doing here, Roger?"

He took a long time to answer. His words were slurred, his movement sluggish. "No family," he said, stopping to burp. "If Sir Geoffrey is truly dead."

"How can he not be?" I asked. "Do you really think William de Ferrers is the type of man to ransom another? And anyway, surely the girl is of marrying age? She must be twenty years old or so."

His face clouded over. "What do you mean? What do you mean by saying that? You filthy bastard. Just because you have that face, you think she wants you? You're finished. You stay away from her, you accursed demon." He reached for me and I gently pushed his hand away and held it on the table. His strength was as a child's, compared to mine. I wanted to snap his wrist. I wanted to grab the jug of wine and smash it into his face. I wanted to sink my teeth into his flesh and tear it apart.

His men were watching closely. The hall was quiet. Forcing a smile, I released his hand.

"I meant nothing by it at all, my lord sheriff." I stood and bowed a little. "I wish you a good night, thank you for your generosity. I shall return tomorrow to discuss how I can help you with the Green Knight."

He waved his hand at me and grabbed another greasy bird off our plate.

Oftentimes, you find that the longer you know someone, the greater the chance that their character will disappoint you.

"I will show myself out," I said to the old servant at the hall door who struggled to his feet and lit a lamp. He held himself as if he had once been a soldier or at least a bailiff used to violence. But he was well past it.

"My lord says I must—" the old man stammered.

"You will stay here," I said, clapping my hand down on his shoulder. He winced. "I would not want an old man such as yourself to risk falling down some steps, unnecessarily."

"But—" he said.

"Ah, yes, I would appreciate borrowing your lamp," I said. "You are too kind. Now sit down."

I had a quick look around the keep but I could not find the

girl. For some reason, I expected her to be skulking around. But I was bored and tired so I gave up.

I was almost out of the keep when Marian stepped out of the shadow of a side doorway near the doorway into the inner bailey.

I pretended to be surprised.

"Come with me," the young woman whispered.

I hesitated and looked around. It was still quiet and very dark.

"I will," I said. "But you should know that if the sheriff's men see us together I do not think Roger will be pleased with you tomorrow."

"I care nothing for what that monster thinks," she hissed. "And neither should you. This way, hurry."

There was a narrow stairway up to the floor above. Along the corridor a short way, she turned the handle into a small parlour. I followed, ducking inside after checking there was no one watching. The room contained a table with a lamp, a couple of plain chairs and not much else. Beyond was a bedchamber.

"Do not trust a word that he says," Marian said, planting herself in the centre of the space. I stood with my back almost against the door.

"The sheriff?"

"Whatever pretext he summoned you on, do not take him up on it."

"Actually, I came to see him," I said. "He is an old friend."

Her face closed up. "A friend, is it? What sort of friend would lie to you?"

"What lies did the sheriff tell me?"

"That my father may yet live."

I stopped myself from saying that her father would have lived up until William needed blood to drink.

"So you know differently?" I said. "I might have expected that a young woman would pray her father be returned to her."

"Oh, do not be an imbecile," she said, her pretty face twisted in contempt. "I could not bear it if you were simple. I loved my father. He was the kindest, sweetest man who ever lived. But he was a fool with money and he trusted far too readily. He took up this foolish mission though I begged him not to."

"I knew your father," I said. "He was indeed a good man. A capable knight. He could not have known the evil he was up against."

"But the sheriff knew," she said. "He chose my father because he wanted me. The sheriff wants me to be his wife."

"You are speaking madness, girl," I said. "Roger is already married. Has been married for years. He has children grown."

"He has sworn his undying love for me," she said, standing up straight. She pointed at me. "There, right there where you are standing he fell to his knees and begged me to marry him. He would divorce his wife, he said. He would have her charged with adultery and a divorce would be simple. He would put a child in my belly, a son who would inherit. He would disinherit his own sons for me, declare them bastards. He would give me the world if only I would marry him."

Some men went mad with lust but it was difficult to believe Roger would risk so much, even for a girl as lovely as the one before me. "Was he drunk?"

"When is he not? I refused him, so the sheriff sent my father off to die but now pretends that he lives."

"How does your father being alive help him to marry you?"

"He sent off my maid and my friends," she said, emotions other than anger creeping into her voice. "One night he forced his way in here, then into my bedchamber. He forced his fat body upon mine. I should never have opened that door to him but I knew enough what to expect to keep a dagger on me all the time. A dagger held against a man's loins is as a miracle cure against his ardour, did you know that? I keep the door barred every night. He cajoles and begs me to move to a chamber nearer to his. I am certain there is a passage through the walls into that chamber, I hear the guards allude to it. It is where he brings his women."

I still struggled to understand. "Yes, but how does your father's life help the sheriff more than his death would?"

"If my father is alive then I am a guest of the sheriff. If my father is dead then I become a ward of the king, who can marry me off to who he likes. And whom he likes would probably not be Roger. Although I suspect the sheriff fears that the king will take me for himself. None of these prospects fill me with joy."

"I do not doubt what you tell me. And I am sorry you have been subjected to this. But I doubt that your father can be brought back to you. The man they call the Green Knight is not one to hold prisoners for long. Sir Geoffrey was a good knight. His shield saved my life once. He stood guard over me after I slipped upon the top of the wall at Acre. I owe him my life."

She screwed up her lovely face. "What madness do you speak? How can you have fought with my father? He was a young man when he took the cross. It was many years before I was born."

"Twenty-five years ago, I would say." It felt like a different life. I had been truly young back then.

"How can this be? You are surely no older than twenty-five years yourself." She wrinkled her nose.

"Forty-seven," I said. "Thereabouts. In truth, I stopped counting years ago."

"I had hoped and prayed that you would take me away from here," she said. "But you are a witless fool and a liar, just as he is. Why would you even say these things? Am I supposed to be impressed? Go away. Leave me to my fate, then. It is God's will, I suppose."

I forced myself to laugh, lightly, as if I was unconcerned by her words. "I swear to you," I said. "I know that I have a youthful aspect. But I knew your father. He had the most beautiful voice. He would sing and a crowd of battle-hardened old soldiers, drunk and rowdy by the fire would fall silent and weep."

She paused and looked up at me. "My father has not sung since my mother died. Ten years ago."

"Then I am sorry to hear that."

She stepped closer to me, tilting her head up. She smelled good. Her neck was exposed to me, the beat of the great veins either side of her throat warming her skin, sending her scent up to my nose. It was the smell of honeysuckle flowers, sunshine on ripe wheat and hard apples. The scent of her neck was different to the scent of her hair and the warm musk of her breasts beneath her clothes. It was the smell of life, youth. Fertility.

"You are truly that age? But your skin is so smooth." She reached up as if to touch my face then pulled her hand back to her breast and held it with her other hand against herself. Her lips were parted slightly, she breathed lightly. She sucked her bottom lip between her teeth and frowned. Her eyes were huge and bright, flicking, searching all over my face.

I was beginning to understand how Roger de Lacy had become obsessed with the girl.

"What did you mean, you hoped I would take you away from here? I cannot carry you away from the sheriff's care. How could I do it?"

"He is not your liege lord, is he? You could defy him. And I am free to go where I please. I am no prisoner."

"He is the Sheriff of Nottinghamshire and Derbyshire. He is the king's representative in the shire where I hold my land. I cannot defy him, he would take grave offence. And anyway, I have nowhere to take you. I ride into Sherwood Forest, into the deep wood, to finish what Geoffrey began. There will be battle, girl."

"Do not girl me," Marian said. "I will take care of myself. I have been without maids or servants for months. I will not get in your way."

"It simply cannot happen. I do not expect all the men I take with me into the wood to survive. I will not lead you to your death, Marian. And I cannot send you to my home, especially if I am not there to protect you. The sheriff, if he is as infatuated with you as you say, would simply go there and take you back. All that would change is that I will have risked my position and my chance to take revenge on the man who has slain your father."

For a moment, as she took a deep breath, I thought she would explode with anger. Instead, she sighed a great shuddering sigh and slumped into a chair. She held her head in her hands upon the table.

"I understand. And thank you for listening to me. But I do not know how much longer I can fend him off," she said, her words muffled by her hands.

She was truly desperate. If Roger had tried to force himself upon her once then it was likely that he would do so again. The young woman was desperate indeed and she had asked me for my help. I did not want to make Roger my enemy. I did not want to be distracted from my task.

I approached where she sat. Her head snapped up and she watched me warily as I sank to one knee before her.

"If what you say is true," I said and held up a hand to stall her protests. "I swear that I shall do all I can to help you. Consider me a friend, lady Marian. But now I must go."

FOUR ~ BROTHER TUCK

I RODE FOR THE WOODLAND two days later. With me were Jocelyn, Anselm, and Swein.

The sheriff had supplied me with provisions and even a few shillings for the paying of bribes but he had provided me with no men. He had, in fact, been distant and surly to the point of rudeness since that first night. No doubt, one of his men had seen me conversing with Marian after all, or even entering or leaving her chambers.

I had gone to see the Warden of Sherwood in his large Nottingham house. The man was too drunk and terrified to be of any use and I had no patience for sobering him up just to beat the truth out of him. He had given me the name of one of his deputies, however, and his village.

"How can the sheriff expect us to succeed without providing

us with a few more men?" Jocelyn was unhappy about the venture, as well he should have been.

"Indeed," I said, absently.

If I were thinking more clearly myself I would have known something was up with the sheriff's strange lack of support.

Instead, I was thinking of Marian.

It was a shaping up to be a lovely day. Bright, warm. The blossom on the crab apples lit up the hedgerows. Fat bees flew about, happy after their long slumber wherever it was that bees went over winter and drunk on nectar.

We rode at a slow pace along the road north from Nottingham, toward York far to the north. The woodland of Sherwood started on the right hand of the road. So close to the town it was well used and coppiced in the under layer and free from brush. It was a light, peaceful, pleasant woodland.

I knew, however, that the place grew dark and impenetrable just a few miles to the north. Inside the deep wood, at the centre, there were few people other than the outlaws. Outside the couple of villages, there was little more than a few charcoal burners and swineherds, if indeed, William had allowed them to continue to live there.

"Or even a servant or two," Jocelyn said. "With our lack of men, we need Anselm to be fresh for fighting so Swein will have to do all our armour maintenance and fetching water and cooking."

If Swein heard him, and he must have done, the young man said nothing.

"Swein must also save his strength," I said. "We will need his bow. We will scrub our own armour when needed and fetch our own water. Come, Jocelyn, you have been on campaign before."

"This is no campaign," he said. "This is madness."

"Yet you come," I said.

"Of course," he snapped. "I have as much right as you to revenge what William did. More, even."

"Then pray that we succeed," I said.

"What about Anselm?" Jocelyn asked under his breath. "Do you really wish to risk the life of the Marshal's son?"

"His fifth son," I said. "Anselm will never receive a thing from his father, except the weight of expectation. He must make his own way in the world, just as his father did."

"In other words, you do not care if he dies."

"Do not direct your anger at me," I said. "Save it for William and his monsters."

Jocelyn rode on ahead. I wanted both us and our horses to be rested, so we stopped at midday to eat the food we had bought in Nottingham and to water the animals. The meat was freshly cooked in the castle kitchens and the bread was freshly baked. We ate largely in silence, other than the sound of Swein slurping and smacking his lips.

Jocelyn stared at him. "He attacks his food like a bull charging a gate," he said in French.

Swein froze and stared, aware of an insult when he heard it, no matter what language it was spoken in. His hand tightened around his hunk of bread, squeezing it together. "What did you say?"

Jocelyn smiled and answered in English. "Speak not with your mouth full, you uncouth swine."

"Jocelyn, attend to your food. Swein, be not so eager to take offence. Turn and watch the trees for enemies, string your bow. Have you forgotten that we are in enemy lands, or close enough? An arrow could find its way into your back at any moment here. This may be the last meal any one of us eats. We must rely on each other. Our enemies are out there. So I will have no more of that, not from any of you."

That sobered them well enough and I finished eating to the sound of blackbirds chirruping in the hedgerows and the sun warming my face.

"They say in the tavern that the sheriff has himself a lovely piece all shut up in his castle," Jocelyn said as we dressed in our hauberks.

"Is that so?" I said.

"They say she is a great beauty. Young and unmarried."

"Indeed?"

Jocelyn stared at me. "I knew it," he wailed. "You have seen her."

I said nothing, strapping my belt around my surcoat.

Jocelyn was outraged. "You spoke to the maiden, I know you did. I can see it upon your face. What was she like?"

"She was a girl," I said. "Old enough for marriage, I suppose."

"Describe her to me," he said.

"You should find a wife," I said. "As soon as is possible."

"That is what I am doing," he said. "Tell me about the girl. Has the sheriff deflowered her yet?"

"For the love of God, Jocelyn," I said. "We have more

important things to discuss. Mount your horse."

The road was deathly quiet, other than the birds and the ceaseless breeze in the twigs of the branches above. The leaves shimmered with an infinite variety of greens upon the browns and black.

"Not far till the village of Linby," Swein said, walking by the horses with his bow at the ready and his arrow bag over his shoulder. "Track comes up down there, then you go into the wood a ways. They cleared out a good few acres for planting years back. Paid old Ranulf a tidy sum for the pleasure. Not bad land, so they say."

"I hope this forester is still here," I said. "Or at least, uncorrupted by William's influence."

"If not, we can just talk to the villagers, right?" Swein said.

"You can trust nothing a peasant says to you," Jocelyn spoke in English. Swein's head jerked up but he said nothing.

"Nor will I," I said. "William twists people to his will, in one way or another. Whether his reach extends this far, we will discover. But you will be respectful to these people. They will have suffered. We will ask for ale and bread and we will eat. And I will ask the questions. Do they know you here, Swein?"

"Some might," he said. "That good or bad?"

"I do not know."

Soon after, we took the track and rode through the trees until they receded into a few small fields upon either side. A spring trickled along the side of the road, growing ever larger. We rode into the village. I counted six houses, arranged roughly in two rows leaving a road down the centre. There was no church or chapel. A pig snorted from somewhere.

"Where are they all?" Jocelyn asked.

"Hearth fires still burning in the homes," I said. I could smell them, along with fresh oat cakes.

"They are all hiding," Swein said.

I strode for the largest house. "Jocelyn, Anselm, stay out here and watch the trees. Swein, come with me."

The ground was muddy and there was pig shit everywhere. I ducked inside the dark house. It was dry inside and smoky. "I am looking for the forester," I shouted. "The warden's deputy. I am come from Nottingham. From the sheriff."

The fire crackled in the central hearth. A slowly bubbling pot swung atop it by a long chain to the rafter above.

Swein shrugged.

Outside, I looked to Jocelyn who waved his left hand low, toward the trees behind the house I was in. It was a sign we had worked out while campaigning for King John. It meant there were men hiding there. Jocelyn must have glimpsed shadows in the trees. His other hand rested on the pommel of his sheathed sword. Anselm stood by him, looking everywhere but where the men were and failing to appear relaxed.

"I have come from Nottingham," I shouted into the trees. "I come to talk. I am not here for outlaws. I am not here to impose fines nor to inspect boundaries."

The only answer was the wind in the leaves.

"I will pay silver for any man who will sit and speak with me," I shouted.

Pigs squealed again. They had been herded into the house

next door, one with the door closed. No doubt, the owners sat inside, trying to silence their animals, fearful of my intrusion. It was as though I had wandered into enemy country yet it was not ten miles from Nottingham and not nearly as deep into the wood as I had to go.

Twigs crunched and Swein placed an arrow on his bow cord and peered through the trees. I held out my hand to forestall him. A man of about forty years stepped through. He was dressed surprisingly well, in a dirty but well-made surcoat over a bright blue tunic. His face was deeply lined, cast in the shadows from his cap. When he drew near, he looked at me most unhappily.

"Never know who's coming, these days," he said, looking at me dressed head to toe in mail. My helm was upon my horse but otherwise, I was ready for war. "I am Ranulf, the forester here."

"And I am pleased to hear you say so," I said. "For it is you that I have come to speak to."

"Ah," he said, looking over his shoulder. "And you are?"

"Thirsty, thank you, Ranulf the forester. Shall we drink some ale in your home?"

He pulled off his cap and scratched the top of his head. The hair was thinning and he had some sort of weeping sore on it. It reeked of wet cheese. "The thing is, my lord, I think it would be best if you spoke to the warden instead of me."

"What a wonderful idea," I said. "Sadly, the poor man was too drunk to speak. When I sobered him up, all he did was weep and vomit until I allowed him a little wine. For a short while, he babbled about a terrible Green Knight in Sherwood stealing the king's revenue and how I should seek out his loyal forester, Ranulf of Linby who would know everything about this knight. What village is this?"

"Linby," he allowed, glum and defeated. "Best come in, then. I suppose."

"Wait here," I said to Swein. "Watch all ways." Swein nodded, eyes already darting about.

Back inside his neat home, Ranulf poured his rancid ale and invited me to sit on a bench at his table. He would not meet my eye but stared at his lazily bubbling pot.

"By all means," I said. "Ask your wife back in here to continue making your stew."

"She is not my wife," Ranulf said. "And the fewer folk seen talking to you, the better it will be for all of us here."

"Seen?" I asked. "William's men watch you?"

"William?" he was confused. "You mean Will?"

"The Green Knight," I said. "Whatever you name him. Where is he?"

Ranulf shivered. "I have never seen him. His men, though. His men come. They take what they want."

"Why do you stay here? Take your woman and go to Nottingham."

"They would kill me. Men have run. They do not get far. They do not die well."

"I can help you," I said. "I will kill the Green Knight and his men."

"You?" Ranulf swallowed. "You and your three men? Forgive me, sir, but you must not understand what you are facing."

"So tell me. What are his men's names? Where do they live in the wood?"

He lowered his voice. "I beg you, please, leave now."

"You are afraid."

"Of course I bloody am," Ranulf said. "Every moment you are here risks my life and the life of everyone in this village, forsaken as it is."

"Perhaps you should be more afraid of me." I spoke softly.

He stared at me, confused.

"You have failed in your sworn duty. You have failed to manage the people of the forest. You have attended no courts for, how long, two years?"

"Two years of Hell upon the earth," Ranulf's voice shook. "Would you rather I had died?"

"Not I but the king demands you do your duty in his forest. Tell me all you know and I will speak for you, help you to avoid punishment."

"Punishment?"

"You may be treated with leniency and allowed to go free with just the loss of a hand or perhaps both hands."

He laughed. "I have lived in terror, day and night, since those monsters came. Nothing you can say will frighten me any further. I will tell you because I have not forgotten my duty, no matter what you say." He drank down his ale and wiped his lips. "Will the Red. Much the Miller. Brother Tuck, the Bloody Monk. And the rest."

"The Green Knight's men," I said.

"Aye, sir. Some of them. Each one of them worse than the last. Mad, terrible, the lot of them."

"Will the Red is red of hair?"

"Red with blood, sir," Ranulf said.

"Did you say one of them is a monk?" I asked.

Ranulf scoffed curling his lip. "He dresses like one. He claims he is one, from the priory just up the way. Maybe he is. But he don't act like one."

"And the third man is a local fellow, too, I take it?" I said. "From the mill down the river?"

"The Miller," Ranulf said. "They call him that as he likes to grind folk up. He carries a hammer. Smashes flesh and bones into pulp in front of others. As a warning, like."

I wondered whether William finds such men or creates them himself. Perhaps his blood makes men evil. Or perhaps it is his way with words.

"Where do they live?" I asked.

"Deep in the wood," Ranulf said. "I have not ventured that way in over a year. But there are caves there. Cabins. Plenty of places for the outlaws to hide. They are all loyal to the Green Knight. Loyal or dead themselves. It was give yourself up to them or become their prey."

"They take people," I said. "To drink from?"

"Drink?" His voice cracked. He nodded. "They took my wife, here in this room, took her then sucked blood from her body and—" He banged the table. "I have been a craven."

I said nothing about that because it was the truth. "Tuck, the Bloody Monk. Does he claim to be from the priory at Newstead? Does he live there still?"

Ranulf nodded, his eyes wet. "Take me with you," he said.

I looked at the cooking pot. "What about your woman?"

"She is an old creature. I allowed her to live here when they took her sons."

"You do not want her to come with you when you leave with us?"

"She is nothing to me," Ranulf said.

"Yet I see just the solitary bed," I pointed out.

Ranulf's face coloured. "The nights are cold."

"I will collect you when I return. I go to the priory to find this Bloody Monk."

"Do not," Ranulf's voice shook. "You shall be killed."

"Monks do not frighten knights."

"They are monks no longer," Ranulf said. "They are much changed."

"You will wait here until I return," I instructed Ranulf. "I will not take you back to Nottingham unless your bedfellow comes with us. I will be back tomorrow."

I spoke with such confidence. Although I knew what William and his men were capable of, I still underestimated his brutality.

∞

That night, our small campfire crackled in the darkness. I was hungrier than I remembered being for years and tore into my bread and hard cheese.

"If we are to rest," Jocelyn argued. "We should do so in the meagre comfort of that shit stinking village."

"The forester believed the place was watched," I said. "I'd not sleep soundly in a hovel that could be burned in a trice."

"But you'll sleep out in the open?"

"Of course," I said. "I can hear enemies coming. I can see into the darkness. We are much safer here. Sleep, all of you. We will approach the priory at dawn."

"You mean to attack?"

"A priory?" I asked.

"You said the forester claimed it was taken over by William's monsters. Why would we not attack it?"

"Even if I trusted the word of a craven," I said. "How can we four mount an attack on such a place?"

"It is a small house," Swein said. "Compared to many such places."

"Seen many priories, have you?" Jocelyn asked.

"A few," Swein said. "This one never had much more than a dozen monks."

"Have you heard of this Brother Tuck?" I asked.

Swein nodded.

"Strange name, is it not?" I said. "What on earth can it mean?"

"Well, spit out your words, lad," Jocelyn said, knowing Swein considered himself a man grown.

"They say he was a bad man, even before. A glutton, a thief, and rapist but he took to the clergy and somehow avoided the noose. He is one of them men what is always jesting and laughing but he does it to make men feel afraid. It makes men nervous, have you met men such as that, Sir Richard? Anyway, I heard they call him Tuck because he tucks into those he kills with great passion. Tucks into them as a man does with a hearty pie."

Sitting beside Swein, Anselm's face was illuminated by the fire. The lad looked horrified. "Tucks in, as in eats them? But I thought they drink the blood, not eat the flesh?"

"Drinks the blood and eats the flesh, with a right savage manner." Swein shrugged. "That is what they say." His face was drawn and his eyes looked through the fire and into the past. "There were a bunch of other monks at the priory. The Green Knight's men killed all the ones who would not follow him. And those that did became like Tuck. Drinkers of blood. Everyone stayed away from the priory after that."

We sat and listened to the fire crackling.

"In the morning," I said. "We will ride to the priory, arrest this Brother Tuck and take him quickly to Nottingham, stopping to collect the forester and his servant. When we get Tuck to the castle, I shall have him reveal all about William's lair. Then he shall succumb to his wounds, dying in agony."

I could feel Swein looking at me and he nodded once when he met my eye.

"Finish eating, sleep. In the morning, we fight."

Jocelyn could be a prickly and proud man. But he was good at heart and generous. He woke himself well before dawn and came bade me sleep myself, for which I was grateful. We rose as the sky was growing bright in the east and a light rain fell. We broke our meagre camp and rode north, for the priory. It was not far from the road and on the edge of the wood rather than deep within but we were parallel with that darkest part of it, between the rivers.

When we arrived at the boundary of the priory, I saw what Swein had meant. Set back from the road in a large clearing, the place was little more than a small timber hall, in a poor state of repair and some equally tumbledown outbuildings scattered around it. There was no wall, nor even a proper fence and the hedgerows were ragged and full of gaps.

The ditch around the boundary was full of leaves and overflowing with stinking, green water. The fruit bushes were wild tangles. Although the gardens were bare, the orchard was overgrown and everything was untended and filthy. The air stank of old death, like a battlefield a week after the fighting had ended. Underneath it all was a faint smell of smoke, suggesting someone, at least, lived nearby.

The path up to the hall was muddy. There was spattered shit from dogs, sheep and deer, all washed together by recent rain into a rotten slop.

"It looks deserted," Jocelyn said.

"Your pardon, sir," Anselm said. "There are fresh tracks upon the path. A man or two or perhaps three, not more than a day old."

"Up to three men in there?" Jocelyn said, drawing his blade.

"How many monks did you say became like Tuck?" I asked Swein.

"Not sure," my new squire said, shrugging. "Half a dozen?"

Jocelyn coughed. "I believe I will wear my helm after all."

"As will I," I said. "You two young men guard the horses. If any man so much as approaches you while I am inside, no matter how far distant that man is, sound the hunting horn, do you hear me?"

"Blow the horn at the sight of any man," Anselm said,

fingering the hilt of his sword.

While I pulled my helmet on top of my mail coif, Swein set to stringing his bow, which he did with a longer cord tied to both ends. I disliked the helm as it restricted vision and hearing so much. Yet, I was entering an enclosed space that was likely to hold at least one of William's monsters and I wanted as much protection as I could get. Jocelyn and I both chose to leave our shields because the rooms and corridor walls could impede us and because we were attempting to abduct a man and needed a free hand each.

Jocelyn and I stood at the heavy door.

"Should we knock?" Jocelyn said. I could hear his smile even through his enclosed helm.

I tried the latch. It clicked up and the door swung outward. It was unbarred.

"Perhaps they think they are safe," I said.

"Perhaps we are falling for a ruse," came Jocelyn's muffled reply.

"Quiet now," I whispered, drawing my sword.

I eased the door wider.

The hinges caught and juddered. I stopped the door but it was too late. The uncared for iron hinges screeched their unmistakable sound, echoing through the house, loud enough to wake the dead on Judgement Day.

"That's that, then," Jocelyn said.

"Silence," I hissed. I could hear sounds within. Men's voices. Laughter. Even singing. "Do you hear that?"

Jocelyn shook his head.

"Sounds as though they are yet awake and drinking," I said. "Just like monks."

"Let us sober them up with a sword through the spine."

"All but Brother Tuck," I said. "We need him alive."

We stepped inside and I waited for my eyes to adjust to the gloom. The building was partitioned with internal walls, painted plaster over the wattle and daub. A short corridor, two closed doors on either side and one door at the end, right in front of us. Once, it had been painted in bright colours but now everything was filthy. Brown stains spattered the walls. The floor oozed underfoot. The stench of death, old death and fresh blood filtered through my helmet.

Voices echoed around. Even Jocelyn, through his helm, coif and under-cap could hear them. Three to five men, I guessed. Easy enough if they were monks, hard odds if they were fighters and worse if they truly were men imbued with the strength of William's blood. I would take no chances.

Pushing in front of Jocelyn, I stepped to the door. The men were on the other side. I considered whether it was worth opening the door and attempting to talk, first. Perhaps I could avoid bloodshed. After all, who knew who these men were, really? On the other hand, we were dressed as if we had come to kill and their first response might be to attack, in which case I had handed our enemies an advantage that should have been ours.

Jocelyn hissed in irritation and nudged me on my back. I half turned to him.

The door opened inward.

A young monk stood, door in hand, staring up with profound

shock at the sight of a huge, armoured knight intruding into his revelry. He was unarmed, wearing a filthy robe. His tonsure had mostly grown out. But his eyes were hardening into rage and I thought I saw William's madness in them.

I smashed his nose with the mailed fist of my left hand and barrelled him aside, knocking him down. I stabbed my blade through his eye, grinding the edges against his eye socket

The hall was as filthy as a pigsty. A milky grey light came from small, high windows, two holes in the thatch above and a few fat tallow candles stuck about the hearth. The floor was covered in smashed pots, bones and rotting things. It reeked of excrement and rotten flesh.

Of the five men who sat about the dying hearth fire, four leapt to their feet, knocking over their stools and a bench. They were dressed like the man I had stuck, in filthy robes, as if they were monks that had climbed fresh from a grave. Their age was difficult to determine through the grime on their faces but they moved fast enough. And I knew men who were ready to fight when I saw them.

The fifth man remained seated, with his feet raised upon the back of a quivering, naked old man. His pale body smeared in black filth and old blood, curled up in a ball. His beard was matted, his head bald.

The man with his feet up was bulky, with a fat, red and grinning face, reclining like a lord in a great chair. He was their leader. He was the man I had come for.

"Ha," that fat man shouted, pointing at me. "Take them, I want that fancy armour."

108

The other four circled wide, staggering in their drunkenness but moving like wolves circling an ageing ox, their eyes fixed upon Jocelyn and on me. I moved to my left to take the two there and Jocelyn went right. I hoped that he knew these men were William's and that despite their pathetically weak bodies and their inebriated state that they would likely be faster and stronger than he would.

I circled, crushing potshards underfoot, stepping through mud and a mass of flesh. The men laughed, though they were unarmed and attacking an armoured knight. They were mad and I chose to slay them. I knew which was the man known as Brother Tuck.

Deciding, I charged the nearest man. My first step was onto a dismembered wrist and my ankle rolled and twisted. Seeing my stumble, the men whooped and charged into me.

I ran the first man through his guts but the both of them bore me down with their fury. I ripped my blade out, spilling blood and bile but both pummelled my helmet with their bare hands. Their blows were like hammers, one was upon my back, knees pushing me down into the filth. I could see nothing and tasted the bloody filth oozing through the eye slits in my helm. They were trying to drown me in it.

I heaved myself up, throwing down the man upon my back. My sword I rammed up into the chin of the other, driving it up through into his brain. My sword jarred against the inside of his skull, scraped, and caught on the bone as he went down. The other one leapt upon me again, tearing at my helm. I elbowed him in the head, spun and backed away and swung my blade at his head. He jerked back but I caught him in the neck, slicing deep and sending him sprawling. I staggered after him and cut the other side, severing his head from his body.

My helm eye slits were half filled with oozing grime. I swiped out as much as I could and peered about the room.

Jocelyn was stepping back, keeping both men away from him. Both men were bleeding from the head. An ordinary knight would have stood little chance but Jocelyn was a superb fighter, his defence with the shield and footwork were outstanding. And the monks, for all their brutality, were not trained in war and nor were they freshly fed on William's blood. So I left Jocelyn to fend for himself a moment longer and instead looked for Brother Tuck.

His feet splashed through the filth toward me, a cry of incoherent rage bursting from him as he charged. The monk must have had his fill of William's blood. He moved like an arrow, shot from a bow. I got half out of the way and raised my elbow as high as his neck. The great mass of the man crashed into me and past me, the impact of his crazed rush smacking into the small space of my mailed elbow. A normal man would have received a crushed windpipe but not William's monster. It was, though, enough to send him sprawling into the filth underfoot. I followed his fall, bore him down and kicked him as he landed. I stomped on his back, popping ribs. I forced his face into the blood-drenched mud. His hands clawed at it, sliding in the slime. He grasped what appeared to be the lower leg of a small child, torn off at the knee. Perhaps he thought to use it as a weapon against me. I ground my heel into his hand.

Across the hall, Jocelyn cried out. I feared he had been wounded but it was a cry of victory, as one of the monks fell, his head cleaved top to bottom.

The final monk, finally seeing sense, turned to flee.

I charged to him, crunching and splashing, and speared him through the back of the neck.

Jocelyn panted from the exertion, muffled by his helm, nodded and waved that he was well. I returned to my prisoner as he was rolling onto his back. I kicked him hard in the balls. Hard, like I meant to kick through to his heart. Hard enough to rupture his stones, I hoped. He racked and jerked in silence, all wind kicked out of him and curled up into a tight ball.

"Get the rope," I said to Jocelyn.

Jocelyn was breathing very heavily and he had somewhat of a wild look about him. The kind of look a man gets when he has faced his own mortality. I realised that his fight against the monks had taxed him. I resolved to not allow Jocelyn to face William's men alone ever again.

We bound Brother Tuck tightly. He reeked like an animal. He growled and spat. I had to thump him in the face and head a few times to keep him still while we bound him wrist and ankle and at elbows and knees. I balled up a rag, stuffed it in his mouth and tied rope tight around his head to hold it in place.

"Quickly now," I said. "We must ride for Nottingham."

"What about that fellow?" Jocelyn pointed to the hearth.

The old man with the matted beard lay curled and shaking in his filthy nakedness. "I had forgotten about him."

"You cannot mean to leave him," Jocelyn said.

"For the love of God," I said. "You watch that one. Keep him on his knees with your sword at his neck."

I removed my helm, placed it upon the large chair, and rolled the creature over. His face was caked in ordure. The stench from his mouth was like rotting meat and befouled eggs. "No," he mumbled through smashed teeth. "No, no, no..."

"Jesus Christ Almighty. Jocelyn, they have put out his eyes."

The broken old man shook all over. "Who? Who?" he mumbled.

"Who am I? I am Sir Richard of Ashbury. Who are you? Do you live hereabouts? Can you hear me? Can I take you to your family?"

"Prior." He swallowed. "I am. Prior. Gregory."

"Sweet Christ, he's the prior, Jocelyn. Hear me, prior, you are saved. We shall take you with us back to Nottingham."

His shaking grew violent and he reached out a hand to me. I grasped the wrist. The fingers and the thumb had all been hacked off and left to fester. The hand was black. I eased his hand back and sat him up. His other hand was missing no more than the thumb but it too was mottled with black corruption.

"Kill. Me."

"I cannot imagine how you have suffered, good prior." I stroked his disgusting head. "But know that your tormentors have all been killed but one and he is not long for this world. Before he dies he shall know suffering as you have known it."

"Bless. You."

"Say your prayers, prior," I said and drew my dagger. When he was done, he mumbled that he was ready and I ended him rightly.

I wrestled Brother Tuck onto a steady packhorse and bound him to it while Jocelyn calmed the beast. I advised Tuck that if he caused me too much trouble I would simply remove his head and after that, he lay largely still.

Wary of the possibility of pursuit, we rode hard for Linby, Ranulf the forester's village.

Upon arriving, we found that every soul there had been slaughtered.

FIVE ~ ENGLAND INVADED

NOTTINGHAM WAS ABUZZ when we returned. I naively assumed they had heard of the slaughter so close to the town.

I was wrong.

"What has happened?" I asked a groom as we walked our horses up to the extensive castle stables. "What is all this everyone is saying about the French?"

There were fine palfreys, much finer than my chestnut riding palfrey than I had brought with me to Nottingham, unused. He was getting old and his gait was never particularly civilised but the palfreys in that yard clearly belonged to a great lord. It was a joy to see the ambling palfreys, their skin full of juice, their coats glistening as they paced softly, gently exercised by the grooms.

There were even two destriers, the most expensive and desirable warhorses for knights. The fine beasts graceful in form and with goodly stature, quivering ears, high necks and plump buttocks. I could not afford one, let alone two. The grooms were taking great care with those dangerous beasts. A destrier was trained to bite, kick, rear and ride right over people and those horses were well known to kill more stableboys than smallpox.

I had to wave coins around to get anyone's attention. A lad found us a corner and set to work while we unloaded.

"The French, lord, the French, have you not heard, lord?" The boy could hardly get his words from his mouth he was so excited. "The French have invaded, lord."

Anselm and Swein shared a look. I hoped that they were becoming friends and allies.

"Invaded where?" I said. "When?"

"London, probably," the boy said, grinning. "The king is riding there to throw them back into the sea."

"London is not by the sea," Jocelyn pointed out.

"Well, wherever, then," the boy said, unconcerned.

I dragged Brother Tuck from the courser, who stomped and whinnied at me.

"You are happy now?" I said to the beast.

"He is not happy, you fool," Jocelyn said as he pushed me aside. "He is angry at you for making him carry that filth." He brushed the courser's grey-white coat down himself, whispering in his ear and neglecting his own war-trained stallion so that mine would be mollified. "If the French have truly landed, Richard, then we must ride to meet them."

I cursed under my breath. "You may do as you wish. I am staying to destroy William. I have waited twenty-five years for him to turn up and I do not mean to squander this chance. Truly, Jocelyn, you must do your duty."

Tuck, bound tightly at my feet, squirmed and groaned. I kicked him in his belly, hard and he curled up in silence.

"And what about your duty?" Jocelyn asked, brushing my horse.

"The archbishop considers me disgraced," I said. "He will not want me where all men, especially the king, can see me and remember Gascony. All his life Hugh de Nonant has fought and clawed his way upward and his life is built upon his reputation."

"And what do men say about me?" Jocelyn grumbled. "Your disgrace is mine by association."

It was true but it annoyed me to hear him be so ungrateful. "Men say that you have dutifully stayed loyal, like a true knight. Like the Marshal himself would have done."

"The Marshal would never have served a lord as lowly as you," Jocelyn said.

I laughed. "True. You never had to stay with me. And you may go and fight the French if you wish it. I will publicly release you, if you wish to join whatever forces the king musters. You will win great fame, I have no doubt. Now is the time to achieve your greatness."

He said nothing while he saw to the horses with our squires and I guarded Tuck, who became fitful every time he recovered from my blows. I hoped that he was almost-but-not-quite dying of thirst and suffocating. I had so many questions for him but no time to ask them so he would have to wait.

"Whose horses are they?" I said to the stable hand, pointing at the magnificent destriers and fine palfreys.

"Why, they're the archbishop's, sir," he said, looking at me as if I was a madman.

"The Archbishop of York?" I grabbed his shoulder.

"Yes, sir," the lad was frightened by my intensity so I let him go.

Jocelyn stared. "Did he say—"

"Yes. My liege lord is here. I must go to the castle. Watch the monk every moment. You do it yourself Jocelyn, allow the squires to do all else but you be sure this monster stays bound."

Tuck was awake and he squirmed violently and shook himself, moaning from deep within his fat belly. I readied another kick but Jocelyn placed a hand on my arm.

"I think he wants to tell us something," Jocelyn said.

"I do not have time for this," I said and untied the monk's gag and withdrew the sopping rag from his mouth. It reeked worse than dysenteric bowel water. I held my dagger against his neck.

"Please," he begged. "Blood. I must have blood."

I stared hard at him. "I heard how you like to jest. I am not amused." I moved to replace the rag.

"I will die." His eyes bored into mine. They were shot through with blood and I would have sworn he was afraid. "I swear, if I do not have blood then I will die."

"What do I care if you do?" I said.

"You need me," Tuck said, his foul mouth gaping like a landed fish. "Need me to talk. About him. About the Lord of Eden. If I am dead, you will never know. A drop is all I ask. Just a drop."

I looked at him, confused that he thought I would stoop so low as to feed him blood and I jammed the sopping gag back between his yellow teeth. He wailed and groaned. I shoved him onto his face to tie the rope about his face. His thrashing about was scaring the horses and drawing attention.

"Be still. Lie still, I say. Very well, here, then," I said, standing and looking around. "Here is your blood for you, if it will cease your caterwauling."

Tuck looked up from the straw, pathetic hope in his eyes.

I kicked him hard in the teeth and nose, rocking his head back. He lay still.

"You killed him," Jocelyn hissed.

"No, no," I said. "It'll take more than that. But I pray he'll lay quiet now."

The horses started and the nervousness spread around the stables. I held up my hand, apologised to the grooms and squires for the disruption, and explained that the man I had abused was my lawful prisoner. The muttering and grumbling continued. It does not do to disturb rich men's horses.

"Sir Richard of Ashbury," Jocelyn said quietly. "Making friends wherever he goes."

"Roll that thing onto his face so that he does not drown in his blood."

"What if he does die?" Jocelyn said. "How will we explain that?"

"I have bigger concerns," I said. "Anselm, clean my armour and have my sword straightened and sharpened. The point may require regrinding. See to it yourself that it is done properly. I go to meet the archbishop."

The castle was a heaving with men, dressed in an array of colours, all talking of the new turn in the war. Most would be Roger de Lacy's personal knights and squires, men that owed him service. Some few wore the archbishop's livery. I was escorted through the castle and into the hall, where I expected the sheriff to be holding court but instead, I was taken back to the sheriff's solar, announced and ordered in immediately.

The archbishop stood by the narrow window. He turned as I entered. He was just as I remembered him. Tall, broad shouldered, going to fat but still full of strength. His skull looked as thick as a bullock's but his eyes were shrewd black pinholes.

"My lord archbishop," I said, inclining my head momentarily.

His eyes were shining with inky blackness. His eyebrows knitted together over his slab of a nose. He did not look happy to see me.

"Roger, how are you?" I said to the sheriff, who looked deeply unhappy. He was surrounded by parchment and his clerks and priest buzzed about him. "So, I hear England is invaded."

"Richard." The sheriff glanced up at me from his seat, no expression on his face. "You have returned." He looked back at his parchment.

In the far corner, a wiry, tall figure leaned in the shadows. One of the archbishop's men, I assumed, though I could not make him out.

"What in the name of God are you doing here?" the archbishop said, his voice deeper and fiercer even than I had remembered. "You were to stay in that hovel you call a home until

I summoned you."

The archbishop was one of the most powerful men in the kingdom and my liege lord, yet I had to fight the urge to leap forward and smash his skull against the wall. "William is here."

Roger and the archbishop exchanged a glance.

"So you say." The archbishop snorted.

"You doubt it, lord?" I said, surprised.

"I do doubt it," he said. "I doubt it very much. As I doubt your sanity and your good judgement in coming here in a time of war."

"I have done as you asked and stayed in my lands," I said. "But my home was attacked. The attackers were sent by William."

The archbishop nodded. "They told you this?"

"Yes," I said, bending the truth.

He scowled. "They said they were sent by Earl William de Ferrers?"

I took a breath. "They did not use his name."

"Ah," the archbishop nodded, glancing at the man in the corner as if inviting him to join him in mocking me.

"It is William," I said. "He is hiding in the deep wood. He has killed or subdued or driven off the outlaws. He is extending his tendrils into the villages. Soon, the roads will be unsafe."

"Absurd," the archbishop said. "Utterly absurd. You were always a little touched, Richard and now you have lost your mind."

"Will you tell him," I said to the sheriff.

Roger rubbed his grey head and sent his clerks away. They closed the doors behind them. "No," he said. "The Archbishop of York is correct. The trouble in Sherwood is the typical outlaw banditry and we shall clean them out in time."

I stared at him. "I disbelieve what my ears are hearing. You and I discussed this. We agreed it was William. Before I left to discover more."

Roger stared at me. "I was mistaken."

The archbishop smirked from across the room.

The sheriff was bitter about that girl, Marian. I had forgotten her and forgotten Roger's enmity before I left. Had he been hoping that I would be killed in the wood? Was that his plan all along? Or had the archbishop poisoned him against me, for some reason?

"And what did you discover?" the archbishop said. "You come into our presence with a filthy face and stinking of mud and manure."

"I rode to question the forester," I said. "In his village. He confirmed the new ruler of the wood was a knight."

The archbishop laughed. "They always claim to be a lord, do they not, Roger? What arrogance. Jumped up peasants strap on a stolen, rusted sword and think themselves equal to a king. Richard, you have no head for these kinds of things, you know this. You are a mighty warrior, every knight in England knows it. But you are a step above simple minded when it comes to the hearts of men. That forester is as corrupt as they come. Ranulf, is he not? The warden tells me the man has been keeping the fines he forces from those living in the forest. He was spinning you tales, son."

There was more to it, of course. I could have explained how the poor folk of Linby had all been slaughtered by William's men merely for speaking with me. I could have told them about the destruction of the priory and the torture of the prior. But some instinct caused me to withhold the existence of Brother Tuck. Perhaps it was the hot rage that spiked through me at the archbishop's moronic, offensive words.

"Do you mean to insult me?" I asked him.

The shape in the corner moved out into the light. It was the archbishop's man.

Only, it was not.

It was a woman.

She wore a hauberk, covered with a black surcoat. She had no mail coif on her head but wore a padded cap ready to take one. She was broad at the shoulder but narrow as a sword blade. I would have taken her for a man but for the fine features of her face and her huge, dark eyes. Some men have a womanish look about them. Other men are as beautiful as a Spanish princess and yet I was certain the figure in the corner was a woman. I could smell her. She reeked like a knight does, of horses and leather. Yet her sweat-stinking linen undergarments smelled strongly of woman. She stared at me with defiance, anger and amusement filling her eyes. The confident stare of one warrior facing down another.

"Insult you? By speaking the truth?" The archbishop growled. "Do not stare so, Richard. This is my bodyguard, Eva."

"Bodyguard?" I said and laughed. She stiffened, like a cat that is ready to pounce. The archbishop held out his hand to her.

"She is more capable than any man and you will watch your tongue. I trust her with my life and she has my full confidence, in all things."

It was suddenly clear. He was swyving her. Every man knew of the Archbishop of York's love of young girls. He usually kept his dalliances to servants and peasants, those who would not cause a fuss and whose families would be easily bought. I had assumed him too busy and too old to keep up with such things but clearly, he had found a new perversion. Dressing up his fancies as knights. I wondered if she screwed him while wearing the hauberk. I would imagine the mail would chafe. Perhaps that was what the old goat enjoyed.

"I understand," I said.

"No, you do not," the archbishop said, scowling. "You will go south. We must slow the Prince's invasion."

"I cannot go anywhere, did you not hear? William has made himself King of the Wood not thirty miles from here."

"Then he will wait," the archbishop shouted. "The very kingdom is at stake. Your personal squabbles are irrelevant."

"Squabbles? He murdered my wife. Slaughtered my brother, his family. Uncounted others. He must be brought to justice."

Roger and the archbishop exchanged a long look.

"You have my sympathy," the Archbishop said. "Certainly, you do. And rest assured, if William de Ferrers is truly in the greenwood, we shall roust him out, Roger and me, shall we not, sheriff? And he shall hang for his crimes. If he is there. But in the meantime, the Prince of France has landed an army upon our shores and he is aiming for London."

I was defeated. I knew my duty. There was no way out of such a command from my lord. It was a perfectly reasonable request and not one that the king would have any sympathy with if I brought my case to him. He would never even hear it.

"The king marches to meet the French?"

The archbishop coughed. "Indeed, he does not."

It should not have surprised me. King John was a capable enough leader of armies who could steal a march on anyone, if he so chose. But he was a far cry from the audacity and vigour of his brother Richard, who was called lionhearted for good reason.

"Where does the king go?"

"North."

That did surprise me. "He is running away?"

"Did I not tell you he is slow, Roger? Give him a castle wall and tell him to get over it and no army in all Europe will stand in this man's way. Give him a simple puzzle and he will stare at for a week, like a dog calculating a dice roll."

The sheriff looked horrified at the insult. The ridiculous, sham bodyguard, Eva, smirked.

"Very amusing, my lord," I said. "The king goes north to deal with the barons there before he faces the French."

"There," the archbishop said. "Not so difficult after all, is it. The rebel barons are giddy with joy. The Scots, in league with the French, have invaded the north of England. The French had sent a few knights and plenty of marks but the Prince has landed with thousands of men. The rebels feel assured that victory is theirs. The king's army is made from the men of us few loyal lords but the bulk of it are mercenaries. And mercenaries have to be paid. The king will isolate and crush each baron on his way north to deal with the Scots. One by one, he will fine those traitor lords for every mark and shilling they have squirrelled away, if they wish to keep their lives and their lands."

Roger and I nodded in agreement. It was a sound and necessary strategy. The Scots could be beaten. They were a rabble, who were used to fleeing at the first sign of resistance. They counted on the lack of forces in the North.

"And," the archbishop continued. "When the king has enough gold to pay for his army for a season or two, he will come south and defeat the French."

"By which time," I said, "the French will be in possession of London and a dozen castles in the south. It could take a year or two or more to grind them out of each one."

"Which is precisely why you must go south and slow the French advance."

"Me alone?" I said it in jest. "Certainly, I can defeat a thousand men with a single lance."

"You should not attempt wittiness, Richard, it does not become you."

"Tell me what men you are giving me."

"None," Archbishop Hugh said. "You will ride south for the Weald, in Kent. South of London. The king has a loyal servant with lands there. His name is William of Cassingham. You will go to him and together you will slow the invasion."

"How many men does he have?"

"It is uncertain," the archbishop said, looking at Roger.

"At least two hundred," the sheriff offered the figure reluctantly.

"Two hundred knights," I said, amazed at the audacity.

"Against ten thousand?"

"Ah," Roger said. "Two hundred archers. Not knights."

"Dear God," I said.

"Yes, quite right, son," the Archbishop Hugh said. "Put your faith in God."

"Why me?" I asked, appalled. I was being given an impossible task. All I could do was pretend to obey and then lay low. Perhaps I would ride to the Weald, find this man and stay back from the fighting while he was crushed. No one could say I was shirking my duty if the Kentish archers were all dead.

"Most loyal knights are flocking to the king," the sheriff said. "We all must throw our lots in with him now. If the French win, if the rebels rise to power, we shall all lose our lands and everything we hold dear. Even our lives."

"What the sheriff means to say," the archbishop said. "Is that you are a great knight. You have fought in countless skirmishes, raids, sieges and even pitched battle. You have the vigour and countenance of a man half your age, with the experience of one twice as old. Who better but you?"

"And unlike many knights," I said, "I cannot say no."

"Indeed." The archbishop stood in front of me, almost of a height with me but bulky beneath his robes. "Think of this as an opportunity to regain your position. When you do this for him, the king will be willing to overlook any past rumours that surrounded you in the past."

"You give me your word that this will happen? That I and my men would be welcomed at court?"

"What do you want at court?" my lord said, looking horrified.

126

"I can teach John's sons the lance or the sword," I said. "Anything suitable that pays well for me and my men."

The archbishop relaxed when he realised my ambitions were so meagre. "What men?"

The sheriff spoke up. "He means Jocelyn de Sherbourne."

"Ah, your son, of course. Yes, of course. Yes, yes. No, you shall be welcomed by the king, of course, and I will myself extend your lands and find you a better place to live than tired old Ashbury Manor. So full of dark memories and tainted with death. You could even bring that beautiful daughter of yours back into the world. She is still of childbearing age, is she not? She would dearly love to converse with ladies of her rank once more, I am sure. A suitable husband could be found. And is your boy married yet? He will have wealth enough to find a proper wife."

"You lay it on thickly," I said. "But I will take you at your word, as witnessed by the sheriff here, is that not correct, Roger?"

"Yes, yes," he said, waving his hand at me.

"Every day is vital, Richard, every single day. You will ride in the morning. I will see you provisioned. Eva, give Richard his money, will you."

The woman moved like a wolf, stalking toward me with her eyes fixed upon mine. I felt that I was the prey.

"Here," she said, her voice deep but clear and strong. She dumped a heavy purse into my hand and slid back.

I hefted it and held it up. It was good to feel such riches, heavy in the palm of your hand. "I will ride at first light for the Weald and there I shall find this knight Cassingham. We shall fight the invasion with our two hundred peasants until the king comes.

This Cassingham knows to expect me?"

"I would not say that he expects you, precisely, no," the archbishop said, walking away from me. "In fact, you may need to encourage him to stay and to fight the French."

"We have prepared you this letter for him," the sheriff said, handing it over. "It has both mine and the archbishop's seal upon it."

I had been given an impossible task but I could see no way out of it. What could I say? I laughed and nodded, tucking the letter away.

"One final thing," the archbishop had the good manners to at least look embarrassed. "You must take Eva here with you."

I could not understand for a moment. "A woman?" I looked at her. "I care not that you bristle, so, girl. My lord, I cannot escort a young woman through England when it is beset by war."

His great forehead knitted together and his voice became a growl. "She is more than capable of taking care of herself. And you will do as I command."

"Very well," I said to her. "I will come for you at the Castle at first light. Do not be late as I shall not wait for you, not at all, do you understand me, woman?"

"Perfectly," she said, her lips tightening, curling up at the edges.

I knew that I had to abandon her.

∞

As I was led through the keep, the bailey and the outer gate, I felt a deep, profound fury at the thought of William slipping away once again.

The sheriff had insisted that I be escorted all the way out of the castle. No doubt, he wished to keep me well away from Marian so I was accompanied by three of his men. Burly fellows with stout clubs, no doubt very good at keeping townsfolk in order. I could have killed all three in the blink of an eye but, of course, Roger knew I would not create a disturbance for the sake of the young woman. But it confirmed how much he was concerned for her.

I looked for her but did not see her until I was well outside the walls.

At the bottom of the pathway up into the castle main gate, a short, stocky servant with stick-thin legs swept the path outside a large, newly built two-story house. It was by that time very dark so it was strange that she be working so furiously when she should have been resting. Bent-backed and swaying, she swept ineffectually, glancing around from deep within her hood. I assumed she had lost her wits.

"Sir Richard," the old lady hissed as she sidled up to me keeping her back to the gate and the guards standing inside far up the slope. She peered out of the shadows of her hood.

"Sweet Jesus Christ," I said. "It is you, Marian."

It took a moment for me to recognise her because she was dressed in a peasant's garb that was far too large for her. Her clothes were bulky and lumpy around her abdomen, like she was a deformed old crone.

"Keep your voice down," she said, her eyes glaring up at the castle walls.

I drew her into the shadow of the house. "What in the world are you wearing?"

She grinned. "My maid Joan brought me some clothes. I have stuffed my own garments inside to make me appear fat. Rather ingenious, is it not"

"It is madness," I said. "How did you get out?"

"I am no prisoner," she shot back. "Well, not precisely. I simply have no place to run to."

"You went through all this to speak to me?"

Her eyebrows knotted together over her nose. "What? No. No, I wish to come with you."

I drew her deeper into the shadows as two squires strode by, their arms full of linen. "I am going to war."

"I know that. I heard them speaking. I had to warn you and beg your help. Please, you must get me out of here."

"Warn me of what? What did you hear?"

"They wish to get you far away from Nottingham. I think they are expecting that you will die."

"You have warned me and you have my thanks. Now you must return."

"I shall not return. If you do not take me, I shall run anyway. I have food, wine." She tapped her bulky body. "My good, kind friend Joan will take my place, calling out through the door if asked. She is old and fat but she has the voice of a girl. She will slip away back to her own rooms at dawn before I am discovered to be gone."

"If he is truly infatuated with you, his men will bring you

back."

"I must act. I must at least try. I cannot simply sit and wait and allow myself to become that man's wife."

"Would it be so bad?" I ventured. "To be the husband of an enormously wealthy lord?"

She set her jaw. For a moment, I thought she was going to hit me. Instead, she softened. "Will you not be a true knight and save a maiden in need of rescue?"

"The ballads are not true to the world. You will find that out in time."

Marian leaned into me, looking up with her big eyes. "They all say how you are a true knight. That you risked your life to save that of the Lionheart. That you risked your life to rid the holy land of an evil band. That you fought bravely for King John in Normandy and Gascony, storming wall after wall—"

"Stop, stop, you think I am so weak as to be won over by flattery? Do you take me for a fool?"

She straightened up. "Yes," she said. "The sheriff is lying to you, using you, sending you into harm's way. Would taking me with you not be a way to set even the score against him?"

I looked at her then up at the castle. Then back at her again.

"Hide your face, look down. You will have to spend the night in the stables."

Jocelyn had paid generously for the stable boys to look the other way. No doubt, word of a blood-soaked monk tied up in the stall would get back to the sheriff by morning but he had troops to muster so I hoped I could be away the moment the gates were opened.

"Who is this?" Jocelyn asked.

"You wanted me to hire servants, did you not?" I said, ushering Marian into a separate stall to Tuck's. The horses were yet nervous of the man but Jocelyn had worked his magic on them and they stood quietly and slept. My grey courser was even laying down to a deep sleep.

"Men servants," Jocelyn said. "Not an old scrubber woman."

I was silently gleeful at the prospect of his regretting those words when he saw the young lady. I felt her resist my hand as I guided her into the stall by the grey but I pushed her gently inside.

"She is joining us and we will have not another word on the matter until we are on the road. Not another word until then, do you hear me?"

Jocelyn understood something was up and he must have died to ask what. I whispered to the girl that I would find her some clean straw and a blanket.

"The monk was groaning," Jocelyn whispered. "I had to knock him about the head. He sleeps now but when he wakes I fear his cries may wake the dead."

"He is perhaps dying of thirst," I said.

"Thirst for blood?" Jocelyn asked, with a heavy emphasis.

"I have only felt I needed it when gravely wounded," I said. "Other times it is an urge I am able to resist."

"You can resist," Jocelyn whispered. "But this fellow appears unable to last much longer. Come and see for yourself."

"It is too dark," I said. "What would I see?"

"He has the appearance of a corpse," Jocelyn said. "I paid a couple of grooms to bring water, wash the fiend and change his robe for a peasant's garb while I stood guard."

"Good man," I said.

"But I saw that his skin was green and mottled, fetid and taught. As if he were dead."

"Yet he breathes."

"I do not like it," Jocelyn said. "And the grooms were as disgusted and disturbed as I was. No doubt word will be spreading that you keep this creature. No, I do not like this, Richard."

"You will like what the sheriff and archbishop said even less."

Of course, I should have known that Jocelyn would embrace the chance for glory. To save a kingdom, single-handed, was all Jocelyn ever wanted. That and fame, riches and a well-bred wife to give him sons while he spent every day out hunting. Not too much to ask of God.

"We must be together at the gate and ride out through it the moment it is opened. We shall be miles away before the archbishop's woman realises she has been abandoned."

"She is supposed to watch you for him," Jocelyn said.

"Of course. But why not send a man? Surely, he must have expected me to reject her and he will somehow later use it against me. Bah, I have no mind for these things. Go, eat, find the squires and send them to me. We must buy up supplies for the road. The prices will be as high as Heaven but the archbishop has bought me with these coins."

Marian slept curled up on the straw without complaint. It was as we mounted at dawn that Jocelyn realised that the old scrubber was, in fact, a great beauty. I thought his eyes would burst from his head but he controlled himself and we rode out as quickly and quietly as we could.

Brother Tuck was almost dead but I bound him in sackcloth and carried him over my shoulder. I told the porter I was taking one of my men home for burial. He did not believe me but he let us through the gate.

Our little company headed west. I meant to stop at home on the way South.

Not five miles along the road from Nottingham stood a knight with his horse, a very fine black courser, waiting for us.

"Is it a trap?" Jocelyn said, drawing his sword and looking all around at the fields beside the road for signs of waiting ambush.

"Of a kind," I said. "That is no knight. That is Eva, the archbishop's bodyguard."

SIX ~ THE WEALD

WE RODE EAST FOR THE MORNING, as I wanted the sheriff's pursuers to think I was heading for Derby and my own land. But well before midday, I instead took us through a narrow track that led roughly south. We weaved our way through wooded hills toward the River Trent, where I knew of a little-used ford used mainly by drovers.

If we avoided trouble right away, we still had two hundred miles or more to go before we made it to Kent. I had decided immediately to avoid London because I was afraid that the French would have taken it by the time we got there. So we would continue to edge west of south from Leicester, perhaps to Cirencester and cross south of the Thames high upstream, then hook around London and keep on east, all the way to Kent. It was the end of May when we left Nottingham and the damp, misty morning turned warm and stayed that way.

A strange company we made as we set out that first day. Eva, the archbishop's supposed bodyguard, had impressed me by stealing the march on us, presumably sneaking out from one of the town gates in the dark or earlier and spending the night out by the side of the road. The archbishop had clearly meant for her to spy on me and she meant to carry out that duty with no regard for her own wellbeing. Women are born to bear pain and they do so better than men, yet they do not endure discomfort with the same fortitude.

Her woollen cloak hung heavy with dew and under it, she wore her full hauberk, black surcoat and a fully enclosed great helm hung from her saddle. It was clear from the way it clung to her when she moved that her hauberk fit her perfectly. There was no doubt that it had been made for her, fitted exactly to her shape, rather than some lad's cast off. It was excellent quality and would have been a significant investment for any knight. In her case, the archbishop had presumably paid for it and he was wealthy beyond the limits of my imagination. At least, before the king had bled him dry over the years.

"I had hoped to leave you behind. But as you are here, well, of course, you are most welcome to join us," I said, feigning acceptance of her outmanoeuvring of me.

"Just as your lord commanded you," she said, looking me square in the face before mounting her fine horse.

She barely spoke a word all morning. I did not ask her questions and she volunteered nothing of herself. She rode well and her gear appeared well worn and well cared for. Barely any rust at all. I doubted I could give her the slip easily but I intended to get rid of her as soon as I could.

Jocelyn was tight-lipped, confounded by her sudden appearance and her arrogant style of dress. But he was barely aware of Eva. Marian had caught his eye.

She was wrapped in my cloak, with the hood up over her own, sitting very well in the saddle of the ageing palfrey I had provided for her. That palfrey was old when I bought him years before but still he had cost a small fortune for his gait was as smooth as a maiden's belly. Aged as he was, I rarely taxed him with my weight but he was an ideal mount for a young lady. Marian had seemed touched by my generosity, offering to ride one of the packhorses instead and I warmed to her even more. She wore the servant garb, still stuffed with clothing and food and the Lord knew what else so she looked as round as a ripe apple. Even with her face down and in shadow, she could not hide her beauty.

"My lady," he said, easing his horse close beside hers. "I am Sir Jocelyn de Sherbourne. It is a great pleasure to meet you. Of course, these are somewhat unusual circumstances. I wish only to say I swear that, wherever it is that we escort you, I shall protect your life with my own."

From the back of the palfrey, Marian looked up at Jocelyn from under the rim of her borrowed cloak. "What a brave and honourable knight you are, Sir Jocelyn. I have never felt safer than I do at this moment. I am so glad that you are here beside me."

I thought his chest would burst. His cheeks coloured and his tongue was suddenly tied. I spurred past them to Anselm, Swein and the wrapped, writhing body of Brother Tuck.

"Anselm, Swein, we must deal with this monk before we get to Leicester. He may die of thirst before we can arrive. But even though he is weak and dying, he may yet retain his unnatural strength."

"Where should we torture him?" Swein said. He was bareheaded, having put his hood away once we were away from the town. "Me and Anselm can take him off into the woods?"

"Anselm will stay with the others," I said. "Swein, you will come with me. Can you sit a horse?"

He looked up at me through his tangle of blonde hair. "Climbed on an ox, once."

"You will lead the packhorse, then, but you must hurry. We will head for the large copse up ahead, do you see?"

"On the little hill?" Swein said.

"Hurry on ahead, run if you need to and I will catch you," I said. "Oh, and be sure to take a cup with you. Do not untie that monk."

"I'm not daft, my lord," he said and picked up his pace.

"Anselm, keep an eye behind for any sign of pursuit. And listen, son. You keep an eye on that Eva woman. If it seems like she's going to grab the Lady Marian then you raise a cry, you understand? Be ready to race after her. She rides like she fancies herself a horseman but I wager she'll not out ride you on that grey lightning." He took the praise well, though he was grinning as he fell back alongside Eva. I waited for Jocelyn to draw near. "Sir Jocelyn, might I beg you for a word?"

"Of course, Sir Richard," he said, throwing his chin up and riding ahead with me out of earshot.

"My hope is we slipped the damned sheriff's men but while I am up there sorting out the monk, be mindful that you might get company."

"Worry not, Richard," Jocelyn grinned. "I'll not let them take her." He patted his sword.

"You bloody will let them take her," I said. His face fell into a scowl. "What will you do, draw blood over her? He might send a dozen men after that girl, do not be a fool."

"God will grant me victory," he said. "I have sworn to protect her."

"Listen, son," I said. "Understand that standing by your word could mean her coming to harm."

"My word is my word," he said, rather offended. "I have a noble name that I must uphold. And I have a noble heart."

"You have a stiff prick and a soft head. If the sheriff's men come for her then you give her up. If your noble heart is set on her you can try for her hand when we return. Roger cannot marry her until he rids himself of his wife."

"I heard what they were saying in the town," Jocelyn said. "He means to have her, marriage or not, at any cost."

"Do not make an enemy of the sheriff and get yourself killed over a girl you have spoken a dozen words to."

"It is you who have made yourself an enemy," he said. "Yet again. It seems to be the only thing you are good at. Why did you abduct her if you mean to simply hand her back?"

"I did not abduct her, she is a free woman. She is simply riding the same route as we do."

He looked over his shoulder. "What about that ridiculous woman? Is she here to grab the Lady Marian?"

"I doubt it. She was surprised to see her, did you notice? And she is the archbishop's plaything, not the sheriff's. Still, she may get an idea about stealing the lady back to Nottingham, so I instructed Anselm to keep one eye on her. You do the same. That horse of hers looks fast but I am sure that she would be no match for your horsemanship. Now, I am going to question the monk before he dies."

I caught up with Swein and we picked our way into a copse upon a slight hill across the field. In a second field beyond the copse, the folk it belonged to looked to be out together as a family, hoeing about their green crops in the late spring sunshine. I hoped they would be too far to hear any cries the monk made.

We secured the horses and I dragged Brother Tuck from the packhorse and dumped him beneath a stand of hawthorn.

"String your bow and stand back over there to the side with an arrow nocked and ready," I said to Swein, who obeyed swiftly and without question. The young man impressed me more every day.

The stench of rot and death billowed out when I unwrapped the sackcloth from Tuck's body. His ankles were bound together, as were his wrists and I had tied his arms to his fat body.

He groaned and writhed. The man's skin was greenish and waxen. His eyes were closed but they darted about underneath the bulging lids.

I slapped his face, hard.

His eyes sprang open and he lunged for me with his mouth. I dodged back. He flopped like a fish onto his face. He snarled and drooled, his jaw working into the mulch.

"Brother Tuck," I said. "I will give you water if you control yourself."

He snarled and twisted within his bonds. I yanked him from his front into a sitting position against the trunk of a hawthorn, the leaves green and the uncountable berries turning bright red above. Tuck's eyes rolled, bloodshot and unblinking.

I poured water from a skin into his mouth. He gagged and coughed on it, spraying it everywhere. He cried and groaned as if I had burned him with fire.

"Swein, you will not need your bow, for now."

"Is this some plague," he asked, coming near behind me. "Something to do with the Green Knight's blood?"

I sat on my haunches, watching Tuck twitching and gasping. "In the Holy Land, William made many men loyal to him. They would drink his blood, once every week on the Sabbath. It gave them great strength and speed and resistance to pain and hunger."

"That is what this is," Swein said. "That is what he did to the men in Sherwood, the ones I tracked to your hall."

"The ones who attacked my hall, yes," I said. "But that is not what this is."

"What is this, then? Lord?"

"I do not know. But I do know what he needs."

Swein sighed. "Blood."

"Take your dagger and cut yourself where you think best. Your arm, perhaps. Drain some into the cup you brought."

The young man stood very still.

"I do not wish to make you angry, Sir Richard," Swein said, stopping and starting. "But can you not use your own blood? I am not afraid to bleed, you know, I don't mind a bit of a scratch, like, but I don't know, lord, I just don't know about this."

"You do not wish to give any to him," I said. "I understand. I am not angry. But I cannot use my own blood."

"Very well." He hesitated. "I do this because I want the monk to tell us where the Green Knight is. And after he tells us I want to be the one to kill him."

"I understand," I said, promising nothing.

As Swein sliced the back of his forearm, Tuck's head snapped up. His nose twitched and his lips curled back. He began to growl.

I drew my sword and held the tip to his neck while Swein collected the blood. "Hand it to me," I said after a few moments. "Stand back and ready your bow once more."

Swein wrapped his arm and when he was set, I raised the cup to Tuck's mouth. "Hold still or I will slice open your neck rather than feed this to you."

The words calmed him long enough for me to pour the thick, hot blood into Tuck's mouth. I wished it were I that could drink it. Tuck drooled and gulped it down, licking his lips.

He let out a shuddering groan and sank back against the tree, unmoving.

"Did it kill him?" Swein asked.

Tuck's mouth moved, twitching and his eyes opened, focusing on me. The sweaty pallor on his skin seemed immediately less, a little red came back into his cheek. His lips formed a word, a whispered croak.

"More."

"Speak and perhaps I shall allow you to live."

"More."

"Tell me about William," I said. "The Green Knight. The man who gave you his blood. Who did this to you? What do you men call him?"

"God." He grunted out what could have been a laugh.

"Where is his camp?"

"Blood."

"What made you this way?" I said. "Why are you dying without drinking blood? What did he do to you to make you this way?"

Tuck grinned and leered at the cup.

"Perhaps we should take simply his head," I said to Swein. "Are you sure you wish to be the one to do it?"

Swein nodded. "I will send an arrow through his skull."

Tuck's eyes swivelled between Swein and me.

"Fine, then." I stood, holding the point of my sword against Tuck's chest. Swein planted his feet and drew back his cord.

Tuck screamed, "No!"

"But you have no use to me."

"I will tell you." Tuck's throat must have been raw, his voice was like gravel.

Swein eased his bow cord. I squatted and gave Tuck another taste of blood. His eyes became clearer. His skin took more colour and he breathed easier.

"Tell me how he made you," I said. "Why are you suffering in this way?"

"I drank the blood of the Lord of Eden," Tuck said, his voice still raw but almost human. "I am now a son of Adam." He grinned.

"But that is how he has always granted his power," I said. "The power of the blood simply fades over time. Over seven days."

Tuck giggled. "That's for the initiates. I'm special. He changed me for eternity."

"And his men would drink normal blood to make it last longer. But why are you suffering like this?"

Tuck nodded. "Now I must drink blood, every couple of days. More than that and I get weak. Sick. By the seventh day, I die. But as long as I drink mortal blood, my gift will last until the end of days. The end of days, I say. Now, give me blood."

"That seems a rather simple cure for your evil," I said. "All I need do is starve you? But how is that change made? What is the method? You get no more of this cup until you answer."

I placed the cup beside me, well out his reach.

He stared at me, his eyes mad, red-ringed and twitching.

Without warning, distant shouting came through the trees from the road.

"Watch him," I commanded Swein, who nodded and pulled a touch of tension on his bowstring.

I ran to the edge of the trees and looked out across the field to the road, which ran from left to right along the boundary.

Jocelyn and Anselm were cantering to the left, back the way they had come. Marian and Eva continued heading to the right.

The shouting came from six horsemen, riding two abreast, who approached Jocelyn and Anselm along the road from the left.

Clearly, we had been pursued and we had been found. The sheriff's men had found Marian.

Those men-at-arms were all in full mail, helmeted, some had shields on their arm or slung on their back.

All six of the sheriff's men drew to a stop in front of Jocelyn and Anselm. Their leader raised his hand to halt his men. Marian and Eva rode on at a walking pace, Eva with one hand on the bridle of Marian's palfrey. Both women looked over their shoulders, tense and ready to spring ahead.

"Let them through, Jocelyn," I whispered, urging him from afar. "Let them take her, you romantic idiot."

I watched, too far away to be heard or to interfere, as Jocelyn drew his sword.

"Bloody fool," I said.

"Sir Richard," Swein shouted from the trees behind me.

I spun, sword up ready to strike at Tuck. Instead, the disgusting fiend was sitting exactly where I had left him. He had the cup of blood to his lips, draining the last of it, his hands at the farthest reach of his bonds.

"Should I kill him?" Swein shouted, half drawing his bow.

"No," I said, running toward the monk. Tuck looked up, blood all around his grinning mouth. I clouted the top of his skull with my pommel, hard enough to cave in the skull of a normal man.

He fell, dead or just nearly. I knew not which.

"Bind him, cover him, put him on your horse and follow me," I shouted at Swein as I ran for my own, unwinding his reins. I led the grey courser out of the thin trees at the edge of the copse and rode out across the field, taking stock of what I had missed.

Blows had not been struck. But three of the sheriff's six men rode around Jocelyn while he remonstrated with the leader and the remaining two men. Jocelyn shouted an order to Anselm, who wheeled his horse around and chased the three men along the road. Those three mounted men were going to take Marian. Anselm looked like a child next to the big men. At least, he had both hands on his reins, sword sheathed.

Marian, on my ancient palfrey, could never have escaped from them and I doubted that Eva would be capable of outriding a man. So the only course of action for the women would be to surrender to the three men-at-arms closing on them along the road.

Eva turned her horse and drew her sword, placing herself between Marian and the approaching riders.

It took me a moment to realise that Eva was going to fight. The idea was absurd. That mad young woman was facing down proper soldiers. Just because she wore the garb of a fighter and had the hilt of a sword in her hand, she thought she could challenge three mounted men-at-arms. By so doing, Eva was in danger of getting herself or Marian hurt or even killed. Men-at-arms were not known for restraint or good judgement.

I spurred my horse and he sprang forwards, released into a gallop. I aimed for Marian, sitting still upon the palfrey, looking at the riders who bore down on her. Anselm rode hard on their heels. I was near enough to hear the hooves of their horses thudding against the packed earth of the road and though I closed the distance rapidly, I was too far away to stop what was happening.

The three riders slowed and reigned in and surrounded Eva. One of the men rode right around Eva and closed to Marian. That man reached out of his saddle to grasp the bridle of Marian's palfrey.

While the other men shouted at her to stop, Eva raked her heels against the flanks of her black courser and the fine animal leapt forwards as fast as a cat. Eva slapped the flat of her blade on the top of his helm, hard. He yanked his own mount back, in panic and anger. Forgetting Marian, he drew his own sword. His eye slits must have been knocked out of alignment, as he waved his blade wildly while shouting.

The palfrey was not trained for combat and the frightened horse shied sideways away from Eva and into the man-at-arms. With a backswing, that blinded, angry fellow hit Marian with his sword.

The girl screamed and fell from her saddle. She hit the road surface and lay still. The panicking palfrey stepping and stamping all around Marian's body, afraid of the shouting around him.

After a moment of shocked silence, the tension on both sides erupted into action.

Eva cried out a challenge, pushed forward and barrelled the blinded swordsmen from his own horse. He fell, arms flailing, his sword spinning from his grasp.

I was closing but still too far to intervene.

The other mounted men drew their own blades. A second of the three attacked Eva from behind, pushing his horse onward, with his sword ready on his shoulder and his shield up.

Anselm urged his rouncey on and slashed that horse's rump with his blade. The animal sprang forwards, trying to throw the pain of the wound from its back. Instead of attacking Eva, the rider dropped his sword into the long grass at the side of the road and held tight to his reigns while his mount leapt away into the far field.

Jocelyn and the three remaining sheriff's men galloped toward the confused melee from the left side of the road. I reached it before them. Shouting at everyone to stop, I forced my courser into the third man's smaller rouncey and simply pushed him out of his saddle.

Eva leapt to the ground, stamped her foot on the fallen man and then pushed Marian's horse away, showing no fear as the animal half-reared. Eva stood guard over Marian, sword out, helm down. She looked like a knight.

I spun to meet the other remaining men as they reined in. Jocelyn and the leader of the six men stopped together. That leader bellowed at his men to stop fighting.

"And stand back," I roared. "All of you. Keep your distance. Put away your blades, for the love of God."

The sheriff's men calmed themselves. Everyone but Eva sheathed their swords. For a moment, the only sound was the hard breathing of men and horse.

"Sir Richard," the leader called to me. "So good to see you." He unbuckled his helmet. It was the sheriff's friend and loyal servant, Sir Guy of Gisbourne.

"Check the girl," I said to Anselm, who leapt from his horse and ran over while we waited. "She fell hard." I glared at Gisbourne, saying nothing.

Sir Guy attempted to hide his discomfort, sitting up straight as an arrow, sweat running down his brow.

"The lady's upper arm is cut, Sir Richard," Anselm shouted,

his voice breaking. "Her head is bruised but not broken. She is too winded from the fall to speak but she breathes."

"You are lucky the girl is not dead," I said to Sir Guy. "Your man there was a hair's breadth from being a murderer."

"I know," Guy said, anger flushing his face. "He will be punished. I am relieved the young lady is uninjured."

"Uninjured?" Jocelyn was spoiling for a fight, his blade in his hand. "She is hurt, you fool. Blood has been drawn. Justice demands—"

"Jocelyn," I said. "Please attend to the Lady Marian." Jocelyn wanted to argue but his lust for the girl overcame his love of a fight. He swung his leg over his saddle and hurried to her, fussing over her like a mother for her firstborn child.

"I apologise for my men's enthusiasm," Sir Guy said, attempting a smooth smile. "Yet you must understand why I am here. Truly, I regret this misunderstanding and placing the girl in danger. But the fact is, the young lady must now return with me to Nottingham."

"She will not," I said.

"I cannot return without her," Sir Guy said.

"And yet you must."

Sir Guy looked at me and past me at my men, such as they were. "We outnumber you," he said.

"We outclass you," I said. "Do you really wish to trade more blows? You will lose men, perhaps even your own life. You would risk harming the lady even more than you already have."

"I cannot return without her," Sir Guy said, desperation edging his voice.

"The sheriff will punish you," I said, nodding. "He must have been angry. He must have threatened you with all manner of consequences should you fail." Sir Guy's silence confirmed my words. "She is free to go where she wishes. And she does not wish to go to Nottingham."

"She is a ward of the crown, entrusted to the sheriff's care."

I eased my horse close to his and lowered my voice.

"No, she is of age," I said. "She is eighteen years old and free. You understand, Sir Guy, that I must defend her freedom. I will do so."

"I have no wish to fight you," Sir Guy said, lowering his voice so that his men could not hear. "I saw you slay half a dozen knights in just a few moments in that campaign. I never believed the rumours about you and the blood but I understood why they said it. You move with unnatural speed, Sir. So I tell you that I know I am no match for you. But the sheriff will not accept that I had her in my grasp only to allow you to leave. You know what the sheriff is like."

"Strangely, I did not know until now," I said and glanced over my shoulder. "Take the woman Eva back with you. Lay the blame upon her in some way."

Sir Guy's face set hard. "I'll not go near that woman."

"Why?"

"She is the archbishop's," he said. "I will not cross him. And she is unnatural."

"How so?" I asked, glancing at her.

"Can you not see? She dresses as a man. She fights in the yard, invites challenges from squires and knights alike." Guy spat.

"Oh? How does she do?"

Guy hesitated. "I will not take her back with me."

I shrugged as if I did not care what he did or did not do. "You cannot have Marian. You will not take Eva. So keep riding. Chase about the country looking for me." I raised my voice. "Find somewhere quiet to spend a few days. Come back to Nottingham having lost me. Having never found me. Your men will want to save their hides also. I will pay you and your men a few shillings to tide you over for the next few days. Why not find a nice tavern somewhere and spend it on drink?"

Guy's men sat bolt upright and stared at him.

Ultimately, I suspect, it was fear of my sword that kept him from forcing the issue. Being known as the Bloody Knight sometimes had its uses.

∞

Swein returned across the field with Tuck bound up across his saddle. I had to stop to gag him once more, which was a dangerous business now he was full of vim once more.

"You did not kill him," Jocelyn said, surprised and offended.

"I am not finished with him," I said. "Your little encounter with Sir Guy rather interfered."

After we patched up the Lady Marian, we went on our way.

We spent the night in local lord's tumbledown hall. The place had a sagging roof and the thatch was brown, wet and stinking. The lord was off with the king but his steward was generous enough, considering the way things were in England.

I could never have predicted but Eva and Marian seemed to make a friendship of sorts and they slept alongside each other. I suppose that Eva felt protective of Marian and the young lady was glad to have Eva's attention in spite of the woman's strangeness. Marian was otherwise alone in the world.

Jocelyn did his best to contain his desires for Marian and his anger at me, for taking him away from his own vengeance, from his chance at a stable life with a good woman and his confusion as to why I carried Tuck with me. Jocelyn was full of unspent forces.

The next day he rode on ahead, keeping clear of the girl. And me.

That morning, I fell in beside Eva as we rode and before I spoke, I shared a companionable silence with her. Anselm rode on one side of Marian, babbling at her. Swein led a horse on the other side, looking up at her almost continuously.

The weather was warm and I could not bear to wear anything more than a shirt and tunic. The sun was wonderful. Blossom burst forth among the uncounted shades of green in the hedgerows. The fields were sprouting their green shoots of wheat and rye and the people were out hoeing the rampant weeds from between them.

Eva was not nervous of me, nor of what I would say and she rode without even glancing my way. It was admirable.

"I was most impressed with the way you protected the young lady," I said to her.

She nodded her head slowly, as if to say, "Of course you were."

I pursed my lips, wondering how to get her to speak of herself.

"I suppose I also wonder why the archbishop's bodyguard would fight the sheriff's men in that way for some unimportant girl," I asked.

She fixed me with her hawkish eyes over the long, straight nose. "If she is so unimportant, why not let them take her?" Eva spoke as if she was a lady who was halfway to becoming a commoner. I guessed that she was somewhat like me and came from the impoverished rump of the knightly class.

"I would have done so, had they not charged in so." I was not sure if I meant it.

"They would never have tried it but they saw you were not there and they thought to seize their chance while they could."

"Sir Guy says that you sought to challenge his men in the training yard?"

She laughed but with little joy. "Did he tell you how I beat them all?"

"Surely not," I said, for it was not possible.

"Try me yourself."

I had to laugh. "Where are you from?"

She scowled, staring straight ahead. "Nowhere."

"You are certainly English," I said. "But where were you raised? Who is your father? Does he know that you ride like a knight? How long have you been training?"

"So many questions," she said. "Let me ask you some, first."

"Gladly," I said. "But you must offer something yourself. First."

"Very well. Yes, my father does know that I fight and ride like a knight. Now, tell me what you are doing with that man tied up in the sacking."

"He is no man," I said. "He is a murderer and when we are south of Leicester he will tell me what I need to know. Then I will cut off his head."

She looked at me then. "You should not trust a man like that to talk. You should kill him now."

Eva spoke as easily of killing as an old soldier might. "How old are you?" I asked her.

"How old are you?" she shot back.

"Forty-seven, I think."

She laughed, her face lighting up. Her mouth was suddenly wide and her eyes shone. She was a striking looking woman. "My father said the same but I did not believe it. How have you stayed so young? What is your secret?"

"Perhaps God rewards my service in the Holy Land. Who is your father?"

"Hugh de Nonant. The Archbishop of York."

I did not know what to say.

"I see."

"Do you?"

I thought about what the archbishop could be up to by sending her with me. Was she telling the truth? Why would he clothe her in such a way?

"He dresses you as a knight?" I asked. "By your presence does he hope to unsettle the men he speaks to?"

She was silent and I chance a look. Her face was drawn tight over her bony face, her lips pressed together. I gathered I had given a great insult.

"Do you mean that you truly can fight?" I said. "As well as a man?"

"Better," she said. "Better than most men. Better than most knights."

I suppressed a laugh, as I did not wish to anger her any further.

"Where did you learn to fight?" I asked.

"It is your turn to answer my questions," she said and she was quite right. "They say that when you were fighting for King John, in Gascony, you would drink the blood of the men you slaughtered. High on a castle wall before the army you swallowed the blood from a knight's severed neck and threw the body down to the defenders."

"I see the tale grows in the telling," I said.

"So you deny it?"

I sighed. It was a beautiful afternoon. By speaking of such things, it was as though I was spoiling that glorious, holy thing. The most wonderful thing in all the world. An English summer day.

"We scaled the walls but only a few of us made it inside. I fought my way down the other side and chased a fleeing group of knights and squires into the ground floor of a corner tower. They were pressed together tightly, I thought I could trap them, kill them. But I was drawn inside. They shut the door behind me, thinking to kill me. There were twelve men in there. Men and boys. I was alone. Surrounded. They were behind me and halfway up the spiral stairway. I killed them all. I cannot remember precisely why I needed to be so thorough. I can recall a few of the survivors, on their knees, begging to be taken prisoner. But when the battle rage is upon you, what can you do? Certainly, I was very gravely wounded. My face was torn open, I could feel my cheek opened and flapping like the sole of a shoe. My knee had been smashed. I'd had my helmet torn away and my skull felt cut and crushed by heavy blows. I would have died. So I drank."

She looked confused. Disbelieving. As well she might.

"You were dying so you drank the blood of dead men?"

"It heals me," I said. "So long as the blood is somewhat fresh. It heals me completely, quickly and thoroughly, leaving no scar. I know that may surprise you. That you will not believe me. But it is the truth. And that is how they found me. They broke into the tower from above, came down the stairs. I looked up over the body I held to see a group of Monmouth's knights crowded on the stairs. Of course, as I am sure you know, Monmouth and my lord the archbishop are enemies, of a sort. Before the day was out I had been denounced, the priests had proclaimed me possessed by a demon or the son of Satan or some other form of evil. They demanded my death."

She looked closely at me, perhaps judging whether I was playing some game. Plainly, she doubted wounds so severe could be healed.

"How did you escape the accusations?" Eva eventually asked.

"There was no crime committed, as such. I denied it. I had fought bravely. I had won the walls. The king sent me home, hoping that the scandal would blow over. God knows, he was right. He has had enough of his own in the years since that it is no more than a rumour."

"A rumour that is true," she pointed out. "How long have you been this way? What does it have to do with the monk in a sack on that horse?"

"It is your turn to answer my questions," I said.

She declined.

It was two weeks of riding to get to the Weald, on the southeast corner of England. We went west and south, then headed east once we were south of London. An interesting journey. I did not press the woman for details and, little by little, Eva revealed her story.

One night, sitting quietly together by the hearth in a hall in Wiltshire, she spoke more about her early life. The firelight flickering orange over Eva's strong features, making deep shadows in the hollows beneath her cheekbones.

"The archbishop is your lord," she said to me. "So you well know his nature. I have often wondered how many brothers and sisters I have in England and France. And Rome, too, no doubt and in every other village in between."

I laughed politely. Yes indeed, I knew what the archbishop was like. And I knew that I was also a bastard, though not raised as one. Not quite.

"My dear mother was just a young girl when my father became infatuated with her," Eva said. "So she says. She was the youngest of a poor knight up in Northumbria and they had very little, other than too many children. And mother was a beauty. Beautiful but weak of body and mean in spirit. I suppose now that they somehow thrust her under the archbishop's nose. He used her, and then when she fell pregnant he put her away. Her brother took us in. And I was born in the cold, up north. And foisted onto my uncle, who was a knight."

"Who was he? Perhaps I know him."

"Perhaps you do," she said. "And that is why I will not say."

"Fair enough," I said. "How did you end up working as the archbishop's bodyguard?"

What I really wanted to ask was why she was telling me everything about herself and how much of it was true. What was her game? Was she really who she claimed to be? Was she still going to spy on us, report to the archbishop?

Surely, I thought, I should not expect her to slip a knife into my ribs one night.

"I am not sure why or how it started. But I loved to play at knights and Saracens with the boys. Even though mother and my uncle beat me bloody so many times. I would hide away, in the stable or go out into the wood and swing a stick around."

"I was the same," I said.

"Were you beaten when discovered? No, you were encouraged. As I got older, the boys did not like me playing with them. My cousins and the other girls would mock me. When I was eight or so, some of the manor and village boys caught me and gave me a hiding."

"A gang of boys can be the evilest thing that walks the earth," I said. "I wager your mother was pleased you'd had some sense knocked into you."

"She was dead by then," Eva said, dismissively. "She died in the winter. Died of her bitterness. She was abandoned by the archbishop and then no other man was good enough so she died bitter and lonely. I did not miss her."

"Your beating did not cause you to give up," I said, nodding in approval.

"I hunted those boys," she said, the firelight glinting in her eyes. "One by one, over weeks. Days, perhaps. Time passes differently when you are young. I took the first boy, Thomas, in the woods by his den. I left his face a pulp. He would not admit who had done it but everyone knew. The other boys knew. They were on their guard all the time but still I got them. John the Pimple was their leader. He must have been twelve years old. He seemed a giant to me. He was canny. Wary. I had to stalk him for days. He thought that he was safe in his father's workshop after dark. He was wrong."

"You seem to be proud even now," I said and she snapped her eyes to mine. "And you bloody well should be." I banged my ale mug against hers and she smiled.

It was the first smile I had seen on her face. It was quite lovely.

"So you were sent away?" I prompted.

"Quite the opposite," she said. "The boys' fathers were livid. My aunt and the women were horrified. But my dear uncle began training me as he would any squire."

"Good God," I said, trying to imagine what my own people would say if I did something similar.

Eva nodded. "The first year or two they all tried to dissuade him. The priests, his wife, the villagers. My uncle never wavered. He told them all to shove off. There were a few of the boys also training. We were quite poor. They would never speak to me, let alone train with me."

"Sounds like an isolated way to grow up," I said, recalling my own chaotic upbringing amongst dozens of pages and squires. "Lonely."

"I was never happier," she said, a smile creeping back onto her face. "Over the years, he taught me the lance, the sword, dagger. Wrestling, riding."

"Ah," I said. "A wonderful existence." For these were the best things in all the world, as well as women and wine.

"Until my uncle went away to fight. He never returned. His wife, everyone else, forced me out. My cousins were triumphant. I had nowhere to go but to the archbishop."

I winced. "I am sure that he loved that."

"He denied that I was his," she said. "At first. He tried to force himself on me. But I fought him, tripped him and threw him down. I thought he would kill me but instead he was impressed. He had one of his men test me with sword and shield. After that, he indulged me. In a certain amount of secret, of course. But even though word got out, everyone is afraid of the archbishop's ire."

"And then he took you into service as his bodyguard," I said.

"You must know what he is like," she said. "He knows that I fight well. Better than most men. But he has me by his side when he speaks to certain men."

"Certain men?"

"Men such as the sheriff," she said. "And other men that the archbishop likes to fluster with my presence. Most of his vassals and almost all of his priests and monks. He enjoys seeing the indignant expressions on their faces, he has told me. He enjoys making them uncomfortable and dares them to make mention of my presence. Dares them to challenge him. But he has never taken me anywhere near the king or his courtiers."

"And he asked you to follow me," I said. "When we left Nottingham. He knew I would not take you willingly."

"Yes," she said, not meeting my eye.

"And you were to do what? Watch me?"

She drank more of her ale. "To see that you did your duty and went to the Weald. He told me to do everything I could to keep you there and I was to stay with you. But if you went north or anywhere else, I was to find the archbishop immediately and tell him. He suspected you would go into Sherwood, or return to your home. I think he hoped that you would flee overseas."

"Would he mind you telling me this, do you think?" I asked, confused as to why he would want me so very far away from Sherwood.

She shrugged. "I do not care what he thinks. I serve him because I know no other who would have me. Have me as a squire or in service as a man at arms." She eyed me over the rim of her cup.

"I would," I said. "I would have you serve me." Of course, I did not have the income to support more men but I was somewhat drunk and her eyes were large, dark, and beautiful.

"You would?" she said, orange dancing over the black irises.

"Of course," I said. "I saw how you defended Marian without a thought for yourself. You stood over her, ready to fight to protect her, though you barely knew her. You ride well, you have your own equipment and you care for it diligently. You would make a very fine man-at-arms. But my lord is the archbishop and he would never allow me to take you on."

"I see," she said. "I understand."

"So we shall not ask him."

We crashed our cups together and drank, smiling.

∞

During the journey south, Eva was taciturn with all of us, except those nights when she and I would sit, drink and talk quietly. I enjoyed teasing words out of her, enjoyed her company very much. I suppose it was because I so favoured her with my presence that Jocelyn resented hers. He thought that her manner of dress was an absurd boast, an affectation that was offensive to any true man-at-arms. Jocelyn continued to hold her in contempt until the day he humoured her with a practice sword fight using a sturdy stick.

She rapped him on the head and the fingers before he realised what he was up against. She was like a willow and as fast as the strike of a night viper I had once seen in Acre. Jocelyn, with his sturdy bullock's shoulders hunched low behind his shield, hammered her into submission. Eva was a fine fighter but Jocelyn was simply beyond her.

Still, she had more than proved her worth to him. What is more, because he was already infatuated with Marian and because Eva was illegitimate he had no lust for her. He accepted her as another squire.

Anselm seemed to be terrified of her. Presumably, he was

either in love with her or saw her as competition. Possibly, it was both.

Swein mistrusted her and kept his distance, without ever explaining why.

For Marian, she was a great comfort, being both a woman and a person she could ask about practical matters such as where to pass water while on the road and other issues particular to ladies.

Marian proved herself stoical and strong willed. The first few days she was close to tears from the soreness of riding and the discomforts of the road. Even my old palfrey's gait would make you sore if unused to riding. But she never complained, not once in my hearing. Jocelyn waited upon her, tended to her every whim, helping her on and off her palfrey, to and from buildings. He cut her meat and poured her ale. He laughed at her jokes and sang to her. He berated an innkeeper to heat gallons of water so that she might bathe and spent my money to pay for it. I had the bath next, though, and I did not begrudge him for his attempts to woo her. To what extent it was working, I had very little idea. Marian often behaved strangely around me, as if she were wary of being close to me. She was deeply disturbed by the writhing creature I carried with us.

All the while, Anselm taught Swein the practicalities of being a squire. We even allowed him to train with a sword, every now and then. The young man was not bad, although he was rather old at sixteen to be beginning his learning and we kept him to swinging a stout stick lest he hurt someone. Untrained swordsmen always want to swing their swords like axes, going for power over speed and control.

But Swein's true talent was the bow.

One fine evening outside Devizes, we stopped to spend the night at the edge of a meadow under cover of a stand of oaks. Swein declared that he must shoot some arrows.

"You have duties," Jocelyn said from a low log by the young fire, rubbing at a flake of rust on the hilt of his second-best sword. "See to them before you play."

"If I don't practise the bow then next time I shoot in anger I might miss," Swein said, taut with contained anger. "You have to practise the bow, Sir Jocelyn, you just have to. What if you need me to protect you and I miss?"

"What did you say?" Jocelyn said, climbing to his feet, his blade flashing in the evening light. "Did you defy me, boy?"

"Jocelyn," I said, tired of his nonsense. "You go ahead, Swein."

Swein grinned in triumph while he strung his bow and bent it, pulling the cord back repeatedly without nocking an arrow.

"You have to warm the bow," he said over his shoulder, aware of how I stared at him. Bows and arrows fascinated me.

His arrows were precious to him and he looked after them as if they were newborn babies, always checking on them, keeping them dry and protected in their arrow bag. He twisted up a big bundle of shoots, wildflower stems, and long grass and laid it in front of a tussock at the edge of the meadow.

He stood fifty yards away and shot a few arrows into it. Every shot was on target.

"Good thing too," Swein said when he came to collect them. "I can make a new bow from a stave, if I have to. And I can make a cord out of almost anything. But I can't make an arrow. Just can't do it. Every single one of them is precious. If I miss the target then chances are I ain't ever going to find that arrow. Not in woods like these."

"So will you let me have a shot with it?" I asked. His face fell and I laughed. "I am only pulling your leg, Swein. But can I try the bow? I always loved shooting a crossbow. Is it much different?"

Swein handed it over and I tested the pull. It resisted. Pulling it back to my cheek was an enormous effort. "Good God," I said. "Jocelyn. Jocelyn, quickly come and try this bow."

I will never forget the look of wonder and blossoming respect upon Jocelyn's face when he attempted to draw Swein's huge bow back to his cheek.

"How can you pull this thing?" Jocelyn asked Swein. "Over and over again? You are as scrawny as a baby bird."

Swein scowled and disrobed for us, taking his undershirt down to his waist. He turned his back and flexed the thick muscles across his back and shoulders.

"Good God," I said, poking at his flesh like I was at a market. "You have shoulders like a destrier."

"A lifetime of using a heavy bow," Swein said over his shoulder. "Every year when I was a boy, my dad used to make me a bigger bow. Took me all summer to get strong enough to pull it with ease. Then next year he'd do it again. It's the only way to get strong enough to pull these big war bows."

Eva cheered from by the fire, asking Swein to remove the rest of his clothes. Marian laughed, clapping her hands and gave voice to her agreement. Swein covered himself up again, his fair-skinned face glowing red. Jocelyn was surprised by Marian's somewhat lewd outburst but there was lust in his eyes, for what man does not want his lady to be a secret harlot?

From the shadows under the trees, the writhing form of Tuck groaned. I sighed and motioned for Swein to follow me.

Brother Tuck had to be fed every couple of days with a few drops of blood. Swein, driven by his desire for revenge — whatever it was he was revenging —gave up his blood gladly. Anselm dutifully contributed when Swein's arm began looking like a ploughed village field.

We removed the sacking wrapped around the rancid smelling figure. He was growing thinner every day, which was good because he was easier to move and contain. I kept his eyes bound but undid his gag. His mouth was fouler than a city gutter.

"Hurry," I said, holding Tuck down.

Swein slit his own arm, held it high and squeezed a trickle into Tuck's gaping maw. Tuck groaned and slurped it down, making noises like an animal.

I bound him up again, looping him to the branched trunk of a solitary yew so he could not get away unseen in the night. Or worse, worm his way into our camp.

Jocelyn scowled at me as we returned to eat. "Why do you keep him? How long has it been? Ten days? It is madness. Either take the monk for trial or, at least, drag him away and slaughter him yourself."

"I will," I said.

"When, Richard?" Jocelyn said. "What are you waiting for?"

"He is the only one who knows where William is," I argued.

"So question him and be done with it," Jocelyn said.

"Carrying him with us is absurd."

"Tuck is raving mad most of the time," I said. "I keep him on the verge of starvation lest he causes trouble when at full strength. Keeping him bound, gagged and covered up drives his wits further from his mind. I cannot question him upon the road. But when we reach the Weald, I will find a secluded place. I will bind him and I will give him a pint or two of blood. That should bring him back to himself so I question him fully. But we cannot do that here. What if he gets loose out here?"

Jocelyn looked unconvinced. Everyone else refused to meet my eye.

"Alright, listen. When we reach the Weald, I will question Tuck and then I will fulfil my promise to that poor old Prior," I said to everyone. "Will that suit you all?"

It was difficult to hide his presence when we rode through towns. He had befouled himself so many times that we submerged him in a river and rubbed his disgusting body against pebbles and sand to clean at least the outside of his clothes.

His presence greatly disturbed Marian. It was many days before she accepted that he could only be kept alive by blood. I explained everything to her. She found a kind of comfort in the fact that her father had been slain by immortal, powerful monsters rather than mere men. Marian had heard the rumours of a darkness in the greenwood, everyone in Nottingham had. It was a nameless evil far worse than the normal outlaw bands. But no one would tell her anything. The sheriff had kept her ignorant and isolated and only ever repeated the lie that he expected her father to be ransomed any day now.

None of them understood why I kept Tuck. Why I refused to question him until we got to the Weald. In truth, I did not clearly understand it myself at the time. But Tuck was the single strand that might lead me to William. And he had been made into what he was by my brother's blood.

My blood.

The roads were infrequently travelled, especially in the south. Everyone loyal to the king had fled or was locked away in one of the many castles that John controlled. We met many men fleeing from the French forces but no one had any useful information, merely rumour and fear. Some men said the king was coming, others that he was in London and others that he had fled for Scotland.

Still, we met no French. Nor did we meet English forces other than the occasional group of men scouting about for their lords. Few men loyal to King John were brave enough to travel deep into Kent.

We asked for directions and arrived in the Weald at the beginning of June.

Kent was a beautiful place. Rolling green hills and rich villages. It was perfect land for farming. It lay between London and the ports of Dover and Sandwich and the routes to France and the rest of Europe. It was the richest land in England, as well as the key to the entire country.

The Weald, however, was a semi-wild land in the centre of that most civilised part of England. It was heavily wooded and hilly, where the rest of the shire around the coast was cleared and heavily farmed. The soil in the Weald was thin and difficult to grow crops on. It was grazed by sheep and cattle in pastures dotted between acre after acre of dense woodland. The ash and oak and beech woods were cut and provided fuel for the towns of Kent, for London to the north and the many charcoal makers working throughout the deep wood.

When we reached that land, we asked for the village of Cassingham and learned that was on the far side of the wood, halfway to Dover. We came from the west and would have to travel miles from one side of the wooded Weald to the other.

We never got that far.

Within the first few miles, walking slowly through that tangled, remote woodland we were surrounded by men armed with bows.

∞

The road was completely deserted, twisting through the dense tangle of old wood, coppiced ash and thick layer of green summer growth. There should have been people around. There were villages, farms, shepherds, swineherds and charcoal burners all over the Weald but I assumed that the Wealden folk had fled or gone to ground after the French invasion. It was approaching the middle of June 1216.

"Do you feel as though you are being observed?" Jocelyn asked me as we rode, our horses' hooves thudding softly on the dry ground.

"I do," I said, peering into the gloom, glad that we were all armoured. All of us that had it to wear. I looked back to Anselm and nodded to him that he was to watch Marian. The lad sat up straighter in his saddle and placed his horse beside hers.

"But is it Englishmen," Jocelyn said. "Or is it the French?"

I fingered the hilt of my sword.

"It's just the Green Man," Swein said, brightly, from behind us. He sat awkwardly on top of his stocky packhorse, like a dog riding a cow. He was an appalling horseman but he loved being in the woods.

"What in God's name are you blathering about?" Jocelyn said, still looking sideways, trying to see further than a half dozen yards away.

"The Green Man, isn't it," Swein said. "That feeling you always get when you're in the woods. That feeling of being watched? That's the Green Man. He lurks, watching. Up to no good."

"A peasant superstition," Jocelyn said, lowering his voice. "It is more likely a man of the usual colour. Perhaps we should ride hard, leave him behind."

I knew he meant Swein, not the watching man.

"It's not superstition," Swein said. "You can see where he's been, all the time. He leaves his mark."

"What mark?" Jocelyn said, attempting to scoff.

"The knots in tree trunks," Swein said. I turned but his face was completely serious. "Knots in tree trunks is where the Green Man has just pulled his face back inside the trunk, after watching you. The tree bark flows like water but the moment you look at it, it turns to solid bark again, only the ripples are marked upon the tree. And he loves the yew most of all."

"The yew?" I said. The trees are massive but squat things with dense, very dark green leaves that are like flatted needles. There was one or more yew outside every church in England.

"The yew is the archer's favourite tree making bow staves," Swein said, stating the obvious. "Because it is the tree of death. The Green Man lives inside every yew, in the darkness under the leaves, between the trunks. Why else would they be green all year round? You know the leaves are deadly, right? You have to keep cattle away from yews or they'll eat them and die. The berries are the colour of bright pink blood and anyone that eats them, man, dog, cattle, dies coughing up bright pink froth. The Green Man is death, he lives in the yew and his magic, his sight, his murder goes into your bow. That's the truth. Every archer knows."

Jocelyn was silent. We looked out. I listened hard, sure I could hear footsteps and sure I could smell bodies on the air. But perhaps, I thought, it was my imagination. It was difficult to smell anything over the stench of Tuck.

"Do not be absurd," Jocelyn said eventually but his heart was not in it.

Marian laughed from behind us, breaking the spell. "The Green Man is a story," she said. "The songs say the Green Man when they mean to say birth or death and rebirth. You know the poems, do you not? Where the leaves burst from his face and eyes, as though he is spring itself, come to life only to be so full of vitality that he dies, that he cannot breathe. Like he is himself a form of folksong. Like a wood in summer. Suffocating in its own abundance. That is all. He is no more a true man than is the sound of a river or the wind in the trees."

Jocelyn whispered to me, "Do you know what she is saying?"

"Of course," I lied.

"Fascinating," Jocelyn said over his shoulder. "Just fascinating, my lady."

"Halt!" A man in the centre of the road said.

I yanked on my horse's reins so hard I hurt the animal. Jocelyn drew his sword.

"Hold it there," the young fellow in the road before us said, looking at Jocelyn.

The man was not tall but he had somewhat of a commanding presence.

I opened my arms wide. "We will not harm you," I said and leaned over to pat my horse's neck.

"Calm yourself," I whispered to Jocelyn. "Watch the trees. Be ready."

"Harm me?" the young man on the road said, grinning. "I am not afraid."

I looked closely at him. The man was strongly built, with a large face. He was dressed in rough country clothes and no armour but he wore a sword at his hip.

"Fine, fine," I said, allowing him his swagger. "We are simply passing through. I am travelling through this land, heading toward Dover. On the road there I believe I will find a village called Cassingham."

"What you want in Cassingham?" the young man said.

"I am looking for a squire named William of the village called Cassingham," I bellowed at him.

"What do you want him for?" the man said, eyeing me warily. "You for King John? Or for the French?"

Leaves rustled and twigs snapped in the trees to either side and there were shadows moving amongst the dark green. Whispers, too, perhaps and definitely the wood smoke and sweat smell of men.

"Who are you for?" I asked the young man.

"I asked you first," he shot back, knowing that I had spotted his men surrounding us. If they were archers then we had no chance.

I stuck out my chin and slipped my hand around the hilt of my sword. It felt good in my hand. I glanced round at Eva behind me. She nodded, her own hand at her hip, reins held ready, her horse high and sensing the tension of the rider. Swein slid his hand toward his bow staff. Jocelyn had his fine horse under masterful control but the beast was quivering, expecting to be charged at any moment.

"I am a loyal and proud servant of the rightful king of England," I said, watching the man closely. "King John."

"Thank God," the man said, relaxing and then he cupped his hands to his mouth and shouted. "They are loyal to the king. Show yourselves."

There was a great rustling and stomping from the thick undergrowth all around on both sides of the road. I was shocked to see more than a score of men push their way through the bushes and stride into the road.

The twenty men wore gambesons and iron caps. A couple had mail coifs. Some were armed with spears, a handful swords and every one of them carried a huge bow and a quiver of arrows. They simply stood and looked at us, many of them smiling at our discomfort.

Jocelyn and I shared a look. We were surrounded and outnumbered but I did not feel as though we were being threatened. But they were certainly enjoying themselves at our expense, the damned commoners.

"Perhaps you'd be good enough to point me toward Cassingham," I said. "Can we reach it before nightfall?"

"You probably could," the fellow said walking toward me. He seemed relaxed, amused even, so I let him come close. "But William of Cassingham ain't there."

"Where is he then?" I asked and the men around us chuckled.

"Why, he's right here, sir," the man said, indicating himself.

I was not expecting a great knight but still I was surprised. The stocky fellow was young, in his early twenties perhaps, with big eyes, a huge nose, and a wide mouth. Although his features were too large, it was not an unattractive face. The man was unarmoured, even less so than his men and his clothes were of poor quality. Strange attire for a man who was supposed to be a squire but then again, a landed country gentleman was one step above a wealthy peasant. At least he wore a sword at his hip, though the scabbard was battered.

"You're William of Cassingham?" I said. "I am Sir Richard of Ashbury. The Archbishop of York sent me to you."

Cassingham stared at me for a moment then laughed. His men laughed with him.

I ground my teeth and fought my anger back down.

"Something amuses you about that information?"

"My apologies, Sir Richard," Cassingham said. He reached up under his cap to scratch his head, sighing. "I am not mocking you. I wrote to the king, to the Archbishops of Canterbury and York. I wrote to the Marshal. I begged for help in facing the French. They have thousands of knights and they are destroying this land. My land. Our land. We have held out in the hope of making a fight of it here, of throwing them back into the sea. But it has been more than a fortnight, waiting for more men. We have fallen back from them, this far into the wood. All the while, we have been praying that an army was heading this way." He looked at me and my small group and laughed loudly. "And then we get two knights, their squires, and their wives. If I say that I wished for more, you will forgive me, sir, that I take refuge in bitter jest."

Jocelyn shook with anger at the man's disrespect but he managed to hold his tongue.

I fought my own anger down and looked closer at the young man called William of Cassingham.

He was filthy, unshaven. His men were lean and their faces were drawn. He had bravely stayed and stood ready to fight. Had no doubt been fending off French raiding forces.

"You wished for more," I said to them, nodding and they nodded with me. "Of course you did. And I wish I was an army of English knights come to save you. I wish that I were here two weeks before now. And I wish I was a great lord in his castle, as rich as the Marshal and married to an Iberian princess who squirts the finest wine from her tits." They laughed, so I scowled at them.

"Wishes are for children. The king is occupied with

conquering the rest of his kingdom from the rebel barons. You asked for help. Here I am. And here I will stay and here I will fight with you. We cannot win the war. We cannot take back Kent. But perhaps we can kill a few wagonloads of the bastards before they kill us. Now. Where are those bloody bastard French, eh?"

"In London," William Cassingham said, beside my horse. "In London, where Prince Louis of France has been proclaimed King of England."

SEVEN ~ THE POISON PLOT

"HOW LONG DO YOU MEAN to keep this up before we can go home?" Jocelyn whispered into my ear in the darkness. "We have been here in the Weald, testing God's will for weeks. For how long do you expect us to get away with this? Look, the guards are even staying awake all night now."

"Precisely," I whispered to his shadow. "So be quiet before the French hear you."

Jocelyn and I lay in the sheep shit and long grass at the edge of a pasture, looking down into the French encampment outside the town and castle at Dover.

Dover was and is the closest part of England to France. The narrowest point of the English Channel at just twenty miles. On a clear day, it is perfectly possible to look from England across the water to the coast of France. Fishing boats bobbed always out there, along with the bigger, fat bellied trading ships running along both coasts.

On that morning, the sun was not yet up so all we could see were shadows in the blackness but the sky to our left was taking on the blue of a clear summer morning and all was becoming clearer.

Jocelyn was quite right. We had been harrying the French for weeks. Most of the summer, in fact. The French camp outside Dover was the largest target we had taken aim at. But Prince Louis and his large, well-equipped forces had taken the royal castles at Rochester and Canterbury, and all the towns of Kent, in a matter of days. London, always siding with the rebel barons, had thrown open the gates to him and welcomed him as the new King of England.

Yet for the entire summer, and despite taking the whole southeast of England, the French had simply avoided the castle of Dover.

The castle was said to be the key to the Kingdom of England and it had been since the dawn of time. Since the Saxons, King Arthur and the Romans, there had been a castle atop those white cliffs. In 1216, though, Dover Castle was vast, modern and well supplied with men and stores.

It was designed to bar the way to any French assault and yet Louis had made a mockery of the whole idea and simply ignored it for the summer. The loyal men inside Dover were enough to guard the walls but not to present a challenge if they ventured outside of them.

Then, when Louis was sure that King John was not coming

for him, he had finally invested in Dover. Or, at least, he had sent his men to do so while Louis languished in John's palace in London.

"There must be thousands of men down there," Jocelyn said softly.

"Possibly," I said.

"Hundreds, at least."

"Let us go back to the men," I whispered and we slithered back down the hill and into the trees. It was so dark in the scrubby wood that I saw little more than outlines and shadow and my eyes saw better in darkness than most.

We had forty men waiting for us, led by William of Cassingham.

Each man was an archer and each had a pony. The beasts stood dozing, a few chomping quietly and there was the occasional gushing patter of horse piss on the leaf litter.

"All is quiet in the camp," I said to Cassingham, seeing the glint of his open-faced, old-fashioned helmet. "This is your last chance to call off this raid. We cannot be sure our man will come out to me. And the chances are your men will be caught."

Cassingham laughed in the darkness. "They have not caught us yet."

His men laughed quietly.

In the middle of June, Prince Louis had marched his army all the way across southern England to the ancient and royal city of Winchester and captured it. After not contesting London, King John had declared Winchester to be his capital, the seat of his authority.

John had fled rather than fight a battle he would lose. It was probably a sound military decision, based on the reality of the situation over his personal pride.

But it had greatly disheartened the men of the Weald.

"What do you reckon on our chances, lads?" Cassingham said, half turning to the shadowy men near him. They chuckled again. A good sign of their trust in their leader.

William of Cassingham had rallied the men of the Weald and called them to him when their lords had gone over to the rebels or the French or simply fled. And Cassingham alone had organised the defence of the villages from the roaming bands of foraging French forces.

His band of archers could see off all but the strongest of French groups. The men were mostly freemen farmers but there were villagers and tradesmen too. But they were all skilled with the bow and many with sword and dagger. A dozen had fought in the Holy Land or claimed to have done.

Few on either side were ever killed in those first scraps with the French and rebel soldiers because no man in his right mind stands to be shot when archers are shooting at him. And why attack a defended village when there were plenty that stood defenceless and deserted?

When the French had landed, Cassingham's men drove sheep and cattle away from the edges of the Weald and deeper into the wooded hills and valley pastures, away from the roads and off the trackways. They carried and carted off sacks of grain and barrels of ale to hidden stores or places that could be better defended.

And it had worked. Cassingham and his men were by the

middle of summer already confident of keeping their families fed in the coming winter.

But the fear was that the French would overrun the Weald. And they could, if they wished. But the men were outraged by the invasions of the French into their homelands. Villages were emptied, farms abandoned and the people came to Cassingham's places, looking for protection.

None were turned away.

Cassingham was nobody. A country squire barely out of boyhood. Too poor to equip himself properly. Too beloved in his parish to feel able to leave to it to the ravages of the French.

And yet his legend was already growing.

When all men of noble birth had fled, he alone had stayed and led.

By the end of July, the French had returned to the southeast corner of England. They would take Dover, and then they would be free to receive all the reinforcements that France could send, completely unopposed and unthreatened. Then, no matter how many rebel barons King John brought back under his banner he would never have enough men to stand. King John's Flemish mercenaries would stay with him only as long as he had the coin to pay them.

All Prince Louis had to do was take Dover and then wait for John to run out of money.

And then the French would rule England forever.

"The most important thing is speed," I said to Cassingham and to the rest. "We must be in and out before they know they are being attacked. We need our head start or their superior horses will overtake ours."

"There is no need to say it again," Cassingham replied. "We all know what to do."

His confidence was reassuring and I did not doubt him but I found his disregard of my advice irritating.

"I pray that you do," I said and called for Swein, who brought my horse and my armour. Anselm brought to Jocelyn his and we shrugged ourselves into them.

Cassingham had his men kneel and pray with his priest. I stood to the side. Jocelyn kneeled with Anselm.

For all their talk and quiet laughter, the men were tense. Cassingham was quite right that they all knew what to do. It did not change the fact that they had never done anything quite like this before.

"The French were sleeping?" Swein whispered to me while the priest babbled on about faith and protection.

"A few guards, I believe. But the camp was quiet."

"Sir Jocelyn thinks this attack is a mistake," Swein said, his voice low.

"He does. What does Anselm think?"

"He thinks that whatever you decide to do is the right choice."

I smiled in the dark. "What do you think?"

"I think I should be in Sherwood."

"As do I," I said. "We will return very soon. Tuck is almost recovered enough to talk. If he can tell me what I need to know and if this raid goes well then I might consider my task complete and return to Nottingham. As long as Cassingham does well."

"He will," Swein said. "They all will."

"Oh?" I was amused by his certainty. "So you are an expert in warfare now, Swein?"

"I know archers," he said, defiantly. "I've seen these men shoot. And Cassingham leads them well."

I thought the same thing but then I had seen twenty-five years of war, on and off, and I had seen the best and the worst of leaders.

"Why do you think Cassingham leads well?" I asked Swein. The priest was finishing his prolonged prayer, asking God to bless their dutiful service for the king.

"When he talks, it seems like he knows what he is doing," Swein said slowly, struggling to put his thoughts into words. "And when he does something, you know that he has done the right thing. In the right way."

It was a garbled but fair assessment. "And do you think that Cassingham relies on what other men think?"

"He listens when his men suggest something or ask a question," Swein said, pondering it. "But he seems like he always knows what to do anyway."

The men murmured an Amen and stood to prepare themselves.

I clapped Swein on the back. "Good," I said to him. "Be sure to remember that when you are a leader."

"Me?" he said.

Cassingham returned with Jocelyn and Anselm. "Sir Richard," Cassingham said. "My men will be in their positions by the time you and Sir Jocelyn get to the camp."

It grew lighter with every moment. Colour coming into the

world.

I mounted my horse. Jocelyn and Anselm climbed upon theirs and I nodded to Cassingham and Swein, who would fight with the other archers, him being close to useless on horseback. I hoped he would be able to cling on to the back of one as we fled.

I walked the horse from the clearing to the road that wound up and then down toward the camp. It was dark. My heart raced. Like Jocelyn, I was not convinced that an attack on a heavily fortified enemy camp with thousands of men was a good idea. I was afraid that I would be captured. I was afraid that Anselm would be killed and that his mighty father would punish me, or at least, never forgive me. The Marshal was the one man whose opinion I respected. And the most powerful man in England, aside from the two kings.

The French camp already stank. The wind blew the cold salt smell of the sea to keep the excrement stench from overwhelming the senses. And even though only a fraction of their forces had arrived at Dover to begin the siege, it never took long for thousands of bodies to befoul the land and air for miles around.

The light wooded hillocks at the landward border of the camp would no doubt be cleared and occupied when the rest of the French arrived. But for now, it would cover our forty archers as they crept within long bow range and would protect our coming retreat.

It was light enough to see the silhouette of the vast castle, a dark shape on the brightening sky. The castle occupied a high mound of chalk that ended in the famous white cliffs on the seaward side. The land descended down to the town on the right, built on lower ground with easier access to the beach.

Between the castle and us stretched the edges of tents and frames of shelters and the siege engines they were quickly throwing up. It was a warm night, despite the cool sea breeze.

It was less than three hundred yards from the shadows to the camp but it felt like the dark moment stretched out like a black cloak, on and on, to the sound of hooves drumming on the thin soil covering the chalk trackway.

The first challenge came out of the dark.

"Stop there. Who are you?"

"Friends," I said in French, pulling to a halt.

"But who?" Two men approached in the gloom. "Name?" They seemed rather bored, which was good.

They also held spears, which was unfortunate.

"Sir Richard of Ashbury," I said,

"English?"

"A knight loyal to King Louis of England," I said. "As are my squires."

I dismounted slowly, groaning and sighing as if I had been riding all night.

They backed away from me, their spears held ready. I wished I could see their faces but they were clearly wary.

"Why are you here?" the closest man asked. He was a seasoned man-at-arms who could be trusted with gate duty.

"I have ridden hard to bring you news of King John's army."

They stiffened. "Tell me, now."

"How dare you speak to me in such a way," I said, feigning anger. "Bring me Sir Geoffrey and I will speak to him here."

The spear-bearing man-at-arms was becoming visible as the dawn grew. He glanced at his fellow spearman.

"Hurry, man," I said. "Come on. If I am an enemy, then how do I know that it is the steadfast Sir Geoffrey that is captain of the gate tonight?"

That appeased the senior man-at-arms somewhat. "Very well. You will come with us, Sir Richard and we shall rouse Sir Geoffrey."

I was certainly not going to walk into the French camp. "I do not obey your orders. You will bring Sir Geoffrey to me here and I will gladly speak to him."

They were confused and suspicious, as they had every right to be. What tired man would refuse shelter and refreshment after a long ride? But their natural deference to their betters asserted itself and the man-at-arms went to find Sir Geoffrey, leaving just the one to watch over my two men and me.

There were other French moving just inside the entrance. Rough ditches had been dug either side of the road and a bank thrown up as the beginning of a defensive palisade. They need not have bothered, for King John had neither the men nor the inclination to contest the south.

Jocelyn and Anselm dismounted, likewise making a show of easing their aching bones. Anselm walked our horses back and forth along the road. He was supposed to ensure they were ready for when we had to make our escape.

It grew lighter. More men woke in the camp and I cursed the man-at-arms for taking his time to grab the knight on watch. Jocelyn was tense beside me, attempting to appear nonchalant.

"What if Sir Geoffrey is not coming?" Jocelyn muttered.

"Any knight will do," I said.

Jocelyn nodded at the camp entrance, the gap in the ditch and palisaded bank stretching away ever clearer in the predawn light.

Sir Geoffrey was a small man, roused from sleep. His clothing was tousled and his cap was pulled down over his head.

Unfortunately, he had brought two large, armoured men with him. Neither wore their helm, at least nor carried a shield but both had swords at their sides with hauberks and mail coifs over their heads, much as my own men and I were attired.

"Who are you?" Sir Geoffrey said, looking me up and down. "What in the name of God are you doing waking me? Come on, out with it."

"King John approaches with his army," I said, speaking loudly enough for the men beyond the entrance to hear me. "Ten thousand men, two thousand horse."

Sir Geoffrey was stunned. His men stared in shock.

"Preposterous," Sir Geoffrey said, looking sideways at me. "You are lying." His men stared back and forth between us. "Take them."

"Jocelyn," I said. Before the word was out of my mouth, my man's sword had cleared his scabbard. He grasped the head of the man-at-arms' spear with a mailed fist and thrust his sword through the man's mouth into his head.

Sir Geoffrey gaped but his armoured men stepped in front of him and came for me.

The second spearman ran for the camp, raising a cry of warning. Jocelyn made to go after him.

The armoured men were wide-awake, battle-scarred veterans and they moved apart to surround me as I drew my blade.

"Joss, take the lord!" I shouted. Jocelyn changed his target to the noble Sir Geoffrey who was likewise attempting to flee.

The bodyguard nearest me charged at me while the other turned to protect his master. I had only one to contend with, so I turned his thrust, stepped inside it and slammed my body against his, grabbing the wrist of his sword arm. I crashed the pommel into his face, then again as he reeled away, pulling him back to me. As he fell, I pushed my point through his nose, grinding against the bones of his face. He was screaming until the blood poured down his throat. I tasted it in the air as he coughed it out.

Jocelyn had tripped Sir Geoffrey and was fending off the other man. Cries were coming from the camp. It seemed to be suddenly brighter. I ran to the armoured man and, having no time for niceties, thrust into his spine so hard that he was thrown onto his face. My blade pierced his mail and I felt it push into his backbone.

The blade snapped. It broke two-thirds of the way to the point, which clattered away onto the road and the rest was too bent to get it into the scabbard so I tossed it away.

Jocelyn dragged up Sir Geoffrey and together we got him onto my horse. He was dazed and bleeding from the head. Still, I had to hold my dagger to his throat as Jocelyn thrust him up to me from below.

Frenchmen came charging out after us as I embraced the knight in a bear-like grip, holding the point of my dagger against his neck and my other hand on the reins.

The whole sky to the east was faint blue and the world about us was tinged in blue-grey as Jocelyn and Anselm mounted. Both of them turned to defend me from the two dozen men that staggered out of the camp toward us, tired and uncertain but armed and willing to kill.

The arrows slashed down, just beyond us. A man was shot through the head, another the chest. Arrows clattered off the road. One that bounced off a stone in the road snapped and hit my horse, spinning but still with enough force to draw blood from his leg.

I urged the grey courser on along the track, between my men and up the hill toward the cover of the trees, holding Sir Geoffrey to me.

Jocelyn, Anselm and I stood our horses side by side on the brow of the hill. I glanced behind at the top of the hill. There were a dozen men lying dead or dying at the entrance and still the arrows arced in.

Dozens of men stood out of range. A score of knights gathered at the edge of the camp, more arriving and mounting with every moment.

"Run," I shouted. "Go now."

Most of the archers fell back to their ponies, mounted and began streaming away through the trees. Crows flying up, cawing in panic at the clattering of hooves and shouting men. A few kept shooting, covering the retreat.

When the knights realised that the rate of the arrows was falling, they advanced, shields up. Arrows bounced off them.

"We must go," Jocelyn said.

We rode hard. The final ten archers behind us were the best riders on the best horses.

They kept pace with us, or almost but the French knights caught up, their huge, powerful horses charging up behind us.

We made the first ambush just in time. The road bent around a low hill, the wood was a dense tangle either side of the track.

The pursuing French were slashing at our rearmost archers when the first arrows smashed into them. Our archers had left their horses on the other side of the hill and were only a few yards from their targets. The force of the arrows crashed into men and horses, the arrow shafts shattering and cracking in a cloud of splinters. Riders were unhorsed. The others fled.

On we rode, falling back through three more planned ambushes. We rode, through field and heath at a trot and at a gallop. We led them away from our defended villages and broke off into smaller groups, seeking to confuse them.

The pursuers gave up at sunset.

"Your friends have given up on you, Sir Geoffrey," I said as we looked out at the riders filing away back to Dover. "Which means you and I can have a nice little chat."

∞

After another night and half a day, when we were certain the French had truly given up, we returned to Cassingham's village in the Weald. The Kentish squire was given a hero's welcome by the men we had left behind to guard the families.

The day after our escape, I bound the French knight Sir Geoffrey up in the small shelter I had built away from the camp proper. I had made sure the place was well out of earshot and down in a dank hollow.

I had built the structure around a deep-rooted stump of oak. It was dark and damp, despite the bright summer's day outside coming through the doorway and the gaps all around the sides. The walls had been made from green saplings and the floor was merely earth with dirty straw atop it. A row of three sturdy posts on either side of the stump held up the sides of the roof. The place was crawling with spiders.

I had built it as a place to hold Brother Tuck.

"This is no fit prison for a knight," Sir Geoffrey said, puffing out his little narrow chest. "You will get your ransom. I demand a house befitting my station."

"What do you think," I asked Cassingham. "He is your prisoner."

"Don't speak French all too well, Sir Richard, truth be told," Cassingham said.

"He demands a finer gaol. Are you certain that you do not wish to ransom him?"

Cassingham, by way of answer, stepped to Sir Geoffrey and looked down. "We know what you did. We know you raped that girl in Rochester. No, you'll not be ransomed, sir. We may send them your balls. But the rest of you will never leave the Weald."

"What did he say?" Sir Geoffrey asked me in French. "Tell him I have wealth. I can pay whatever price he sets."

"I would not be so quick to offer that," I said. "We know that you raped that young girl outside Rochester. Everyone there knows it."

"I deny it," Sir Geoffrey said, his voice shaking.

In the far corner of the hovel, I found the bound form of Tuck and dragged him into the light before Sir Geoffrey. A thick rope ran between the oak stump and the scrawny form of my starving, mad, bound prisoner, Brother Tuck.

Cassingham stood just outside the door, leaning on the frame with his arms crossed.

"You see, Geoffrey, the only thing you have to offer is the stuff flowing through your veins. I have had a problem with our monk, here. He refuses to tell me what I need to know, without me giving him a proper drink. One that will bring him back to himself."

I took Tuck's sack from his head and the monk's twitching eyes fell upon our new prisoner. Tuck growled behind his gag.

"Silence," I said and cuffed his head, thumping him down to one side. "You see, Sir Geoffrey, Brother Tuck has knowledge that I need. And he is remarkably resistant to torture. Show him your hands, Tuck."

The monk held out his shaking, bloody hands. I had removed the tips of most of his fingers. Even the thumb and forefinger of his right hand but still he protected his master's secrets.

Sir Geoffrey recoiled and horror crept up his face as he realised he was being held by madmen.

"I have promised Tuck that he shall have as much blood as he can drink, should he answer my questions."

Tuck gurgled and heaved, his eyes bulging. He was laughing.

Sir Geoffrey pissed himself, which was the proper reaction.

"Please," Geoffrey said. "I will tell you everything."

"No, no. You misunderstand me," I said. "I do not need anything from you but your slow death."

"King Louis has given me Rochester," Sir Geoffrey swallowed. "And other lands hereabouts. If you ransom me, I can assure you that not only will you receive a significant payment, you shall have lands of your own under me when the war is won."

Cassingham and I looked at each other. "You think you will win?" I said to Sir Geoffrey. "You and Prince Louis?"

"Yes, King Louis." Geoffrey stammered. "That is to say, Prince Louis of France. I know his plans. I will tell you, I swear it. All his plans."

"His plans?" I glanced at Cassingham. "He plans to take Dover Castle before winter. Then he in spring he means to take the rest of John's castles, one by one until John is forced to flee or is captured. Then Louis will be King of England, for ever."

Tuck giggled behind his gag, his eyes bulging.

"Quiet, you mad bastard," I said to him. "Am I not correct, Sir Geoffrey? Of the siege, it looked to me that half of Louis' men will guard the town of Dover while the other half invest the castle. The engines being assembled were mangonels and perriers. It looked as though a huge tower was being made, with wattle sides. Louis has sent his fleet to sea, perhaps back to France, lest it be trapped by John's ships if they decide to attack. You had men digging in the front of the castle. No doubt, you intend to undermine the great barbican. A sound plan, I am sure. Is there anything I have interpreted incorrectly? Is there anything of substance that you can add? You see, you are not here to tell me anything. You are here because the good folk of Kent want a little justice. And, also, because I need your blood to feed to my monk."

Tuck giggled again, drool soaking through the bonds at his mouth and down his chin, glistening in the gloom.

"Do not despair," I said to Sir Geoffrey. "You will have a few days of bleeding yet."

I took out my dagger and the knight screamed.

∞

The French siege of Dover Castle dragged on. By August 1216, they had already breached and captured the castle's barbican. A great success for them but then they still had the gate beyond to take. Later, one of the mighty gate towers was brought down by the mangonels but still the French could not get through the castle's defences.

Dover Castle had cost a fortune to build and John had invested thousands in enhancing the place during his reign. Clearly, it had been worth every mark to the crown. It was the only place in southern England the French had failed to take.

All the while, our Wealden archers denied the French foragers access to stores inland. We ambushed, captured and killed dozens of them even when they began riding in force. Eventually, the foragers avoided the Weald altogether and we had to venture out into the rest of Kent to disrupt them. Our efforts certainly helped. Late in the year, the storms grow strong and regular enough to disrupt the short crossing from the French coast. The French would be without resupply from the sea for the autumn and winter and so the besieging forces grew desperate to take the castle before the bad weather forced them to become self-reliant.

At the start of October the garrison, led by the brave lord Hubert de Burgh, still held out, throwing back every assault on the walls. The longer the strength of the French was focused on Dover, the longer King John would have to strengthen his own forces.

All that time, I tried to put the pieces of Tuck's mind back together. An impossible task, though my hope was I could do enough to find out where William de Ferrers was and what his plans were.

But I waited too long. I had already kept Tuck in a state of starvation and isolation for three months. And it took three months more of feeding Sir Geoffrey's blood to Tuck to get anything close to coherent answers from him.

Even then, his mind was so ravaged that almost everything he said was incomprehensible. I had to keep Sir Geoffrey alive an awful lot longer than planned. Tied up in the dark with Tuck, being bled every day to feed him, Sir Geoffrey lost his own mind.

Cassingham was a hard young man but it was too much for him. His honour would not allow him to be part of my torture of Sir Geoffrey, the severity of whose continued punishment went beyond the law and common decency. Cassingham spent his days and weeks leading his men on raids against the foraging French and spying on the siege from afar. Swein rode with them and I was pleased, for the young man learned much about that particular kind of warfare.

All that summer and into the autumn, Jocelyn could barely tear himself away from Marian's side. But when he was with her he found his tongue tied and his jokes and witticisms were painful to behold. Although I met her only rarely, Marian seemed formal and distant with Jocelyn, far more than she was with any other person, noble or common, man or woman. Whether that meant she could not stand Jocelyn or that she was in love with him, Jocelyn could not decide. Neither could I, for that matter.

Whenever we could, we knights and squires trained Cassingham's men in the art of war. Most of them could shoot an arrow through a barrel hoop at a hundred paces but few could ride or fight effectively with a bladed weapon. No doubt they were good in a wild scrap for they were strong and fearless. But any idiot can swing a blade around. It was restraint they needed to learn, and control and how to defend. Even the ones who knew the sword had to be taught how to properly align the edge of the blade and how to cut with a draw or a push rather than hacking as if chopping wood. And these self-proclaimed swordsmen were the worst. When a man believes himself knowledgeable on a subject not all the true experts in the world can change his mind. It must be beaten out of him with rapped knuckles and clouted skulls.

Eva had learned proper martial techniques from knights and though she had rarely used them in anger, she could instruct just as well as any of us. Many of the Wealden men would scoff at the idea over their ale, or make bawdy comments but they would listen and gravely obey her in the cold light of day. Especially after she knocked them on their arse five times in a row.

After a long day of hard training in early October, I sat with Eva on the edge of a high pasture watching the sun falling over the trees. We shared a jug of ale and some bread. She wore a cap with her hair gathered up inside it.

We had taken off our mail and gambesons and sat in our undershirts, our bodies hot and stinking. She smelled much like a man did after a day of work, only it was different. Better. Whenever she was without the weight of her mail on her, I could not help but notice the swell of her breasts beneath her clothes. She rubbed and scratched at her chest. Through the open side of her shirt, I caught a glimpse how she had bound her breasts down with a wrap of linen.

"They are an impediment," she said, unsmiling.

I realised I had been staring and looked at the sunset once more, my face no doubt taking on the colour of the clouds. I began to mumble an apology. She waved a hand at me, telling me it was unimportant. She was not offended.

"I imagine it would be," I said, coughing. "Though it does not seem to slow you down nor restrict your skill. You are better than many a man I have seen named a knight."

She nodded, accepting what she knew to be true. She fingered underneath the side of her linen wrap. The skin beneath was as pale as moonlight.

It was a sort of madness, her carrying on as if she were a man. Without first her mother's brother and then the archbishop to pay for her, keep her hidden, and suppress talk, she would never have managed to carry it on. Of course, I would never have said such things to her. The woman was as prickly as an old holly tree.

But I liked her. She was the only person I knew, other than Emma, who would speak to me properly. She and Emma, though they were so different, shared a directness of speech that was so rare. Without Emma's effortless courtesy to temper it, Eva's bluntness was mistaken for rudeness and she found herself without many friends. I liked especially how she never seemed to want or expect anything from me.

"How is Marian?" I asked, keen to change the subject.

"Ask her yourself."

"You were well trained to fight," I said. "But never to converse, I see."

She snorted her derision. "Says you, Sir Richard, who speaks to no one unless it is to command or to terrify them."

I stared at her, wondering if that was truly how she saw me. "Perhaps you have the right of it," I said, drawing a suspicious look from her. "Marian will not speak to me."

Eva shrugged. "You frighten her."

"Me?"

"You frighten everyone," she said, peering over at me.

"Is it Tuck?" I said. "I do not wish to keep him there. I know what they say about him. About me."

"Yes," she said. "Of course it is Tuck. And Sir Geoffrey. It is wrong. It is madness. But it is not simply your torture of those two. Nor is it your nobility that scares them, for you are barely rich enough to warrant your title."

"What a kind thing to say," I quipped. She ignored me.

"Everyone knows that you are different from normal men. They have seen how you move. They have seen you lift a barrel of ale, without effort, by yourself. The story of you snapping that bow is whispered. Then there are the rumours. No one knows why you were disgraced. I certainly have said nothing. But the folk here say you were known as the Bloody Knight. That you drank the blood of the dead while on campaign in Gascony. They say you fought with the Lionheart and that you are sixty years old though you look like a man of twenty and the secret is that you drink the blood of maidens. That last part, I suspect, is one reason why Marian stays away, despite how she truly feels about you. But every day that you keep those two locked up together only further confirms it."

"That I am the Bloody Knight?" I said. "I do not care what these people say about me."

"You should kill Tuck," she said, her eyes cold. "He is mad beyond saving and evil. His presence is poison. And what you are doing to Sir Geoffrey in there is evil too. He deserves death. Not what you are doing to him. That is true whether people are saying it or not. Surely you see that?"

I looked in her eyes. Her face was dirty with grime and sweat. The skin beneath shone with health and vitality, stained brown by the sun.

"I will kill him tomorrow," I said. "Both of them."

"Good," Eva said. "Is what I am saying unknown to you?"

"No," I said.

She sighed. Her face was softer, more open than I had seen it before. "I wish I had been taught how to make conversation."

I thought of Emma, for the first time in months. That I had not thought of her surprised me, because usually she was never

199

far from my thoughts. But it was because I knew what she would have said about my abduction and preservation of Brother Tuck and my treatment of Sir Geoffrey.

"You tell the truth," I said to Eva. "And the value of truth is greater than the art of conversation."

I stood, finishing my cup of beer.

"Where are you going?"

"I will end those men now," I said, standing. "Why put it off any longer?"

For a moment, she looked tempted to come with me. But even her warrior's heart balked at two grimy executions in the dark.

Mine certainly did.

"And I am not sixty years old," I said to her as I walked into the wood, treading the familiar path to the dell with my greenwood gaol.

When I stepped inside with my sword already drawn, Sir Geoffrey wept. His lips muttered a prayer. He was filthy, thin as a bow stave and his beard and hair were matted and wild. His arms were lined with half-healed cuts and scars where I had drawn his blood for Tuck.

"Sir Geoffrey," I said. "You raped a child. You and your men killed loyal Englishmen. But your punishment has denigrated us both. This ends now with your death."

"Oh, thank God. Thank God."

He was still muttering when I drove my blade through the base of his skull.

I dragged Tuck from his corner and unbound his eyes and mouth.

200

Tuck wailed at the death of Sir Geoffrey. In his mad, lonely state, Sir Geoffrey had been Tuck's only friend.

I felt a sudden weariness and horror at what I had inflicted upon both of these men.

"The time has come, Tuck," I said.

"To be free?" he asked, looking up like a dog at his master's homecoming.

"In a way," I said. "I know now that I have wronged you. That I damaged your mind by starving and confining you. Damaged beyond repair. You have told me nothing. You are not capable of telling me what I need to know. So now I will free you from the bonds of William's blood. If you have any sense of God left in you, take a moment to pray before I end your days."

"No!" Tuck screamed. "I will tell you. I will tell you."

"It is too late."

"The king, the king!" Tuck shrieked. "The Green Knight will kill the king."

I hesitated. "What new madness is this?"

"Not madness, my lord, not madness. A man. The big man. He came to Eden. He came to the Green Knight. He begged my lord for poison. My lord said no. The big man said he would pay any price. My lord agreed that he would do the poisoning himself, if the big man would name the man to be poisoned. The big man was quiet. But Tuck heard it. Tuck hears all. Tuck is a good monk. Tuck says his prayers. Tuck likes to do a shit at vespers but don't tell the Prior, don't tell the old prior or else Tuck—"

"Who was the big man?" I cut in.

"Didn't know him. A man. Big man," Tuck said.

"Who was the victim?"

"The what?" Tuck looked startled, confused.

"The big man's target. Who was the Green Knight going to poison?"

"Oh, that," Tuck giggled, covering his face. "I told you. I told you. The king, of course. Bad King John. King John is to die, I heard it in Eden. My lord will do it when next the king comes to Nottingham."

I leaned against the wall, smelling the damp, earthy fungal smell of the greenwood posts. Tuck was mad. There was no doubt. He was deluded as to where he was and what he was doing. But because it was William de Ferrers he was talking about, I thought it might be true.

"Listen to me, Tuck, you must tell this to the sheriff. Or to the Marshal, yes. Yes, that is what I will do. You must come with me." I cursed myself for killing Sir Geoffrey too soon. He could have been witness to Tuck's words. "You must say to them what you said to me."

"What I said to you?" Tuck asked. "I behave myself. I only drink when my lord commands."

"You must tell the king that the Green Knight means to poison him in Nottingham."

Tuck's face fell into the deepest horror that a man could show. "I told?"

"You told," I said. "But I will protect you from him. I am your new lord now, am I not?"

"What did I tell?" Tuck said.

I sighed and spoke patiently, as if to a young child. "You told

202

me that your master, the Green Knight, is going to poison King John in Nottingham."

"No," Tuck said. "No, I did not. I would never. I could not. I never said. Anyway, it'll be some other great lord what does it."

"Who?" I said. "Do you mean Hugh de Nonant? Or someone else?"

He ducked his head down and rocked back and forth. "No, no, no."

"I will get you all the blood you need," I promised. "But you will tell the Sheriff of Nottingham or William Marshal what you told me."

Tuck's groan started from somewhere deep in his bowels, like the lowing of a cow. Quicker than I had ever seen him move before, he leapt up, tearing through the rotting rope around his arms and leg.

Before I could bring up my sword, he threw me aside and rushed Sir Geoffrey's body. I assumed he was going for the blood but instead he crashed his head into the central oak stump. The hut shook. Tuck cracked his head twice more before I recovered my wits enough to drag him away. The ancient oak had cracked and so had Tuck's skull. His nose was split, smashed flat. I could see shards of bone and the pink stuff of brains flecked in the wound before the blood welled out, filling his eyes.

I thought that perhaps he could recover from such an injury, if I could get some blood down his throat immediate.

But I would not. I knew Tuck. After so many months breaking and then nursing his broken mind. I knew he was telling the truth about the poison plot. And I also knew that no court would take the words of the man as anything but raving lunacy. And the thought of dragging him across the country again was more than I could take.

I forced pity from my mind. This creature had committed tortures and terrors against the innocent and even against the holy. The suffering I had inflicted upon him was fair, even if he had been serving as a proxy for my revenge against William.

About to warn him once again that he was about to die, I decided not to bother. I did not see what difference it would make.

I killed him and cut his head from his body though I doubted he could rise again. I buried Tuck and Sir Geoffrey both, in the wood by their summer prison, hacking through roots with my sword.

Then I gathered my men and the next morning before sunrise, we set out for Nottingham.

I had to warn the king that he was to be murdered.

EIGHT ~ THE DEATH OF THE KING

"I AM HERE TO SEE THE KING," I said to men at the gate of Newark Castle in Nottinghamshire. The town lay behind the castle and to the north over the wall I could see the top of the church tower as I stood before the gatehouse.

Newark was a small but sturdy castle built on the banks of the River Trent, rising it seemed straight from the waters. Upriver to the west, the sun was low in the sky above the wooded hills, casting a smear of orange light on the rippling surface. The castle was square and compact and still looked like new, having been built in stone only twenty years or so before. We approached from the south and crossed the bridge that the castle guarded.

A stocky man-at-arms with a mace hanging on his belt came

forwards and looked me up and down, taking in my filthy, mud-spattered clothes and rusting armour.

I had ridden all the way from the Weald prepared for war, not trusting to the safety of the roads. Potentially saving the life of the king and catching William in the process was worth days of sweat and discomfort and we had arrived at Newark by the middle of October.

I hoped that the hard riding had not permanently damaged our horses. Sometimes it took them days or weeks to fall ill and die. Jocelyn was already close to weeping for his precious bay courser.

"And who are you, sir?" The man-at-arms said and looked beyond me as if to query why a lone knight could possibly be important enough to want an audience with the king.

"Sir Richard of Ashbury." I wanted to bash his face in with his own mace but I was too tired to put him in his place. He was the sergeant of the guard and served the crown rather than the local lord, so I had to pay him the proper respect or I would end up in gaol instead of before the king.

Still, mention of my name had a satisfying effect. Colour drained from his face. The two guards behind him whispered to each other, glancing at me.

"Are you staying at the inn, Sir Richard?" Though his tone was more respectful, he looked pointedly at my legs. They were caked in black mud.

The town and castle were packed full of the leaders who followed the king from place to place though the bulk of his army was camped miles out of town. The common loyal men and mercenaries spilled over into the villages for miles and tents were up in fields all around.

"I know that I am unfit for the king's company but please impress upon the king's men that I have urgent business. I have knowledge of the highest importance. Knowledge that must be heard now, or the king's life—" I broke off, fearing I sounded like a lunatic. I cleared my throat. "I have hurried hard. There are no rooms where I might clean and dress for court. Hence my appearance. I shall wait nearby with my men. But I must be seen. Ideally, by the Marshal, if he is here, or William Longspear or Ranulf of Chester."

I pointed to Jocelyn, Anselm, and Swein who waited with the horses pressed against the base wall of the castle wall below. They all looked miserable and exhausted, the horses' heads low as they dozed. I had pushed them all hard on the ride north.

The sergeant cast a final, withering look at me and went away in conference with one of his men.

"Don't want much, does he," I overheard them say as they passed through the gate.

Night was falling when the sergeant returned and allowed us to lead our horses into the castle courtyard and stable our horses. Newark Castle was essentially a large irregular square with a large hall, stable, chapel and other buildings inside. The outer walls were thick enough for chambers, storerooms and quarters on all four sides and there were, in addition, five towers plus the gate tower. There was enough room to house scores of knights with their retinues of squires, pages, grooms, servants, and chaplains but even still, it was now full to bursting.

The castle stable was heaving with the fine horses of the king and the courtiers. The beasts were spilling out from the stalls and the grooms struggled to find places for them. Most were riding horses that the great lords paid fortunes for. The court was never in one place for more than a week and being with the king meant a whole day in the saddle every second or third day. But there were knights' horses there too, straining at the excitement of being near strange mares. We kept well away from those creatures. Everyone knew enough to avoid a trained warhorse, even I would retreat into doorways to avoid being bitten or kicked by beasts who were as violent as a drunk man-at-arms or a wronged wife. One huge, black-coated stallion with heavily muscled hindquarters steamed in the cold, quivering in a high state. Barely contained, it snorted and moaned, lunging at the mares nearby while the grooms strained to contain the chaos.

"Whose horse is that?" Jocelyn asked no one, as if his heart ached with longing for the magnificent animal.

The sergeant escorting us shrugged. "Came in with a bunch of lords last night. He's not one of the king's," he said. "But if he claps his eyes on it, no doubt he'll want it."

"Some rich fool," I suggested. "With more money than sense."

"That is Geoffrey of Monmouth's horse, my lord," a passing groom said, his eyes full of wonder and terror.

"There you go then," I said, for I had heard how the young Monmouth was enormously rich but not at all a fighting man. "The idiot will like as not get himself thrown."

"What a waste," Jocelyn muttered, talking about the horse and not the loss of the courtier.

208

"Wait here, if you please, Sir Richard," the sergeant said. "They will send for you."

My men all fell asleep in the corner of the yard amongst our equipment and supplies. Our precious horses were tended to and they too lay down to sleep where they could, on mounds of straw and covered with blankets. I hoped that they would all recover soon. The men were young and the horses expensive and well cared for by the castle and royal grooms so I trusted that they would.

I sat on my cloak on the floor, leaning on my saddle and wishing I could drink blood. Just a little bit. I wanted my strength back. I wondered if anyone would miss the smallest groom.

I woke.

"Sir Richard," a servant with a lantern stood in the darkness before me, the flickering light illuminating a miserable old warty face. "My lord will see you now."

Still half asleep, I followed the servant through the castle until he told me to wait through a door somewhere deep inside. Squires, priests, and servants hurried up and down through every corridor and the place resounded with shouting and the clashing of feet. The room was an antechamber with nothing but two stools and a side table, a slit window on the wall opposite the entrance door and a door on each of the other doors. It was bare but clean and I sat on a stool, a shower of mud flaking off the links of my mail. I was aware of the sour stench of my body.

One side door opened and two lords walked in. I jumped to my feet. I did not know them but by their dress, they were vastly rich and therefore powerful men.

"You are Richard of Ashbury?" one man said. He was about thirty years old and plump, soft of the body. But he had the eyes of a murderer.

"I am."

"You lie," the plump man said, his lip curling. "Richard of Ashbury fought with the Lionheart. You are little more than a boy. I should call my men to throw you in the Trent."

I overtopped him by a head. I ground my teeth and held myself still until my rage subsided. Striking the fat little lord would no doubt mean my death. "I am Richard of Ashbury. I have a youthful countenance. I am known for it."

"That is true," the other man said. He was probably younger than thirty but his bearing showed no deference to the other man. This one was a fine looking fellow and stood straight and tall. Indeed, he looked familiar but I was tired and I could not place him. "They say you made a pact with the devil in exchange for your strength in battle."

"They do that, yes," I said, shaking my head. "Often I decide to take it as a compliment instead of an insult."

There was fear in his eyes for a moment before he laughed. "I am William Marshal," he said. "It is an honour to meet you." He noticed my confusion. "Ah, my father is the Earl of Pembroke, the famed William the Marshal. I am merely his firstborn son and barely worthy of his great name." He smiled but there was a hint of bitterness under his levity.

"Of course, my lord," I said. "Forgive me, I have ridden far to bring news."

It was also the fact that the last time I heard of the Marshal's son, he was with the rebel barons. Clearly, he had been pardoned and welcomed back into the king's arms. The great William Marshal was the king's most powerful supporter, despite how badly the king had treated him over the years. The king owed the Marshal more than a few favours and I supposed Marshal the elder was calling them in.

In fact, all his five sons but Anselm had been with the rebels and they had all suddenly changed sides.

The plump lord interjected. "You do not mean that you believe him, William?"

William Marshal the younger peered at his fellow lord. "Richard of Ashbury, this is John of Monmouth."

"I have heard of you," I said. "I am glad that you are here."

"Heard of me?" the pudgy little goat turd said. "What have you heard of me?"

"Simply that you were raised at court. I knew your father, in a way. You are a favourite of the king. That is good, for I have news that concerns his safety."

John of Monmouth sneered. "You could be anyone."

"Bring me to a man who knows me," I said, fixing young Monmouth with a stare. His lordly father had been the one to engineer a scandal about my blood drinking. His son was not my enemy but still, he shared his father's blood and, it seemed to me already, his father's character.

William Marshal nodded. "Your lord is Hugh de Nonant. The Archbishop of York."

"Perhaps not him," I said. "Someone else can confirm who I am."

"You see?" Monmouth said, sneering. "He lies."

"Why not your liege lord?" Marshal said, placing a hand on Monmouth's arm.

"I am not sure that I can say," I said, keeping my face set hard lest I give anything away. "I have information that should be heard by as few men as possible. My lord would force me to tell him and that may not be in the best interests of the king."

"What in the name of God are you blathering about?" Monmouth said. "Are you feeble minded? Are you drunk?"

The son of the Marshal rubbed his nose. "How is my little brother? Is he well? Is he learning his duty?"

"Your brother?" I was tired. "Oh, Anselm? Of course. He is here. In the courtyard, sleeping in the stables. He is very well. He is a very fine squire and there is no doubt he will make a good knight."

"Ah, that is good to hear," William Marshal grinned. "I have not seen the boy in years. I will have him brought to me. I am glad to hear he will make a good knight in time. The Lord knows we need good fighters right now and I fear we will need them still when he comes of age."

"Anselm is already a good fighter, my lord," I said. "We have been fighting for the king in the Weald. Anselm has fought this whole summer. I have lost count of the number of Frenchmen he has killed."

Satisfyingly, the Marshal was shocked. "He takes after our noble father then. Good."

"Yes, yes, how very proud you must be," fat little Monmouth said. "Yet another witless killer, just what England needs. What vital news do you bring? The messenger said it concerns the king's life. Was that all nonsense? If all you hoped for was a chamber for the night then you shall be very much—"

"Poison."

Monmouth gaped.

William Marshal froze. His whole body went rigid and his eyes darted all over my face, searching for something.

Neither man spoke so I continued.

"A while ago, I captured a prisoner. He was from Nottinghamshire but he only gave up what he knew shortly before he died. He told me of a plot to poison the king."

"Who was this man?" Marshal asked, his welcoming, conversational demeanour abandoned. He was intense. Fearful, even.

"A monk from a priory in Sherwood. A monk who had abandoned God. And common decency. He was with an outlaw leader when that outlaw was propositioned by a lord to carry out the poisoning. It was to be the next time the king passed through Nottingham."

"Who was the lord?" William Marshal said, his eyes boring into mine.

"The monk did not know him," I admitted. "But he said he was a big man. A big man and a lord."

Marshal the younger pressed his lips together.

"And you say this monk is now dead?" fat little Monmouth said. "So we have your word alone?"

"Yes."

"How convenient," Monmouth said, sneering. "But I suppose

something must be done."

"Word of this must reach the king," I said, glaring at both of them. "It will reach him, immediately, one way or another."

Young Marshal was irritated by my presumption, glancing at Monmouth as if weighing a decision. He chewed on his lip for a moment. "I suppose the word of this monk can be trusted?"

I nodded. "He was not trustworthy. He was a criminal. He lost his mind well before his end. But I knew him well enough to know he was speaking truthfully. He expected nothing in return. It was not to save his life or to make any gain. And I would not have ridden this hard and fast to bring this news if I did not think it was worth relaying. I may have made a pact with the devil but I am not a fool. I know that I put myself in danger by telling you this. I know I expose myself, to mockery at least and possibly worse. But I felt it my duty to come. If the king was killed and I had done nothing..." I was tired. I wanted blood. Or, at least, a large cup of wine.

"Sit, Richard, please," Marshal guided me onto a stool. "I understand."

He called a servant, ordered me brought food and wine and also that Anselm and my other men be found a place to sleep that was better than the stables.

"We will speak to the king himself," Marshal said to me, his friendliness restored although I detected that his manner was forced and likely had been from the moment we had met. "Yes, yes, we will speak to the king and as few others as we can. Wait here, eat, rest."

As they left, Monmouth looked at me with anger but he no

longer mocked me. In fact, he regarded Marshal's retreating back with a sort of brooding wariness.

I could make no sense of their true feelings but reading my enemies' intentions was always a problem for me in my first one or two centuries.

That night I had no strength to ponder it so I ate, drank and slept sitting with my head upon the table until a squire shook me awake.

"What is it?" I said, bleary eyed and grabbing the man by the arm and pulling him down toward me. "What is happening?"

"Marshal the younger sent for you," the squire said, shaking with fear. "You have an audience with the king. Please, my lord, please do not hurt me."

I looked down and realised I had my dagger pressed to the inside of his thigh.

"Sorry, son," I said, putting it away. "Take me to the king."

∞

Once he checked his balls were still attached, the squire led me through the castle again. It was dark. The young man's lantern was a candle surrounded by translucent, waxed parchment and it gave off a meagre, smoky light. The keep was quiet, though still clerks, knights and priests shuffled by us carrying lanterns and candles of their own.

At a door guarded by two sturdy men-at-arms, they took my sword and my dagger and I waited while the squire went inside.

After a few moments, young William Marshal slipped out of it, closing it softly behind him. His face was grave.

"The king wishes to see you," Marshal the younger whispered, his eyes fixing me with an unreadable stare. "I warn you that he does not believe in you. And my father is with him. And also your lord, the Archbishop of York is there."

As if I was not nervous enough at facing the king, the knowledge that Hugh de Nonant would be present made me fret indeed. I was as certain as I could be that my lord was in league with William. How could I possibly accuse the man while he was in the room. It was close to a disaster.

"I see," I said.

"There was no avoiding it once the king got wind that you were the bearer of the warning," young Marshal said, a strange look in his eye. "Perhaps you should play this threat down, Richard and avoid the archbishop's ire? I pray, though, that you are given leave to pursue this plot up in Sherwood, eh? Anyway, you must go in. And I must get away." He smiled, patted my arm and opened the door for me.

Candles flickered from the motion of the door and shadows danced over the three great men inside. It was a solar, a day room given over for use by the king, with other chambers unseen beyond. A roasted meat smell rolled over me. My stomach churned from hunger and nervous excitement.

The king himself sat at the far end of the long central table. John, by the Grace of God, King of England, Lord of Ireland, Duke of Normandy and Aquitaine, Count of Anjou. The titles came to mind, I had heard them announced so many times and they had a familiar rhythm, as if they were an old prayer. But no one spoke them aloud anymore. He held almost all those titles by claim but not in fact.

There he was, the man who had kneeled in Westminster Abbey seventeen years before and sworn to observe peace, honour and reverence toward God and the Church all the days of his life, to do good justice and equity to the people he ruled, to keep good laws and be rid of all evil customs.

He was eating, his head down, slurping up wine from a shining cup and sucking grease off his fingers.

On one side of the room stood the Marshal himself, the Earl of Pembroke, the greatest knight who ever lived. He was over seventy years old but stood straight and tall and was still an intimidating man.

On the other side of the room loomed the archbishop, my liege lord. Massive, bulky, wearing fine, glowing church robes resplendent in white with gold crucifixes. Above his finery was his bull's head face, red and angry.

I did not know in which order to address them, nor what to say. So I stood in the doorway, hesitating like a maiden crossing the bedchamber threshold on her wedding night.

"Come in, you Godforsaken fool," the archbishop roared. "And shut the damned door."

The king paused in his eating to take a drink of wine. He glanced up at the archbishop. "You are the least holy man I ever met, Hugh."

"Thank you, Your Grace," the archbishop said, his voice rumbling from his chest.

The king smirked into his goblet and waved me over to him. I approached on the opposite side to the archbishop, nodding at William the Marshal who gave me the faintest hint of acknowledgement. He wore a fine sword at his side. He wore brilliant green over bright red.

I reached the king's side and knelt. King John sat in a huge, solid chair carved from oak and stained a brown so dark it was almost black. He paused for a moment and looked down at me, fixing me with that stare that he had. His eyes were pools of ink. Always, he bored into your soul with those eyes, searching yours for plots and threats and signs of disloyalty.

The moment that King Philip of France had heard the Richard the Lionheart was dead, he had invaded Normandy. That had been seventeen years before and John had been fighting, in one way or another, for his kingdom ever since. The kings, dukes, and counts of France had turned against him. His own barons had jostled and provoked him.

Since taking his oath, John had fought and lost in Poitou, Gascony, Anjou, Brittany and Normandy. He had invaded and subdued Wales, Scotland, and Ireland. I had fought for the king in most of his campaigns and had watched his struggles and his failures take their toll. But in the two or three years since I had last stood before him, the king had aged a decade or more. He had grown remarkably fat. His face had a yellow tinge. He seemed old, older than I would have believed. I remembered right then that he was of a similar age to me, almost fifty. His black beard had gone grey. His hair had receded and his cheeks had sagged. There were lines around his eyes and bags under them. The rebellion and the invasion were sucking the life from him.

"You are truly in league with the devil, Richard," the king said, searching my face. "Are you getting younger with each passing year? Dear God, your face makes me sick to my stomach."

He waved me to the bench alongside the table and I eased myself onto it. The table was laden with plates, half eaten pies and roast birds and fishes. It was very late to be eating such a meal. I wondered if the king had lost his wits or if he had completely succumbed to gluttony. Judging by the great mound of his belly and the fat under the beard at his neck, I guessed it was the latter, at least.

"So," King John said after cuffing his mouth. "Someone is trying to poison me?"

It took all of my will to not look at the archbishop so I just sat there, dumb.

The king glanced at the archbishop. "Would you look at the state of your man, Hugh?"

"My apologies, Your Grace," the archbishop said. "He did not come to me first or I would have never allowed him into your presence like this."

King John waved him into silence. "Richard is a man of action, a bringer of death and terror to my enemies, is that not right, Richard? Yes, I can well forgive a little filth at my table. I live with the reek of horse sweat in my nose, do I not? So, out with it, what is this plot against me?"

"I know little of any plot, Your Grace," I said. "Simply that an outlaw of Sherwood has been tasked with poisoning you when you returned to Nottinghamshire."

The king regarded me. His dark eyes were unfocused. Whether through overindulgence in wine or through age taking his sight, I knew not. The candlelight danced as servants came in to take away dishes and bring more. The king did not offer me any, for which I was glad. He slurped away more wine.

"What do you think, Hugh?" the king said, still watching me.

The archbishop sighed. "I think that someone is playing my dear Richard for a fool."

The king nodded and glanced at William the Marshal, the Earl of Pembroke.

"Almost certainly, this plot means nothing, Your Grace," Pembroke said with confidence. "Almost certainly the plot does not exist. And even if it did, there is no chance some outlaw could ever attempt to get close to you. But would a little prudence not be in order? Perhaps we should take care with your food and wine while we are in the shire. It would hurt us none to do so."

King John looked up at the Marshal through heavy lids. "Do you mean to say that you do not take care with it now?"

"Of course, Your Grace," the Marshal said smoothly. "I only meant to post guards over the wagons. And in the kitchens."

"What a lot of fuss over nothing," the king said, wafting away the threat with a bird's thighbone. "Do I not carry my wine with me, everywhere I travel? The food is procured locally but prepared by my own staff, is it not? Well then, how could I ever be poisoned? Richard, how could you ever imagine some vile peasant outlaw could ever get anywhere near my royal person?"

"It is not a peasant, Your Grace," I said. "This new leader of the outlaws was once an earl of England. He—"

The archbishop spoke over me. "He thinks the outlaw is William de Ferrers."

The king looked between the Archbishop of York and me. "You killed him in the Holy Land."

"Your pardon, Your Grace but William de Ferrers escaped," I said. "I looked for him for years but I never found him."

"That is because he died," the archbishop growled, his huge thick robes rustling like parchment. "He died in some shit stinking hole in the middle of some shit stinking land, you imbecile. You think that he still lives simply because you failed to kill him yourself? What arrogance. You have no proof that William is the outlaw that plagues Sherwood. You simply wish it to be true. Please, Your Grace, I cannot apologise enough for wasting your time with this."

The king held up his hand. "The latest outlaw chief in my forest, yes. I remember that he has been preying on the Great North Road, has he not? Taking coin and messengers. Taking travellers. Churchmen. What is being done about this?"

The king addressed the archbishop, for he was the most powerful lord of the north.

The archbishop bristled. "Sheriff Roger de Lacy has sent men to clear Sherwood but they were all lost. The year before last, I believe. The sheriff has sent almost every man of his to you for the war."

"I know what de Lacy has sent me, you fool, and I asked what is being done about the outlaws." The king burped and rubbed his fat belly, sighing with satisfaction.

"I cannot answer for the sheriff," the archbishop said. "But I believe he has not the men to do anything until you win the war."

The Marshal, behind me, snorted quietly but the king did not seem to mind.

"You believe the outlaw leader is William de Ferrers?" the king asked me.

"I am certain of it," I said. "His followers know him to be a nobleman."

"All these peasant leaders claim to be some exiled lord of somewhere or other," the archbishop said. "It is preposterous."

The king yawned and rubbed his eyes. "What do you say, Marshal?"

"It does not matter who the outlaw is," the Marshal said. "He threatens the road north. I agree with you, Your Grace. Sherwood must be cleared, immediately."

The king nodded as if he had suggested such a thing be done. "You make other knights nervous, Richard."

"I do not mean to, Your Grace."

"Have you stopped slurping up the blood of the slain?" he asked.

"I have, Your Grace," I lied. "It was the momentary madness of battle, after I had taken the walls for you."

He waved down my justifications. He had heard them before. "They say you are cursed. When men see that your face is ageless then they will know that they are quite right. My armies are crushing the barons, one after the other. Soon I will be ready to drive the French from England, for the last time. But things balance on a blade's edge. I cannot bring you into my armies again. But your magnificent abilities can be of use to me. What's say I find a handful of men who would fight under you. What would it take, Marshal?"

"To clear Sherwood? Richard could do it with twenty knights and squires and say, fifty bowmen. I am sure we could spare them."

"There," the king said. "Would that suit you?"

I could not believe my luck. The king would give me the men I needed to destroy William.

"It would, Your Grace." I bowed my head.

"Fine, you do that and then we will see about you serving me once again, what do you say? Yes, yes, of course, you say yes. Go now. Let me sleep. Someone see this man out. Marshal, you will organise the men for Sherwood? Yes, yes."

I was led out. I would have the men. My revenge was at hand.

I rushed to tell Jocelyn the good news.

That very night, the king was taken ill. A bloody flux, they called it.

I was nervous but everyone seemed sure the king would recover. He often had digestive problems, so they said. So we prepared our equipment, cleaning and sharpening. I met a few of the men that I would be leading. They seemed good enough. I had not been sold a duck after buying a pig.

Two days later, in the castle stables, I was seized by a half dozen men. I did not fight, for they were John's own men. They escorted me through the castle, downstairs and, to my complete surprise, they threw me into the castle dungeon.

"But why," I shouted as they closed the door. "For the love of God, you bastards, tell me why. What is happening?"

One man held the door open a crack, his candle casting his face in yellow and black dancing shadows. He spoke four words before the door slammed with an echoing boom.

"The king is dead."

NINE ~ OUTLAWED

I STEWED IN THAT BLACK DUNGEON, not knowing it was night or day. Barely knowing if I slept. A few times, I was brought water.

"What is happening?" I asked the gaoler but he ignored me.

Once or twice, there was bread.

I measured time by the level of piss and shit in my bucket but since I barely ate and my lips were cracked with thirst, I was not sure if I had been there two days or two weeks. It was like being buried alive. All I had for company was the scurrying rats and my memories. I saw, awake and asleep, my wife murdered over and over. I saw the men I had slain. I saw the gallons of blood I had spilled in a massacre in the Holy Land.

No wonder Tuck had lost his mind.

I woke to the searing light of a single candle and was brought up into the world again. Outside, it was dawn. A thin, steady rain gusted down in waves of countless tiny needles. It felt wonderful.

I expected to be brought to the archbishop or to the scaffold.

Instead, it was Jocelyn and Anselm waiting in the rain in the castle courtyard, holding our horses at the ready. Swein was there too, his old brown hood soaked and heavy on his head. He grinned at me over Anselm and Jocelyn's shoulders. My armour and weapons wrapped and loaded upon my horses.

My men gave me wine and a chunk of tough cheese and I followed them out of the castle gates, holding my tongue until we were gone.

It was strangely quiet. More than subdued, as would be expected, Newark felt deserted.

Guards looked away from us as we rode out and off from Newark Castle, heading west along an empty road. The swollen Trent flowed by to the left, down the hill, rain patterning all over the mud-brown surface.

"Tell me," I said to Jocelyn after we were well clear of the castle and town, pulling to a stop in the rain right on the road. There was no one around.

"The archbishop had you taken into custody before the king was even cold. We could do nothing. His household knights took the king's body away to Worcester for burial. And immediately all the great lords fled in the night. They raced each other to be the first to reach Prince Henry, who is all the way down in Salisbury or thereabouts. They will be there by now, I don't doubt."

I looked back at the castle. "The archbishop had me taken. And then I was just left there?"

Jocelyn and the others exchanged a look."

"You are charged with treason," Jocelyn said. "But no one knows precisely why or any detail. You were supposed to be held."

Treason. The word hung as heavy as a roll of lead.

"They think that I murdered the king?"

"No man says it is murder. He died of the flux. He has been long on campaign. He ate too much and drank too much wine and he fell ill and died."

"But it was William," I said. "The king was poisoned. It was just as I said. Just as Tuck said."

"We tried to tell them," Jocelyn said. "Anselm told his father and his brother."

"You did?" I asked the young man. I knew he was terrified of both of them. The Earl of Pembroke frightened everyone by his fame alone. And the elder four sons of the Marshal were all mad enough to have joined the rebellion, however briefly and Anselm was confused and intimidated by disloyalty. "You have my thanks, Anselm."

"That is not all he did," Jocelyn said. "Tell Richard what your older brother did."

"He gave me gold and silver," Anselm said, rain streaming down his face. "For bribing the guards."

"It took us a couple of days to find out who were the right men to pay off," Jocelyn added. "And they made Anselm swear to wait until the archbishop and the last of his men had themselves left."

"What treason am I supposed to have committed?" I asked.

"The precise charges are unknown," Jocelyn said. "But I heard it was because you abandoned your task in the south."

"The grooms are saying it's because you are swyving the archbishop's daughter," Swein said, grinning. "Stole her away from him."

"I see," I said. "How do they know about Eva?"

Swein shrugged. "Servants talk, lord."

"It is simply a means to do away with you, lord," Anselm said. "My brother said the archbishop wants you to stay away from Sherwood. And your lord knows you would obey the Marshal rather than be loyal to him, if it came down to it. In an open war between the two Royalist factions."

"The archbishop and the Marshal are enemies," I said, seeing the extent of their rivalry for the first time. "What will they do now?"

"Think about it, Richard," Jocelyn said. "They are going to crown Prince Henry as the new king. Do you know how old Henry is?"

"Young," I said.

"He is nine years old, Richard. And whoever controls the boy controls the kingdom," Jocelyn said. "The king's loyal barons have been fighting a war of access to the Prince for years. Every maid, page, and lady within a mile of the boy are in the pay of Anselm's father or your lord. Or both. Or some other baron."

"So goes the rumours," I said.

"We spoke to my brother about it before he left," Anselm said. "He told us all."

"So freeing me does what?" I said. "What does the Marshal want me to do?"

Jocelyn pointed south, as if we could see my liege lord. "The archbishop has brought the charges against you himself. With his resources, the archbishop will win. You will be denied the right of appeal through trial by combat and you will be killed. The archbishop is disposing of you. Legally, perhaps, but he has declared you an enemy. The Marshal wants you to fight for him instead."

"For him and for the Prince and the kingdom," Anselm said, proudly.

"So I am fleeing justice," I said. "I am making myself an outlaw?"

My three men looked at each other. I was struck by how they seemed to be friends, companions, comrades. One was the son of a great lord, one a knight who would have a fine career without being sworn to me and one was an outlawed commoner. Any of them could have fled while I was locked up. I would have been convicted and no man would have condemned them for breaking an oath to a treasonous lord. Instead, they had not only stood by me but had worked hard to break me out and save me from the fate that the archbishop had arranged.

"Richard, we have no choice but to flee," Jocelyn said. "But you are not fleeing justice. You would be found guilty. Do you want to be tried when you cannot win? Is temporary outlawry not the better choice?"

"Temporary?" I said, grasping the word. "Are you certain of that?"

"No," Jocelyn said, glancing at his squire.

"My father is certain that he will make things right," Anselm said. "He will soon be in a position to help you."

"So long as he seizes control of the boy king before the archbishop," I said.

"The archbishop is known for governing well, for making his own lands richer and for passing on his wealth for others. The barons all want to be rich," Jocelyn said. "Yet we are still at war with the French. There are two kings of England, one French and the other a young boy. The barons will want a warrior in charge. They will turn to the Marshal as they have before. He is the steadiest hand in the kingdom. He wants you. He will have you. Legally. We simply need to wait it out."

"A perfect time to go to Sherwood," I said. "I will be out of sight and we can dig William out of his hole like the parasite he is."

"For the love of God, Richard," Jocelyn cried. "Will you forget William for once? How can we four take him? We do not all have your strength. You think only of yourself. What about your house? You manor? My sister? Have you considered her at all? Emma has been running your manor all summer. What happens to her when your property is seized?"

"But the archbishop is not here," I said. "His attention will be on young Henry, you said so yourself."

"Come, Richard," Jocelyn said. "He has a practice of taking lands. From his own men. From anyone. He has men who do this for him. Men learned in the law, from London. They will be acting upon the archbishop's orders to take everything you own. Anselm's brother told us."

"I will fight them," I said. "We shall man the walls of Ashbury and fight off any man who comes."

"That is your answer for every challenge," Jocelyn said. "A blade will not work in this case. Will you kill men acting within the law of the land? Will you cut down men armed with writs and lawfully charged bailiffs? You will never climb your way back from outlawry then."

I sat and looked at the soaking land around me. The hedgerows hanging heavy with water. Fields running with tiny rivers downhill toward the Trent through the lines of alder and willow along the banks.

"You are right. Let us go and collect Emma and everything we can carry. With no income and nowhere to go, I will not be able to take any servants. They will have to serve their next lord."

"Only until we return," said Jocelyn.

I prayed that he was right.

∞

It was two days before we arrived at Ashbury to collect Emma and put my affairs in order. By that time, we had almost dried out and the sun struggled through.

The thought of abandoning my manor was unsettling. Approaching my home along the familiar lane was something I had done countless times but every detail was imbued with significance. We forded the stream that had burst its banks at the bottom of the hill and flooded the woods at either side. It had always been a boggy area, surrounded by bladderwort and bog myrtle but when I was very young I had tried to catch sticklebacks as they darted over the pebbles.

All woods are wet places. Even in a summer drought, go into an English lowland wood and you may immediately plunge your fingers down into cool, wet earth, full of fat worms, perfect for tempting fishes and making girls scream. Two or three spade depths and you are into sucking black water amongst the tangled roots.

The pigs from the village snuffled at the edge of the wood and hedgerow, gobbling up the acorns and beech mast, roaming under the loose guidance of the local swineherds.

In the hedgerows around my manor house, I had encouraged my men to plant blackthorn. I loved blackthorn though my servants and villagers thought the wood half-evil or, at least, magical and, therefore, to be mistrusted. Perhaps they were right. The wood certainly burns like the devil.

That stuff was dense and hard and made the best walking sticks and poles for sword training. It kept the sheep and cattle out of the gardens. I always enjoyed the way it blooms before Easter and before any leaves grow so the white blossom explodes over the bare black branches. In autumn, my servants picked great basketfuls of the blue-black berries harvested and boiled them with fat game from my woods. That day, I noticed that no one had picked the berries.

Snails clad in their yellow and purple armour spotted over the sodden timbers of my gateway as I rode through at midday. Bert the Bone's pack of elderly dogs howled and bounded around me as I dismounted, scattering the chickens.

Would I ever see any of it again?

Although it had been well over ten years since we built it, the palisade around Ashbury manor house still felt new. I had dug out the ditch and piled up the bank alongside the rest of the labourers from the village and beyond. Those that did not know me had not liked it. They thought I was showing off, making them look bad by throwing more muck than they did. And also, that I was there to keep my eyes on them continuously so that they would work harder and take few breaks.

My own servants had explained to them that I simply enjoyed a physical challenge. That I liked being up to my knees in mud, seeing how hard I could work, testing my strength and endurance. I well remembered being struck by how well they knew me and I felt immoral for having to abandon them to an unknown fate.

"Some of you stood by my family after the tragedy that occurred here twenty-five years past," I said to my gathered servants in the hall.

It had turned into a warm, bright autumn afternoon and the doors and windows were thrown open and the golden light flooded in across the men and women standing together.

"More of you came after, trusting that there was no curse in this place and no curse on me. I am sure that some of you do believe me cursed, because of what they say about me. And that I have a youthful countenance though I am as old as a grandfather. Well, perhaps you are right. But no matter what you believe in your hearts, you have stood by this place and you have each done your duty. You have served me and I hope you feel I have served you well in return. I have tried to be fair in my judgements. I have tried to give to you as much as I could."

I was pleased to see nodding heads and hear murmurs of assent. I took a breath.

"It is also a lord's duty to be often away from his home. And whenever I have been on campaign or on other business, you have continued to serve faithfully under good stewardship. This past summer you have done without me once again and I am certain you have followed the Lady Emma's commands as if they were my own. Indeed, you all know she makes a better job of things than I ever have." They laughed yet it was unfair of me to seek refuge in levity. "But now I must go away again. Only, this time it will be different. You know that we are in a time of war, our land divided. I have had a disagreement with my liege lord, Hugh de Nonant who is also the Archbishop of York. He has brought a charge of treason against me."

Their astonished muttering rose to cries of alarm and I waved them down into low murmuring.

"I am told by other great lords that my enemies conspire to find me guilty, no matter the evidence I can bring before judges. And so I must flee. In fleeing, I condemn myself to outlawry. My property will be confiscated. That means this house and these lands will be sold by the crown. Soon, you will have a new lord. You must serve him well, whoever he is. With no income from these lands, I can take none of you with me. But, I swear to you, I shall return. I shall defeat my enemies and I shall claim back my home. For now, I ask only that you all help me and my family to prepare for our absence. With the steward, we shall work out how what is left can be shared amongst you all, rather than fall into the hands of the next lord of Ashbury. God be with you all."

They clamoured again and begged me for more words but I could not face them and I pushed past into the courtyard.

"That was the longest I ever heard you speak in my entire life," Jocelyn said, grimacing as he walked out with me. "You are not very good at it."

"Pack your things," I said. "I must have a word with the prior."

∞

I walked through Ashbury's fields, then the Tutbury Wood and waded the Stickleback Stream to go to speak with Prior Simon before leaves for outlawry.

Simon was young to be a Prior, as I understood it. But he had been at Tutbury since he was a little boy. He had always shown a great aptitude for monkish things. The young Simon had even travelled away somewhere or other to study for a few years.

The man, when elected Prior by his brothers, had become a nuisance to me. Always he was seeking to improve the lot of the priory, which in practice meant pressing me for more money or for more rights or privileges. Money that I never had.

His monks worked hard for him. He was a Godly and practical man both and I admit that I admired his resolve and his aptitude.

I never liked him as a man.

"Where will you go?" Prior Simon asked in the privacy of his own house.

"Away," I said. "Just away."

"You do not trust a man of God to keep your secrets?" the Prior said, with absurd familiarity.

"It is better for you and everyone else if you do not know, surely?" I said, attempting to keep the irritation from my voice. "I came simply to ask that you do what you can to help everyone through this period."

"Of course, Sir Richard," the Prior said. "It is my God-given duty to do so. Do not think of it as a favour to yourself."

His self-aggrandising and pretentiously pious answer made me want to smash him in his chinless face.

"Before you flee into the wilderness," Prior Simon said, shifting closer in his seat and lowering his voice. "You should unburden yourself. Your life's tragedies weigh upon you, I know that they do. I have seen it."

He leered at me, his lips wet with anticipation.

I considered tearing his throat open and drinking him dry.

"Whenever thoughts of my life's tragedies occur to me," I said, speaking truthfully. "Or if feelings of anguish intrude upon a waking moment, I simply do not think on it any longer. I ignore the thought. I push away the feeling. Such things are too much to endure."

My answer seemed to excite him.

"God wishes you to face your sin," Prior Simon said, placing his sweaty palm on the back of my hand. "That evasion is your guilty heart. God wishes you to be unburdened of your crimes. Tell me and feel free."

"I am guilty. I have sinned," I pulled my hand from his sweaty grasp and stood. "And yet it is not my own crimes that concern me but those of enemies. And I will be the instrument of God's vengeance upon the guilty."

"Which enemies do you speak of?" Prior Simon asked, his eyes looking up at me, voice wavering.

"All of them."

∞

Two days of activity at Ashbury later and we were heading south once more. There was only really one place in all England that I could hide and also give me a chance to fight my way into a king's pardon.

I had to go to Kent.

There was little news of what was happening elsewhere in the kingdom. It seemed everything was happening far away. Whether our king was to be King Louis the French prince or King Henry the child.

Emma had taken our sudden flight with good grace. All her life, God had thrown bad luck at her. Her father had died when she was a baby. Her mother killed, violently when she very young. Brought up with Jocelyn by family she barely knew. Married young to an older man, whose seed had been weak. Pregnancies came to bloody ends. Her husband died leaving her nothing but debts and a manor that was overrun by Saracens. When Jocelyn had failed to claim his Poitevins inheritance, she had come to Ashbury with him. Through it all, she had remained remarkably accepting and had not turned bitter. She prayed often. Perhaps that was her secret.

I tried to speak to her of it, our first day riding.

"Good grace?" she said to me, her eyes flashing. Suddenly, she looked very much like her mother. "Taking it all with good grace? How else am I to take it, Richard? How could I have changed anything with public anger? Or displaying self-pity? When I say I am going to pray, it may mean that. Or it may mean I am weeping in the darkness. But what difference does it make how we accept God's will? You are a knight with a disagreeable temper. You charge your lance at anyone who offends you and then you end up friendless and alone, just as I am."

She spurred off to ride beside her brother, who threw me a look. For a moment, I was reminded of him looking at me that way many years before, when he was a small boy after I scolded him for his wandering attention.

"But I was thinking about being a knight," the young Jocelyn would protest, as if the content of a daydream was relevant.

I had failed them both. When they were children and since they had come to me, penniless and desperate. All I had needed to do was find each of them a good match. Both had plenty of promise for any prospective knight or young lady. But I was poor and friendless through my own lack of grace. And I had been lonely and I had welcomed their company. I had never truly wanted them to leave. I had been selfish. Taking them into outlawry with me was a new low for them as it was for me.

I had to make it right, somehow. I urged my horse beside theirs.

"And what are you two talking about?" I said, grinning, certain they had been cursing my name.

"I am not convinced that our destination is the right one," Jocelyn mumbled.

"Yes," I said. "I know. But you know why we must go."

"Because," Emma said. "You are almost entirely without friends."

"Correct," I said. "It is curious, is it not, that if the archbishop had not previously forced me to Kent then I would have nowhere to go at all. It is most fortuitous."

"Fortuitous?" Emma said. "That your liege lord wishes you dead?"

"You know what I mean," I said. "You call me friendless but I know one man who will welcome us."

"You hope," Jocelyn said.

"I do," I said. "I might even pray for it."

From the corner of my eye, I watched them both smile, just a little.

"But the truth is," I said. "I would go south no matter what. Whether I had the fortune to know Cassingham or not. My only hope now is for a pardon from the king. From the regent. When I have made war on the French. I will have a great victory and then no man can deny me my place as a faithful lord and knight."

Jocelyn sighed and nodded. "But I swear," he said. "Sometimes your arrogance borders on madness."

Never a truer word spoken.

∞

It felt like a long ride. I could not wait to get stuck in against the French. I did not declare myself anywhere that we went and I stayed out of the towns. Emma, who rarely rode and almost never travelled, was exhausted from the start. She never complained. Not to me, anyway. Jocelyn was giving up a lot to throw in with me. But he strove to be a good knight who did his duty by his lord. And, I suspected, he had his heart set on returning to Marian who awaited us in the Weald.

But I worried that Swein chafed at fleeing south again.

"This will be the last time," I said to him one night, sitting out under the stars. "I will make things right and when we go back north, we shall destroy William. Together."

"Yes, good." Swein poked at the fire with a long, blackened stick. He did not seem pleased at my promise. "I understand."

"Do you no longer wish to attack Sherwood?" I asked. "Has your heart gone out of vengeance?"

"No," Swein said, looking up at me. "Those men will pay for what they did. But I have missed my fellows in the Weald. You are not an archer, my lord. You wouldn't understand. Just chatting with others who know their business as well as you do, or even better."

"I can't shoot a bow," I said. "But my trade is the horse and the lance. My passion is the sword and the shield. I know well enough what you mean. I am pleased you found good company. I pray we find them well."

"They'll be alright, Sir Richard," Swein said, with the certain confidence of the young.

Of course, he was quite right.

Cassingham and his band of archers had kept up their attacks on the supply lines of the French.

He had set up winter quarters in a hall in a village deep in a wooded part of the Weald. One of the many manor houses that some lord had abandoned in flight from the French. We had found our way to him, village by village, as if they were stepping-stones through a river. Cassingham's men had built defences and stocked stores inside, enough for hundreds of hungry mouths through the coming winter.

We arrived late one morning in November and were welcomed like old friends. It was all rather heart warming. Marian and Eva stood together in the cold, Marian with a huge smile on her face. Eva scowled at me.

William of Cassingham rushed to meet us and welcome us into his hall.

"I apologise for bringing more mouths to feed, William," I said.

"We have had plenty of food from the French," Cassingham said, grasping my arm. "And even if we were starving, I would feed you, Sir Richard, from my own plate in order to have you fighting with us. Come inside, let us eat. You must tell me what is happening beyond London. We hear little."

Later we were seated, full of food and halfway drunk on stolen French wine.

We were crammed against each other at the top table.

Cassingham sat opposite me, with Emma seated on his right,

then Jocelyn opposite Marian and Anselm. On my side sat Marian, and then beyond her Swein and Eva sat at the far end, not speaking.

Marian seemed to have grown ever more beautiful since I last saw her and many eyes, it seemed, were drawn to her as well as to Emma.

Whereas I was very aware of Eva at the far end. I wanted to speak to her but it was difficult to do so at the best of times.

"That was a fine thing to say when we arrived, was it not?" Swein whispered to me, leaning over Marian like the bumpkin that he was.

"Cassingham is only a country squire," I said in a low voice as I pushed Swein out of Marian's face. "But he has more of the true knight in him than many a rich lord, I assure you."

Swein's eyes shone as he looked over the rim of his cup at Cassingham. Marian's did the same and I wondered what I had missed while I was away. I glanced at Eva who sat with her arms folded across her wonderful bosom. Jocelyn stared at Marian like a drowning man stares at a rope.

"What has happened with the siege?" I asked Cassingham who sat opposite.

"The French have abandoned Dover for the winter. The French brought down the gate, beyond the barbican, and they stormed the breach soon after you left for the north. Every attack they made was thrown back. The defenders made a timber wall inside the destroyed section of wall and there they fought back assault after assault. The fall rains came in late October and the French, dispirited, signed a truce. They would lift the siege and attack no more for three months and the garrison promised to not attack them in the same period. The French have now dispersed into the castles they took in the summer and also into London, which still celebrated Louis as king of England."

"I am astonished that the people yet support Louis," I said. "I will never understand those merchants of London."

"But the heart is going out of the Lords and merchants of London who supported Louis in the summer," Cassingham said.

"Why do you say the fight is going out of the rebel barons?" I asked. "How can you know, stuck down here? In this lovely wood."

Cassingham laughed. "It is not all of them. But the barons were at war with King John. It was King John that took their wealth and their lands and did as he pleased. Already, many are cooling their support for Prince Louis, who is granting lands as king of England to his own French lords. Already, so they say, many of the prominent men of London are sending word to King Henry and to the regents William Marshal and the Archbishop of York."

"But who says?" I asked. "You are living in the middle of a woodland, William, how on earth do you know what the barons of London are thinking?"

He grinned at my ignorance. "A handful of their servants have come to us. They are proud Englishmen and women. Many in London suppose that their lords might as well be French as English, so long as their rights are respected and their profits continue. Which is a fair argument for a merchant in London. But many here have been wronged and it is our duty to see them right."

Marian beside me stared, enchanted, at Cassingham. "If ours were a just world, you would be lord of these lands after you throw the French back into the sea."

She tossed her hair back over her shoulder, exposing her neck.

Cassingham blushed. "My lady, you are too kind. But I am far too lowly to hope for so much."

"Anselm will put in a good word for you with his father, won't you Anselm," I shouted down the table.

"Yes, Sir Richard, I will indeed," the lad said, speaking with absurd slowness and at far too great a volume yet still not entirely disguising the slurring.

"Jocelyn, do not allow your squire any further wine and punish him tomorrow."

"Oh, I will indeed, Sir Richard," Jocelyn said, mimicking Anselm. He clouted him round the head.

"Even though the lad cannot handle his wine, I am honoured to have him fight with us," Cassingham said. "It makes the men proud. They feel they are fighting on the side of right."

"It makes me proud too," I said. "When I was a boy, his father was at the peak of his fame in the tournaments. They say he bested five hundred knights across Christendom. Can you imagine such a thing? We would charge about the courtyard, legs astride a stick, shouting, I am William the Marshal, no, I am William the Marshal."

Jocelyn laughed. "As did we, twenty years later, in the Holy Land. Truly."

"What makes him such a great knight?" Swein asked, turning

abruptly to me. "My lord, if you don't mind me asking? Sorry, my lady." He elbowed a boiled turnip into her lap and she swatted him away, laughing at his eagerness and ineptitude.

When she turned away, I noted how lovely and soft her neck looked. I could almost smell the blood beneath her skin.

"William the Marshal?" I said. "He won, first and foremost. He would never have been more than a minor son of a minor lord, had he not won his riches at tournaments. Then he went to serve the old King Henry and he served him with absolute loyalty, even in the final days when all the king's sons rebelled. Did you know the Marshal unhorsed King Richard the Lionheart? Only man who ever did. Of course, he was just Prince Richard back then but still. He could have killed Richard, had he wanted, but instead William Marshal killed his horse, just to prove the point. But then he served Richard with complete faithfulness. Then came King John."

"Who treated him appallingly," Anselm said, loudly.

"Give him more bread, Jocelyn and shut him up. And King John mistrusted the Marshal and treated him badly as Anselm says. And again, the man does his duty and puts the king and the kingdom first before himself."

"That is not to say he has not feathered his own nest every step of the way," Jocelyn said to Cassingham. "He has played the games of power as skilfully as he ever did in the tournament."

"Yes, yes," I said.

"But how did he win so much?" Swein said. "Was he a big man in his youth?"

"Not especially," I said. "I have heard it said that he claims only to have a hard head. His single greatest talent, his one God-given ability that sets him above all others is that he can take a blow from the mightiest arm and yet stay on his feet and keep fighting."

"An ability that is rare for a man," Emma said. "Yet present in all women." I laughed, as did Marian but the others looked disturbed. "I am speaking poetically," Emma explained to Cassingham.

"Ah," he said.

Jocelyn took up the tales of the Marshal. "After winning a tourney in Normandy once, the blacksmith had to lay his head on his anvil and hammer his helm back into shape just so he could remove it from his head."

We traded stories about the Marshal while his fifth-born son lay slumped and snoring on the table. The meal had lasted until nightfall. More and more, I turned to Marian's lovely neck beside me. She smelled wonderful and the wine had thinned her blood and caused the skin of her face and neck to become flushed with a fetching pink hue.

I felt Eva's eyes upon me.

When it was late, she came and dragged Marian up from the table. I fell into Eva's dark eyes but the women said it was time to retire. The ladies shared a bedchamber attached to the hall but when they were gone, I could think of little else but Marian's neck and Eva's magnificent bosom. I remembered her sweat and her linen wrap from the weeks before.

That first night, I slept in the hall but I knew I had to get away from people. There was too much temptation. I wanted blood, to taste it, to feel it in my mouth and in my guts and limbs.

"I must find somewhere to live," I said to Cassingham. He himself occupied the bedchamber at the rear of his hall and, as far as could tell, he shared it with no one. "Somewhere away from anyone else."

The village houses were fully occupied but two men offered to give theirs up for me as I was a knight and they were no more than freemen farmers. I declined, though I was touched by their generosity. Cassingham had clearly put them up to it so I stressed to him again that I wanted somewhere miles away from the village.

What I did not tell him was I wanted somewhere that I would be no danger. Far from Eva and from Marian and everyone else.

And I wanted somewhere private.

Somewhere that I could feed.

∞

When Cassingham understood just how alone I wanted to be, he pointed me toward a cabin up on the side of a hill a few miles north from the village along the valley.

It was an abandoned oak cabin in an oak wood, in need of serious work. It had until a year or two before been a hunting lodge and belonged to the lord who owned the wood. The lord had died and his heir had been so caught up in all the unrest that he had never claimed it.

The wood was mostly oak but had a dense understorey of holly and coppiced hazel. Along the ground were straggly remains of blood-red crow's foot, almost died back for winter and a thick carpet of bright green dog's mercury. It was a working wood but empty of workers. The winding route up to the cabin was along a disused charcoal burners' path.

The hazel and ash had clearly been used by the charcoal makers but still, the oaks ruled the wood and acorns were everywhere underfoot. The local swineherds were about with their pigs who snuffled up and crunched acorns for miles around. The leaves were falling or fallen by the time I moved in, the architecture of the oaks revealed. Winter woods are stark, the lines and angles are skeletons bared to the bone, like the corpses of crucified men. The bones of the wood stood out like ruins.

My cabin was a sturdy place built from thick oak boards and beams, put together when the locally felled oaks were yet green. The single door faced south into the valley and through a cleft in the hills, I could see the sheep grazing the grass on the other side. The cleared area in front of the cabin let the sun warm my plank walls on the few warm days, causing sap to bleed down from joints and pegs and filled the air with the scent of life and summer, though the days were drawing in.

It was a steep valley, or as steep as it gets in the Weald. Out of the windows beside the door, I could look at the stream nearby that provided my water as it ran down the hill to the river flowing along the valley floor. Buzzards sometimes swooped along the length of the valley, often high up but also shooting low, hunting mainly at dusk. One dawn I watched a buzzard drinking from the stream, flicking the water up into its mouth and shaking water from its great dark feathers.

I would lay in bed and listen to the constant sound outside, through the walls and roof. Whether it was the rain or wind in the trees or the trickling of the stream, it was a never ending, reassuring humming of the world. At night, it would be the owls hooting in the branches high above. In the daytime, the blackbirds would flit between the holly and the ash, ever agitated, perhaps afraid of the coming winter. Always, over it all, were the rooks.

Rooks, birds of carrion and harbingers of death prefer elms, the taller the better, but a big group had made their nests in an oak glade close to the cabin. Even at night, I would hear them in their nests cawing in the darkness, jostling and pecking, stretching their wings. Each pair bedded down together in their nests, safe from the madness of crow society for the span of the night. Whenever there was a high wind, I used fallen rooks nests for kindling.

Rooks have a thundery call, like the rough accent of the backwoods Sherwood folk or the voice of any man who hailed from north of the Humber. A rasping, raucous, leathery old cry halfway between a hoarse complaint and a throttle shout of greeting. It reminded me of the men swarming up on scaffolds when churches and castles are being built. Bawled conversations consisting of endless oaths and laughter. Rooks are the most sociable of birds and they like people's company as much as they do their own. They were pleased that I had moved in.

Of course, this only confirmed my own darkness and unpopularity. Wealden folk, if they are proficient with a bow always shot rooks on sight. If not, they will go as far as sending boys up the trees to smash the eggs or throw down the chicks for the dogs to gobble up. I would not allow such practices for my rooks.

As the winter grew colder, the birds ate worms, pests and anything that crawled. Only at harvest time was it they prey upon farmer's grain and it seemed unfair to punish them for taking a little of what they needed.

"They enjoy my company and I theirs," I explained to Cassingham one time, who looked at me like I was mad beyond measure.

"But what about rook pie?" he asked, aghast.

"Any lad shooting my rooks can expect a hiding."

Swein gleefully told me that the men called me rook master. No man was stupid enough to say such things to my face, no matter how drunk he was. Though I gladly took up their name of the Crow's Nest for my woodland home. It was perfect and their name for it, created by them from fear and spite, made me care for the place even more.

The cabin itself was full of little mice and enormous spiders, who all came out to creep around in the darkness as I lay alone with my thoughts.

Scattered throughout the oak wood were wide flat clearings dotted with a collection of blackened stones, many shattered by the long heating from whatever it was charcoal burners did. They made excellent areas for practising the sword, once I had stamped down the bracken, stitchwort, dying foxgloves and saplings.

The cabin was damp and took weeks to dry through, burning through great mounds of fuel. I stuffed up the windy cracks with moss and clumps of wool.

I built a stable, of sorts, for my horse. It looked awful but I was mightily proud of it and I prayed it would not only survive the winter but also keep my dear horse safe and warm too. I would have happily brought him into the cabin, had it been warm enough.

Mostly, I chopped wood and brought food up from Cassingham's village.

As well as preparing for a lonely winter, I had other plans. I intended to ride north to the nearest French occupied town that remained unfortified. And I would bring myself back a Frenchman to feed on. I could keep him bound and gagged, much as I had done with Sir Geoffrey for Tuck. I would feed off him, taking a little at a time. And if the man died, I could bury him in the wood, unseen and I could take another man and another.

When the winter was over, I would be stronger than I ever had been. Strong enough, perhaps, to take on William by myself.

∞

After Christmas was well over, I rode north and spent many days exploring the tracks and routes that I could use to bring a man back to my cabin unobserved.

There was a village a dozen miles away. French knights had been there, they told me, and forced rent from the villagers. Their English lord had run away and left them to their fate a year before and they had no one but Cassingham to protect them. But even he and his men could not be everywhere. The French were due to return to collect further payments in kind, the villagers told me, begging me for help. All I could do was advise them to pay what was demanded and then I rode away.

But not far. There was a wood nearby. A mixed wood of elm, hazel, ash, oak, and elder throughout. Elms stood together in circular thickets where goldcrests and chaffinches sang.

There I hid and waited for the French to return. I lay shivering in the bare branches of a wych elm, watching a family cutting back a portion of their ash trees. Wych elm trunks often branch near to the ground, which makes them perfect for easy climbing. When I was a boy, I used to try to get girls to climb up them with me so we could be secluded in the wide boughs.

That day, though the branches were bare, I lay high up and well-hidden. I kept one eye on the family at work below me and one eye on the distant road, praying for a visit by a Frenchman full of warm French blood.

Coppicing must be done in winter, or at least before the sap rises in spring. I watched that family collecting every piece of the wood they cut down. The poles had a thousand uses. Thatched roofs required rods to secure the stacked bundles of thatch. Poles were used for making and setting eel and fish traps. Even the brushwood trimmed off the sides of the poles was gathered up by the children into tight bundles, bound together from twisted lengths of bark or from nettle twine. Those bundles would be used to get a young fire burning quick and hot. They piled fallen leaves over the cut stumps to protect the hazel shoots in spring from the browsing of deer. Moss showed everywhere, vividly green and shining around the stumps. The children chatted incessantly while they worked, recounting old scores and battles won by them against their enemies, the children of another family nearby.

Two days, I waited, shivering in the trees, hoping that the French would come raiding or raping so that I might prey upon them. My poor horse was miserable, though I covered her with a thick blanket and walked her about when it was quiet.

The French did not come. On the third morning, angry, hungry and eager for the taste of hot blood in my mouth I returned to my cabin.

On the way back, in the afternoon and almost at my oak wood, Eva found me.

She was beside the track, hacking at a fall of deadwood with an old, bent practice sword. Her black courser stood behind her, dozing, a thick blanket over him.

"Eva," I said, totally surprised. "How did you know where I was?"

"You can't do anything in the Weald without someone seeing," she said. She was wrapped up in a cloak with her hood up over her cap but her cheeks were flushed pink with the winter's chill.

It was an awkward, wild part of the wood with the hill rising steeply above, too steep to harvest the wood. Dead trees up there had fallen down over one another in tangled jumbles, slumped like piles of corpses after a siege. Leaning trees, partly-felled by great storms or the toppling of their elderly fellows, are called widow makers. When felling an already-leaning tree the immense forces on the trunk can cause it to suddenly twist and spring out at you, knocking you flat and sending your axe spinning into your face. A half-fallen tree though providing a haul of dried, seasoned wood, is dangerous. It is neither alive nor dead. It has no future but destruction and yet it will fight it all the way down. And it will betray the unwary.

Did Eva suspect what I was up to, I wondered. Was she ambushing me? Was she going to try to kill me?

"Why are you here?" I asked, fingering the hilt of my dagger.

She could not meet my eye. "You have not been seen for many days now. Not since Christmas. Some of us were wondering if you were well. Perhaps the French had come up here to raid."

"No one is travelling," I said. "And if they did I would kill them. This strikes me as strange?"

She sighed. "Life in the village has become somewhat tedious," she said. "I have no conversation and no man will train with me."

I relaxed, slightly. "You do not converse with Marian? Have you fought over something?"

"No, no," Eva said, irritated with my misunderstanding. "She only has time for Jocelyn, Cassingham, and Swein. And I knew you would be hungry. I brought you bread and cheese and wine."

"I suppose you better stay with me tonight," I said, ungratefully cursing that God's will had confounded my search for blood. "It'll be dark soon."

"What a generous, gracious knight you are, Sir Richard," she said and we rode single file back to my home.

"Where were you going to stay if I had not come along?" I asked her.

"Do not think me some helpless maiden," she said. "Finding a sheltered spot and starting a fire is simple enough."

"If you say so," I said. A part of me wondered if I could murder her and drink her blood. Although she was a stranger and not well liked, she was far more popular than I was. If she disappeared, then men would know who to blame. Of course, it would also have been completely immoral and I would never have done anything like that. The very thought was unworthy. Shameful, even. But I felt empty and weak and I wanted instead to be filled with power.

"I am stiff," I said when we had stabled our horses. "And there is daylight yet remaining. I will stretch my limbs and warm myself with some sword practice before eating."

"I will join you," she said, shrugging off her cloak.

We sparred in the open space between the stable and the cabin before going inside. She had improved and I was impressed by her ability. I had trained with dozens, possibly hundreds of squires and knights in my time. Eva was skilful. She was as strong as a young man was and had a long reach.

Her greatest attribute was her quick mind. She anticipated attacks. Her footwork was superb.

We sparred and clashed shields and I let her rap me upon the helm. Somehow, when we were breathing heavily, our breath misting the air, I made her laugh.

Twilight came. The gradual softening of the bleakness of the day turned into the still blackness of night. We had no candles outside and no lamps to fight by, but even while the western sky was a deep blue we could see by the light of stars in the crow-black blanket of night right above. When we became two shadows fighting each other, we could put it off no longer and went inside.

It was cold. I built up the fire while she sat on a stool at my rough table, not speaking but drinking down ale. I felt her eyes on me. The silence stretched out.

While the fire grew, I poured out a little of the water I had drawn that morning into the washbowl by the hearth. We had trained together, as men did so I decided to honour her by continuing as if she was a man. At least, that was what I told myself. With my back to her, I shook off my hauberk and continued to disrobe until I was naked and I washed the sweat off my body.

She moved behind me, rustling as she stood but I did not turn. I heard her shrug and shake herself out of her mail, which swished and thumped as she dumped it on the table. Even though my heart thudded in my chest, I admired that she had kept her steel off the damp floor. Then her doublet dropped and I wondered how far she would go.

Still not looking, I dropped to a knee to lay thicker sticks upon the fire. They caught as one and the flames lit up the room as bright as a yellow sunrise.

I stood. Her skin glistening and beaded with the cold water, she unwrapped the final circuit of the linen strip that enclosed her torso. As it came clear, her breasts spilled out, full and heavy and round. They bounced a little as they came to rest, freed from the binding.

She took the cloth from the bowl, bending at the waist, her back and flanks catching the firelight and shining along the hard muscles. There was not an ounce of spare flesh upon her, nothing but the whipcord of ridges and pits that came from hard training and never enough food. She was muscled like a knight and with her long limbs and square shoulders could have passed for a young man. But underneath that frame hung her huge breasts. She stood and washed them, wiping the cloth about them so they lifted and fell. She wiped her ridged flanks and under her arms, sighing and tossed the cloth into the bowl.

Fixing me with a stare of defiance, she thrust her hands on her narrow hips and stuck out her chin. She was shining like a statue of bronze, her belly flatter and harder than mine was, running into the shadowed triangle beneath. Her eyes began searching my own body. She smiled.

"Good God," I said, bewitched by her beauty.

She shook her head, laughing but not probably not with joy. I was unsure what to read from her eyes, dark and flashing.

"Good God, I said again, praying for words or thoughts to enter my mind. I knew what was going to happen and I welcomed it but I wanted to preserve the moment for eternity.

She sighed. "You are utterly witless."

Thankfully, she was not.

Making love to her was perfectly wonderful but a somewhat strange experience. Her body was hard. Her backside was small and all muscle. And she was strong. Strong of body and strong willed.

After pushing me down and sitting astride me, she issued curt commands throughout, telling me where to place my hands. I found it difficult to keep them from her voluptuous breasts, they being the only pliable part of her and also a sight in themselves that would have made St Paul spill his seed under his bishop's robes. She pushed my hands from them and into the moistness of her body and she made me grasp her by the neck. My own pleasure in the act appeared to be of secondary importance to her own. I can only suspect that my face wore an aspect of ecstatic bewilderment throughout.

At the end, she ground herself down against me, throwing her hips back and forth, flinging her black hair, and arching her back. I held tight to her as she gasped and lay against me, hard but for the giving softness of her chest.

"You may plough me until you are yourself finished," she whispered and rolled onto her back.

It was mere moments until I hurriedly withdrew and spilled my seed upon her belly. I collapsed beside her in a state of exquisite surprise.

I was cleansed. Complete. Whole, for just a moment.

It was dark but for the light from a smoky candle on the table. The fire I had started had died into nothing.

She wiped her stomach with the corner of a blanket and rolled over and leaned her hot skin against mine. "Build the fire."

She took a blanket and went outside to piss while I built the fire. When she came back, she cut bread, sprinkled it with salt and brought it back to the bed with the cheese and a skin of wine. The bed was narrow and she pressed herself against me after passing me the platter.

The fire grew and threw light on us. It all felt rather domestic. I was not sure what was happening or why it was happening now

258

but I was contented enough to live with it. We ate in silence. I could smell her body and I waited for her to begin to talk, to tell me about herself. I knew well that women loved to speak in the darkness. I was ever happy to listen and even to join in on occasion but rarely could I speak much myself. They always wanted more than I could give. I was never good at that sort of thing.

"May I sleep here?" she asked after we had eaten.

"Of course," I said. "I would be happy with the company. It has been a long time since I had the pleasure of—"

"Good," she said and lay down, stretching out alongside me. In just a few moments, she was snoring.

Not knowing what else to do, I lay beside her and wrapped her in my arms. In her sleep, she pushed her sinewy body against mine while I held her magnificent breasts. Somehow, I slept too.

And slept late. She woke me at dawn by whispering what she wanted and then doing it to me until I woke enough to return her passion. She wrapped her legs around me and sighed when I rolled on top of her.

A voice called from outside. "Richard?"

It was Marian. I froze. She was calling through the door and her voice carried through the thin walls.

"Richard, Eva did not return last night. Jocelyn said not to worry about her and also that I should check with you. Have you seen her?"

Eva lay under me, her hand across her mouth, eyes filled with mirth.

"Yes," I shouted back. I hesitated, wondering what else to say.

The silence stretched out.

"I see," Marian said and she stomped off without another word. Hooves pounded on the hard earth as she cantered away.

I lay down to Eva's laughter. "You've done it now," she said.

"Done what?" I said.

"Broken her heart."

"What in God's name are you talking about?"

"Did you not know?" Eva seemed genuinely surprised. "You really can be witless, Richard. For some time now, Marian has had her heart set on marrying you."

I leapt from the bed, pulled on my shirt and flung open the door into the frosty morning. I called her back. Her horse was already gone and she did not return.

The sun shone over the hilltop and shone through the wood, catching the crisp bare blackthorn branches, dark holly leaves and skeletal oaks standing their guard around my cabin. The winter sun throwing flashes of silver frost and outlining every twig and leaf, illuminating every blade of grass, existing in its own right even when attached to the whole plant and tree.

As I called Marian, the rooks in the wood erupted with the most raucous of choruses. The great black birds swooped in the dawn light and cawed on the wing, as if they were mocking me. Crows take flight before the dawn, swooping through the dark like spirits. Is it the crows' duty to wake all the other bids? If all the crows were to die, would all the other birds wake later, after sunrise?

"Richard?" Eva called me from the doorway of the cabin, blankets wrapped around her. "Come back to bed."

While the raw chorus of dark birds in the canopy sounded above, I noticed the warbling, sweet, delicate trilling of robins, chiffchaffs and blackbirds in the understorey and bushes.

∞

I gave up my hunt for blood. I did not take a Frenchman and feast upon him. Instead, I exhausted myself with chopping wood, practising the sword, caring for our horses and ploughing Eva.

It was a long winter. When the snows came, I chopped wood for fully half of every short day just to keep us from freezing overnight.

A tawny owl would cry from a favourite tree nearby. On still nights, his fellows could be heard calling back from far away through the wood, keeping in contact like archers waiting to spring an ambush.

Those nights I spent with Eva were long and pleasant, huddling under blankets by the fire. I cannot say I grew to know her but we grew comfortable around each other.

By the time of Lent, I was sure she had no secret motive, that she was not working for the archbishop. As sure as I could be, at least.

We rarely spoke of the past. Never of the future. For a while, I wondered if she would bring up marriage but she never did so I said nothing of it. Whether it was her intention to get with child or not, she did not do so. I could not tell if I was relieved or disappointed but I think she was a little sad.

Of the others, we saw very little, although Eva forced me to visit them as often as the weather allowed when we went down to collect more salted pork and flour.

Jocelyn courted Marian, without success. At least, they did not marry and it seemed to me that he grew impatient and angry, driving her further from him. What advice could I offer him, me who knew so little of women? Nevertheless, I tried. One night before Easter, we sat drinking together by Cassingham's hearth fire after mostly everyone else had fallen asleep.

"These stupid moths," Jocelyn said, giving me a significant look. "Waking from their winter slumber only to plunge straight to their deaths. Why would they do this, do you think?"

I had the feeling his comments were somehow aimed at me. No doubt, a part of him was hoping to stay in the Weald and keep trying with Marian rather than attacking Sherwood. And I knew what part.

"Moths are in love with the moon and the stars, son," I said. "They are creatures so mad with lust that they will fly into anything that remotely resembles it, even a candle flame or campfire. They want light. They want it so much that they do not mind if it will lead to fatal disappointment."

"Disappointment?" Jocelyn said, laughing. "Is that what you believe is waiting for me? That I am a moth to a flame? Listen, Marian is a perfectly suitable woman and I am a suitable husband. Or will be as soon as I win myself land. If any man here is a moth, it is you with that woman. Mark my words, she is the archbishop's, body and soul. She comes from his seed, you fool. She will give you up. Betray you. Betray us. Mark my words."

"You are wrong," I said, dreading even the thought of it.

"Calling me a moth," Jocelyn said, scoffing. "You are the moth."

Marian was always civil with Eva and with me but there was no doubt we had both offended the young lady by abandoning her to spend the winter with each other. She spoke to me very rarely.

We went into the village for most of the holy days, important saint's days and feast days. Every time I saw him, Swein chafed to get north. He and Marian both wished vengeance upon the Green Knight and his band of evil men. They drew together, as far as their stations allowed. Swein could make her laugh, which was more than Jocelyn would ever be capable of.

"When can we return to Sherwood?" Swein asked me one cold March day in Cassingham's hall. The others were with me and we shared the last of the stolen French wine, which was souring into vinegar but was better than no wine at all.

"I have been long thinking on that," I said. "In order to hire enough men to scour Sherwood, we need money. And in order to overcome my outlawry, we need a glorious military victory. And the French can provide both."

A large part of me wished I could stay in the Crow's Nest forever, swyving Eva, chopping wood. Getting old. Perhaps my seed would one day grow in her belly and we could live as man and wife. I said nothing of the sort to Eva, fearing scaring her away from me. She never mentioned marriage or a future together so I assumed she was not interested in one. So it was all just a dream. I had been playing all winter, pretending to be a commoner, pretending to be a husband and half-hoping to be a father. It would never happen.

Instead, duty beckoned. William had to receive the punishment he was owed. The monster had even slain the king. When the blossoms bloomed all over my wood, I knew it was time for me to fly the nest.

In late spring, the French returned to Kent in force. Cassingham gathered his men from all over the Weald.

It was time to fight.

TEN ~ THE GREAT
DOVER RAID

"THE FRENCH ARE COMING," I said to the assembled leaders in Cassingham's adopted hall in early May 1217. One of his men had come charging in that morning. The fellow upon a steaming horse with word from the coast. The news he brought with him had stirred the hornet's nest that was the Weald.

"They mean to take Dover once more but this time, they shall finish the job," I said. "Your man's report is clear. The siege engines are being carried ashore. The first are already being assembled. We must strike now before the fighting men join them."

Jocelyn rapped his hand upon the table. "Sir Richard is right. The longer we wait to take action, the stronger their position becomes."

Cassingham and his men were disturbed, exchanging glances.

"We have been taking action," Cassingham said. "For many months have we been fighting the French while our king fights the barons of the north and the west."

"Skirmishes and minor ambushes," Jocelyn scoffed, waving his hand.

Cassingham's lip curled into a snarl.

I stepped in. "You have performed magnificent deeds," I said, raising my voice so all in the hall could hear me clearly. "You have harmed the enemy with raids, you have stolen his supplies, you have protected villages. Punished crimes. But now is our chance to destroy him. To truly change the course of the war. If we do this, Prince Louis will be denied Dover Castle, for months at least. We can destroy his engines, kill his engineers."

"It would delay only," Cassingham pointed out, "you say it yourself."

I carried on, unperturbed. "They have unloaded their supplies at Dover. Supplies of food, wine, oil, bolts and swords, engines and horses are being brought ashore as we stand here and speak. If we destroy them, Louis will be without the things he needs to fight the war. He may have thousands of knights and bowmen but what use will they be if he cannot move them, supply them and fight them where they are needed?"

"If we do this," Cassingham drummed his fingers upon his table. "The Marshal could move to isolate the barons. Without the promise of reinforcement from Prince Louis, he could invest in a siege."

One of Cassingham's captains spoke up. "Our men in London say the barons have taken the city of Lincoln."

266

"But not the Lincoln Castle," another said. "That, the rebel barons yet besiege."

"Precisely," Jocelyn said. "Many of the barons and their men are gathered in a single place."

"We must move quickly," I said, encouraging them to see it all. "We must strike at the French and then the Marshal must destroy the barons before Louis can recover his supplies. Speed is the key to this lock. We must strike now and we must send word to the Marshal right away."

"Send word that we mean to attack the French camp?" Cassingham asked.

"We must send word that we have destroyed it. The riders must go out immediately. Today, if possible. Tomorrow at dawn if not."

There was a minor uproar that Cassingham waved down.

"How can we give word of a thing that has not happened?" Cassingham said, aghast.

"But it will have happened," I said, "by the time that word reaches the Marshal."

Cassingham did not like it. It seemed immoral to him. As though he would be lying to the Regent.

"It is a moot point. We cannot attack a camp of that size," Cassingham said. "Even if it is undermanned we would be hugely outnumbered."

"You are always outnumbered, Cassingham," I said, grinning. "All of your men, all of last year, all this past winter. It has never stopped you before. This is not so different to when we took Sir Geoffrey last year and led them into the woods."

"That was a mad chance," Cassingham said. "We never expected it to work as well as it did. It should not have done. In our favour was the fact we were on the far edge of the camp, we killed barely any of them and led them to where we were strongest. Carefully prepared ambushes, in the woods. It was little more than a gesture. And still they hunted us for weeks, we were always on the run. And even then, Sir Richard, we planned that raid for days. Now you ask us to muster hundreds of men and to mount an attack on a fortified encampment the moment we arrive at it."

"It is the only way, Cassingham," I said. "If we delay even a little, there will be hundreds of knights, hundreds of bowmen, thousands of men and our chance will be gone."

"You wish only to better your own standing in the eyes of the regent," one of Cassingham's captains said. "You are accused of having a hand in King John's death, are you not, my lord? You would risk all our lives for your own ends."

Jocelyn leapt to his feet. "How dare you?" he cried. "Who said that?"

I stood too, slowly and waved Jocelyn down.

Crossing my arms, I looked around the room, into as many eyes as I could. All were silent. I found my accuser, recognising the captain as one I had fought beside before and saw him shrink under my gaze.

"We should each of us be thankful to God," I said. "When duty and glory align. I fight for our young King Henry. Which man here says I do not?" I let the silence fall. Eyes flicked about. "We can win glory. William of Cassingham will win fame. Sir Jocelyn, too. You men who are not knights or not of noble birth, you will win whatever riches you can take from the French. And you will win the chance of a great story to tell when you are old and fat, about the time you saved England from a false king and his pillaging armies. You men are the finest archers in all England, or so you like to tell yourselves. You decided to fight with William of Cassingham when your lords ran and hid in the king's castles. One day soon, this war will be over. What will other men say of the Wealden Archers? Will they tell of a band of big-mouthed oafs who sat through the war with their arrows shoved up their arses? Or will they sing songs of the common men who threw down a French prince and pissed in his face? Come with me, or stay here. The choice is yours. If you stay then I will simply have to keep all the spoils for myself."

We rode for Dover at dawn.

∞

Cassingham knew that I was right. Once we were committed to making the attack, we had to carry it out and get away before the French arrived in force.

All the first day while we rode through the Weald with over a hundred archers, I allowed Cassingham to take charge and admired how he harried his men, harangued them for their slothfulness, inspired them, bawled them out, praised them and kicked their backsides into a frenzy.

They knew him. They loved him. Me, they still did not know and few of them liked or trusted me. I was a knight, from far to the north. Some of the Wealden archers had fought in Gascony, Normandy, Ireland, Wales and the Holy Land but most had never left Kent. Amongst those men, outsiders were mistrusted. And I was an outsider amongst outsiders.

It was safe to say that the men under my temporary command obeyed me with some reluctance.

Watching them that day I noted that Swein was welcomed and accepted, despite his Yorkshire accent and youth. He was a brilliant bowman, through and through and when he talked, men listened. He had matured over the winter. His clothes were better than they had ever been and he had taken or purchased a gambeson and a decent helm with a huge nosepiece. Still, he wore a hood over the top of it but, at least, he had found a new, green one.

The second day we met with other groups in the woods outside Dover. We were almost two hundred and fifty of Cassingham's men waiting in the darkness before the dawn a few miles from the edges of the French camp.

Cassingham and his captains, who it seemed now, included Swein who was supposed to be my squire, checked their men's equipment and kept up their spirits in the dark.

"Hope it don't rain," Swein said to me, looking up at the grey clouds rolling in from the sea on the dark sky.

Wet bow cords lose their potency. But I doubted Cassingham's huge band of archers would be shooting many arrows that day. We wanted the rains to stay away so that we could burn the French camp.

There was no way to hack that many siege engines to pieces.

So we carried oil and most men carried bundles of kindling. With any luck, we could get in amongst the siege works and make such a blaze that they could not put it out before their vital equipment was destroyed beyond repair.

But only if the rains stayed away.

"I might even pray for it," I said to Swein and he grinned.

"Do not mock prayer," Cassingham's priest said, overhearing. "Not this day, Sir Richard. God will not be mocked."

"I never mock God," I said. "Only men who believe that He cares about their whining."

The priest cursed me under his breath as Swein laughed.

"This is why you never have any friends, Richard," Jocelyn said. "Most men do not take such things lightly."

"But my man Swein here takes God as lightly as I do," I pointed out, "and he has made plenty of Wealden friends."

"Swein is a commoner among commoners," Jocelyn said, grinning. "And he can make conversation on subjects other than war, which is more than you will ever achieve."

Swein had the good grace to laugh. I did not.

"You are in fine fettle this morning," I said.

"We will win a victory," Jocelyn said. "And perhaps even take a knight or two as my prisoner. And this time, I shall ransom him and finally put some marks into my purse. I shall be on my way." He looked back along the dark road toward the village of Cassingham as if he could see Marian from all those miles away.

Eva had wanted to come with me before we left.

"I know that you wish to test yourself against real foes," I had said. "And know that all your training has made you a fine man-

at-arms. But you should stay with the Lady Marian. There will be few enough wounded men left behind to protect her, should the French raid here while we are away."

"Do not condescend me," Eva had shot back. "I know I am a fine man-at-arms. I want to kill Frenchmen."

"And that is why you are needed here."

Even though I knew she was stronger than most men, certainly better with sword and shield than any of the Wealden archers, still I treated her as though she was a weak and feeble woman. In time, the poor woman would pay for my condescension of her.

But Eva had stayed with the Lady Marian. Already I missed her long, hard limbs and her hot skin against mine. I would much rather have been naked and abed with her than lurking in the dark woods dressed for war.

Cassingham called his men to him.

"Some of us have been here before," Cassingham said to them. "This one, though, will be the biggest raid any of us has ever been on. You all know what you must do so I will not repeat it. I merely remind you that if we succeed in our task this morning we may save the garrison in Dover Castle. And if we save them, we may save all England. Our battle cry will be King Henry."

Their murmuring grew towards a shout and Cassingham growled at them to shut their idiot mouths until we attacked.

They knelt for prayer and for once, I joined them. While the priests wittered away, I asked God to make my enemies stupid, weak and fearful that morning. Please, Lord, I said, let the French have drunk themselves insensible last night on their fresh wine. God likes it best when you ask him for very little.

272

Cassingham and I divided our forces into three groups and agreed on the signal for starting the attack and the signal for withdrawing.

I would attack the centre of the camp. Cassingham would lead his men around the left flank and come in from the north. The third group was on my right hand, attacking the southern side of the camp. That group would attempt to hold that entire side of the camp and also to watch the town for any counter attack from French forces garrisoned there.

My group would drive into the centre of the French, straight for the largest of the siege engines.

I had eighty men under my command. They were nervous, excited, grim. They tested their bows, checked their swords, daggers and other weapons. I did not give them a speech. They knew their jobs.

We led our horses toward our group's mustering place outside the French camp, under cover of the thin trees, already much cleared from the year before. The French camp was unseen over a rise but I could see the battlements of Dover Castle's highest towers, dark against a lightening sky. A light mist drifted through the deep green, grey of the morning, settling dampness over the shimmering nettles, goosegrass, grasses, sedges and ferns. Ferns were everywhere.

I drew next to Jocelyn. "If this succeeds then we will have to ride north. We will have to bring the news to the Marshal."

"What about the messengers you made Cassingham send?" Jocelyn asked.

"They were vital but they will not be believed."

"And you will?" Jocelyn shot back. "You are outlawed."

"They will believe you," I said. "You are known to be a true knight."

Jocelyn scoffed. "A true knight? No man of import knows me as anything."

I did not argue. "Anselm will tell them, won't you, son," I said over my shoulder.

"Yes, my lord."

"So you better not get yourself killed this morning, you hear me, Anselm? I do not give you permission to die. Stay behind Jocelyn or you and Swein will guard the horses."

"Yes, lord."

"You too, Swein. I know these men are your friends, now but I want you with me when I go into Sherwood."

"Don't worry about me, Sir Richard," Swein said. I could hear the grin on his face. "This ain't my fight."

"Quite right."

We gathered just as the light was growing and waited for Cassingham's signal to attack. The other groups all had to get in position so that we could all attack at once.

The trees about us were young, well coppiced and much of the brush had been cleared. Along the floor was the last throws of the intense mauve-blue haze of bluebells in the wood. There had been an extravagant profusion in my oak wood because the deer grazed the undergrowth, the boars chewed and stamped down bushes and saplings leaving the ground layer clear for the strange plants to flourish. Outside Dover that morning, the pink campions and goosegrass spread along the ground, ringed by a wide layer of bright green nettles in the deep shade at the edges beneath the trees.

The woods were full of birds singing in the dawn. Rooks and crows gathered above our heads, scaring the pigeons and blackbirds into flight. We waited for the signal to attack.

"How do they know?" Swein asked me, pointing to the carrion birds. "That they will feast soon, I mean."

Before I could answer, a Kentish priest growled his own opinion. "Because they are evil."

"They are wise," I said, ignoring the holy idiot's huffing. "They have seen from their own experience that when men gather like this, blood is spilled."

Swein nodded, accepting this truth.

"They are beasts," the priest said. "They cannot be wise. It is blasphemous to think otherwise."

Jocelyn glared at me. He was right. It was no time for an argument with a priest, no matter how much I enjoyed them. I held my tongue and wondered if I would get a chance to drink some blood of my own, along with the crows.

We waited for the signal.

On the horizon, beyond the camp, the familiar silhouette of the great castle resolved out of the darkness. Upon its huge mound, the castle looked down upon the landing area for the ships below the famous cliffs. Southwest, to my right, was the town, on much lower ground and overrun by French.

The messengers had told us how the beach below the town was covered with fat cargo ships pulled higher than the tideline up the sand and shingle. Many of the ships had already been unloaded. I half dreamed that we could go down there and burn them too but I knew we had to be realistic. We were but two hundred and fifty men against perhaps two thousand between the siege camp and the town.

I mentioned my thoughts to Jocelyn. He called me mad for even thinking it.

"How do you get down to the beach?" Swein asked, cutting in.

"Jocelyn is quite right. It is beyond us," I said. "We would have to attack between the forces of the camp and the town, being trapped between both. The cliffs are low by the town but it is still a steep, narrow slope down to the beach. Then we would have to burn the ships and fight back up that slope. I saw it from afar last summer when we scouted the camp. The lowest part of the cliff is thirty, forty feet high. We would never make it back up while under attack."

Swein laughed. "Now that would be a feat worthy of a song."

"Indeed," I said. "It would be a beautiful thing, though, would it not?"

"You have a strange idea of beauty, Richard," Jocelyn said.

A thin drizzle started, then stopped. Then started again.

"These God-forsaken peasants," Jocelyn muttered in French. "What is taking them so long?"

"Be patient," I said, fingering the hilt of my sword.

"Perhaps they have run away," Jocelyn whispered. "What can they be doing?"

The men around me fiddled with their clothing or pissed where they stood. Anselm went a few paces back to take what must have been his fourth shit of the morning.

276

Swein chuckled to himself and spoke in a low voice. "How can you even take a shit while wearing a coat of mail?"

"It can be awkward and messy, squatting in a hauberk," I said. "But all you need do is hold your small clothes aside. And anyway, it is preferable to shitting yourself during the battle."

"Does that happen?" Swein whispered, amused, no doubt, at the idea of knights soiling themselves.

"It happens very often," I said. "Would not be a battle without the stink of shit. I seem to remember doing it myself once or twice."

"You do it every time," Jocelyn said.

"Shut your mouth."

In truth, I was growing nervous at how light it was getting. It was only a matter of time before the watchers in the French camp saw us. They would see hundreds of men spread in a broken crescent about the edges of their camp, crouching in the shadows of the brush. No doubt, we would run into the first French work parties at any moment, coming to chop wood and cart it back to the camp.

Jocelyn fretted too, mumbling to himself. "What is taking them so damned long?"

A hunting horn sounded far to our left.

Cassingham's signal.

I nodded at our man, standing at my shoulder and he blew his horn just as the third to my right sounded, halfway to the town.

"Thank Jesus for that," Jocelyn said and jammed his helm down over his head.

Leaving a few lads to bring up and guard the horses at the

palisade, we streamed into the camp on foot. The place was laid out much as the previous summer. A rough circle half a mile away from the castle, which rose high on its mound with the mighty walls and tower after tower around it. The town of Dover was half a mile to my right, lower down the hill.

The camp in front of me was protected by a narrow ditch and a low bank, topped with a half-hearted attempt at a palisade of steaks. Roads crisscrossed inside between the rows of canvas tents. Latrines and piss-trenches lined the downhill side.

On the far side of the camp, beneath the walls of the castle but outside of bow range were the great war engines that the French were building. Black struts and beams stuck up into the dawn. Mostly half-finished and dwarfed by the walls of one of the greatest castles in the land but still impressive structures.

They were our targets. We would have to fight our way clear through the entire camp to reach them. And, more to the point, back out again.

All of a sudden, I was struck by the madness of it. I saw our attack through Cassingham's eyes and the eyes of his men. But I had cajoled and browbeaten them into the attack and it was too late to back out now. Withdrawal without first attacking them would have been disastrous, leaving them free and full of confidence to chase us down.

Most of the men with me were archers in the prime of their life. There were a handful of boys with us, and a couple of priests and at least one woman had snuck along with us, too. It was not Eva.

The men who were supposed to be guarding their gateway

278

were lax indeed. If there were men watching the approach at all, then they had fled at the sight of us and had not even paused to spread the alarm.

We had declared our presence with horns but we did not cry out yet as we streamed into the camp. We saved our war cry. But we made plenty of noise as we shouted instructions to each other.

"Walk," I shouted to my eighty men as the ones in front starting pulling further ahead. "Save your strength. Stay together, stay together."

French men pushed aside the flaps of their tents, blinking in the overcast dawn light, looking confused. These first few men received arrows for breakfast or were cut down with our blades.

We were quite deep into the camp when the first proper, martial French cries came, their shouts of warning, their own horns sounding and warning bells started clanging.

A line of bleary-eyed soldiers jostled each other into place, blocking the roadway between the tents. We had to get beyond them. There were a dozen, then twenty and thirty of them. Many were without mail armour, some without even gambesons and others had no helmets but there were plenty enough armoured men-at-arms there to frighten my men back from them.

We had to cut them down before they inspired more men into making a stand. Although the camp was barely populated, we were still vastly outnumbered and the French organising against us would be our undoing. We had to break them.

"Stay together," I shouted, drawing my sword and pointing at the line ahead. "And kill them. King Henry! King Henry!"

I ran ahead, trusting they would support me. Arrows cut the

air right by me and felled every man in the line before I could reach them. An arrow at close range can pierce mail, especially the cheaper sort and some of the men wore none at all. The arrows thudded and slashed into their bodies. They cried out, some screaming. A few turned and ran but were brought down by arrows in the back. Most of the fallen were wounded but not dead so I finished them off, stabbing them through the necks and eyes and armpits. Jocelyn and Anselm came up beside me and together we made short work of those unlucky survivors. French who had been coming to their aid backed away, looking to make a stand elsewhere or, hopefully, flee to safety.

"With me, with me," I shouted to my wonderful archers.

We made our way further in. There was no chance of us killing them all. Indeed, we did not wish to do so. We wanted only to scare them away so that we could do our burning of the engines and the food and wine and shoes and arrows and other supplies.

I had insisted to Cassingham and his men that we needed to leave the French a route of escape, toward their fellows in the town garrison. But they were not fleeing as swiftly as I needed them too.

"Burn these tents," I said to my men. "Stir up some camp fires. Get the boys to start blazes here. Let's scare them back into the town, come on. Make a noise, you bastards. Show them who the men of Kent truly are. For the Weald! For Cassingham! King Henry!"

They took up the cry, shouting for their homeland, for their leader. They kicked over tents and lean-to's and threw burning brands into them. Fires flickered and grew. Black smoke drifted across the dawn light. The rain stayed away.

The gathering French ran. In ones and twos and then, seeing that so many of their fellows fled, dozens at a time swiftly followed. They ran for the town, plodding down the hill.

"To the engines now, to the engines, men, with me, with me," I cried. "King Henry!"

The engineers, those experts who constructed and then operated the mangonels and other engines, were proud men. They were men who brought down castle walls, towers, and gates. They were men who brought down counts and dukes and kings. A few brave fools defended their half-built mangonels from the trenches they had dug about their engines. They shouted challenges, brandishing huge mallets and iron spikes and long, heavy wooden levers.

"Leave," I shouted at them. "Go join your friends."

Reason said that I should have killed them anyway, because if they were dead then who could build the replacement engines for the French? But I admired the way that they stood defiantly in the face of such odds and I offered them the chance to live.

Instead of taking it, they mocked my men and were full of contempt, for they could see how poorly dressed we were and they knew us for the peasant rabble we were.

But these peasants were deadly beyond any that could be found in France.

"Kill them quickly," I told my archers. The men cheered and they murdered the engineers in moments. The bowstrings thrummed and the arrows crunched through the clothes, skin, flesh and bones of those men. The arrows ripped through them like the hand of God had smitten the engineers. After the single volley, the archers leapt into the ditches to finish them off by hand.

"Good God," Jocelyn shouted to me. "Why do we not have archers with us every time we fight? With a thousand of these men behind us we could conquer all France."

The Wealden men in earshot roared their approval and Jocelyn's standing was immediately improved among the peasantry.

"Shut up and burn these machines," I shouted. "Burn them now, burn them well. Come on, hurry. This is why we are here."

I took a dozen men and we kept up the madness of the attack to keep the French away and afraid. We whooped, cried, kicked over barrels and tents, and threw down everything that was upstanding and tore up anything planted in the earth. My men doused the timbers of the machines in oil and set fires about them. The flames licked up and took hold.

But something was not right.

There was no great store of food and weaponry and equipment.

"Bring me a Frenchman," I shouted and they dragged a wounded engineer over to me. He seemed young but it was difficult to tell as he had taken a cut across the forehead and his face was covered in a torrent of blood.

"If you ransom me," he said, wiping his eyes and peering up at me. "My father will pay you handsomely, my lord. He is a rich burgess, a craftsman in—"

"The best you can hope for," I said, "is that I end your life swiftly. If you do not tell me true answers to my questions, then I swear to you that I shall throw you onto that fire."

He started shaking. "No, no, no, please, I know nothing, I know—"

I slapped his face. Too hard, knocking him senseless for a moment.

My hand was covered in his blood. I fought down the urge to lick my fingers and suck the blood from his face. My men were all around me. I had to fight it down.

I grabbed him. "Where are the supplies?" I asked him. "Where are the stores of grain? Where are your barrels of oil?"

"On the ships," he said, gibbering and whimpering. "The beaches ships. Not yet unloaded. We need the grease, also, to coat the parts before we assemble the gears..."

I stared down toward the sea.

"What is it?" Swein asked beside me. "What did he say?"

"The supplies are on the ships."

The men's shoulders slumped.

"A partial victory is a victory still," I said though I did not believe it. The smoke billowed up into the air, catching the sea wind and drifting across the camp.

An English voice shouted from over by the burning engines. "A counter attack! They are coming, knights and soldiers are coming this way."

I ran to the men who were calling, shouting at them to fall back to me. It was all falling apart. We were going to be driven off and I would be robbed of the great victory I needed.

"Where?" I shouted, looking toward the town.

"There, my lord," the men shouted, pointing up the hill.

I laughed and clouted them about the head.

"You great, bloody fools," I shouted. "Those are Englishmen. That is the castle garrison, riding out to fight with us."

And so it was.

They were glorious to behold. The knights of Dover Castle streamed from their castle gates on their fine horses and down the steep slopes towards us. Lances held aloft, pennants streaming. They had dressed for war quickly.

I called for my horse and Anselm ran back and brought it up to me. I rode up to meet them as the sun broke through the layer of low cloud.

There were twenty or so knights and twice as many squires, all mounted.

Their leader advanced his destrier to me. "I am Hubert de Burgh," he called. "Constable of the Castle."

He was a small man, rather young for his position but he came from the best stock and his entire family were loyal followers of King John. His oldest brother had taken half of Ireland and another brother was the Bishop of Ely. Sir Hubert was dressed in magnificent armour and cloth but his horse looked thin and weak. Horses suffer in sieges.

A few of his knights and squires stayed with him but most of the others rode by us, toward the French camp, to join in the slaughter and the destruction.

Hubert de Burgh and I spoke from horseback.

"My lord," I said. "I am Sir Richard of Ashbury. I have heard nothing but fine things of you, my lord. We were all mightily impressed by your resistance to the French last year."

The Constable frowned. "You are Richard of Ashbury? Are you the son of the Sir Richard who fought beside the Lionheart?"

I sighed. "My lord, we have come to raid. We are only two hundred and fifty. Freemen of the Weald, for the most part. We cannot hold this position, not for very much longer."

"I can see that," Hubert de Burgh said. "And we are too few to risk becoming too much embroiled in your fight. We do not have long. We cannot be caught out here. But we came to hold off their counter attacks while you burn as much of the damned place as you can before their master arrives."

"Our scouts and spies told us the camp was full of supplies but in fact, much of it remains onboard the ships below. I mean to go down there and burn them."

"Good God, man," the Constable said, looking down toward the distant beach. "We cannot help you to do this."

I pushed my horse closer to his. "Your men can hold the French back from the town while my men burn the ships."

"But you have no time," the Constable cried. "Prince Louis is about to land."

"What do you mean?"

"Look," Hubert de Burgh shouted, pointing out to sea. "Are you blind?"

The sun was near its zenith. The day had half gone in the blink of an eye while we had fought and burned. Out to sea, beyond the roofs of the town and further along the coast to the southwest, crept a scattered line of dark shapes.

"Ships," I said.

"Prince Louis," de Burgh said. "The false king of England. He is coming. He is coming here. And he is coming now."

"Then we had best move quickly," I said and dragged my horse around to tell my men to gather so that I could tell them the change in plans. I was half expecting them to tell me to stick my ship burning idea up my backside and I wondered what I could promise and threaten to get them to risk being killed or captured.

But when I turned, Swein was already shouting at the men. They were gathered about him as he stood atop a wagon. He had his bow raised in one hand and one foot up on the sideboard of the wagon.

"... and we're going to go down there and we're going to send them back to France with their arses on fire. Now, grab your kindling and every arrow you can find. For the Weald!"

The men shouted as one, "For the Weald!"

Swein turned, saw me and grinned. He leapt from the wagon and strode over to me as I dismounted.

"I suppose it would be churlish of me to ask you hold my horse," I said.

Swein laughed.

All men are afraid of battle, unless they are mad. But some men can also enjoy it. Many great warriors do not love the madness of battle. But the very best do in fact revel in it. Not in the way a madman does but with the certainty and surety of a man who is doing the thing he loves. Much as a blacksmith does when fully occupied by his art or a carpenter consumed by the procession of his carving or when one is riding a horse at a full gallop and you fall into a state of perfectly flowing clarity. For some few of us, the madness of war makes perfect sense. I was always one of those few. I was surprised to find young Swein amongst our number also.

"Find two men to take a message to Cassingham that we go for the ships," I said to Swein, for he knew the men more than I did and I trusted him to pick the right ones.

"I will."

"And tell the rest to bring all the kindling and fire that they can carry."

Anselm looked after the horses and with four men and all the boys, he held by the edge of the French camp under the castle walls. Other than Anselm, all were archers and they would keep any roaming bands of French away from our few mounts.

The Constable led his forces down the hill away from the camp and toward the town below. There were hundreds, if not a thousand or two thousand men down in the town and still more filed down to their fellows from the camp. The Constable let them go and his men spread out, ready to charge down any attempted counter attack.

We were about sixty as we trotted down the path to the beach. What unburned skins of oil we had remaining were slung about a few shoulders. Others carried bundles of twigs or smouldering brands and all of us carried tinder.

The younger men ran forwards and shouted back what was ahead and below but I saw for myself soon enough.

A dozen, fat bellied traders' ships in a row high up on the golden sands. Just as the messengers had asserted. It was a narrow beach, with the tide high and licking at the sterns. The salt spray of the sea blew right up the cliff.

The path ran down along the crumbling, chalk cliff face switching back halfway down. The cliff was angled enough to grow bushes and great clumps of sedge. It was narrow but we could make two abreast for most of it and we ran down as fast as we could.

Seagulls swooped about us, crying and squawking. It was nesting season and the gusting clouds of black smoke above had wound them into an even greater frenzy than gulls normally felt. Beyond there were more wheeling birds in mixed flocks of sanderlings and dunlin.

One of the men paused to take aim at one of the birds, being cheered on by a comrade at his elbow. I kicked the archer up the arse, cursing them for their delay and both of them picked up their feet and scarpered down the slope.

The sailors and guards had seen us streaming toward them and were already leaping from their vessels and trudging away down the sand, leaving the vessels unprotected.

I pulled off my helmet so my voice would be heard above the surf and wind. "Five men to each ship. Each group needs kindling, fire and oil if there's enough." I shouted to Swein and Jocelyn, who began organising and directing the men as they came down off the slope. "And kill any bastard who tries to stop us."

I did not dare to hope that we would burn all the ships before we left. Likely, we would only get a couple going with a blaze so big that it could not be put out. As our men split up to take the ships, I trudged toward the nearest one, keeping a look out up behind us.

On the top of the cliff below the walled town, men were massing. Heads and shoulders looking down at us. Whether they were French or surviving English townsfolk, it was hard to say. They made no move to interfere, they simply watched. Many heads swivelled away from us to down the coast. From so low on the shore, with the enormous ships blocking my view, I had no sight of the fleet of Louis' ships. But I knew they must be close.

"We have to be quick, Swein," I shouted as I came into the shadow of the nearest ship. The hull was covered with tiny shells and green stuff, although much had been scraped off and was lying about in the sand. The hulls of the older of the beached ships were chewed and gnawed at by gribbles and shipworm.

The sailors had set up little campfires. There were ropes strung everywhere, hanging laundry and supporting sailcloth shelters. There was the usual camp detritus underfoot, discarded smashed pots and animal bones amongst the driftwood. No sailor used driftwood for fires unless he was desperate. The flames of a driftwood fire burn green and blue, haunted by the spirits of the drowned.

The men had been lazing about for a couple of days, no doubt getting their fill of the supplies before their master Prince Louis of France showed up. I would be willing to bet the ship masters had been busy selling some choice stuff to the townsfolk, too.

Swein leaned over the side of the nearest ship and cupped his hands to his mouth.

"There's oil here," he shouted to the men. "Pass the word, this ship is full of oil. Come and get it. Pass the word."

Jocelyn, his helm under his arm, shook his head. "You are the luckiest sod who ever lived."

"I have been called many things in my time," I said. "But lucky is not one of them."

"Not in life," he replied. "Clearly, Richard, you are not lucky in life. Merely in battle."

"Is that what this is?" I said. "A battle? Come on, you lazy oaf, let us make a bonfire big enough for Louis to find us. Use some of this driftwood."

We slung casks of oil between Swein's ship to the farthest ship in either direction.

"This is taking too long," I muttered, as the fires started to catch inside the ships.

Oil is all very well but much of it will not burn until it is heated. There were hundreds of small casks of almond, poppy, and olive oil that the men were pouring all over the decks. There were stinking ones full of rendered animal fat that they smashed and dumped into the flames. But our fires would have to burn big and hot before they caught.

"Come on, hurry, lads," I shouted up at them. "Pile the fires high and let us go."

"Sir Richard," men were calling me from up above the ships near to me and pointing frantically up at the cliffs behind me.

Our men were up there, waving and pointing and calling. Black smoke billowed above them. They were jabbing their fingers out to sea and jumping up and down.

"Time to go," I roared. "Swein, get them out of here. We fall back now. Leave the fires unburnt, come on, to me, to me."

I walked backwards, waving the men off the ships.

Swein shouted the orders and the word was passed down. They did not have to be told twice. They leapt from the smouldering ships and ran back to the cliff. We counted them all back in and Swein and I were the last to trot up the steep cliff path. The gulls squawked and dived at us.

At the top, I saw how close the French fleet was. They bobbed so near, their sails half full and men packed the decks and were shoulder to shoulder at the rails, staring at us while the spray frothed under the keels.

My men were tired and covered in soot and oil.

Looking down from the cliff, the beached supply ships had small fires glowing in the holds, the smoke from them blown flat by the offshore wind.

"God damn those French ships," I said. "Everyone, we fall back."

Hubert de Burgh rode up, scattering my men as they fled back toward the French camp. "Sir Richard, the French grow lively. They are emboldened by the arrival of their comrades. We cannot hold them and I will take my men inside the castle once more. On behalf of everyone, I humbly thank you for your efforts today. You have set Louis back by months, I pray."

"The leader of these men was William of Cassingham," I said. "A squire of the Weald. He brought these men together, he leads them. Remember him, my lord, when the war is done."

"Truly? William of Cassingham, you say? Then I will certainly remember him," de Burgh said, "and you also."

His men were urging the Constable to flee when a crossbow bolt thudded into the flank of one of their horses. The knight wrestled the horse from panic and rode away for the castle.

Hubert de Burgh's squire rode up and held out the Constable's helmet. More bolts clattered in. They were being shot from long range, down by the town walls. There was a gusty wind and there was little hope for accuracy but the French had found their courage and it was truly time to flee.

"God be with you," the Constable of Dover Castle shouted through his helm and he and his men rode off.

Anselm and his lads were rushing to us with our horses.

"Thank God," Jocelyn said as they approached. "Come on, Richard, we're the last men here."

"It is a shame about those ships," I said. We were so close to wiping out tons of vital supplies. I had a mad urge to run down there and stoke the fires.

Jocelyn clapped me on the shoulder and shoved his helm back onto his head. He fumbled with the chinstrap. "It was a good effort. The whole camp is burning, or near enough. This was a successful raid. Now, let us go."

"I suppose so," I said.

We mounted and turned, ready to weave our way through fire and crossbow shot, back to our men.

There was a roar, like a great rushing wind and I turned back in time to see the closest ship, the oil-laden ship, go up in a white-hot burst of fire, like a dragon had incinerated it. The flame grew and grew and it seemed as though the very air burned, shimmering and wild. I felt the heat of it through my armour and doublet and clothing from hundreds of yards away.

As if by some signal, the other ships also ignited, one after the other, with great rushes of light and heat and in moments, every ship upon the shore was engulfed in a terrible inferno.

I had never seen anything like it.

"Like looking into the unquenchable fires of Hell," I said, hearing the rising passion in my voice as I spoke.

"Come on, Richard, you mad fool," Jocelyn shouted. "Or we shall see the real thing for ourselves."

We rode out through the smoke, with bolts clattering about us and Cassingham's archers sending their own arrows back toward those who were coming out to see us off.

As our full force gathered on the road back to the Weald, we found the French garrison suddenly losing heart. The men slung their crossbows over their shoulders and slumped back to Dover.

"What has plucked their goose, so?" I asked.

Cassingham himself told us when we met up with him under the cover of the woodland. By then, the sun was low in the sky. The day had almost gone without me really noticing the time passing. Such is the way in battle.

Cassingham was grinning, clapping every man on the back as he came to us. His priest was praising God, for we had won a great victory and, though we had many wounded, we had not lost a single man.

"Are we pursued?" I asked, for my fear was that our exhausted men, without mounts, would be overtaken and slain.

"It seems not," Cassingham said, hands on his hips.

"Why not? What about the reinforcements?" I said. "They were practically on top of us. I could smell them over the smoke."

"The French ships abandoned their landing," Cassingham

said, laughing. "Our brave King Louis must have thought twice about landing amongst that inferno."

"Praise God," I said, mad with the flush of victory. "Now is the time. Jocelyn, Anselm, Swein. We must take the women and ride north. With this victory, the Marshal as Regent will surely grant me a pardon. Then we will take Sherwood and destroy William de Ferrers and his band of blood drinking bastards."

It seemed so simple.

ELEVEN ~ THE BATTLE OF LINCOLN

"WE WILL NOT BE SAFE HERE," Eva said, crossing her arms in the doorway of the small hospital, the small dormitory where travellers could stay when visiting or passing by the priory.

Eva and Marian would stay there, at the Priory of Tutbury, near to Ashbury. After riding north from the Weald, I had nowhere else nearby that I could take them. Nowhere that I could trust. Nowhere that was not under the influence of one great lord or other.

Thankfully, Emma had elected to remain safe in the Weald. She told me she had decided to stay. There was no discussion. She did not seek my permission nor approval. Cassingham had sworn holy oaths upon a local relic that he would defend the lady's life and her honour.

"You expect me to trust your words because you grasp a box with some old saint's rotten knuckle bones inside?" I had said to Cassingham in his parish church before I rushed north.

"Blasphemer," Cassingham's priest had hissed at me, his words echoing from the plastered walls. "You should fall to your knees and beg forgiveness from the holy bones of Saint Bertha."

"You can shove Bertha's bones up your holy arse," I said. "Now leave my presence immediately or I shall drink your blood."

When Cassingham gave him no support, he backed away and then fled, condemning me and my offspring to terrible punishments.

"You are not welcome in the houses of God," he shouted from the doorway. "The Lord shall cast you down onto your belly and you shall be smited by His mighty hand."

I laughed loudly and the priest slammed the door behind him.

"The men love how you fight," Cassingham said, unimpressed with me. "But many people here will be glad to see you return to the north."

"Take care of Emma," I said, grasping his shoulders and looking hard into his eyes.

"I swear I shall," he said. I believed him.

Marian and Eva, on the other hand, would not stay in Kent. But I could not risk taking them into the arms of my enemies. Before riding directly to the Marshal's gathered forces I had to hide the women somewhere safe for a few days. If I was arrested or killed, they could be seized too. Once I was sure of their safety, I would collect them from the priory.

Strictly speaking, Tutbury Priory was on land granted by my family yet it was Hugh de Nonant who held ultimate authority. But he had not visited the place nor shown any interest in twenty years. It was a small house but it had always been attached to the lords of Ashbury.

"No one will know you are here but the monks," I said, confident that Eva was concerned over nothing. "You will be safe in this hospital. The monks will keep an eye out for you."

"It is precisely those monks that we will not be safe from," Eva said, throwing her chin out. "And I know where their eyes will be looking."

"I have seen you fight," I said and reached up to stroke her face. She slapped it away.

"You are making a mistake," she said, crossing her arms.

"My family has kept this Priory since it was founded," I said, gently. "The new prior has been here since he was a boy, on and off. They are not dangerous."

"Not to you, perhaps," she said. "You are a man. A lord."

"They are men of God."

"They are men. And I cannot stay awake all night, every night."

I sighed, desperate to be away. "It is only for a few days."

"You are a fool," Eva said, unwilling to part on good terms and she would not kiss me.

Jocelyn fared little better with Marian, who was angry at being left behind. She wanted to come to Lincolnshire with us and I spoke to her too before we left.

"I must have the Regent's pardon before I can return to the

world," I said to Marian at the gates of the priory while Jocelyn waited, already mounted, out on the road. "If I remain an outlaw I could be killed on sight. Once I get the Marshal to agree, I will return for you both and we will take the fight to William, I swear it. But none of that can happen unless it is I that tells the Marshal to his face that I have won a great victory for the king. Jocelyn and me both, that is."

"You come back quickly," Marian said, pointing her finger up at my face. "And you bring Jocelyn back to me. And Swein."

"Good Lord, girl," I said. "I promise nothing."

Though I was in a great hurry to be off, I pulled young Prior Simon to the far side of the gate and extracted oaths sworn upon Christ's bones in Heaven that he would keep the women safe and well cared for. Just words to me but binding for him, I believed. To make sure and secure an earthly loyalty, I made a small donation with what little coin remained to me and promised more upon my return. It was in his financial interest to keep them well and monks loved nothing more than money. Foolishly, at the time, I did not follow that thought through to its inevitable conclusion.

"What is happening at Ashbury?" I asked the prior in his house. "I hear there is no new lord yet."

"A steward arrived," Prior Simon said, not meeting my eye. "Sent by the archbishop. A hard man but a lively one. Full of jests but not kind, I fear. John is his name. Tall as an oak, he is. He brought a couple of servants with him. Rough types but they have not caused any trouble and I pray that they will look after your manor until you can make your proper return to us."

"What about Cuthbert?" I asked.

"Ah, your old steward has gone to live with his daughter's family in the village."

"That God damned bastard bishop," I said.

The Prior looked up at me while attempting to look down his nose at the same time. I wanted to smash that nose and suck out the blood but I need him to keep Eva safe so I swallowed my pride instead.

"I apologise, Prior Simon, I spoke without considering first," I said, with as much contrition as I could muster.

The Prior, who I had known since he was a boy and given money to keep him and brothers in their house for decades, grudgingly forgave me.

Then he betrayed me.

∞

It was two more days of hard riding from Derbyshire to Lincolnshire, something like sixty miles. The roads grew ever busier with scouting and foraging groups and levied men coming to muster with their lords.

The Marshal's royalist forces were pouring into a camp around the village of Stowe in Lincolnshire. The village was barely ten miles north from the great city of Lincoln, where the rebel barons had concentrated their forces.

When I reached the camp, the men-at-arms guarding the road by the camp forced me to surrender my arms in the name of

William Marshal, the Earl of Pembroke and Regent of England. I told them that I had a vital message that the Regent must hear.

"Are you alone?" the chief knight among them asked. It was strange to them that a noble knight would have no retinue.

"I am," I said, not telling them that my men waited in a woodland a few miles away.

They took me at once, through the great mass of men and horse, all the way into the Marshal's presence. His quarters were in the tumbledown hall outside the village. The roof was sagging and the place reeked of damp, despite the warmth outside. A fire smoked away in the centre of the hall, which was crowded with lords, priests and attendants and the immense noise was like a pot filled with angry bees. The Marshal's men escorted me through that chaos and into the presence of the great man himself, who turned from his conversation at the top table to peer at me as I was introduced.

I recognised many of the men around him. There was his son, also called William Marshal, who had helped Anselm to free me from Newark Castle, smiling yet raising his eyebrows in silent remonstration. Also, there sat young Geoffrey of Monmouth, smirking at me as if he knew what was in store for me. He was an odious little shit but the size of his lands guaranteed him a seat at the table. I recognised William Longspear, the illegitimate son of the old King Henry and brother of Richard the Lionheart and King John. Longspear was as tall as me and a great knight and leader, though he had commanded over the disastrous defeat at the Battle of Bouvines a few years before. Ranulf of Chester sat beside him, the great lord and slayer of Welshmen. There were also a dozen or more bishops and priests in all their finery, scowling at the mention of my name. Those holy men I did not recognise.

Those great lords and priests looked at me with surprise and waited for the Regent to make his response.

"You do not much understand subtlety, do you, Sir Richard," the Marshal said as looked up at me. "Do you understand that I must have you arrested now?"

Geoffrey of Monmouth snickered, and looked round at the others. Only the priests shared his glee.

I froze. "I had hoped my great victory in Dover would prove my loyalty to the Crown."

The Marshal sighed. "You never needed to prove it to me, Richard. But there are ways to do these things. Our good friend the Archbishop of York would use it against me if I did not have you seized."

"I apologise, my lord," I said. "I cannot allow you to do that."

"I am sorry, I believe I misheard," the Marshal said, blinking up at me. "What did you say?"

"How dare you," the pudgy Monmouth declared in a shriek, slapping the table hard enough to wobble the wine. "Good Lord, man, you should be hanged for such treason."

"Be quiet, Geoffrey," the Marshal snapped, without bothering to hide his irritation.

Monmouth collapsed into his seat and hung his fat head. Longspear laughed.

"My Lord," I said, dropping to one knee by the Marshal's chair and speaking earnestly. "There is no man alive who I respect more highly than you. As a knight, as a warrior and as a loyal servant of the crown, you have no equal. So understand that when I say I must be allowed to destroy William de Ferrers. He is hiding in Sherwood, he is killing or enslaving the good folk of the king's forest. He is so close I can almost taste him. He is preying upon the king's loyal forces, you know this, my lord. And it must be I who slays him. I have sworn it. I swore it twenty-five years ago. I am begging you to allow me to fulfil the oaths I have made to the innocent dead."

The Marshal stared at me in disbelief.

"Everyone, leave us." He spoke softly but somehow everyone around him heard his order and fell silent. The great lords and knights stood and filed out, taking everyone in the hall with them in a cacophony of muttering and clattering feet.

Geoffrey of Monmouth stiffened and leaned in to the Regent. "My lord, I beg—"

"Get out, I said," the Marshal shot back at young Monmouth, steel in his voice.

Geoffrey stomped out, glaring at me over his shoulder.

A couple of silent men-at-arms stood at the back wall ten feet away, ready to defend their lord. As if any man in their right mind would attack William the Marshal, even as ancient as he was. I noted how his upper arms were thick with muscle and his shoulders were broad though the rest of him remained slim and straight.

"I have never been entirely sure of what to make of you, Richard," the Marshal said as everyone left, leaning back into his chair. "You can fight, anyone who has seen you has attested to that. But since your return from crusade, you have had little ambition."

"The Archbishop—" I started.

"Yes, yes. Your liege lord has kept you repressed," he said. "Yet if you had any ambition to change the facts of your situation, you could have changed them."

"When I returned from crusade?" I said. "I did not know that you even knew my name, my lord, let alone that you had any interest in me so long ago."

"I take an interest in all promising knights," the Marshal said, grandly. "But after a year or two of inaction, I ceased to expect anything from you. You were content to slumber in your hall, living a quiet life. There is nothing wrong with that. I expected you were growing old. But when you mustered for the king's campaign, I was astonished to see you looking so young. And now, what has it been, more than ten years later and I see you have not aged a day. No wonder the men turned on you when you were caught slurping up the blood of the dead. Do not deny it. Men whom I trust told me themselves that they saw you. Your perversions are a matter for God and for yourself, as far as I am concerned but the men did not like it. The old Monmouth, he did not like it. They were jealous of your fame and then they were jealous of your eternal youth and your ability. And instead of protesting more than a little, you were content to hide yourself away again. It smacks of a certain moral cowardice, does it not? But perhaps you were right to hide. And now that I see you once more, I am struck that there must be some truth to the rumours."

"That I have made a pact with the devil?" I asked.

He stared expectantly at me.

"May I sit, my lord?" I asked.

The Marshal stood, grabbed a jug of wine and two cups and sat down himself again. Not in the chair at the centre of the table but on the bench at my end. I sat opposite and he poured us both a cup of wine.

"My true father was Earl Robert de Ferrers," I said.

The Marshal spilled a little of the wine he was pouring. He set the cups before us. "I see."

"I only learned the truth of it while I hunted William near Jerusalem. And then he confirmed it to me himself when he had me captured."

"He captured you?" The Marshal said, for I had never really spoken of that part of the story.

"But for a moment," I said. "After I had slaughtered most of his men. But the truth is that William and I share the same father. And I do not know why but both of us aged normally, until the day we were each killed. He died at the Battle of Hattin and when he rose again, he was immensely strong and he did not age a single day after that. And his own blood, when ingested by other men, granted them increased strength also. And speed and endurance and it seemed to addle their brains. They believed him Christ reborn. It may not have been the blood that made them believe. William has a way of twisting men's minds."

"And you believe yourself to be the same as he?" The Marshal said, looking warily at me. "With magic blood?"

"I am the same. William and his foul beasts killed my wife and then they killed me. I was being buried by my surviving servants when I awoke."

"Yes, I heard this part, I recall it now. Sometimes, you know, Richard, these things happen. Your servants should have called in a physician."

"I was dead," I said. "I died and I rose again. Since that day, I have had great strength. I have not aged a day. See for yourself. I was twenty-two years old. Today I am forty-seven or so."

The Marshal stared at me for a long time. "And what did you have to do to gain these gifts?"

"My pact with the devil?" I asked. "Nothing. I was killed. I awoke, like this. That is it. I met no devil. William believed it a gift granted by God. It often seems more of a curse. But what can I do? This is what I am. They call me evil for drinking the blood of my enemies, men already slain. Well, I admit it. What other evils do I do? I do not kill the innocent. I seek to do right by my lord, my family, my household. I support the Church. And I loyally serve my king and his regent."

He drank while he observed me closely. "What of this blood drinking? Why do such a thing?"

"The desire for blood is always in me," I admitted, speaking freely to the most powerful man in England. "But I resist it. I do not kill for it. It seems that every time I drink, the desire for it only grows. And it rarely lessens. When I drink, my strength is increased even further. My speed of arm and mind both rise. And with blood, my body heals from terrible wounds in mere moments. I have been run through with blades, pierced by arrows, sliced and cut upon the face, arms, body and legs and yet I have no scars."

"And William de Ferrers has these same... abilities?"

"He may be stronger than I. In fact, I am certain of it for he has no compunction about taking blood from men, women, and children. He revels in it. In the Holy Land, he scoured the countryside taking families to feed upon. To drink dry and then discard. This increased his strength and also allowed him to make an army of men. Knights and men-at-arms who would be unremarkable in combat were it not for their ingestion of William's blood. He is most certainly doing the same in Sherwood."

The Marshal drummed his fingers on the table. "But why? Why here and why now?"

"Who knows what his plans are or what his ultimate goal is? In the Holy Land, he was on his way to creating an army. He wanted to carve out his own kingdom. Perhaps he has similar plans for England."

"Do not be absurd," the Marshal said. "This is not Palestine but England. One man cannot overcome a kingdom, no matter how much blood the fellow drinks, no matter his own strength. Nor how many blood-swilling swine he ensnares."

"I do not believe he is one man alone," I said. "I believe that there is, at least, one man working with him. The most powerful lord in the north of England."

William Marshal wiped his mouth with the back of his hand. "There is no doubt," he said after a long pause, "that the Green Knight of Sherwood is in league with the Archbishop of York. I had my suspicions when it was my men and the men of other lords who were disappearing on the Great North Road by

306

Sherwood and yet the archbishop moved freely up and down many times in a year. When he had you arrested, I knew for certain."

"And I knew for certain that it was he that planned the king's poisoning," I said. "It seems strange but William de Ferrers poisoned his own father."

"Robert de Ferrers was killed by poison? But why?"

"My brother Henry killed William's wife and child in the Holy Land," I said. "I now know Henry was no true brother. We shared only our mother and he well knew it when we were children. In the disorder after Hattin, he slaughtered William's family. It drove William mad. He returned after a couple of years."

"The Massacre of Ashbury," the Marshal said. "It was always said there was no reason behind it."

"Reason enough for a madman," I said.

"And now you wish to continue the slaughter," the Marshal said.

"I want justice," I said.

"You want his death."

"More than anything," I admitted.

"He should be tried," the Marshal said, looking at me intently, judging my reaction. "This is England, not some Saracen backwater. We should bring William de Ferrers to justice. But perhaps the kingdom requires certain men to face a quieter fate. A simpler solution, for the good of the realm."

"You believe me," I said, not realising he was getting at something else. I was quietly thrilled, as I never expected anything but derision.

"No," he said. "I cannot believe the half of it. Magical blood? You are some form of lunatic, I do not doubt. But there is enough truth in your words to reinforce my own conclusions. The Archbishop of York is colluding with an outlaw band in Sherwood. The archbishop, I believe, poisoned King John. The sad truth is, the archbishop may have saved England by his treachery."

That gave me pause. "What are you saying?"

"John may have triumphed in the field, eventually. He was a competent enough commander of men. But I can do better without him. And with him out of the way, I have reissued the articles of the barons in the name of Henry, with a few corrections, of course. I have pardoned all men who come back into the king's peace. Once we throw out the false king Louis, England shall be at peace with itself once more. And all because John is not here to poison his own well."

"That may be the case," I said. "It does not excuse the fact that the archbishop is a regicide."

"Of course it does not," the Marshal snapped. "Do not top it the morality with me, you blood slurping madman."

William Marshal was my lifelong hero. Still, I felt an urge to twist his head from his shoulders and drink from his severed neck. I closed my eyes and allowed the anger to pass.

"How will you prosecute the archbishop?" I asked. "I would be happy to speak my evidence at a hearing."

The Marshal laughed at my naivety. "I can never prosecute him. Even if I thought that such a thing would work, which it would not, England has enough open fighting amongst itself. All

I can do is isolate him from the king and continue to outspend him."

"That seems somewhat uncertain," I pointed out. "Would a knife in the dark not be the better option?"

"Perhaps. And yet who would do such a thing?" he asked, speaking lightly and taking a drink of wine without looking at me.

I understood what the Marshal wanted from me.

"A man who would expect little in return," I said. "Merely a warrant to clear Sherwood of outlaws. And perhaps a very small payment. I am nearly out of money."

"I doubt he would let you near him," the Marshal said, looking at me once more.

"Perhaps I know someone who could," I said, wondering what Eva would say. She did not like her father but I feared she would feel somewhat displeased about me murdering the man, let alone helping me to do so. "Or perhaps I could take him on the road, as William has done with so many other travellers."

"Spare me the details," the Marshal said. "I suspect that the archbishop is content to wait until my death, as old as I am. He's playing a game that will last longer than the players."

"He must be of an age with you, my lord," I said, thinking back to when I first met the archbishop. He was already old, or seemed so to me at the time.

"I suppose that he is," the Marshal said. "Yet he wears it well. Like you, he seems to have not aged in the last ten or fifteen years."

The silence drew out as we stared at each.

"He has not aged," I said, deliberately.

The Marshal rubbed his eyes and leaned forwards to pinch the bridge of his nose. "Can it be true, what you say about William's blood? The truth now, Richard, is it not some conjurer's trick? You wear some secret eastern face paint or perhaps you are the true Richard's son?"

"I swear it," I said. "I will swear any oath, holy or otherwise. William's blood, my blood, can arrest ageing if ingested. But how precisely, I do not know. Only that it seems to be effective. And I believe that for it to continue to work the archbishop must be drinking blood regularly. The blood of who, I do not know but a man of his power could be using servants or, come to think of it, those that William takes into Sherwood."

"Good God." The Marshal looked all of his seventy-plus years. "What can he and de Ferrers be working towards?"

"It seems our purposes are one and the same," I said, planting my hands on the table. I would kill William and if I had the chance, I would kill the archbishop as well. And I would reap the Marshal's reward. "I am ready to leave for Sherwood immediately."

"Do not get ahead of yourself," the Marshal said. "Sit down. I have to take Lincoln first. And you will help me."

"You must have hundreds of men here," I said, warily. "You do not need me."

"I have close to four hundred knights," he said. "But you are worth ten more, at least."

Frustration boiled up. "I am honoured to hear you say so yet—"

"And there is your wife's son, Sir Jocelyn, plus the three

squires and a score of archers you have in the woods a few miles away. My youngest son is with you also? Yes, I have exceptional men who saw your approach and shadowed you all the way from Nottinghamshire. All of you would be most useful. In fact, I have a task for you. Do not argue. You fight for me at Lincoln and then I will see you restored to your lands and you will have your warrant for Sherwood."

"And a manor for Jocelyn."

The Marshal stared me down. Then he sighed. "Fine. Now, listen."

∞

The walled town of Lincoln was in possession of the rebel barons, led by Thomas the Count of Perche. The castle of Lincoln was in the centre of the town and that, however, was in the possession of royalists, men who had been loyal to King John and had continued to be loyal to young King Henry.

The Marshal, after he had heard from our Wealden messengers that the French had been repulsed and delayed by our daring raid at Dover, had decided to take back the town of Lincoln and save the brave garrison of the Lincoln Castle.

"He was greatly impressed by the Dover raid," I said to the archers. "So he wants us to fight for him here, too. In a way, that makes use of your abilities."

"And what is our task?" Jocelyn asked, impatient as always.

We stood in the shade of a copse of alder where my men had

made their own camp. There were hundreds of such groups of men all over the fields all around us to the north and the west of Lincoln. There seemed to be a few mercenary crossbowmen about but few enough English archers.

I wanted to let our men know what they faced. They were strangers in this part of England.

"We're to fight our way through to the castle," I said to him and to others, gathered together now in the Marshal's lively camp. "The Marshal wishes us to scale the western wall of the town while his main force attacks the north gate. Once inside we will gain entry into the castle, freeing the garrison to attack from the rear while you men shoot down into the town. You will have only as many arrows as you can each carry up to the walls. There are thousands of men-at-arms in Lincoln so I suggest you choose important targets. The Marshal prays that our disruption will distract and distress the defenders. There are hundreds of crossbowmen in the city. If they are within range, the Marshal suggests we consider shooting them instead. And we are to exploit whatever opportunities present themselves. You men know I am no archer. I will leave the details up to you, Swein."

The archers exchanged nervous looks.

"Perhaps you fellows are regretting following us into the north. But out of all Cassingham's men, you twenty wanted glory and wealth the most. I allowed you men to come with me because Swein asked for it and because he swears you are all gifted archers and brave men. I know you expected to be fighting in the woods, against outlaws, not storming the walls of a city and fighting knights. But this is your opportunity. Fight well and you will be rewarded. When the city falls, you will be amongst the first to take what you can from the fallen and from the rebel citizens."

A few of them, at least, began nodding and standing straighter. I would leave it to young Swein to inspire them further.

"You truly expect the city to fall just like that?" Jocelyn said to me. "We simply scale the walls and attack thousands of knights with a score of archers? No offense, my friends."

Jocelyn was making out as if he was angry but I could tell he was excited. He was eager to prove his worth. I had not yet told him what the Marshal would give him were we to succeed. I did not want him to risk his life more than necessary.

"I admit, it is a difficult task," I said. "But they are sending us a local man, a mercenary named Falk. And long ladders for the wall. So we will complete our task and we will all win glory for ourselves. And then we will finally destroy William. Then you can marry Marian, Jocelyn and be lord of your own manor. Your dream come true, son, and all of it within grasp."

"I very much like the sound of that," Jocelyn said, smiling.

Swein scowled and turned away to speak to his men.

I bet you do, I thought. "You know, when all this is over, I might even ask Eva if she would like to stay with me."

"Not marriage, surely?" Jocelyn asked. He could not imagine marrying so far beneath himself.

"Why not?" I said. "She likes me."

"Now you arc dreaming," he said and we laughed.

God must have been laughing too.

∞

313

Two days later, on the twentieth of May 1217, my men and I stood ready across the fields from the western walls.

Lincoln was a magnificent city. Lincolnshire is one of the flattest parts of all England, a wet, boggy, flat place. Yet there is a great limestone ridge running straight as an arrow through almost the whole county up to the River Humber. That great escarpment is cut through by the River Witham and at that point stands Lincoln. Lincoln was also the crossroads of two of what were England's greatest roads. Ermine Street ran straight south all the way to London and the Fosse Way ran southwest diagonally across the country to Leicester and then down to Cirencester and beyond toward Dartmouth. On the northern bank of the river stood the walled city of Lincoln, which spread from the bridge at the bottom, up the steep escarpment to the plateau of the ridge above. On the edge of the escarpment was the castle, on the western side and the great cathedral on the eastern.

Its location and geography were the reason the rebel barons had taken the city. It was of vital strategic importance. By controlling Lincoln, they could control not only the county but also control access to the rest of England.

And that was one of the reasons the Marshal wanted to take the city back. But really, he wanted a great military victory to finish the rebellion and King Louis for the last time. Crushing the thousands of men in Lincoln would break the resolve of those who held out for their rewards from a victorious King Louis. They had to be persuaded that England was now under the command of the greatest knight who ever lived and that they had no hope.

Win Lincoln and we would win England.

Yet, the city would be a tough place to crack. The rebels had got inside because the citizens had thrown open the gates and declared themselves for Louis. Storming it by force would be a different matter.

We stood at the edge of a copse of alder on the western side of the city looking across fields and a scatter of isolated houses to the walls, the castle keep behind them and beyond the tops of the stunning towers of the enormous cathedral. The walls of the city fell away on the south, down the escarpment towards the River Witham. It was a huge place.

"We have to take that?" Swein said, gawping. He and the archers from the Weald had never seen Lincoln. It was only forty miles southwest to Nottingham but in those days, you never went to a place unless you had good reason to.

"No," I said, misunderstanding him on purpose. "Those men have to take the city. All we have to do is get up on the walls."

To the north, across the fields of the ridge, we could see the Marshal's army as it approached Lincoln's north gate. He led about four hundred knights with their attendant squires plus another thousand armoured, non-noble men-at-arms and a thousand or so levied men who were lightly armoured. Most were making the final approach on foot. Those who yet rode would dismount before they got within bow range of the north wall.

The Marshal's forces included four hundred mercenary crossbowmen who approached in front of the knights. The crossbowmen would cover the assault by keeping the heads of the defenders down behind the walls while the ladders were scaled and the walls assaulted.

Bands of mounted soldiers roamed around outside the walls on all sides, no doubt there to cut off any attempts at escape and to relay any clues to troop positions. Down the escarpment on the other side of the river, there were more horsemen and groups of soldiers, although who they belonged to I had no idea. They were too far away to be concerned with. Battles always draw gawkers.

The rest of the Marshal's forces were held in reserve to the north. No doubt, he hoped he would not need them, or perhaps he feared to cause too much damage to the beautiful, wealthy city. But I knew they were there if needed.

In my group, we had four men-at-arms, including myself. I led Jocelyn and Anselm who were armoured like knights. Swein commanded our twenty archers, armed with their huge bows, laden arrow bags, and swords or daggers. Between them, they had a pair of ladders twenty-five feet long. They looked spindly to me. I prayed to God that they would hold us as we scaled the wall.

We were being escorted by my last man-at-arms, a mercenary named Falk. The Lincolnshire man was a commoner who had risen to knighthood over a brutal career fighting from Wales to the Holy Land and wherever there was state sanctioned murder to be had. He was rough of manner and ugly as hell, a rolling lump of a man. His blade was a dirty great falchion, nocked and rusty but sharp as sin. His surcoat was emblazoned with a griffon design but it was partly hidden underneath a thick layer of grime and old blood. I was glad to have him.

The Marshal's forces charged onward, out of sight. The shouts of battle grew.

"Let's be off, Richard," Falk said and spat out a quivering glob onto the trunk of the tree beside me.

"We move quickly," I said to the men. "Even if they see us, we keep going. Even if we do not have surprise on our side, even if they shoot crossbows down at us. We are getting up that wall."

Those of us with helms jammed them on. We tightened our buckles and straps, knots, and we trotted on foot out of the tree cover and cut straight across the field. To our right, the ground fell away steeply down to the river. There was a road down there that ran parallel to the river with houses all along it, leading to the river gate.

It seemed a long way to the wall. A long way to be completely exposed.

Please, God, I prayed, please do not let them see us.

We crossed into the final flat meadow field, an open expanse that led right up to the base of the wall. There was a narrow postern gate there but we would not waste time attempting to break it down. Surely it would be sealed with rubble and boarding.

Our target section of the western wall loomed up higher and higher the closer we got. The top of the castle keep, with it's loyal, royalist garrison still holding out, poked up behind. The crenellations like the shattered, rotten teeth of Falk, panting beside me like an old dog.

There were heads up on the top of the castle tower, between the gaps of the crenellations, but they were all pointed northward. I prayed that those men were still loyal to their young king and would be spurred into taking up arms and joining us.

And if they were not, I meant to force them to do so.

It would only take one of the rebel heads inside Lincoln, on any of the long section of wall, to glance our way for the cry to go up.

Jocelyn next to me panted. His shield, like mine, was slung over his back. Our hauberks were heavy. But I rarely tired. Jocelyn was about thirty years old but he was strong and he trained every day that he could. Anselm was dressed as we were but he was so young, he could run all day and not tire. Falk was lumbering beside me, panting like Jocelyn. The man was battered and scarred and he ran with an awkward, limping gait but he kept up with us.

The lightly armoured Wealden archers trotted along with their ladders, their faces grim but focused on the wall ahead.

I expected a face upon the wall to turn. A shout to cry out. A horn to sound. Arrows and bolts to slam down into us.

But we reached the base of the wall, unnoticed and unopposed. We lined up in the clumpy, long grass, backs to the wall, looking up.

Panting, the men looked down the line to me.

I jammed my mailed fist upward, indicating the top of the wall.

The archers hoisted their ladders against the bottom of the crenellations at the top of the wall, about ten feet apart. We wanted to come up both ladders together.

I moved to mount the ladder nearest to me. Jocelyn grabbed me.

"Wait for the men to go first," he said.

I knew he was worried that the ladder would snap under my

weight. And more to the point the top man would be the first to cop a rock or bolt to the face or be run through as he clambered over the top.

But I knew that a fall from such a height would not kill me as it might a normal man. Also, if the ladders did break after other men had climbed then I might be stranded. Without me to lead them, they would struggle. And I had to have a victory. It had to be mine. Personally. I had to be free to kill William.

I shrugged Jocelyn off. "You wait until last. Your task is to protect Anselm."

Though I could not see his eyes through his helm slits, I could imagine the look in them.

"Falk, you get up the other ladder," I said.

"You do not command me," Falk said, his crude voice muffled by his helm. Nevertheless, he leapt upon the ladder. It bowed and creaked under his weight. The fifth rung snapped and he fell, catching himself on the other rungs, his weapon and armour clanging and clattering. The men holding the ladder wrested it back into upright position, dragging the top against the stone at the top of the parapet high above. Falk clambered back up.

"Go softly, you fool," I hissed at him and swung myself up my own ladder.

I trod as lightly as I could. My breath was loud inside my helm. The ash poles of the ladder creaked and cracked. I wondered if I should have left my shield behind rather than wearing it strapped upon my back. It would no doubt catch on the top but then while I fretted away, I had reached the top. My hands at the top of the stone. My instinct was to hesitate, to peer over to see what awaited me.

But speed was vital. If there was a man there then I could not wait for him to leave or turn away. I had men mounting the ladder behind me. It was a matter of go up and over or go home in defeat.

So I threw myself up, onto the edge of the wall, grasping the far side with outstretched arms.

My wrists prickled and my heart was in my mouth, expecting a sword blade or an axe to come chopping down to sever my arms.

I pulled myself up so I was face down on the top of the wall, the crenellations rising up each side of me. Hiding me, or so I prayed, from anyone looking along the wall. I was laying stretched out, imagining a blow aimed at the mail covering the back of my neck. I wriggled forwards and heaved. The corner of the top of my shield caught on the crenellation and screeched as I pulled myself in and fell on the other side in a jumble of arms.

A shadow fell across me and I drew my dagger.

Falk was there, standing over me. "You know, they told me you moved like a warhorse on the charge. I see they were lying, as usual." He laughed inside his helm and stomped away along the wall to the north, fiddling with the chest strap holding his shield to his back.

I rolled to my feet as our archers clambered over. I helped the first two to make a more graceful entrance than I had, then left them to help the rest over.

I looked inward, across the castle bailey and over the other castle wall into the city. The castle keep was on my right and the magnificent cathedral towers were right ahead, in the centre of the city.

The attack on the north gate was already raging. Arrows and bolts clattered and flew. Men shouted and pushed from atop the north wall. I could not see down into the city by the gate, for all the buildings in between, but I could hear them well enough.

I slung my shield upon my arm and walked south along the wall to the point where it made a right angle turn toward the castle keep.

Everyone else, the squires and archers, went north after Falk.

Two men climbed from inside the city farther along the wall. When they saw me, both froze. They were well-armoured men-at-arms, wearing great helms and I was sure they would attack. Instead, they stopped atop the wall by the steps.

"Who are you? What are you doing here?" The first man shouted in French.

"A loyal servant of King Henry," I roared and drew my sword, bringing my shield in to cover my body.

The two men looked at me, looked at the archers streaming away along the wall behind me, then up at the castle keep. And then they ran back down the way that they had come.

I turned to the sound of cheering. The men at the top of the keep were cheering my minor victory. I took the right angle junction of wall and hurried to the wall of the keep. There was a small, very thick, iron-banded door there. I hammered on it, hard, over and over.

"You in there," I called. "Time to get your swords wet."

The men at the top shouted down.

"Who are you?"

I removed my helm and shouted back. "Sir Richard of

Ashbury. William Marshal, the Regent of England, has sent me to request that you men join him in attacking the traitors holding this city."

It did not take them long to open the door and join me. There were twenty-six men at arms in all who came out to fight. They were led by a young knight named Sir Stephen of Cranwell. The young man and his fellows were spoiling for a fight, their eyes mad with desire to smash into the men who had taken their city and their families and kept them besieged in the small keep for so long. They had been fully armoured and prepared all day, in case the fight spilled into their keep.

"You will all listen to me and do as I command," I said. "But only until you are unleashed upon the enemy. Then you may each prove your worth as you see fit."

Sir Stephen was wound as high as a young stallion but he nodded in agreement.

"Have you fought in a real battle before?" I asked as we moved off.

He scoffed at me.

"Do not worry," I said. "Remember your training, all of you."

They were greatly offended. I recalled how young I appeared to those who did not know me. They thought I was topping it the grand knight when I was younger than they were.

You just wait and see, I thought.

I led them north along the wall toward the section where Falk had halted our archers.

The castle wall surrounded a roughly rectangular bailey that sat against and inside the larger city walls. Inside the bailey were the usual hall, stables, workshops and open ground for training in the centre. That bailey took up a full quarter of the upper city, with the cathedral opposite it taking up a huge area across the open square between the two great structures. The lumpy Falk had led my archers and men northward from where we climbed in, all the way to where the castle wall led inward to the centre of the city.

There, at the northeast corner of the castle bailey, was a circular bay atop the wall where our twenty archers plus the rest were gathered under the shelter of the battlements.

Sir Stephen and Falk exchanged a terse greeting and I peered over the wall.

The noise of battle is like nothing else in all the world. The noise was like a storm wind howling through a woodland. It was like the crashing of ocean waves onto a rocky shore. And it ebbed and flowed like both. So much so that it was possible to understand at what stage a battle was at by the sound alone. The early stages of a battle were composed of individual shouts and insults and the sounds of feet and hooves running to and fro. Toward the end of a battle, the air would be filled with groaning, moaning, weeping and men begging for aid, for a priest, for their mother.

In Lincoln that day, I heard the sound of battle in full swing. The clash of iron upon iron. The thud of iron on wood. Horses hooves stamping. Bowstrings twanging, crossbows clacking, arrows splitting the air, tapping, and clattering against stone and wood. The loudest noise was the shouting. The noise that thousands of shouting men can make is breathtaking. A cacophony of insults, orders and incoherent cries of rage as men try to murder other men and to stay alive themselves that build to a roaring the likes of which exists nowhere else on earth. It is a humming of discord that fills every octave, rising, falling, and rising sometimes into a strange and beautiful harmony, just for a moment, before crashing into a thousand cries once more.

I peered over the parapet toward the north gate.

There were hundreds of men in the street below, from right underneath the wall all the way up to the north gate. The walls were yet being fought for, with our loyal fellows still climbing over the walls one by one all along it.

Our men were pushing them back, though. The walls were being taken.

"We should attack from the south," the young Sir Stephen yelled into the side of my helm.

"Shut up and get down," I said and dragged him into the cover of the crenellations. "We will do so but not yet. We must wait until they are committed. We have to time it correctly, do you understand? The timing is all-important. We must shock them with our attack, shock them into breaking their will. They are far from that yet. Now, where are the men guarding the castle?"

"What do you mean?" Sir Stephen said.

I cursed God for sending me a fool for an ally. "The men who kept you all from breaking out."

"Honour kept us from breaking out. We could have fled at any point over the wall and away in the darkness. But we knew we must hold. There are men-at-arms always by the bailey gatehouse, however, if that is what you mean?"

I shouted to Falk. "Gatehouse for the bailey?"

"East wall," he said, shuffling over to me. "Near the southeast — keep your fat heads down, you sons of Kentish gravelkind bastards — near the southeast corner of the bailey by the tall square tower, do you see?"

"I do. And that is our way off this wall and into those men below."

"And here I was thinking you were going to leap off this wall into the middle of them and just sort of slay the lot of them," Falk said.

"Do not give Richard ideas," Jocelyn shouted.

A hunting horn sounded and then another and more joined. Over and over, they sounded while we poked our heads over the parapet.

The rebels were falling back. They had lost the north gate.

"They run," Sir Stephen shouted, so elated he jumped to his feet and shouted down at them. "Yes, run, you sons of meretrices, run all the way back to London. Run back to France and drown along the way—"

I kicked his legs out from under him but it was too late. His men, taking his lead, leapt to their feet and began shouting.

We were spotted immediately. Men pointed up as they filed past.

"Cease your shouting," I yelled, as did Falk and Jocelyn.

"They are not fleeing," Jocelyn said as he dragged down the ones nearest him. "They are falling back in good order. This is part of their plans."

"What did you do to Sir Stephen?" the nearest man growled

from behind his helm. I wished to tip him from the wall. Instead, I ignored him and he jerked from a metallic ping against his helmet. He ducked down.

Crossbow bolts clattered off the stones and we crouched low again.

There were bowmen scattered across the city in the roofs of the tallest, largest buildings. Some sat on the thatch and tile, most had hacked their way through the bottom of the roofs and were shooting from inside, well hidden and well protected.

"Archers?" Swein shouted.

"No, do not waste your arrows," I said. Crossbowmen and archers were hardly worth bothering with when we had so many knights upon the field. "We must take the bailey gatehouse."

"They are stopping at the square," Falk said, dragging me away from my part of the walled, circular corner of the wall. Bolts fell around us but he paid them no mind. "Look." Falk pointed south along the wall to where the rebel men were falling back to.

"They have built a wall," I said.

"I heard you was a sharp lad, Sir Richard," Falk said. "There's not nothing get past you, is there."

Between the wall of the castle bailey and the corner of the cathedral, the rebels had built a wall from carts, barrels, house timbers and whatever else that could be jammed and hammered together. The knights, squires, and men-at-arms clambered carefully over certain lower sections and then took up places on the far side.

"Hardly the walls of Jerusalem, is it, Falk," I said.

"Don't need to be, does it," he said, pointing east along the length of the cathedral. Along that road were gathered dozens, no, hundreds of horses. They were held by grooms, pages, and squires but as the mass of men fell back, I watch knight after knight hurry to his own horse.

It was immediately obvious what the enemy intended to do.

"Good plan," I said.

Falk grunted.

"What is it?" Swein asked.

"Our enemies down there are preparing to charge the flank of the Marshal's men," I said. "They will wait and wait and then they will smash into our tightly packed men-at-arms when they reach the palisade."

"Charge like that will crush our lads," Falk said. "Kill a lot of men, make the rest run off. For a bit, anyway. Good plan, aye."

I thought about it for a moment. The bolts kept coming, clattering about us.

"We have to clear a section of the palisade for our men," I said. "If they break through quickly then we still have a chance."

Swein's archers looked deeply unhappy. So much so that I laughed. I laughed at their misery and their fear.

I stood and walked to the centre of our circular corner. At once, the bolts came at me. One glanced from my helm, then another. It was good iron and my hauberk was as expensive as I could possibly afford. The rings that made up my mail were thicker, smaller and denser than most men would wear. The better the protection the heavier it was, which cost men speed and mobility and made them tire faster. But with my strength and stamina, those were not concerns I shared.

A bolt or arrow could still bust a ring apart and enter my quilted, linen doublet underneath and if it pierced that and somehow entered my body deeply, then as long as I could find some blood to drink before I died, then I would live.

My helm was enclosed but for the eye slits and breathing holes, yet an arrow could find its way in or buckle the metal. My greatest concern was blindness, however, as I was unsure whether I would be able to regrow an eye, even after ingesting blood. So I turned my back to the city. Almost every bolt shot at me missed but the ones that hit me and bounced off my mail still hurt. An awful lot. But I had to make those talented but inexperienced archers believe that they would live through the day. They might not have my armour but perhaps I could give them a little of my courage.

"Our enemy is luring William Marshal into a trap. The Regent's men are chasing headlong into a barrier that is built clear across the space between this wall and the cathedral. That wooden wall will be manned by hundreds of armoured men. When the Marshal's forces are pressed against the barrier, our enemy will charge his horses down to take our lads by the side and by the rear with lance and with sword. We will not allow that. We are all going out of the bailey gate and we are going to sweep that wooden wall of its defenders. What do you say, do you want to shoot some knights up the arse from ten yards away?"

They cheered and followed me down the wall toward the gatehouse.

"You have bolts stuck in your hauberk, Sir Richard," Swein said from behind me.

328

"Well, bloody pull them out, lad," I said.

We had to fight our way out into the street. No man was killed, we just shoved them out of the gate towers and cleared the arched gateway of men huddling in it. The gateway was wide enough for two wagons to pass through abreast of each other. I shouted at them all to get out and pushed and shoved them away.

No one there had any idea who we were, or if we were a threat. Even when we burst out of the bailey gateway amongst them, they assumed that we were on their side.

A battle is a confusing place. You can see no more of it than your immediate surroundings and the mass of men around is always surging and changing. And attacks on castles and towns are even more restricted, by buildings and by the funnelling effect of the streets. From approaching along the wall, we had had a rare view of it from above and so I understood as much or even more of what was occurring than the enemies on the ground.

By that point in the battle, they were thoroughly engaged along their front. Behind the makeshift palisade, squires and servants waited with water, wine, and food for the knights. Wounded men drifted away. Fresh men waited their turn at the front.

I wondered when the rebels would spring their trap and charge the Marshal's flank. If I was commanding the mounted knights then I would save it until the latest possible moment until the king's men were exhausted. The charge could be disengaged and repeated but the first shock of it would be the most important moment of the battle. It was impossible to hear anything but the shouting and the clamour of battle. Perhaps the charge had already been launched.

Few of the enemy paid us much mind. Some of those that took note of us backed away, with the instinctive wariness of men when facing the unknown. A few seemed very interested in our presence, nudging each other and pointing.

"Alright, you men," I shouted to those under my command. "We may have to make a start."

I lined my men up in the open gateway of the bailey, archers and men-at-arms together and told them what I wanted them to do. All the while, I hoped that we would not be attacked in the rear from inside. I had seen no one in there behind us but it pays to expect the worst while you hope for the best.

Sir Stephen, his pride wounded but not his person, assured me that his men would perform admirably.

"I have no doubt," I shouted over the roar of battle and clapping him on his shoulder. "What fine fellows you all are. Make your fathers proud."

A group of men-at-arms approached us, their shields up and walking together shoulder to shoulder. Six of them, well armoured behind their shields. Swords drawn.

They knew that we were enemies.

"Hurry, Swein. Ten men shoot there and ten at our six new friends here," I said and stepped back against the wall of the gateway.

The archers shuffled together as closely as they could and drew their huge bows. Half aimed at the rear of the men fighting up on the palisade.

The others aimed at the six men who were only ten yards away.

Our archers called out their chosen targets to each other and then released, almost as one. Twenty of the great war bows sending their heavy arrows into knights and men at arms.

I had never before that moment truly appreciated the power of those things. Months I had been around the archers of the Weald. I had tried my hand at a few of the weapons and I was always astonished that these mortal men could pull them back as far as their ear and further and then do it over and over again.

For sport, the archers would compete to see who could shoot the farthest. Invariably it was the strongest men who had the heaviest, thickest bows who would win. Other forms of competition were to see who could shoot five arrows into a target the fastest. But the war bow was not meant for long range shooting. Nor was it meant for shooting quickly, as arrows were very precious things indeed and every one would have to prove its worth.

The war bow instead was meant for shooting at close range and punching their iron arrowheads into anyone who stood in their way. The arrow shafts themselves were huge things, longer than my arm and thicker than my thumb. Most of their arrowheads were shaped into stubby points, diamond shape in cross-section, designed to force its way into a ring of mail and, through the force of the bow, burst the ring of iron mail apart and carry on through into the man. Of course, under the mail, a man would wear a gambeson, a coat of many layers of linen over the body and arms and cap of the same material under the mail coif worn overhead, with the helm over the top. Our legs were also padded under the mail leg coverings that were like iron trousers, held up by thongs attached to the waist.

An arrow that broke through a mail ring would very likely be stopped in those layers beneath. Some men even wore another thick, padded linen gambeson worn over the chest and back which might stop a blow from ever reaching the mail beneath. But over everything would be a colourful surcoat, adding another layer primarily for protecting the iron from the elements, as well as for decoration and recognition in battle. But a surcoat could also help to catch the shaft of the arrow and stop it penetrating further.

All these layers in combination were counted as armour. And armour worked. If you were a fighting knight, that was the reason you bought the best armour you could afford. You would spend a fortune on having it made to your measure, with the best rings and made by an armourer with a good name. Your armour would save your life against blows from edged weapons, especially slashes and cuts. It could save your limbs and ribs from being broken. Mail worked. Often, when wearing the full harness with every layer included you felt as though you were invulnerable.

The weakness of mail was in stopping penetration, which is why the lance was so powerful a weapon and so feared. The weight of a horse on the charge, pushing a spear point into your armour would run a man through. Our swords could be thrust into mail, though you needed a mighty blow and a lucky one to break through a hauberk.

The other way through was the head of an arrow, whether shot from a war bow or a crossbow. An arrow could never have anything like the penetrating power of a lance. Although I had seen men wounded and killed by arrows and bolts, I had also seen men with ten and more arrows sticking from their armour who swore they could feel nothing, as the arrows had been stopped before pushing into their skin even a little.

So, while I trusted that our Wealden archers would disrupt the enemy and perhaps panic them, I was fully expecting that my knights and men at arms would have to step in front of the archers after the first or second volley and hold the gateway. The archers had orders to fall back up the stairs and shoot from the crenellated walls above down onto the men who attacked we real soldiers.

The six knights who approached held their shields out, just in case we were enemies. I can only assume they thought to push us off our spot or to ask us what on earth we were doing and where we had come from. If they meant harm, they would have charged us, heads down. I expected our archers would drive them away with arrows in their shields.

Instead, they murdered them.

Ten yards was spitting distance. The thick ash shafts thumped into the six knights. Two fell back as if struck by charging horse. Arrows pierced the eye slits of those two men. One dropped, dead, as if he was struck down by a vengeful God. The other screamed like a child, the yard-long shaft waving around.

A third man took an arrow to the centre of the thigh, ripping through his mail and flesh and into the bone, no doubt shattering it. He fell to the side with a cry loud enough to tear his throat to ribbons.

Another man took two arrows to the shield, the force powerful enough to stop him dead, he dropped his sword, clutched the shoulder of his shield arm, and backed away.

Another knight took a blow to the top of his old pot helm with an impact that knocked him senseless and staggering like a drunkard. The final man had been rocked by something or other so vigorously that he reeled backward and then sat down on the cobbles, dazed though seemingly unharmed.

Our other ten archers shot into the rearmost ranks of the men upon the palisade. I turned and peered past the gatehouse wall in time to see armoured men there falling backward. One man flung his sword aside as he fell with an arrow shaft sticking from what must surely have been his spine. Other men fell where they stood.

There was not much of a reaction from the survivors, who were fixated upon the Marshal's men charging the other side of the barrier. Crossbow bolts and arrows flew in from either side but they were shooting in an arc, at high angles and without much force.

"Again," I shouted but they needed no urging from me and they were already shouting their targets to each other and nocking their next arrows.

"Blue coat, left."

"Mine's the tall lord."

"Bare head, far right."

"Fat arse."

"Shiny helm."

After they called their men they bent their backs into the next shots and heaved back the cords to their ears and further. I jumped back, well out of their way.

This time, all twenty of them shot into the backs of the enemy fighting.

At a distance of around twenty yards, shooting into their rear, it was like a magic spell. Ten men dropped in an instant. Wounded men screamed and their cries added to those of the first lot down. The survivors edged away, looking over their shoulders.

The noise from the battle was intensifying. More of the Marshal's men were coming and no doubt, the rebel trap, the heavy horse charge into the flank, was ready to be sprung.

"That got their attention," Falk shouted. Faces and helms across the square were turning to face us. "Right lads, up the wall you go."

"Wait," I shouted. "Stay here. Keeping shooting, keep shooting."

I wanted to see how much carnage they could wreak. Some knights peeled off the palisade and edged toward us.

"Drop any man who comes near," I shouted to Swein but so the archers could hear me. "But keep shooting that wall. Keep killing them."

Arrow after arrow ripped into the men of the palisade. No knights could approach us without coming under the hail of iron.

They were edging away, afraid of the murder we did. Men who stopped to help their comrades were shot. Men who thought to stand were driven away. There were ten down, then twenty and then I lost count of the men who had fallen. Some of them were already dead. More and more, the enemy was aware that they had foes at their rear. The word was shouted between them to get away from us and we had cleared the nearest end of the palisade.

It was magnificent.

"Getting low on arrows, Sir Richard," Swein shouted.

"Stop shooting," I commanded. "Get behind us, not up on the wall. Save your last arrows. If they start using their heads, we may need to scare away crossbowmen."

I got the knights and men of Sir Stephen's castle garrison lined up with us, shoulder to shoulder across the width of the gateway.

I stood in the centre of the line with Falk on my left and Jocelyn on my right. Anselm tried to take position beside Jocelyn but the knight pushed the squire back and rapped him on the top of his helm with the flat of his blade.

Before us, the rebels were gathering to assault our position, where we were so few and they were so many.

"Stay together and stay in the gateway," I shouted. "If any of you breaks our line then I will run you through myself. Do you hear me? Tell me you hear me, you men."

They shouted they did.

"King Henry!" I cried. "For King Henry!"

The men took up my cry. We slapped our blades upon our shields, clapping in time. A few of us shouted insults and jeered, which was a fine thing to hear. It showed our enemies and each other that we had spirit, that we welcomed the fight.

Our challenge was answered at once by a growl of the knights who had been cowed by our archers. They saw our bowmen had fallen back and they surged forwards to finish us off. There was a roar as they rushed onward, twenty, thirty, and then fifty men advancing on us.

My heart raced with the thrill of it. Every sense alive to the clangour and stench of the battle. I felt strong and light. I wanted

336

blood. I wanted to strike the heads from every man before me and I wanted to drink the blood from their necks and devour their flesh.

They charged, so close I could hear their heaving breath and the rattle and rustling of their clothing, their swords bashing their shields as they ran, their shoes slapping on the stone cobbles.

Occasionally, in battle, it seems as though you are in a dream. Can this truly be happening, you wonder, can I be here while this terrible thing occurs?

Coming straight for me was a huge, tall, broad shouldered knight. He was dressed in a bright blue surcoat, stained with fresh blood that was not his own. His shield was half blue and half black. His mail had been scrubbed to a shine, his helmet was silvery like a mirror. The man's sword looked particularly long and very wide at the base, a sword, perhaps, made for thrusting through armour. I was the tallest in my line and perhaps I was clearly the leader of our little band and he had sought me out, jostling his fellows aside for the glory of killing me himself. His men beside him were finely armoured also, in similar colours of blue and black. Perhaps they were from the same place, the same family, even.

And then they were upon us. We stepped into the attack to take their first, mightiest blows on our shields.

My knight in blue made as if he was charging up with a powerful thrust at my head, which meant that his true attack would be anywhere but there. And he checked his thrust at the last moment, slamming his shield into mine so as to force it up and he shoved his blade low, to strike up below the bottom of my shield and into my groin and thighs.

He was strong, his weight was like being knocked by a horse. But I bent my knees, took the force of his strike and forced his shield back. I thrust his sword away as it snaked up toward me and counter attacked with a strike of my own, which he deflected well with his shield.

My strength might have been greater than his but I was as limited as anyone by the strength of my blade. If I struck with all my might, I knew from experience that I could snap my sword blade, or, at least, bend it out of usefulness. I thrust and blocked, waiting for an opening.

More men arrived behind the first line and pushed them against us.

I struck blows against the blue knight, jabbing against his armour. My shield was being chipped to pieces. Jocelyn and Falk by my sides fought their own shoving battles. My helm was smacked and then again by someone, somewhere.

My anger grew. Frustrated, I pushed back, hard. My feet I jammed into the gaps between the rutted cobbles and heaved against them. I could not be resisted. I pushed the blue knight's shield aside and stabbed my blade into the inside elbow of his shield arm and pushed the blade through into his flesh. I reversed the blade backhand into the side of his helm, ringing his head like a hammer on a bell and I followed up with a lunge up beneath the bottom of his helm, sliding up against his coif and smashing into his chin. I twisted and thrust again as he reeled back and I forced him away further, twisting and ripping my blade out downward, tearing his throat. Blood gushed out and he staggered back into the melee.

Another man forced his way into his place and then I edged back to my line and fought again.

Falk breathed heavily, his breath whistling inside his helm. Even Jocelyn was tiring. The men we fought could afford to rotate out of the attack when they tired and the man behind would take his place. Yet we had no replacements but a score of archers and a squire behind. Our line was a single man thick. While we stood firm in the centre, the men to either side were pushed back by the weight of numbers.

Soon, all I heard was my breath in my ears and the muffled shouts and grunts of desperate men. I could taste blood on the air. I wanted it. I needed it. I wanted to break away from my men and take on the whole army. I fought on while Falk and Jocelyn took their first steps back. I had to go back with them to avoid breaking the line.

I had no breath to shout anything to inspire my men to fight harder. Then again, they already fought for their lives, what more was there?

Yet they would break at any moment, I knew, I could feel it in the way the line moved. They were beyond the limits of their endurance.

Perhaps I could give my men a chance, or brief respite at the least, if I fought my way out, break through the enemy and so cause them to react to my actions. As I thought it, I did it. I shoved aside the three men surrounding me and stepped forward into them.

A mass of armoured men surged toward me, seeing a fool and

an easy kill or a good ransom. There were dozens of them, in rank after rank and I realised I had made a mistake. There was nowhere to break through to, any more. It was a sea of armoured men all the way to the cathedral. Perhaps I would not kill William after all.

Perhaps, after all I had seen and all I had done, I would die at the gate of Lincoln Castle.

I hoped, prayed, and pushed forward, swinging my blade like a madman. I pushed them back, smacked heads and arms, I aimed for hands to smash and knees that I could stamp on. I took blows to my helm that clouded my vision with ten thousand swirling stars and still I kept moving, spinning, shoving them back, breaking out further from my men and hoping to bring the enemy knights with me.

My arms felt broken. My shoulders burned. I could see almost nothing.

I was alone. Arrows smashed down about me. The knights around me backed away, struck by a hail of shots from above. They held their shields up over their heads and I struck them from below.

And then the enemy melted away.

The attacks on me grew lighter and fewer for a moment and then they were gone. I straightened my helm, lined up the slits with my eyes once again and watched them running full tilt down the steep hill, down the road toward the river and the bridge that crossed it. Hundreds of men squeezing together between the buildings.

The Marshal's men had cleared the palisade and were over it, chasing the fleeing rebel knights and men at arms.

A group of knights swerved toward me, their blades drawn.

"King Henry!" I cried, throwing my arms wide and backing away. "I fight for Henry. For the Marshal."

Still they came at me until Falk rushed to my side, yanking off his helm.

"Hold fast, you fools. This is Richard of Ashbury."

They left me alone and I stood while my men approached, exhausted, battered, and wounded, to watch the flight of the enemy.

Swein led his archers down from the wall where they had saved me by shooting down into the attackers that had surrounded me.

"Good fight, that," Falk said, still wheezing.

Jocelyn clapped me on the back. "Let us go capture ourselves a few knights, shall we?"

"You go," I said. "You and Anselm, make some money. Oh, and find me a good sword. Mine is quite ruined."

I looked around for a body that I could drag into the shadows.

∞

Swein and his archers were plundering the dead and retrieving their arrows from the men they had shot in the battle. It was only fair that they took whatever else they could.

Jocelyn looked at me as if to say that he knew what I would be doing and he did not approve of it. But I cared nothing for what he thought. The air was full of blood and I needed it. I needed it.

While the dead were plundered, the living were chased through the city and captured for ransom by whoever took them. Knights were found hiding in cupboards, cellars and roof spaces. Many were drowned in the river while in flight over the bridge that led out of town.

Those who escaped on horses fled south. Those that fled on foot were largely rounded up by the Marshal's knights, held in reserve on the south side of the city for just such an eventuality. Inside, the city was plundered from top to bottom.

Noblemen, knights, men-at-arms, squires, pages, crossbowmen, archers, grooms and servants lost their minds once they had taken the city and all plundered it three ways from Sunday. Everything of value within the city was stolen, no matter who it had belonged to. Wine and ale casks were smashed open and men grew drunk and sang. Of course, it is often the way when a city falls though I was surprised to see Englishmen carrying it out upon an English city.

As soon as the day after that first mad evening, men were referring to the plundering as the Lincoln Fair. As in, do you see what I got at the Lincoln Fair? And, prices were low at the Lincoln Fair this year. Their glee, I felt at the time, to be somewhat unseemly, although I would never be one to judge on account of how I spent my own first evening after the battle.

When the looting mobs had rushed beyond the bodies at the gatehouse, I dragged the corpse of the blue knight by the ankles through the gatehouse and into the bailey. He felt heavy as a horse and I was tired but I was also thirsty so I moved him rapidly. I dragged him over the cobbles into the bailey and then quickly pulled the body into a dark armourer's workshop and stripped off his helm.

He was younger than expected. Perhaps not much over twenty. A young knight who fought like an experienced one. I wondered if he had been English or from France or elsewhere.

I took off his coif, seeing that I had, in fact, split it entirely through at the throat, breaking open the mail rings with my blade. It was sticky with blood. I salivated and checked that I could hear no one in the bailey. Pulling down the mail at his neck, I bent my mouth to his wound and sank my teeth into the sticky, congealing mass.

I drank down the hot blood, it gushing into my mouth. It spread through me, like climbing into a hot bath, like warm spiced wine after a winter trek, like a dream coming true.

Something was wrong but I did not know what it was until the young knight groaned and moved.

I jerked away from him as his eyes opened and tried to focus on me. His right arm rose slowly toward me. I slapped it away.

I had never killed a man just for his blood before.

But I had not had my fill, and I meant to have it.

I sank my teeth back into his throat and held him still while I drank down his blood, sucking it from his body. He coughed a spray of blood and without looking, I held my hand over his mouth. His body wracked with spasms while he died. I drank until my belly was full to bursting and sat back.

If I were discovered again drinking blood after a battle, it would mean the end of my position in England. My name would be destroyed. I would have to go to the Holy Land, take a false name, and fight as a mercenary. Any chance at revenge would be over. I wiped my mouth, stripped the surcoat from the body, and stuffed it deep into a dark corner of the workshop.

The knight would be recognisable, I supposed but I would do what I could. I hefted up the anvil from its block and smashed the knight's face in until it was a cavernous, bloody mess. I took his rings and tossed his scabbard behind the workshop when I snuck out.

I kept to the shadows. Few people were in the castle bailey. Two servants walked from the keep door, hurrying out through the gate, no doubt eager to join in the plundering.

No one noticed me.

I gave the rings to Swein, who said nothing but understood. Perhaps he thought I was buying his silence but I was not. In fact, I wished to reward him, for he had done exceptionally well and he deserved a rich reward. Not least for sticking by me, no matter what.

The blood surged through me. I felt stronger than ever. The day's exertions had flowed from my limbs and I stood and listened while the Lincoln Fair was in full swing. I thought I should probably join in, as money is always useful. But I had no will for it.

I saw the blue knight's face staring up, sightless, before I crushed his face in.

Was it even murder, I wondered? He had been trying to kill me in the battle and he would surely have died from his existing wounds in time anyway. But no matter how I justified it to myself,

344

I felt like a genuine murderer for the first time in my life.

But he was dead and I was not going to confess to the crime, nor would I admit it to some priest. They were all in some man's pay. Like every other horror I had seen and done in my life, I would simply push the thought of it away and pretend it had never happened. And if I never spoke of it to God then perhaps He would forget as well.

∞

The next day, I found the Marshal's tent, which he had erected to the north of the city while he oversaw the cleaning up and sorting out and tallying the costs and gains from the action.

The hangover from a battle is a strange thing. The aches and pains start in on a man, his elation at surviving a slaughter becomes melancholy that he himself has killed, or known a man who died or perhaps he did not perform well or committed a crime in the anarchy after. Men sat slumped and quiet talking of things to come, sharing bottles and hiding their spoils.

While I waited outside, along with two dozen other men on their own business, Falk approached. He had not changed out of his armour, had not removed his blood-soiled surcoat.

"Good day, yesterday," he said as he stomped up to me. "Reckon that's the war over, then."

"You think so?" I asked.

"Got to be, Richard," Falk said. "We killed or captured most of the leaders. There's not enough loyal to Louis to carry it on.

And the Marshal, you know what he's like, he'll sue for peace on almost any terms, just to be done with it, mark my words."

"I do," I said. "And now I will speak to the Marshal, accept my warrant and go clear Sherwood of outlaws."

"The Green Knight," Falk said, nodding.

I was surprised he had heard about him.

"Course I bloody have," Falk said. "He's taken enough of my men off the road, last year or two when we went up to York and Scotland. I hope you take the bastards and skin them all alive, the Green Knight especially. Green Knight, what a laugh. Rip his tongue out."

"I will," I said. "Nothing can stop me now."

Sometimes, you say something and as you speak, you know you are mocking God.

"There's a messenger in the camp looking for you," Falk said. "Looks like a priest. Monk, I reckon. Poor lad looks like he's shitting himself. I said I'd dig you out for him. The lad's gone down to the cathedral to wait there."

I had a terrible feeling and I left word that I would be back to see the Marshal as soon as I could.

There was blood everywhere before the cathedral. It was massive, stretching to Heaven above me, like God Himself staring down in judgement on what I had done. I dreaded entering that holy place. I was not sure I could take it but I did not have to.

The monk hurried over to me from somewhere out of the way by the side of the cathedral. He led his tired pony. Both beast and rider were covered in dirt and sweat, suggesting a hard ride.

I recognised him as a brother from the Priory.

"Brother Godfrey, is it not?" I said.

"Sir Richard," the young man mumbled, would not meet my eye. "Prior Simon sent me to find you."

I stepped up to him, grasped him by the front of his robe and dragged him close to me.

"Speak. Tell me all. Quickly, man."

"The women. The women, the Lady Marian and the other one. They were taken, my lord. Taken in the night."

TWELVE ~ INTO
SHERWOOD

"WHERE IS HE?" I demanded at the gate of Nottingham Castle, two mornings later.

"We are not to let you enter, Sir Richard," the captain on the gate said, swallowing hard. He had an open-faced helmet on his head and I imagined what would happen to his warty nose if I smashed my mailed fist into it.

"I am going through that gate," I said, advancing upon him. "And the three of you are welcome to try to stop me. But you should know I am in a killing mood."

The captain stepped back a full step. "I am merely doing as commanded," he said.

"Please attempt to stop me," I said. "I beg you to draw your swords and try, please. I want to feel my sword slicing through a man's flesh."

348

The captain and his two men stepped aside and I strode through. They followed after me at a distance, keeping pace with me and whispering accusations at each other. Servants scattered from me. Entering the keep, two of Roger's clerks stared at me down the corridor. They clutched their scrolls to their chest, spun on their heels and fled with their robes flapping about their scrawny ankles.

I pushed through the doorways and climbed stairs until I came to the Great Hall. It was almost empty but for a few men sitting at the table. The chief amongst them I recognised.

"Guy of Gisbourne," I shouted. "Where is the sheriff?"

He stared for a moment then leapt to his feet. "Sir Richard," he said. He looked to one of his men who nodded and ran off through a door at the back of the hall.

"Where is he?" I said, striding forward toward the top table behind which he stood.

Guy spread his hands. "Please, Sir Richard, there is no need for you to be angry. Sit, I beg you, let us drink together and talk."

"They say you are a brilliant swordsman, Sir Guy," I said, placing my hand upon the pommel of my new sword. "I would love to see how you fare against a man who would test your ability. Shall we wager? If I beat you, then you tell me where the sheriff is."

Guy swallowed and placed his hand on the hilt of his own weapon, shifting back away from the table. "And if I win?"

I summoned as much contempt as I could muster and I threw back my head and laughed.

His face flushed red and I watched with satisfaction as the rage filled the man. I had insulted him gravely. I wished to beat him into submission and draw the truth out of him like blood.

He stepped back further from the table and drew his sword.

Three men rushed into the hall from the back door. I recognised them vaguely as Guy's men.

Alone, I could beat Guy into submission without killing him. But with four men, I would risk killing a man who could tell me where the sheriff was hiding.

I decided to frighten them into subjugation.

Without drawing my sword, I stepped forward to the huge table, bent my knees into a squat and, with a roar straightened, and heaved the massive oaken thing up into the air, longways onto the end nearest Guy's men. Plates and cups slid and flew and smashed. I hurled with such force that the massive, ancient table spun and crashed down on its top, scattering Guy's men aside. The sheriff's chair fell backward with a bang and the benches clattered away.

While Guy stood in shock, I ran to him and seized him by the arms, pinning them to his side.

His eyes were wide as platters and all colour drained from his face.

"Where is the sheriff?"

"Sherwood," Guy said, his throat tight.

Guy's eyes flicked behind me.

"Stay where you are," I shouted. "I will rip his arms from his body."

Guy, his neck tight, nodded at them and I heard them back away from me.

"So he's in Sherwood," I said, my nose half an inch from his own. "I could have guessed that. Where in Sherwood? Where has he taken them?"

"Taken his men? He knew not where."

"What are you blathering about?"

Guy frowned. "He goes to find the Lady Marian. He took ten men before dawn, leaving me and a few of us here to guard the castle and the town."

"Find Marian? But he is the one who took her from me."

Relief washed over Guy's face. "He did not. The Green Knight took her."

"The sheriff is in league with the Green Knight."

"He is not," Guy said and I squeezed him. "I swear, I swear it, on God's teeth, I swear it."

"But the sheriff is in league with the archbishop," I said.

Guy peered at me warily. "The archbishop is here often," he said. "But they are two of the most powerful lords of the north, why would they not be?"

"The archbishop is working with the Green Knight," I said.

Guy simply gaped at me.

I shoved him away and turned around. The three men at arms stood with their swords out. I ignored them and straightened the sheriff's fine chair. I sat myself down in it and thought.

"The archbishop sent a steward to Ashbury after I was outlawed," I said to Guy as he inched around to where I was. Guy waved his men back and pulled a bench upright, quite far away from me. "The new steward was a big man, a very big man named John. I did not think of it at the time but after the women were taken, I recalled the sheriff saying he had sent his chief bailiff, a man named John into the Greenwood. John the bailiff was a big man, correct? And he's the sheriff's man?"

"Bigger than you," Guy said. "Little John they called him. But he went into the wood. He never came out."

I nodded. "I understand now. He was not the sheriff's man after he came out. He was William's. William de Ferrers, the Green Knight. He has made the bailiff, Little John, into his own man. And somehow, William has sent his man to Ashbury, on request of the archbishop. But how did the sheriff know that Marian had been taken?"

"He pays a man who lives near Ashbury. He sends reports, every now and then."

"Reports of me? Who is this man?"

"I would rather not say," Gisbourne said.

"My dear Guy," I said. "I am sorely tempted to cut off your head and then kill your men here. Are you on my side or are you not?"

"He is the Prior of Tutbury. A monk named Simon."

"That sneaky little bastard," I said. "He told the sheriff Marian was there, and the sheriff sent a man to take her, am I right?"

"He sent me," Guy said, sullenly. "Only, when I arrived she was already taken by the new steward, this fellow John."

"You bunch of sly, traitorous bastard dogs," I said. "You have been conspiring behind my back."

"I do only as I am commanded by the Sheriff of Nottingham and Derbyshire," Sir Guy said. "I am a loyal servant."

"You are as cowardly as a woman, Guy," I said. "And as

faithful as a snake. Be thankful your head is yet attached to your body. Tell me, where was the sheriff going first, to look for Marian?"

"Linby, first, then on to Newstead Priory."

"He will find both places empty of life," I said. "Where would the sheriff go next?"

"On to Blidworth, I should think."

"Then I ride to Blidworth," I said.

Guy leapt to his feet. "I will accompany you," he said, then paused. "That is, if you agree, Sir Richard."

"Your lord commanded you to stay here, did he not? All Nottingham is entrusted to you."

"My men can be trusted," he said. "Can you not, boys? If the sheriff's good wine is so much as looked at then I shall cut off your hands myself, do you hear me?"

"Fine," I said. "But you do as I say at all times."

"I swear, Sir Richard," Guy of Gisbourne said, the lying sack of shit.

∞

"First, we find the sheriff and his men," I said to my own assembled band. We were all mounted, on the road north of Nottingham and were ready to set off. It was midday and I ached to be gone already. "Then we will combine our forces, find William and his monsters and save Marian and Eva."

We were Jocelyn, Anselm, Sir Guy of Gisbourne, Swein and

sixteen Wealden archers. Four of the original twenty had elected to return to Kent with the wealth they had taken at the Lincoln Fair. The sixteen that were left were young men all, good fighters, excellent bowmen. I was glad to have them but I feared I was leading them to their deaths.

"Any man who wishes to return to his home is welcome to do so," I said. "I have a royal warrant to defeat the outlaw band and we will all be rewarded. But none of you should think this will be an easy way to make money."

"Sir Richard," Swein said. "My men want to save Marian and Eva as much as you do. The women spent the whole winter with us. There's not a man here who would not give his life for the Lady Marian."

"They are your men now, are they?" Jocelyn said.

"They are," Swein shot back.

"And you consider yourself a man," Jocelyn said. "But if you think the Lady Marian looks upon you as anything but a boy then you are very much mistaken."

Swein reached for his bow and I rode forward, pushing my horse in between the two of them. I kicked Swein's horse on the rump and it jerked sideways. Swein, being such a poor horseman, fell from his saddle and landed hard.

The archers, all mounted, sat up straighter and a couple put their hands to their daggers.

They were Swein's men indeed.

I had not meant for him to fall but I could not apologise now without appearing weak.

"I will have no fighting in this company," I shouted, making some of the horses nervous, and their riders too. "We will be fighting for our lives this very day. Save it for William's men, you flaming bloody fools. Get up on your horse, Swein, and try to stay upon it."

"I told you peasants make poor horsemen," Jocelyn said.

I glared at Jocelyn. "You are supposed to be a knight. Act like one." His smirk fell from his face. "And get rid of that absurd lance, will you, man? We are riding into a woodland, you will find no place for a charge."

"I am a knight," Jocelyn said, sticking his nose in the air. "And the lance is a knight's weapon."

Swein clawed his way to his feet, his eyes full of murder as he looked up under his cap at me. I hoped I had not made an enemy of the lad by shaming him in front of his men.

"Swein, you know the Greenwood better than any man here," I said. "Please lead us onward to Blidworth. Let us move quickly, we have less than a half a day's light left."

The lad mounted and nodded, somewhat mollified.

Sir Guy raised his eyebrows as we rode out. "Not a word from you, Gisbourne," I muttered and he lowered his head to hide his smile.

We knights and squires had good horses, capable of comfortable gait. But the archers and Swein had their sturdy, short-backed ponies. They could keep pace with us but they were much jostled. All had complained bitterly in the long, fast journey north and then every day that they had mounted since. Although, I had to admit they had all grown into their saddles, learning to move with their mount and as we rode north from Nottingham I was pleased to see them riding fairly well and without complaint. For I would need them in fighting form the moment that they dismounted.

"Your so-called squire grows big for his boots," Jocelyn said as he rode close beside me. He spoke in French and, even then, he kept his voice low.

"You will stop this absurd rivalry with the lad," I said. "What has gotten into you? You are a famed knight and he will only ever be a commoner. No doubt, he will end his days on the end of a rope yet you treat him as if he is a threat to you. I know, son, you are afraid for Marian, of course, you are but why release your ire onto Swein? What has he done to deserve it? We need him, he was an outlaw in these woods. And, as you are too blind to see it, those archers are indeed his men. Did you see him when we raided Dover? Did you see him leading them in Lincoln? They were Cassingham's men once but the lad has brought them over to himself. They are here with us because of him. If you truly want Marian back, then you will treat Swein as a friend, not your enemy."

Jocelyn said nothing for a long while and I waited for him to argue. Instead, he eventually agreed. "You are right," he said. "It is just that he and Marian have been often found talking together and laughing together. I could never make her laugh. I am ever awkward with her."

"He is an outlawed son of a freeman," I said. "She could never marry him. You must be patient with her. She will know that you are a good man and would make a good husband, you will see."

Jocelyn hung his head. "She is likely dead, is she not? Or at the very least, she is raped by those beasts."

I thought that Jocelyn was probably right. "More likely they have taken her to William, who will drink from her," I said.

"But his men," Jocelyn said, his face twisted in anguish. "His men will take her, will they not?"

"All that matters is that we get her back alive," I said. "And Eva too."

We rode into Linby. It looked the same as the last time we were there after Ranulf the forester had talked to me in his home and then been slaughtered for it. The whole village had been butchered, with bodies in the houses and in the gardens. It was still deserted. The bones of the dead had been dragged away by the beasts of the woodland. There was no smell of smoke. No animals squealing and being hushed. A pair of goldfinches flitted through the open doorways.

"The sheriff and his men's horses came through here," Swein said, dismounted and looking at the disturbed ground. "No sign of a fight, as far as I can tell."

"Onward to Blidworth," I commanded Swein. "Every man be ready from here on out. Keep your eyes open."

"As if we weren't already," one of the archers muttered.

We picked our way along the track from Linby toward Blidworth. The sun slid behind a cloud but the wind was still warm. The overwhelming scent of immense clusters of elderflower filled the air with their heady smell, so strong that it was unpleasant.

Once out of the village the trees grew close to the track. The woodland by villages is always coppiced and often free of tangled undergrowth. No animal larger than a field mouse is found in such domesticated wood. It was late May. Blossom bloomed in the hedgerows and at the edges of the wood. The whitebeam blossom formed loose domed clusters of small white flowers. Hawthorn shrubs and small trees were more numerous than any other. The dense masses of flowers form white in May but I knew they would turn pink as they matured, as if in the promise of the vivid red berries that they will become, turning the colour of old blood by Christmas. I wondered if I would be alive to see it.

Bullfinches flitted through the branches, crying out at our intrusion with their mournful, single-note call.

And yet for all the new life in it, the woodland outside of Linby felt deeply threatening. I imagined all manner of men and beasts waiting just out of sight and sound in the darkness between the dense trunks and green understorey.

"How far to Blidworth?" I asked Swein, who rode at the fore of our band.

He glanced at me. "Not far," he said. "Half of half a day on foot?"

"A quarter of a day," I said. "So, seven miles?"

"Sounds right," he said, shrugging.

"What is this place like?" I asked.

"Just a village, Sir Richard," Swein said. "A village like any other in Sherwood. A village subject to the king's laws of the forest. Subject to the whims of the warden, foresters, and the verderers." Swein spat off the side of his horse to show me what he thought of those men.

"Like that man Ranulf," Anselm said, from behind me. "He

was a landowner in Linby. What did the folk of Sherwood think of him?"

"The folk of Sherwood?" I asked. "Like Swein alludes to, Anselm, the folk of Sherwood are the same as the folk of anywhere. They moan and gripe about the laws that govern them and likewise complain about the loyal servants of the Crown who must enforce them."

Swein shook his head. "The laws are wrong, my lord, they are wrong. Outside of the king's forests, there are laws, traditions long held. Inside the forest then there is another law. A law where a man is sentenced to maiming or even death for simple actions like trespass or the killing of a deer. I ask you, Richard, what kind of law is it where a skinny old doe in winter, not a day from a natural death, is equal to the life of an Englishman?"

"No fair law," Anselm said.

"The king's law," I said. "Now hold your flapping tongue still for a moment, will you? Who is the verderer at Blidworth? Not Ranulf too? He did not seem important enough to be forester and verderer both."

Swein looked at me strangely. "Did you not know? It is your friend, Sir Guy of Gisbourne." Swein jerked his thumb behind us.

Anselm started to turn about. "Do not look at him, Anselm or I will take your eyes."

Swein grinned. "He's a right evil bastard, that one, my lord."

"He is the verderer at Blidworth?" I asked. "Why would the sheriff not take him to his own village?"

"Perhaps because all the verderers in Sherwood are corrupted," Swein said. "The sheriff is supposed to have no legal authority in

Sherwood but he and his friends have seen to it that every post, from warden and verderer to forester and on down has been one of the sheriff's men."

"But the verderers are elected by the county courts?"

"And who rules them, my lord?" Swein asked.

"It is true," Anselm said. "Swein has told me much about this. I think I shall have to speak to my father."

"For the love of God, Anselm," I said. "You are a good lad and a fine squire but you will never change the way of these things. Men's hearts are corrupted and so their hearts corrupt their posts. So the priests tell us." I lowered my voice. "Now, fall back slowly and warn Jocelyn to watch out for Sir Guy. Speak softly, out of Guy's hearing, draw Jocelyn away. Warn him that Guy may have been left behind to lead us into an ambush."

Anselm's eyes widened, all noble thought of justice for the peasants forgotten. He moved to the edge of the path and slowed his horse to do as I asked.

"An ambush?" Swein asked, scanning ahead.

"Do you know of any likely places?" I asked.

He scratched his nose. "A few, perhaps. There is a dell, a couple of miles from Blidworth. The rocks climb high above the track. And the village has fields on all sides but the houses are in two rows, either side of the road. Men could hide there for us to enter, trap us between the buildings."

"And between here and there is all woodland?"

"I recall a patch of moorland on the high ground up ahead."

It sounded as though we might be ambushed anywhere. I wondered if I was overreacting. Perhaps Guy never considered it

360

important enough to mention. Certainly, if his post existed only to increase his personal wealth and to keep Sherwood as well as the county in his sheriff's hands, then there was little reason to bring it up.

And yet why would Roger leave his best man behind in Nottingham? As Guy had said, his men would look after such a quiet, stable place as Nottingham. Guy was quick enough to volunteer to accompany me into the woodland. Had I been manipulated? Was the sheriff even in Blidworth at all? Perhaps I was being led far from where Marian and Eva really were.

"Every man who has a helmet," I said, turning my horse to face the archers. "Put it on. String your bows. Loosen your arrows. Distance yourselves further from each other. Watch ahead and to either side. Sing out if you hear or see anything at all. Do you all hear me?"

Sir Guy showed no obvious sign of distress at our preparations.

Thus arrayed, we continued on.

I myself chose to go without my helm to preserve my exceptional sight, hearing, and sense of smell. However, I did not pretend to myself that my powers of healing would cure an arrow through my head and I remained rather concerned as we proceeded.

I was thirsty for blood. I wondered idly what Swein would say if I asked him for some of his own, as he had fed Tuck. He would probably not agree.

In the narrow band of moorland between the wood, we went single file, in three separate files moving parallel to each other. The central one I led along the path. Jocelyn the left and Swein on the right.

We sprung no ambush.

At the dell, we found a mix of ash, alder, goat willow, holm oak, strawberry tree, suckering elms, spindle tree, dogwood, elder and white poplar woven together in a rich limestone scrub by a scramble tangle of wild hops, dog-roses and brambles that could have hidden a thousand crouching monsters. I sent archers up and around both sides to discover any waiting bowmen.

There were none.

We approached the village of Blidworth with caution. As we came out of the wood, to either side of the track was a large strip field with rows of barley. The sun was setting over the woodland behind us, sending our long shadows before us as we rode up the hill toward the village, which remained out of sight over a hump in the road.

The clash of iron came on the wind.

I pulled up, straining to hear.

The men, needing no instruction, reined in behind and beside me.

Jocelyn turned his helmeted head toward me.

"I hear the sound of battle," I said. "Up ahead."

"The sheriff has found William," Jocelyn said.

"Or the other way around," I said, speaking quickly. "Jocelyn, you and Anselm lead your five archers up the left through this field. Swein, you take six of your fellows and take up position to the right of the village. Sir Guy, come along with me and these five fine fellows here. We knights to close in from three sides, each covered by the bowmen. And if any of you archers shoot me in the back, I shall rip your giblets out. Move now, quickly now."

The archers all dismounted and the three groups spread out from one another, the outer two circling through the fields to either side of the village.

Unslinging my shield, I advanced my horse slowly forward on the track, right up the hill toward the centre into the main street. Sir Guy rode beside me on his sturdy little rouncey.

The sounds of battle grew as I reached the top of the rise.

Inside the village, men were dying.

The sheriff's men were fighting for their lives.

Two rows of houses, a wide street ran through in between the rows. In the centre, a small group of knights and men at arms fought back to back. Bodies, limbs, and entrails lay at their feet in pools of blood. Their horses were lying dead or dying all over the village, some still kicking their feet and thrashing, blood streaking down their flanks. In the rear of the village, one horse walked slowly left to right, dragging her entrails along the dirt behind her.

A group of men attacked them with darting and jabbing with swords, swinging blades in scything motions. Seven of them, with another man standing apart. All wore iron caps. A couple had spears, another a quarterstaff, and a couple with clubs. Most wore filthy gambesons, the rest in those green tunics. They moved like William's monsters.

They were laughing, jeering, and cheering each other on.

Sheriff de Lacy was in the centre of those men, covered in blood, without a helm, parrying attacks with a bent blade. The men with the sticks were darting in, clouting the sheriff's men with them and dancing gleefully out.

Sir Guy of Gisbourne, all credit to the man, cried out, "Roger!" and spurred his horse straight down the track toward his master and friend.

"The sheriff's men are the centre group," I shouted to the archers and raked my heels back.

My horse had been trained fairly well for the charge. He was often nervous and in high spirits around any sort of excitement and this time, he did not fail to be himself.

He swerved away from the track, trying to avoid the stench of blood and shrieking of the dying. I could not control him so I allowed him to veer to the left.

As he moved aside from the track, the arrows shot past me and sank into the jeering attackers.

A couple of the shots hit their marks, making that wet-solid sound of meat being punched through by steel. Those men went down, staggered and knocked back.

All the attackers broke off, spinning about, looking for the archers.

Guy bore down on them, his sword point forward and low, ready to spear it through the nearest man.

But Guy of Gisbourne had no true notion of the speed and power of the men he faced. What was a charging horse to the power of men filled with William's blood?

The three nearest men charged forward and swarmed Guy's horse, knocking it aside and bearing the beast down, with the rider crashing hard into the street. His sword spun aside, glinting as it momentarily left the long shadow and reflected the blood-red setting sun behind me.

I left my horse and ran toward Guy, the sheriff, and his men.

Arrows slashed through the air from behind me, most hitting home, smacking into the men.

More arrows from the left and right, shot from the flat, slapping into William's men, who snarled and jeered.

The three nearest broke off from Guy and his horse, which was bleeding from the neck, the coat shining and sleek with it.

The boldest of the men wore a gambeson with a mail coif and he was faster almost than even I could see. He swung a rusted falchion at my head as I drew near, which was a terrible mistake on his part. A falchion is a single edged meat cleaver and wonderful for cutting open the flesh of non-armoured opponents. Whereas I was in full mail, shield, helm, and he should have retreated immediately. Instead, I took some of the weight of his blow with my shield, rolling with his wild swing to guide it past me, then pushed his blade away, throwing him off balance. I thrust at his open side, piercing him through the gambeson under his ribs and he screamed, reeling away. His two men were on me, one with a sword, and the other with a sturdy club. Both had arrow shafts sticking from their body.

They were savage and quite clearly trusted their speed and strength to overcome their paltry arms and armour. After all, they had just butchered the sheriff's men, who had been all armoured as well as me. But they had not encountered my speed before.

I gutted the swordsman and took a huge blow to the side of my helm from the club, which shattered the wood and knocked my eyes out of alignment. I could see enough to pull the back edge of my blade through the swordsman's throat.

The falchion-armed man I had run through ran away back to his fellows, as did the man with the broken club.

I straightened my helm in time to see William's creatures fleeing from the centre of the village. They spread apart from each other and away from the sheriff and his two surviving fellows. At first, I assumed they were fleeing from us, from me.

Instead, they were seeking cover between the houses so that they could approach the three groups of archers. They leapt over the wattle fences to the pens and gardens and rushed my men.

They stayed away from me.

Most of the archers stood and shot their arrows but a few scattered away from the rushing men. Swein loosed an arrow into the head of the man charging him, dropping the man at the last moment. The young outlaw ran from the next man and dived into the barley, his archers filling the pursuer with arrows.

Across in the other field, I turned in time to see Jocelyn take the top of a man's head off just as Anselm was borne down under another.

Footsteps slapped behind me and I swept my sword out, cutting into the arm of a charging man and knocking him aside. I was on him, stamping down on his hand and driving my sword through the base of his neck.

I was struck on the back of the helm, sending me staggering. I whirled and lashed out but I was hit again, high on the back near my shield shoulder. I caught a glimpse of a man's face twisted in fury, wielding a heavy blacksmith's hammer.

No mortal man can strike with such force. I was thrown from my feet into the dirt. I fell awkwardly, my shield under me and my sword arm flung out to the side.

I was blind, stunned, starting to panic when the hammer smashed down on my elbow.

The pain was incredible. The crunch of the bones was like a white-hot lance spearing through my body and into my brain. Even as I screamed and writhed, my instinct took over and I rolled to my left, over my shield arm and kept rolling so my shield was across my body. The hammer crashed into my shield with force enough to crack it.

My ears were ringing, I could not see.

I kicked out, purely on instinct and connected with a leg, a knee that crunched.

The man fell on me, pinning my shield to my body. I was afraid, I could not feel my arm.

Had it been cut off?

The body on top of me was not moving. I shoved up with my shield arm and threw him off me.

Screams, shouts, and clashes sounded through my helmet and I rolled to my feet, agony spearing through my arm once more. I wheeled about, shield up from the figures around me. I had to tilt my head back and look sideways to see out of my eye slits.

"Richard, Richard," a voice shouted.

"Jocelyn?" I cried back, spinning around, trying and failing to lift my sword arm.

"Richard, we are victorious. Now sit down before you hurt yourself."

∞

They had to hammer the side of my helm back into shape to remove it from my head. I laid my helm on the stone threshold of the nearest house and Anselm tapped a bad dent from the side with the pommel of his sword.

"There," Anselm said, laying his sword down. "I believe that is it."

"Get this thing off me," I shouted. "Hurry up."

When Anselm eased the helm from my head, I reached up and shoved it off, grinding the edge against the tender part of my skull.

"You took a bad hit, there, Sir Richard," Anselm said, touching my scalp.

I slapped his hand away and stood up, swaying and blinking around.

We had won. William's men were mostly dead. Of the living, the sheriff and Guy sat together, side by side on the threshold in the doorway of the nearest house, holding on to each other. Both were covered in blood.

The centre of the village was drenched in the stuff, red soaking into the packed earth.

Jocelyn stood guard over two survivors, two men bleeding and bristling with arrow shafts. One man had two arrows through the neck and mouth, as well as three through his chest. The man had his eyes closed, breathing slowly and holding himself perfectly still upon the floor.

The other man was not much better off. Five arrows had

pierced his shoulders and upper back at various angles. The left side of his scalp from the crown to the ear had been sliced off. It was a flat, red slab, shorn of hair and skin down to the bone. Blood leaked freely from the wound, soaking the entire left side of his body. His face was white yet he looked around with clear eyes, fully alert.

Surrounding them stood Jocelyn, his shield and sword ready. Four archers stood back, arrows nocked upon the strings, five others stood with their blades out.

My sword arm was broken, very badly. My elbow was smashed and with every movement, I shivered.

"How many did we lose?" I asked Anselm as I stepped gingerly over to Jocelyn.

"John Redbeard and Bull," Anselm said. "Struck dead in an instant. These men, their speed. Their power. It is astonishing."

I was surprised that we had not lost more but still their deaths angered me. "Jocelyn," I said. "Stand ready."

Cradling my right arm with my left, I stood and looked down upon the pair of survivors.

"Who are you?"

The man with the arrows through the neck and mouth blinked up at me, unable to speak. He glanced at his friend. That man smirked and spoke for them both.

"My name is Much," he said. "The tongue-tied fellow here is Will."

"Ah," I said. "You are Much the Miller? And he is Bloody Will?" I shook from the pain in my arm and the anger at the men before me.

"Will the Scarlet, so he likes to be told. His name's Bill Scatchlock. Though you certainly is bloody now, ain't you there, Will?" Much was putting a defiant face on things but he was losing more blood every moment and he would not last for very long.

I wanted to kill them immediately but I needed them to speak. "Where is William?"

Much the Miller stared up at me, nodded at the one with arrow shafts through his face. "Right here next to me."

"Another William. The former Earl of Derbyshire. Where is the Green Knight? Whatever he is calling himself, you know who I mean."

"Robert, his name is," Much said. "Sir Robert. He's nobly born, he is."

"That was his father's name," I said. "His real name is William."

"Christ almighty," Much said, staring up at me, his eyes bulging. "You know what, lord. You don't half look like him, you know. Are you his son?"

"Where is he?" I said, shaking with the effort of containing my anger.

"Might be here, might be there," Much said, pausing to spit a little blood onto the street. "Never know with him. Who are you to him, then?"

I kicked Much in the stomach and bent to the one called Will the Scarlet. With my one good hand, I grabbed the shaft sticking through his mouth and yanked it out. The barbs caught on the man's back teeth and those were ripped from his jaw.

Blood and teeth gushed out and Will bent over lest he drown

in it. I braced the man against my leg, grabbed the arrow coming from his neck and yanked that one out. The barbs tore a great chunk of his neck as it came free, leaving a tattered and wet sucking hole.

I sank to my knees, grabbed the back of Will the Scarlet's hair and held him up on his knees while I drank down what remained of the blood within his body.

It was like fire, that blood, like fire and ice and the first flush of the night's wine in your belly, multiplied beyond counting.

And it was more. More than I remembered, better than the knight dressed in blue back in Lincoln. It reminded me of a cave in Palestine when I had drunk from my brother William. It was not the same. It was not as powerful but it was a faint echo of that blood. I drank until the spurting blood turned to a trickle. It did not take long.

I stood, letting the drained body fall. My elbow itched and I straightened it out, extending it as it popped back into shape. I sighed as the pain left my arm and my head and all my weariness fled from my limbs. My vision and hearing snapped into a sharpened point, colours warmed and glowed, edges popped.

"You are full of William's blood," I said to Much. "The Green Knight, you drank from him. Tell me all you know of him, now."

"What can you do you me?" Much said, smirking. "No matter what I say, I'm going to end up like Bill, there, ain't I?"

"You will certainly die," I said. "But if you do not tell me then I shall remove the skin from your face, take off your hands and feet, smash your teeth out and leave you here to die slowly. Or I can take off your head. Which would you prefer?"

Much glanced at the body of Bill. "What do you want to know?"

"Where is he?"

"Eden," Much said.

"Do not play games with me," I said, through gritted teeth. "Where is he?"

Much grunted. "Eden is the name of the place. The Green Knight rules it, as Adam ruled the first Eden before God and woman betrayed him. We sons of Adam live within the walls of Eden. Sir Robert lives in the sacred dell beneath the palace."

"What palace? There are no palaces in Sherwood. Are there?"

"The Palace in the Green," Much said. "In the green heart of Eden."

"Where is this Eden?" I said, barely holding to my remaining patience.

"Up beyond Mansfield," Much said, jerking his head back. "Not really a palace, I suppose. It's a hunting lodge what belonged to some fat lord before Sir Robert took it over. The old lord run off years ago, no one went there, not for something like fifteen years or more. No servants, nothing. Nothing but deer and boar for miles all around. And us. The sons of Adam. We gone back to the way things was, back at the start of the world."

"And how were things then? Adam was a homeless outlaw, was he?"

The mad creature nodded. 'The Green Knight came to us to gift us his gift. To bring us all back to our own land. We who was thrown off it by lords like you, who took everything from us and demanded more. Well, not no longer. Now we're the ones who have the power of life and death. We overcome it. We are the hunters and now they are the prey. Them, you, and everyone who ain't us."

"This is no more than the typical William nonsense that you are spouting," I said. "You hear me? I say he has filled your head with nonsense, man. Tell me this. You were living in the wood as an outlaw? And he took you and gave you his blood?"

Much nodded. "He done that but he done kill me first, then he saved me after, when he saw that I was a man who believed in the world being the way it was in the beginning, once again. I will help you return the earth to its true self, upon my oath, I said to him. And when I was empty of blood, he filled me up with his. His blood of fire, poured into me, flooded through my veins like quicksilver. It was the greatest gift a man can receive. See, the Christ come down and he told us we had to wait for eternal life, had to wait to have it in Heaven when we wake on the day of the last judgement. But that was a lie. The Christ lied to us. We can have it now. We can live forever. All we have to do is let the Green Knight into our hearts. Obey, faithfully, and we live for eternity, here on earth, with all the pleasures that God has given us. All of it flows from the Lord of Eden."

"You murder innocent folk for their blood," I said. "That is not Heaven upon the Earth. That is base. That is plain murder."

"It ain't murder if we don't kill them," Much said. "We only kill the ones who refuse to open their hearts to the Lord of Eden. And them what offend us. And when we want to see their blood and bone smashed flat and ground up into a pulp. Blood and bone, marrow and flesh, ground up all nice and lovely. A taste worth killing for, ain't it not? If we're going to talk more, lord, I might be needing a little drink. Maybe just a cup's worth off the floor, hereabouts? I can drink it right off the ground before it drains away and dries up. I'm right parched."

"Where are the two women he has taken?"

"Two? Got to be right many more than two. More like two hundred, ain't it, Bill? Oh, sorry, Bill. Poor old Bill. Poor old, dead Bill."

"Two women of noble birth, taken recently," I said. "You must know of them. Where are they?"

Much shifted his weight. "Don't know what you mean."

"I'm going to take your eyes and slice the skin off your face for that," I said.

"No, no, I know I heard what was what," he said. "John's got them all locked up."

It was all I could do to resist caving his skull in. "Where? This is your only chance to speak all you know."

He nodded, grinning. "Do you know a man named John? Little John the Bailiff?"

"Go on," I said.

"You know him?" Much said. "He's a bad one, lord. You stay away from him. He's a giant. A giant bastard, too. He's not right in the head, that Little John. Not right at all. Not fair, neither, not fair at all but he's lord of Mansfield, now. The Lord of Eden granted him the village and fields, just like he done with Blidworth and dear, dead Bill."

"The ladies?" I said, holding myself still lest I shake the words out of him. "The noble women he took."

"Yes, yes," Much said. "I heard all about it. He's bragging about what he done. He went away for a few weeks. Then he come back with them women. He's got them in Blidworth. In the church. And I heard about you. The knight who is coming to save them. Well, big old Little John is in Blidworth. Waiting. Waiting for you and your men. All set up. You'll go charging in to save them and you'll be surrounded. They're going to get all of you in one go. He's a clever one, that John. You got no hope against him, let alone the Lord of Eden himself."

"You have spoken," I said. "You have told me many a useful thing. I will allow you to have a drink. And perhaps I will even allow you to live."

"My eternal thanks, my lord," Much said, looking about, as if fearing a trick.

"First, before I allow you to drink, just tell me. You say the Lord of Eden lives in a hunting lodge north of Mansfield?" I asked.

"That's right," Much said, licking his lips.

"And he warned you to expect me?"

"Expect you, lord? Well, perhaps I was told all about you. Perhaps they been talking about you showing your face round here for months, now. I don't rightly remember. Maybe there is a plan for you and maybe there ain't. Maybe you'll be gutted, lord. Maybe you'll be cattle, lord." Much grinned. "One thing I do know is, you won't get past Mansfield. None of you will." He giggled.

"My thanks," I said. "You are a murderer of the innocent. You have slaughtered entire villages. I wish I had more time to make you suffer properly but this will have to suffice."

I forced him onto his face, snapped the arrow shafts off and held him down while I smashed his limbs with his own hammer. He screamed loud enough to wake the dead. With my foot upon the back of his head, I smashed his feet and his knees. I smashed his hands and his arms. The skin split apart in a half dozen places at each joint. Bone shards ripped through his skin like bright red shards of pottery. His muffled screams were incoherent wails. I crushed his spine and his ribs and still he bucked and wept.

I rolled him onto his back, seeing he yet lived. William's blood keeping him alive and awake beyond what mortal men can endure. Still, he cried and begged me to stop so I smashed his jaw and teeth into a quivering mass that tumbled into his throat and stoppered his screams. And still he writhed around, living through an ordeal. I thought to leave him like that. I even considered trickling blood into his ruined throat to see if I could prolong his torment. But as I looked about for a cup and a likely body, I saw the archers and my other men staring at me in profound horror. At once, I found myself without the heart to continue torturing the man. I almost felt shame but not quite.

I turned to Jocelyn. "Even if it is a trap, our women will be in Mansfield. If not, they will be in this hunting lodge to the north. This place William names Eden. We should leave immediately."

Jocelyn stared back, dismay on his shadowed face. Confused for a moment, I looked around me.

My men were turned away from the violence I had done, their shoulders hunched, collected in small groups on the outskirts of the village. Jocelyn stared at me, Swein and Anselm were turned away.

I realised then that I had drunk from the body of Will Scarlet, in the open, in front of everyone. In front of Jocelyn, in front of Swein's archers. In front of Anselm Marshal. I had devoured blood before Roger de Lacy, Sir Guy, and their two surviving men. My wounds had healed before their eyes. No wonder they either stared at me or looked away in horror.

My secret was truly out. The stories told about me were revealed to be true.

I felt a wave of hot nausea before I realised that I did not care.

"Richard, it is almost dark," Jocelyn said, his face in shadow. I knew from his tone that he thought I had gone too far, that I had thrown away my future but in that moment, I cared not what Jocelyn thought.

"So?" I said. "We can travel at night, we have done so many times. It is imperative that we move quickly. Perhaps we can beat this trap before it is set."

"Richard," Jocelyn said, lowering his voice as he stepped up to me. "You may not know weakness or fatigue. Especially after gorging yourself on the blood of evil men. But every other man here does. We must rest. There are wounded to take care of. Not least your friend the sheriff. And Sir Guy."

"Fine," I said. "Swein, tell the men to take turns on watch. One or two up high, upon the thatch. The rest of them get fires going inside the houses. Eat, drink. Rest. We will leave well before dawn. We will need the darkness."

Swein exchanged a glance with Jocelyn and nodded to me, going off to carry out my instructions.

We dragged the bodies out of the village, separating the

sheriff's dead men from William's creatures, and led the nervous horses in.

My men lit the hearth fire in the largest of the abandoned house in Blidworth. Most of us gathered inside, to rest and eat. After checking the archers on watch at the edges of the village, I came inside and sat by the fire on low stools beside the sheriff and Guy. Both men stared at me, saying not a word. Roger seemed miserable, no doubt hurting physically but also wounded in his pride. He had failed in his rescue mission.

Roger was wounded all over. His mail had been pierced and rings torn apart into a gash at one shoulder. The way he held himself suggested that he had broken ribs and no doubt his skin would be a mottled, purple bruise from neck to ankle. If he ever made it back to Nottingham, he would be abed for a week or more.

"Roger," I said to the sheriff. "Before dawn, you will take your two surviving men back to Nottingham, along with Sir Guy."

My tone, perhaps, shocked him out of his silent contemplation and his wariness of me.

"I am the sheriff. You do not command me where to go, nor when. You vile fiend. How dare you?"

"Roger," I said. "You must understand that you will not be the sheriff for very much longer. The Marshal is Regent now. Your agreement with the archbishop, whatever its nature, has not worked in your interest. The Marshal will win the struggle for power. The archbishop will be dead. You will be removed from your post."

"Nonsense," Roger said to me. "Nonsense," he repeated to Sir Guy. "The archbishop has power that you cannot—" he stopped.

"Well, perhaps you can conceive of his power. But he is the richest man in the kingdom. He has—"

"He has made a pact with the devil," I said. "He has conspired with William de Ferrers, the Green Knight, this Lord of Eden, to murder King John by means of poison. The archbishop has schemed with you to grant William the run of the king's forest of Sherwood in return for what favours? Immortality for the Archbishop and riches for you. And for the hand of the Lady Marian. So cheaply bought, Roger? What else were you offered? A bright future for your children? A position at court? A castle or two?"

He twisted his face and mumbled. "And a divorce. He would free me to make Marian my wife."

I shook my head, amazed at his folly. "Well, it will all come to nothing. The only reason I have not killed you so far is because we were once friends. Or were we? Perhaps I was never anything to you. How long have you and Hugh been scheming like this? Since before John was king?"

"If you murder me," Roger said. "Then you would have to kill Sir Guy and my two men."

"Would I? Perhaps if I was going to remain a lord and a knight after all this, I suppose I would. You know, in fact, you will all spread the tales of my drinking blood, of my torturing a prisoner and the rest. I think it really would be best if I killed you all. By freeing you, I am only doing myself a disservice."

Roger failed to hold my gaze. "What do you demand in return for our silence?"

"Nothing," I said. "I will let you go because it is the

honourable thing to do."

They stared at me and traded looks.

"You are in league with the devil," Roger said, warily. "We all saw you. How can I believe you wish to act with honour?"

Sir Guy did not meet my eye but he nodded.

"You do not believe me but I am trying to be a good knight," I said. "And anyway, it does not matter what I do, your time as sheriff of any shire in England is over. The Regent will replace you. Do not worry, the Marshal is not a vindictive man. He will allow you to return to your lands and live. You, Sir Guy, will have to decide whether you stay in Nottingham. I am certain the new sheriff will want a man who knows the shire. Or perhaps Roger can find you some quiet employment on his own lands."

"I will tell them," Roger said, quivering with indignation or perhaps with fear. "I will tell everyone that are the monster everyone always said you were. I will swear, and so will my men, that we witnessed you murdering prisoners and drinking their blood. You will be charged with murder. Stripped of your lands but properly, this time."

I nodded. "You may say what you wish," I said. "They will not believe a disgraced man. But if they do, it does not matter to me. I do not want my lands. I am not going home. You have nothing to threaten me with, Roger. And I am done with you. Get some rest before you ride."

Roger de Lacy stared for a moment, gathering strength for an argument. Instead, he sighed.

"All this for a woman," he said. "A stupid, stuck up little girl holding on to her precious maidenhead as if it was the Holy Grail.

The Green Knight can have her, the filthy little bitch."

My mailed fist smashed his face and threw him down. I felt the bones of his cheeks crack and a number of his teeth break loose.

When I left before dawn, Roger was breathing but had not woken. His face appeared to be rather a mess. Sir Guy swore he would take Roger back to Nottingham, though it was doubtful de Lacy would be much use for anything ever again.

"You know," I said to Guy as I mounted. "That was a courageous charge you made for your friend."

"Bloody stupid," Guy said, rubbing his neck. "You evil bastards have the strength of the devil."

"That we do."

We rode north, for Mansfield. The village of the giant they called Little John. The man who had taken Marian and Eva. The man who waited for me and my men to come to him.

I was going to cut off his head and I was going to drink from his severed neck. And I was going to do it before my men, not caring that the rumours would get back to the lords of the land.

For what I had said to Roger was true. I knew that once I had gone into the depths of Sherwood that there would be no going back for me. For years, I had denied it but I was not a knight like any other and I could keep up the lie no longer. After I killed William and destroyed his followers I would leave England forever.

THIRTEEN ~
HEART OF EDEN

"SURELY, THIS ENTIRE ABDUCTION WAS meant as a means of luring you into Sherwood?" Jocelyn said as we rode slowly in the darkness, his voice low. "All of us, in fact. Of killing all of us in a single attack. There must be a better way of approaching this problem."

We rode in almost complete darkness, finding our way down the path to Mansfield by feeling the overgrown hedgerows on either side of the road.

"I would have been in Sherwood a year ago if the archbishop had not kept me away," I said. "Him sending me away was for William's purposes. Taking Marian and Eva, I do not know what that could be other than a warning, or as a means of staying my hand should I corner him once more."

Jocelyn's voice grew louder. "That man you tortured told you explicitly that the ladies are bait on a hook."

"He was a fool and a liar," I said, whispering. Our horses were so close that our knees bashed together. "We can trust nothing that he said."

"You will believe anything so long as you think it leads to your vengeance."

"Our vengeance, yes," I said. "Yours and mine both."

"Even if it means risking Marian's life? And Eva's?" Jocelyn was as impassioned as he could be while keeping his voice down.

"William knows that by taking her, harming her, he will enrage you into attacking him," Jocelyn said. "And we are."

"If he was going to kill them, why not do it at the Priory? Or anywhere else and leave the bodies to be found? And why would their deaths enrage me? Marian is a dear girl and I know you are smitten with her but she is hardly anything to me. And Eva. She shares her bed with me but not her heart."

"Come now," Jocelyn said. "You care for that woman much more than that."

"Perhaps," I said, for of course I cared for her. "But William cannot know that."

"William knows you will come to rescue a lady in distress," Jocelyn said. "You said that even when you were a boy, you always loved the ballads where the knight rescues the lady. William knows that you came for me and Emma in Palestine. He is playing you like a harp, Richard. Both of us. We are riding directly to where he wants us to go."

"I do not say you are wrong," I said. "But what else can we do?"

"All I want," Jocelyn said. "Is to get Marian back. I do not care if she decides against marrying me. Who can blame her? Who can blame her when I have so little to offer for our future? But I must do this thing. And not because it is like living some blasted ballad or poem, do not say it is. I do not wish to be a tragic hero and I do not expect her to throw herself into my arms. But I do care for her. I do. Truly. And I will get her back. I will save her. No matter the cost."

Our men ahead slowed down and we reined in a little

"You know," I said. "I have been thinking about my own future."

"You do wish to marry Eva," he said. "I knew it."

"No," I said, even though I would rather have liked to do so. But she was better off without me. "Far from it."

"What future, then?" Jocelyn asked, shifting in his saddle.

"I must move on," I said. "After I kill William. And the archbishop. I shall have to go away. Take the cross, perhaps. And I was thinking that I would renounce my claim to Ashbury. You will get the place anyway, when I am dead, you are my heir and you have been since soon after you came to me."

"For God's sake," Jocelyn whispered. "Do not throw your future away for me."

"You are a good man," I said, for I knew he wanted Ashbury. "But unless I fall in battle, I will not die. Never, Jocelyn, do you not see? I will never age. How long will my servants put up with me? Leaving will be for the best, that much I have decided. And of course, Ashbury must go to you. Just promise me that you will take care of your sister. And please take care of the servants, the labourers, and the village. Or allow Emma to do it until you find her a good husband and then let Marian do it after she marries you."

Jocelyn grunted. "I pray we find her soon. Wait, what should I do about Tutbury Priory?" he asked.

"You may pull down the Priory, stone by stone," I said.

He chuckled. "You cannot mean to give me Ashbury, Richard," Jocelyn said quietly though he could not keep the excitement from his voice.

"I do. And I will," I said. "I have decided. You will have the wealth and position you need to get a good wife. The Regent knows you, he will use you well. You can get a knight or two of your own, take on a couple of squires, a page, a groom, a servant. Your very own shit-bucket carrier. Everything a country gentleman needs to live a full and proper life."

"Richard," he mumbled. "I do not know what to say."

"No need to say anything," I said. "Even just thinking about it has made me feel happy. We will get the women back, kill William, I will go away and then everything will be right in the world."

Swein, ahead of us, held his horses on the side of the road until he was abreast of us, a dark shape against the darker background.

"Perhaps I can make a suggestion about how to attack the village of Mansfield, Sir Richard."

"Oh," Jocelyn said, his words full of his smile. "The peasant has been studying strategy."

"I have," Swein shot back. "Studying by observing William of Cassingham. Perhaps if you yourself had—"

"Enough," I said, tired. "What do you suggest, Swein?"

"You mean to ride into Mansfield at dawn, with all our forces surrounding the village and trap Little John and his men. But that way risks Marian's life. And Eva's. They can hold a knife to Marian's throat and we will be able to do nothing about it."

"You see another way?" I asked. Stratagems always intrigued me because I could never think of any by myself.

Swein's voice grew excited in the darkness. "Why not send in a single man, or perhaps a pair, disguised as beggars. Or monks? Or some other sort of travelling folk, perhaps a man selling pots. That way we can discover the lay of the land, the positions of the enemy and where the women are being held. Then we leave and relay said whereabouts back to you, my lord. That way, we could creep in tomorrow night, snatch the women and flee with them without notice. We can ride hard for Nottingham or some other place of safety. Lincoln, maybe. Hide the women with Anselm's father or some other great lord. Then we can go back for the Green Knight."

I waited for Jocelyn to pour scorn upon the suggestions, yet he did not.

"I commend you for your creativity, Swein," I said. "And your ideas might work against mortal men. But we are facing men who can see and hear and smell better than you. And these blood drinkers would see a stranger as a walking meal. A beggar or pot seller wandering into their village at dawn would be nothing more to them than a pleasing way to break their night's fast. And if we took the women and attempted to flee then they would catch us. A mortal man could outpace a horse over a day in a woodland such as this. These men could catch us before we got away from Sherwood."

Swein took a deep breath, ready to object and to argue for his ideas. I spoke over him as he began.

"Yet you make some good suggestions. You have a natural capacity for cunning and no doubt have a long future ahead of you as an outlaw. Let us push on. In order to do what must be done, we need to be at Mansfield before it is light. And dawn approaches."

∞

I crept through the shadows between houses just as a rosy dawn grew in the east. I would have been quieter without my armour and I would have seen and heard better without my helm but I simply could not bring myself to go without either.

The village of Mansfield was quiet. Like Blidworth and Linby, the folk were clearly dead, enslaved, or terrified into silence and abject misery. The houses were quiet. The few fires, from the faint smell of the dry smoke, were burning low. There were no animals in the pens by the houses. There were few crops growing in the gardens. The middens still stank, of shit and rot, corpses and old blood.

Jocelyn and Swein had both argued that it should be them sneaking in alone. Or that I should take archers with me, at least one or two, who could watch my back while I stole back the women.

Once, months before, Jocelyn had accused me of being so arrogant that it bordered on madness. Confidence turns to arrogance when your view of yourself becomes warped beyond truth. It becomes madness when your view of the world itself is warped and that night, my madness had reached a new height. I told my men that I alone was strong enough to fight my way out if anything went wrong. I believed that no man, not even William's men, could stand against me. Had I not proved myself better than them at every turn? What a ludicrous notion.

My anger and my fear played their part in robbing me of my reason. My anger at William and his men for taking Eva and Marian paled in comparison to the anger I felt at myself for putting them at risk. My fear that they would be hurt was almost overwhelming. That fear was greater than I was willing to admit even to myself.

Secretly, I was also hoping that I could find and rescue both women by myself. It would be a way of redeeming myself to both of the women and to myself but I did not admit such vanity to my men, of course. So I browbeat their objections down and, like a mad fool, went into the village alone.

The top of the church caught the first dim light of the morning, the sandstone glowing softly as if catching the light from the air. The door was half bashed in, hanging awkwardly, like a broken tooth.

If Much had been telling the truth, that was where they were.

I picked my way carefully, slowly. Breathing lightly, still I could hear my own breath hot in my ears. Every step I took further into the centre of the place, the more I doubted that Marian and Eva could truly be held inside.

What did William want from me? What was I walking into? I realised that, whether riding into the village at daylight or sneaking through in the dark, I had been drawn into William's web once again. But how could I do anything different? What move could I make that would confound him?

But why did I even need to? I had been caught up in the schemes of Swein. That lad admired and aspired to cleverness. To stratagems and gambits.

I did not. I wanted the women back. William — or his man John — had them.

All I need do was kill any man who stood in my way.

I kicked down the wattle fence before me and strode into the village.

The black rectangle of the church door beckoned. I jogged up the steps and yanked open the broken door, which gave with a shriek of wood on wood, loud and jagged enough to wake the dead.

Inside was dark. It reeked of death. Of rotting flesh and blood that was fresh.

Muffled movement at the far end.

Ambushers or prisoners, either way, the makers of the noise had to be approached. I stepped forward and there came a cry, a stifled cry from that end.

The blackness at my feet was complete. My helm restricted my sight even further. I held my shield up and strode forward, sword point before me.

A woman's voice, her throat tight with terror, cried out.

"Help!"

She was at the far end of the church and I ran forward toward it.

And I tripped.

Like a blundering fool, like a child in a game, I tripped over a rope set for the purpose. It caught on my ankle and my momentum carried me forward and down.

I fell hard on my shield.

Then they were on me.

William's men sprung from the darkness on either side, with a weighted net and ropes at the ready. They struck blows on my back and my head with sticks and bludgeons and staves, over and over.

My sword was not in my hand when I swung it, so instead I swung my fists. I struck out with my feet, my elbows. But they were so many and I was struck about the head so often that their blows knocked me senseless.

I fought, of course. Though I was blinded and knew not which way was up, I wrestled and thrashed and heaved and struck down one after the other.

But the men set upon me were freshly fed with the living blood of the villagers. I was dragged out into the street.

A knife found its way to my throat. The cold iron nicked my skin, drawing blood and searched around under my jaw.

I was utterly certain my throat was to be cut. My final thoughts were wondering what my final thoughts were going to be, and thinking about how paltry those thoughts were. I wondered if I should instead think of my wife or her children, Jocelyn and

Emma but I thought of how I had failed them all and failed the two women I had set out to rescue and I hoped that Swein, Anselm, and the men would get away.

But the knife instead sawed away at my chinstrap and my helm was twisted from my head. I blinked in the slight glare of the predawn sky.

There was a great giant of a man there before me. A head taller and twice as wide as I.

"He said you was a great knight," the huge man said. "He said you was to be feared. Never to be fought, not even a score of the sons of Adam could face you. But I know knights. You all want to save a lady from a dragon, don't you? Well, I'm the dragon. And you ain't saving no one, my lord."

With his giant's strength, made unnaturally strong by William's gift, he brought a cudgel down onto the back of my head.

∞

When I awoke, I was on my back, on the cold ground.

My head was throbbing with every breath. It felt as though my skull was caved in at the back. A tender mass of broken bone shards and swollen skin.

There were men around me, voices, the stench of blood and death.

It was dark, still. But the sky above was pink with the morning and quickly turning to blue.

I was in chains.

They clanked as I raised my hands to feel my head only to find my hands bound to my body. My legs were likewise wrapped.

My mouth was stoppered with a rag tied tight.

"He lives," a man's voice said.

"Thank the Creator for that," another man said and I was kicked in the side of the head.

The pain shot through me. I ached all over and wondered if my arms and legs were broken. My sight was impaired in some way as the figures around me were blurred and smeared. I realised I had blood in my eyes but I could not move my hands up to wipe my face.

Still, I saw the big man move into view above me. He faced away from me, down the street and bellowed.

"You men out there. As I'm sure you can see, I have your master Richard of Ashbury in chains. Attack me or any of my men and I will slit his throat. I see a single arrow. I hear the twang of a single bow. I slit his throat. I see one of you following us, I slit his throat."

The big man, Little John the Bailiff, turned and mumbled to one of the other figures.

I guessed there were at least a dozen men around me and a few moved off toward the church.

Jocelyn would not give up on me, I thought, he would not back down. Neither would Anselm. They would keep their distance.

Swein and his archers, I did not know what they would do.

Swein wanted revenge for the hurts he had suffered at the hands of the men about me, or their friends. Whether he would seek to avenge me when it was a lost cause, I could not guess.

But Jocelyn, surely, would attempt to save Marian and Eva, no matter if I were dead or alive.

Two women were dragged from the church. I could not see properly but both had heavy hoods tied down over their faces. They had been dressed in filthy old robes. The women whimpered under their hoods as they were brought to Little John.

I writhed and tried to sit up but the men guarding me struck me and a filthy old man sat upon my chest, a rusty dagger held to my throat.

"You want these women?" the giant shouted out. He glanced at me and grinned through his thick, black beard. "You want both these women, do you not?" He laughed. "You follow me and both of them will get this."

John grabbed the woman nearest to him and wrapped one mighty arm about her from behind. With his other hand, he stabbed a knife up into her throat and sawed back and forth.

Rolling over, I threw off the old man on my chest, his dagger slicing deep into my cheek, all the way through until it clashed against my teeth. But the other men pinned me down, held me on the ground and allowed me to watch the murder.

Blood gushed from beneath her hood. It poured out, soaking John's arm and the woman's robe. Her body sagged against him and he held her to him.

A great cry of anguish sounded from outside the village.

Jocelyn or Swein watching from afar, afraid that it was Marian rather than Eva. We always fear the worst, when those we love are concerned.

Little John shoved the body of the woman into the hands of his men, who gathered about her with two buckets. They between them held her upright, pulling her hooded head back so that the blood spurted into the buckets. When the pulse faltered, they picked her up and held her body so that the feet were higher than the head, draining as much as they could.

"Can we string her up, John?" one of the men said.

"No," John said, his voice like the falling of a tombstone. "We ride for Eden. Bring the body."

I was picked up by rough hands and heaved onto the back of a horse, face down and I was tied onto the beast.

The woman who yet lived was wrestled onto a waiting horse and slapped around until she ceased struggling and complied.

The body of the woman was tied onto another horse near me. As they tossed her on, the horse shied away and the body slipped. They grabbed it and shoved it back on top with a stream of curses. The hood fell away for a moment.

As the men and horses filed out of the village of Mansfield, with me along with them, I knew I had failed. The feeling was worse than any wound I had suffered.

But in any case, the woman who had been stabbed was not Eva.

And it was not Marian, either.

Little John had murdered some other woman, for my watching men's benefit. What it meant, I knew not. Perhaps Eva and Marian both lived. Or perhaps they were already dead.

It seemed I was being taken to William and to the place they called Eden.

∞

I had imagined myself storming William's lair. In my fantasies, I had been sometimes alone, sometimes charging at the head of a mounted band or with archers' arrows flying past me to bury themselves into William's monsters.

Never had I expected to be dragged there in chains.

My wounds were bad. My skull pounded with every step of the horse.

To distract myself, I attempted to count Little John's men by the sounds of their voices and the smell of them. Not all of them spoke and they all stank of blood, so it was difficult but there was a score, at least. The horse I was tied to was a swaybacked old mare with mud splattered all over her coat and shit all around her hindquarters.

The sun rose to its midday peak above the green leaves overhead. My view was of the track beneath the horse, her mud-caked hooves and a short way in front or behind at the men who had captured me. All flowed past me in a flickering of dappled sunlight. A jay's blue wings flashed as it swooped through the dappled splashes of sunlight.

Soon, the woodland gave way to open fields and then a hard-packed track surface. I must have dozed for a while and was woken by the horse's hooves clattering on flat cobblestones. I peered about me, wincing from the wounds, remembering my failure.

Our procession had reached a stone pathway, the surface was large, irregular pebbles with flat tops embedded into a hard surface. What we called a pitched path. It was quite common in castle courtyards or the homes of the wealthy but was completely strange in the middle of the wild greenwood.

Looking ahead, I was shocked. The trees all around me had thinned and ahead was a high timber wall across the path with an open gateway in the centre. It was a hunting lodge. One of the few I knew were deep in Sherwood that the king could use as a place to stay while he hunted deer and boar.

The lodge was a rambling stone and timber complex that seemed to grow from the wild profusion of vines and scrambling plants climbing over the walls. The woodland around it had been cut back, coppiced and cleared of brushwood but still the trees were huge, gnarled and ancient.

The men around me were strangely silent, the only sounds were of hooves and leather shoes upon the stone pathway that took us through the gate and into the huge courtyard of the lodge.

Pillars of limestone, carved at the top and bottom supported a gateway in a thick timber wall that stood at least ten feet high. The outer face of the wall was plastered and painted with leaf patterns though it was crumbling everywhere. The wall seemed to extend a long way in both directions before turning to make an enormous square enclosure. The weathered limestone columns had turned green and were pitted from the climbing vines around them.

"You are honoured, little man. As you pass through these

gates, you are leaving England. And you are entering Eden," Little John said from beside the old horse. I knew he was talking to me. "You will obey the law of this land or else I will have to punish you. I trust that you will behave yourself? Good, good."

Beyond the gateway, there was a massive open space, all of it paved with the solid pitched surface of flat cobbles. But filled with a great mass of living green plants. Servants tended to them. The cobbled surface had been pried up all over the place to reveal the soil beneath.

Ahead was the main hall, a long, low single storey building of stone on the bottom half and timber on the top.

Many of the other buildings were constructed similarly. To the right of the hall was a big storehouse or barn, roughly built but sturdy. Between the hall and the barn was a thick hedge of raspberry bushes, tangled and overgrown. Beyond the barn, I could just see the corner of what was clearly a huge stable.

The other side was obscured by the horse but I caught a glimpse of workshops. The walls of all the buildings were covered with vines and climbing plants.

It was tough to see far because everywhere was overflowing with plants, crops, bushes and trees.

John clapped me on the back with his meaty palm, hard enough to knock the wind from me and make my head swim.

Little John leaned down to speak into my ear, his hot breathing reeking of death. "We have a special place reserved just for you. Cost us a fair old bit of trouble, getting hold of all that iron. But then what my Green Lord wants, my Green Lord gets, right? Anyway, hope you like it, Sir Richard, as it's the last place you're ever going to live in. If you can call it living."

He laughed. A big, belly-shaking, rumbling laugh that scared birds from the trees above. His men laughed with him, the silent spell broken.

I was struck upon the back by clubs, wrestled from the horse, dumped onto the ground and struck again. Powerful hands dragged me to my feet. Blades were held to my throat and the men pushed me forward through the courtyard of the lodge complex.

I got a better look at the main building as they dragged me toward it. It was a squat hall built from the local sandstone with a timber and tile roof on top. Other buildings around the courtyard were a mix of timber and others stone.

The truly astonishing, peculiar thing was that beside and between all the structures was an abundance of green leaves. Overgrown hedges and sprawling young trees grew against every building. There were apple trees and wild raspberry bushes. Clumps of cereal crops were planted around lines of grape vines.

Before the front wall of the main hall was a wild garden of herbaceous plants and weeds. I recognised henbane, hemlock, monks' wood, foxglove, datura, and hellebore.

I could see little order to anything and the growth seemed overgrown and almost wild.

Throughout the enclosure, amongst the crops and herbs, were William's servants. Men, women, young and old. They were slumped like slaves, their faces pale and their eyes dark. They clutched hoes, rakes, and scythes to their chests, glancing up at us from under their eyebrows.

"Walk," William's men said and shoved me on through

398

toward the hall. Little John strode before me, sending the slaves scurrying in panic.

They dragged me into the building, yanking open the door. Instead of a grand open space, it was a long corridor down the centre with doors along each side and a single door at the far end.

"Guess what we got in here, then?" Little John shouted. He stomped past the first pair of doors then banged on the ones after, hard enough to rattle the beams locking them shut. "These are the cattle pens. Our cattle are the folk of Sherwood, the outlaws, the villagers. You hear me in there? They serve us or they feed us. Don't you?"

I prayed that Marian or Eva would be there but saw neither. Surely, if they lived, William would have a special place for them.

Although, I recalled how William had rounded up the locals in Palestine and penned them in a single large room underground. A young Jocelyn and Emma had been flung in with the Saracens and forgotten about. They were the children of a Frankish noblewoman and yet for William they had no more value than any of the other Saracens that he and his men used for harvesting blood.

Palestine was a land of war, a land of Saracen heathens who the Pope had declared enemies of God and Christ, so in a way, William's scouring of that land made a perverse kind of sense, to himself at least.

That he could get away with the same thing in the heart of England, making slaves and cattle of good Christians, astonished me.

Through the door at the far end of the corridor, they pushed, dragged and beat me down a stairway into a deeper darkness. It went down, under the ground. There were caves everywhere in Sherwood. It was one of the ways outlaws escaped detection and found shelter in the greenwood. The place Little John called Eden was built on limestone and the caves beneath the buildings were either natural or had been hacked out.

The roughly carved spiralling steps led down and down further. The stairs bottomed out into a short corridor carved from the limestone bedrock and they pushed and beat me along it. Little John squeezed his bulk through the cramped space and at the end he threw open a heavy door. I was beaten down again then dragged inside, leaving a trail of blood on the floor behind me.

The final room, our destination, was long, wide, low and carved directly from the limestone bedrock. The space was lit with lamps and candles in alcoves cut into the walls. All around, those walls were carved with shapes of acorns and oak leaves and attempts at rich, leafy woodland canopy. The leaves were arranged so that here and there, the gaps between appeared as pairs of eyes.

The chamber was dominated by a central altar. The top was a solid piece of thick, dark oak, like some kind of giant table top. It sat atop four wide limestone pillars. The wide edges of the altar were carved into the shapes of bones and skulls, arranged in the shapes of writhing bodies. The skulls eyes had their mouths opened as if they were crying out or perhaps preparing to sink their crazed grins into living flesh. The limestone pillars supporting the central oak altar top were carved like bones. Both the wood and the stone were stained with dark red and brown.

400

Lines were carved into the stone floor, long parallel lines, leading from one side of the room to near the altar, where there was a bowl-shaped pit cut from the floor. They were discoloured with a dark residue.

On the far side of the room beyond the altar was a heavy door with iron bands reinforcing it, of the kind used on a treasury, strong room or dungeon.

And there was a cage. On my side of the room, near the door that I had been dragged in through. A strongly built, black iron cage with wooden pillars at each corner holding it in place. The side of the cage was open.

It had been prepared for me.

They cracked me on the head again and set about stripping me of my armour. They took my hauberk, coif and all my mail, punching me repeatedly to keep me disoriented and weakened. They took my gambeson and all my padding. While I was yet dazed they threw me into the small cage.

"Do you like this?" Little John said. He banged the bars above my head. "We had it made just for you."

I looked at my cage. The flat iron lengths made a cage about five and a half feet tall and a couple of feet wide and deep. I could only stand with my head bent low, the top of my hunched shoulders touched the top of the cage. My shoulders were almost touching the bars of either side.

Outside, on each long edge, the cage was fixed to the floor and ceiling by sturdy oak pillars.

"I hope that you do like it," Little John said. "Because you will never leave this cage." He laughed, phlegm spraying past his black beard.

"When I get out of here I shall smash your face into pulp," I said. It hurt just to speak.

Little John laughed but his eyes were shining pits. "Here is your prisoner, my lord," he shouted, sneering.

The massive door at the far end of the room, beyond the central table, crashed open. A massive force had flung it open from the other side.

William.

My brother, my enemy, the man I was sworn to kill. He strode from the room beyond, wiping the corners of his mouth with a rag. His black hair had grown long and he had a neatly trimmed beard. He wore a dark green tunic, a white shirt underneath. He looked in the prime of his life, had not aged a day since I had seen him last, in a cave in Palestine. I had crushed his chest with a blow that sent him crashing across the room and set the place ablaze. William had escaped, from the cave, from the Holy Land and from my life.

And there he was again, standing behind the central altar, tall and straight, broad-shouldered and slim. The master of his domain. While I was filthy, beaten and hunched in a cage.

"Brother," he said, tossing a rag to one side. "Finally, you are here. I am relieved. You do not know how tiring it has been without you."

I had been waiting to face William for so long. Yet in my imaginings, it had been me in the position of power and William cringing in chains.

I found that I did not know what to say.

402

"Come, Richard," William said. "You must accustom yourself to the feeling of defeat." His voice had a sonorous, resonant tone that washed over you like a wave. He fixed you with an intense stare when he spoke. His men were all staring at him, transfixed by his every word.

"Just kill me quickly, will you," I said, wincing. "I do not think I can stand to listen to more of your mad ravings."

Little John smashed his huge fist into the bars of my cage, rattling the thing. "Mind your own words," he said. "Show respect. Or it'll be me smashing your face into to a pulp, tough man."

"John," William said, calmly. "There is no need for threats."

"But he won't even need his face to give us his—" John started.

"Silence!" William roared.

My ears rang in the silence that followed.

William continued in a softer voice. "Richard, you look quite broken. Please, rest for now. I shall have blood brought to you so you may heal."

"I would rather you choke on it," I said, though I wanted it. "I will have no part of your murders."

"Murders?" William said, as if shocked I could suggest such a thing. "Who ever said anything about murders? The blood is from the living, freely given."

"Freely given?" I said. "From those slaves out there? Spare me your lies."

"There are no slaves here in Eden," William said, spreading his arms wide. "This is Paradise upon Earth, brother."

"You have killed and murdered across the land," I said. "Your men have slaughtered and enslaved whole villages. You poisoned

403

the King of England, you mad fool. You have created a Hell upon the Earth. Just as you do everywhere you go." I took a shuddering breath. The back of my head, where John had cracked it, felt like it was made from porridge.

"I poisoned King John?" William said as if he was genuinely confused. "What on earth can you mean? It was the bloody flux, was it not?"

"You would know," I said, bitterly. "You, more than any man. The archbishop and you conspired. You poisoned King John or you sent a man to do it. I noticed your poisonous garden outside this place."

"Ah," he said, smiling. "Have you ever wondered why so many woodland plants are poisonous?"

"Wondered?" I said, not understanding the question. "God made it so."

William sighed, like a priest teaching me Latin. "Yes, Richard, but why?"

I was irritated. William had a way of twisting words and minds. Even mine. "You think you can know the mind of God?" I said.

"Of course," he spoke with sudden passion. "Why else would He create us in His image if not to know His mind? We must take back our rightful place, as lords over mankind."

"We?" I said.

"You and I are not made as are mortal men," William said. "God made us immortal, as was Adam in the Garden of Eden."

I had never paid much attention to the priests. "Adam was not immortal," I said.

"Of course he was," William said. "And how was Eve made?

From Adam's body, just as we make more like us from taking from inside of ourselves."

"We use blood," I said, astonished by the way he twisted the word of God to match his own mad needs. "Not our ribs."

"It is a story meant to reveal truth," William said, lecturing me in that priestly tone. "The sons of Adam lived for hundreds of years. Clearly, you and I are from the same stock. Neither of us has aged a day. Not a day since God brought us back. Since then we have both suffered wounds that would kill even the strongest man. I have gouged chunks of flesh from my own body and watched it grow back together. I have consumed gallons of poison, chewed deadly leaves and walked away."

I wished I could tear him apart. "Which of those plants did you use to kill your king?"

William threw up his hands. "My king? Mine? I swore no allegiance to that fool. Why should he have remained king when he could not hold on to his kingdom? I could protect England far better than he ever could. And, in fact, I will protect it. I shall be the greatest king that England has ever known. Imagine it, Richard, a strong crown year after year, decade after decade. I will rule for centuries and England will be the greatest land in Christendom. I will make the Pope one of my men. Imagine what I can do with the Saracens."

I stared at him in disbelief. His eyes seemed to shine with the flicker of the candlelight, boring into me, searching me, and almost pleading with me to see what he was seeing in his future.

"You are mad," I said. "You will be a king? The King of England? Absurd. You mean to poison so many lords that the

405

crown comes to you, is that it?"

"Hardly necessary. When I have built my army, with your blood, we will simply take the kingdom from the young Henry. Who can resist us?"

"The Marshal," I said. "Longspear, Ranulf of Chester."

"Oh, Richard," William said. "You have so much to learn. The Marshal is old and mortal. His alliances will fall when he does. I have many men in place, helping things along."

"Men like the Archbishop of York," I said. "I know you are working together."

William laughed. "Together? The fat fool has had his uses, though he has been misbehaving. Keeping you away from me, Richard. I think he is fond of you."

"What in God's name are you talking about?" I said.

William pursed his lips, looked around the room and pointedly ignored my question. "This is a sacred oak grove, Richard. An ancient place. A holy place."

"We are underground," I said, leaning back in my cage. What could I do but listen to his madness? "This is no grove."

"The roots of the oak are its strength," he said, indicating the sinewy carvings on the walls. "And in the oak is the strength of our faith."

"Madness," I said. "Just madness." There was blood in my mouth. I spat it out.

"Did you know that the Tree of Knowledge was the oak? Eve's knowledge was that from death comes life. She knew why the tree bore the fruit. So that it would live again, after death, just as you and I do, Richard. We are the children of Adam. You and I alone.

We are the inheritors of God's first creation."

"You and I are?" I said. "Is that why you freely murder everyone else?"

William nodded. "Those that take on our blood after losing their own become sons of Adam also."

"Your man Much the Miller told me. As did Tuck. Before I killed them, as I killed so many of your precious sons of Adam. And when I get out of this cage I will kill everyone else here. Then I will kill you."

He stared at me for a long moment.

Then he laughed.

William ran his fingers over the surface of the thick oak top to the central table before him. It was a huge thing, dark and solid as iron, three inches thick. Only God knew where he had got such a thing but it was as thick as a castle gate.

"Here is the altar where we both reap and sow our gift of blood," he said, his voice resonating and echoing from the walls. "Sin is poured out here at the Altar of Oak and the blood of Adam is given in its place."

"Come closer," I said. "Come and open these bars and I will drink yours again. Then you shall reap what evil you have sowed."

"Oh?" William started as if I had wounded his heart. "And what evil have I sowed?"

I laughed in disbelief. "King John, for one."

William shrugged. "What is a mortal man compared to us, Richard? We are the inheritors of Adam's gift. God has renewed His gift, through us. Only, you refuse to recognise the truth. You persist in your attempts to live as a knight and a lord of your pathetic manor. Why is your ambition so small? You could join me and together we could take a kingdom and remake the Garden upon the earth. And yet you never will. So this is how I must use you. In a cage. I will use you. Use your blood. I pray that you never forget that you brought this on yourself."

I stared at him, feeling tired. Tired and close to defeated. "You may believe that nonsense. Use me? Never. I will not allow it."

William tilted his head. "You do look weak. You have not been drinking enough blood, have you, Richard. Enough for now. You are tired. So rest, drink as much blood as you can stomach. It is important that you are healed and that you stay strong. I will have it brought to you. See to it, will you, John?"

William turned to leave.

"My lord," Little John said, taking a hesitant step forward. "I must speak to you privately."

William turned back. "You may speak in front of my little brother," William said. "After all, what can he do from in there?"

John nodded his huge skull. "His men followed us through the greenwood."

A thrill surged through me at his words. Of course, my men would not abandon me. Thank God for Jocelyn.

"So?" William said.

"Well," John replied. "It is just that they are out there right now, my lord, keeping watch on us."

"And what exactly do you think they can do to us?" William asked, laughing. "Do you believe them to be a threat?"

"There are a dozen or more. A score, perhaps. Who knows what mischief they could get up to? They could take one of my men on the road. Or they could go and tell the location of Eden."

"Tell?" William asked, glancing at my cage as if inviting me to join in mocking John's ignorance. "Who would they tell?"

"Don't know," John shrugged, looking down. "The Marshal?"

William sneered. "That old man is not long for this world," he said. "But I know how much you love to kill, John, dear boy. Go and murder Richard's men. Kill all you like, drink them up. If you feel like bringing back prisoners then we can always use more soldiers or cattle for our pens."

John nodded and turned to leave, as did William, in the opposite direction.

I knew Jocelyn and Anselm, Swein and his archers were fine fighters. But they had no hope against men imbued with William's blood.

My men were as good as dead.

"William, wait," I shouted, heaving on the bars, ignoring the pain from my bruised limbs. "What is the meaning of all this? Why not just kill me now? Do you mean to torture me? Why am I here?"

William turned back, sighing as though I greatly inconvenienced him.

"Why are you so dense, Richard? How can you be so quick of limb but slow of mind? I am tired,' William said. "I am so tired of giving up my blood to make more of my faithful men. But your blood is the same as mine. We grew from the same seed and our blood is the stuff of eternal life. Now I finally have you. You were meant to come last year. I sent a bunch of bumbling incompetents right to your door so that would you find your way to me. And then our friend Archbishop Hugh stuck his fat face in between us and sent you far away. He knew I wanted you. He was trying to strong-arm me, can you imagine? I will show him soon enough."

I stared at him. "I had forgotten that you were always mad. Your words are nonsense. Forget I asked."

William shook his head. "I have taken one of Hugh's bastard daughters. His favourite, by all accounts. But you know the woman I mean, do you not, Richard? You came running here for her, just as her father will. It took a long time but praise God, you have returned to me. Now I can extract all the blood I want from you and use it to build my army. We will pour good, clean blood down your throat by day and by night we shall milk you dry, brother. Rejoice, for from your lifeblood, from your gift, you will make an army the likes of which the world has never known. We will take the North, we will take the boy king and then his kingdom. Now, is that clear enough? Ah, but I get ahead of myself. Please, sit, rest. I will have your food and blood brought in. See to it, won't you, John?"

William nodded, strode back through his heavy, iron-bound door and slammed it shut behind him.

Before he did so, he called into the dark chamber beyond.

"A thousand apologies. Now, where were we, Lady Marian?"

410

FOURTEEN ~ TREE OF KNOWLEDGE

MY CAGE WAS STRONGER THAN I. The bars were flattened iron strips, half an inch thick. They crisscrossed each other so close that they formed squares barely wider than my fist. Where they crossed, they were riveted together.

As soon as I was alone, I gripped every piece of iron in that cage in turn, pushed, heaved, and sweated trying to bend it. I braced my shoulders against one side and pushed at the other with my arms, feet, knees.

The small door was the most obvious weak point. But the cunning smiths had reinforced that section. The hinges were hidden behind plates on the outside of the bars. The door overlapped the bars perfectly and the bolts securing it ran the whole depth and width of the cage where they were locked into the stone floor and the timbers on either side.

Nothing would budge.

All I managed was to tear off a couple of the more important fingernails and leave my shoulders and hands bruised.

I sat. The strips of bars on the bottom fitted into recessed, carved sections in the stone floor.

There were other lines carved into the stone, lines that ran from the cage floor and out into the cave, meeting in a carved depression by the table in the centre.

I wondered what they had been thinking of constructing when those lines hard been carved into the stone. Perhaps, I thought, they had intended a larger cage or one with a triangular point stretching in front but I could not conceive why they would do such a thing.

As I have mentioned before, I have no gift for creative thinking, nor logic neither.

All I really noticed was that the base of my cage was comfortable and I settled into it.

Little John said the thing had been made especially for me. I supposed I should have felt honoured to require such a thoroughly impregnable gaol.

I strained to hear of any noise coming from the room beyond, where William had called out to Marian. Had he been making a jest, in order to wound me? If Marian was in there, where was Eva?

William had said he held her so that her father would come to save her. But why would he? She had betrayed him by fleeing with me and staying by my side and in my bed. Surely, he would not come to save her.

Unless, she had never betrayed him at all. Perhaps Jocelyn had been correct. Perhaps Eva had always been spying on me for the archbishop, sending to him messages of my whereabouts and intentions.

But I could make no sense of it.

I reflected upon my own stupidity for some time. I considered carefully how inadequate was my ability for planning. I ruminated on the sour knowledge that I had only ever succeeded in ventures requiring a sword and shield and an enemy standing directly before me.

Jocelyn was not a complicated man but I was sure even he could outwit me. Anselm came from the best stock yet retained a perplexing innocence, even in the face of brutality and the knowledge that I was an unnatural, blood-drinking fiend. The lad was a fine squire but his trusting nature meant that a commoner like Swein could bend Anselm's ear on the supposed plight of the common man and the lad's heart would bleed for the imagined suffering. And even such a credulous fool as he was a wiser man than I.

And Swein. A man of no more than eighteen years, who had received no education, no training of any sort other than the bow and probably the plough until a year before. Even a man such as he possessed greater skill at reading men's intentions that did I, a lord over twice his age, with decades of fighting experience.

There was no way out for me. If they ever opened the cage door, I could attempt to fight my way out and I would. But I had no illusions they would be taking chances with me.

Upon stripping my armour and weapons, they had also removed every sharp object from about my person, so puncturing a large vein and bleeding my precious blood everywhere was out of the question. I was relieved because I had no desire to take my own life. I wanted to live. I still wanted to kill William. It was the only thing I had left.

I rubbed my wrist against the edge of the bar in front of me. Perhaps I could grind the skin away until I bled enough that they would remove me from the cage and then I would fight my way free. But the edges of the flattened bars had been forged or hammered or ground smooth.

Defeated once again, I slept.

When I woke, it was to the sight and feel of sword blades held against my throat. The blades had been eased between the bars by three of William's men, their faces leering down at me.

"What are you doing?" I asked, holding perfectly still.

"Don't you try nothing," one said, in an almost incomprehensible northern dialect. He was probably Cumbrian, which was barely one step up from a Scotchman.

"What could I possibly try?" I asked, astonished that they would send in three men who were clearly slower and dimmer than even I was.

"We know you're a tricky one, lord," one of the others said, a young lad no more than fourteen.

The third man, older, nudged him, hissing. "You don't got to call no one lord in Eden, Nobby."

"Oh, right you are, Sid."

The first man, their leader, cleared his throat to gain the upper hand. "You hold still while we feed you, right?" He nodded at the boy, Nobby, who withdrew his sword and bent away behind myself and came back holding a basket.

"Here you go, lord," Nobby said.

"He can't see it," Sid said. "And he ain't no lord, not no more."

Nobby giggled.

"So," I said. "You're the mighty soldiers of your lord William's great army, are you?"

Nobby grinned.

"We are," Sid said. "Or we will be when we're turned into sons of Adam."

"He's making mock," the first man, the Cumbrian said. "You might be a lord and all. But Big John said you can't talk to us like that."

He pressed the point of his blade against my Adam's apple. I pushed my head against the bars and twisted away but I had nowhere to go and he drew blood. There was a look in his eye that suggested an inability to control himself.

I grabbed his blade with both hands and pushed up as hard as I could.

The blade bent where it met the underside of the bar. It bent a long way and then snapped, clattering to the floor of my cage. I swept it up, holding the half-blade in my bare hand.

I shoved it through bars of the cage and on through the Cumbrian's neck before he could jerk away.

Sid swung his own sword from out and sent my broken blade crashing down, out of reach beyond my cage.

We all watched as the Cumbrian held his hands to his throat, that familiar confused expression on his face as the hot blood flowed out through his fingers. The smell filled the air along with

415

the cries of his fellow.

"What are you doing?" William was out of his room, charging over to my cage around the central altar. "What in the name of God are you cretins doing?"

"John asked us to feed the prisoner," Sid said. "Little John, so it was. He said to keep the lord under our sword points while we gave him his food. But he done broke Tom's sword and shoved it up him."

"So I see." William looked at me as if I was a misbehaving child. "Well, get a bucket under him before we lose it all in the floor. Tom, can you hear me, Tom? Do not look so worried. Once you die, you shall finally be one of us. You should rejoice. Look at me, Tom, you will die and then you will live forever. Let yourself go, brother."

"Why save his life?" I said, standing as best I could in my cage. "Let the fool die. He is incompetent. Is this the sort of man you wish serving you? He is not worthy of my blood."

The giant, Little John lumbered in, ducking under the lumpy, rock-hewn ceiling.

"Incompetent?" William said. "He is a little too keen for my favour but that is no bad thing. You were loyal, Tom, were you not? Why would you kill this man, Richard?" William eased the man to the floor as he spoke. Tom yet held his hands to his throat, though the life in his eyes was fading. "He was bringing you food. He was helping you. That is it, Tom, let yourself die, there's a good man. Do you know, Richard, why you killed him?"

"He is your sworn man," I said. "That is enough."

"You killed him because you are a murderer," William said.

416

"Just as much as I am. Only, I am also a creator. I am building a new world, a new Eden. Without me, all you can do is destroy. I am helping you."

"You are building a manor in the king's wood," I said. "And filling it with slaves. Do not delude yourself that you are doing anything great."

"Have you not seen our Eden?" William said, indicating the world above us. "I have made my own Garden, as described in the Book of Genesis. The Lord God made all kinds of trees grow out of the ground. Trees that were pleasing to the eye and good for food. In the middle of the garden were the tree of life and the tree of the knowledge of good and evil. Well, we have trees aplenty but the tree of life is here, it is our blood. The tree of knowledge is that which we grow in ourselves."

"This is no Eden," I said. "This is a hunting lodge, belonging to some baron that you have ousted. Growing crops, all crammed inside the gates, does not make an Eden."

"There were the four rivers of Eden and we have our own four around our Eden here. We have our Pishon, Gihon, our Tigris, and Euphrates."

"You mean the rivers of Sherwood?" I asked. "You have utterly lost your mind."

"No," William said. "It is you who has failed to grasp what we can make of this place. This wild place, where those from the world of men fear to enter. We who dwell here live as Adam did in the Garden. Without sin, without death, without fear."

"Without sin? All that you do here is sin."

William shook his head. "John, draw us plenty of blood out

of Richard. This will be as perfect a time as any to do this."

"To do what?" I asked but I knew, really.

"Lash Tom to the altar," William commanded and the men that crowded the small room lifted up and then eased the dying form of Tom the Cumbrian onto the table in the centre of the room.

Little John leaned his face against my cage. "I don't suppose you will be going to give up your blood willingly, this first time?" His voice rumbled low, from deep within his guts.

"Try to take it," I warned him. "Open my cage and you shall see what happens."

"Ah," Little John said. "I do so enjoy fighting talk." He laughed and grabbed a short spear from one of his men. "Come on lads, time to earn your keep again."

"I will shove those spears up your arses," I said, as the men with spears manoeuvred themselves about my cage. My heart raced, watching the iron spearheads catching the lamplight.

They thrust through the bars from all angles. There was little I could do to stop them though I made as good a fight of it as I could. It was not a matter of will, or strength or speed. I was so very limited by the manner of my confinement. It was, indeed, a matter of geometry.

With my palm, I broke the shaft of the first spear that lanced through toward my chest. But I was stabbed in the back.

I pinned another spear against the bars with my shoulder but another gouged out a lump from my thigh.

I was speared through the shoulder, the legs. Blades sliced my scalp and my chest.

418

The pain was white fire, slashing through my flesh. I was cut a dozen times. I growled, shouted, and slammed against the bars, swearing I would kill them all.

They laughed and stabbed me again.

"Enough," William's voice crashed over their jeering. "We have enough."

They stepped away, clapping each other on the back for their good work. I hunched on all fours in the bottom of my cage, watching the blood drip from the wounds of my head. The drops splashed down between my hands into the shallow pool of blood under me, dark red on sandstone and black iron. My breath would only come with my chest juddering, betraying the weakness and despair I felt.

The blood pooling under me ran into the carved lines in the floor. The blood collected in them, like drainage ditches or gutters, then rolled, and flowed through the bars out into the cavern.

Of course, that was what they were. Channels, catching the blood and funnelling it away from me and into a bowl-shaped depression carved low into the floor by the table.

Upon the table Tom, the Cumbrian lay dead, or as close to it as made no difference. His throat was destroyed and the skin of his face was white as chalk. Tom did move, his fingers flexing and his mouth gaping open and closed like a fish slowly suffocating upon the riverbank. The huge, solid oak table was drenched with his blood.

William himself kneeled by the pool that collected my own and scooped out a cupful. The cup he used was wooden, ornately carved with intertwining oak and vine leaves, big enough to hold

419

a pint or more.

"Behold," William said to me, holding the cup up. He moved to the other side of the table. "Hold him," William said to his men. "We must move quickly while he retains the strength to drink."

William held up the back of Tom's head and gently poured the blood into Tom's mouth.

The Cumbrian coughed and blood — my blood — sprayed out of his mouth but William continued pouring, holding Tom's head. Other men held him down and ropes wrapped around him at chest, hip and knee. Still, Tom writhed and still William poured it in, his face as rapturously proud as a mother spooning porridge into her baby's mouth.

"Dear God of Eden," William said, his sonorous, echoing off the carved stone walls. "The God of the Green. The God of the oak and the vine. The God of the rivers and the earth. Take this acolyte upon your holy altar and find him worthy of your gift. The Oaken Altar, carved from the Tree of Knowledge, is ready to accept this sacrifice. This man has given his essence and poured out his sin here at the Altar of Oak in the place of the blood. The sacrifice of his life and his blood is offered up to you, freely. We pray to you, the God of the Green, that you sanctify his sacrifice with the gift of eternal life so we may welcome this man who is called Tom into our brotherhood and into our immortal band as a son of Adam."

When all was gone, Tom fell back, twisting in his bindings.

William peered at Tom and then pointed at me. "We must have more blood," he said.

For a long moment, I was afraid they would slash me open further. But my blood had not stopped flowing. My shirt was drenched with it. It ran down my arms and down my legs, into the channels and the bowl by the table was filling up.

Twice more, William poured a pint of my blood into Tom until finally, William was satisfied. He stepped back, wiping his bloodied hands on his bloodied tunic.

"That should do it," he said. "Now, we wait."

I looked up across the room, holding myself still so my wounds would not gape open and further. My breathing was loud in the small space. My head ached. I had a raging thirst.

"That was not such a bad thing, was it, Richard?" William said. "You do look quite a mess. I shall have my men bring you water and so on. See to it, John. And now, Richard, you will watch the magic that our blood works. Our blood, with its power to bring life to the dead. To raise them up to be stronger, faster, all but invincible. And immortal."

"You make them like us," I said, my voice weak, for I knew from Tuck some of what was done.

It struck me, then, how what I had inflicted on Tuck and Sir Geoffrey—the rapist Frenchman who had been my prisoner in the Weald—was in some way being revisited upon me. It was God's punishment for my crimes. A man who injures his countryman, as he has done, so shall it be done upon him. Fracture for fracture, eye for an eye, blood for blood. It was the Lord's justice but I had brought it down upon myself.

"I make them almost like us, brother, almost," William said, a small smile in the corner of his mouth. "Our blood fills up their veins, once their own are emptied. They will not age, it is true, if they ever wake from their slumber. Sadly, they must then consume blood themselves or else they will die. One day, I shall discover a means of freeing them from such bonds. But until then, we must feed every man with blood every other day, or he begins to lose his strength. In a week or so, he will die. That is why we must keep these people in the pens above. We have tried the blood of pigs and cows and sheep and goat but nothing works, not fully. Human blood. It must be. So to build my army I must build my feedstock. A man slaughtered and drained will provide seven or eight pints but he can do so only once. From a living man, we can draw off a couple of pints every other day. It is a wonderful system. One blood slave can feed one of my men, day after day. Is it not wonderful? Do you see what we can do here? What we can do to all England? We have no limit on what we can accomplish. But it all starts here, in Eden. So you shall heal and grow strong and then we shall speak again."

William nodded, smirked and strode back through into his chamber beyond and slammed the heavy door shut behind him.

They brought me water, wine and cloth to wipe some of the blood from myself. I took it all without fighting, for I needed it.

"Here," John said, thrusting another cup through the bars.

I took it without thinking, such was my thirst, and threw it down my throat. I gagged.

"This is blood," I said, stupidly, though I had still swallowed what I had in my mouth. From one of your faithful servants?"

"Do you wish to heal your wounds or do you not?" Little John said, that smirk across his lumpy great face.

He was quite right. William knew me well, even then when we were so young.

I drank the whole thing. It was quite beautiful. That thick liquid, sliding down my throat. When it hit my stomach, the ache was like the longing for a lost love. The warmth spread through my body, caressing me from inside, glowing and tender.

My flesh drew together, the bleeding stopped. I sighed and leaned back against my bars, holding the empty cup to my chest.

"Enjoy that, did you?" Little John said, his grinning head up near the stone ceiling. "Lovely stuff that, ain't it. Funny, you wouldn't think a scrawny bitch like that would taste so sweet. That's right. That was your Eva's blood you just drank." He laughed so hard his whole body shook, his great barrel chest sounding like a bell.

My head snapped up. My sight burned with clarity. Every filthy pore on his face was as clear as a mountain stream. The sweat on his brow, the lines around his eyes, each of the night-black hairs of his beard.

"Don't worry," Little John said, his lips wet and sneering. "We ain't killed her yet. We ain't done nothing to her but drained her of a little blood. Our lord don't like us fiddling with women. And anyway, she scared the lads off from raping her after what she done to poor Alf. See, we need her alive and whole, right? We need her to make sure her old dad comes here to rescue—"

I threw the cup at his face. I could not extend my arm and I had to fling it through the square space between the bars but I had a belly full of blood and my eye and hand worked in perfect harmony.

The wooden cup flew like an arrow, at the perfect angle, and cracked him on the bridge of his nose.

Little John screamed like a girl, throwing his head back and his hands up to his face. Blood streamed from his nostrils and his eyes watered.

I laughed so hard that I thought the wounds in my head would open up again.

"You will pay for that," John said, his voice nasal and swallowing his blood as he spoke. "No, your bitch will pay for that. You hear me, you lord's bastard, your precious woman is going to pay the price for that."

"My precious woman?" I said, still laughing. "Is that truly what you think?" And I laughed harder though my heart ached.

John kicked the bars of my cage, his huge strength rattling the thing in its timber frame.

"You don't fool me," John said, blinking through his tears and the bars above my head.

"I would wager there is little that does not fool you, John the Bailiff," I said. "You are as thick as two short planks. Is your great head no more than solid skull all the way through?"

He roared and kicked my cage again. The iron bars shook and shifted before settling back.

I wished to rile the monster further, hoping that he would inadvertently break my cage loose from its moorings. Instead, his fellow men drew him off, muttering about disturbing their lord and glancing at William's door.

"You will bleed and bleed," John said, his huge voice lowered to a rumble. "You will bleed for days and months and years and we will make an army from your blood. You will be in here when England falls. You will be in here when Ashbury burns to the ground. You will be in that cage until you are mad with grief and weak as a woman. You are nothing now, not a lord, not a knight. You are cattle."

His men drew him away while John sneered down at me. Then they were gone.

All of them, they left me alone in that underground chamber with no one to watch over me and no one to watch over the other body. Tied to the table was their comrade, Tom the Cumbrian, covered in blood. His own was mostly outside his body, yet he had a belly full of mine working inside him.

The candles guttered and the room grew darker. The first thrill of the blood faded away and I sat and observed the body of the brute called Tom, wondering if he would ever awake and what he would be when he did.

William's followers were a mix between his monsters, changed forever, and those who were not. No doubt, William would feed those who were not changed forever with his own blood when he wanted them to be strong for a short time. Perhaps he fed them from his own veins, on every Sabbath, just as he had decades before in the hills of Palestine.

I did not know how many of each type of follower William had in the lodge he named Eden but there were enough. With the group that had taken me in the village, the men who guarded the wall as I was brought in and the other faces I had seen in the overgrown courtyard and grounds, I would guess two or three dozen. Thirty or even fifty men, all brutes, some of whom were possessed of strength similar to mine. Some had been soldiers.

I prayed that Jocelyn would flee Sherwood, find William Marshal, the Regent, and beg him for a force large enough to take Eden.

But Jocelyn was not a man to back down from a fight. Not when the woman he wanted to marry was in danger.

Of course, Jocelyn would be certain of gaining victory. He was convinced that the moral rightness of a man's character would endear him to God. Surely, a knight on a mission of such importance would receive God's strength.

But then, Jocelyn was never very bright.

Just as I knew that he was sure to make the attempt, I also know an assault on Eden was doomed to fail.

Sure enough, as I slept curled in the bottom of my cage, he and the rest of my men hatched a plan. A plan destined to end in disaster and death.

∞

"Tom? Tom?"

I woke. Some time had passed but whether it was day or night, I had no idea. Without sunlight, the measure of time is almost impossible. The candles had guttered but William stood on the far side of his altar table, leaning over the body of Tom.

Little John stood by William, holding up a lantern. Other men shuffled around the edges of the ornately carved room.

I had slept heavily and I ached from the prolonged

confinement of my limbs. My back cracked as I stirred.

William patted Tom's face.

"He is dead," William said. "The true death. The final death. My brother's blood did not work."

All eyes in that cavern turned to me.

I yawned. "Good morning, my dear friends," I said. "Which of you shall I kill today?"

The men did not like that and they stirred into anger.

"Perhaps," Little John said, his rumbling voice hesitant. "Perhaps, my lord, his blood is not like yours after all."

"Perhaps," William allowed, his head tilted to one side. "But look at him. That man in that cage is fifty years old, thereabouts. Is that not proof enough of his blood's potency."

"I need a piss," I said.

"Could it be," John said. "That your blood can change another man, my lord, but Richard's does not?"

William appeared thoughtful. "No," he said. "It is the same blood. Our father's blood. This time, it simply did not take. It has happened to me too, has it not?"

"It could be that he lacks the will to put his magic into the blood," John suggested. "You, my lord, you wish us to be changed. And so we are changed. Our base bodies are transformed into the bodies of the sons of Adam, through your will. And that man in the cage does not possess that same will."

William pursed his lips. "You could be correct," he said. "But all we can do is try again. Get this lump of flesh off my holy altar. Cut him up and feed him to the blood slaves."

"But—" John started.

"Bring my brother food and ale," William said, glaring at John. "And blood. Then we will try his blood on another potential."

William went into his chamber opposite my cage. John and most of the men left by the other door, carrying the body.

"I need a piss," I shouted.

One of William's minions jammed a bucket against the outside of my cage.

"Put it inside," I said to the men. "I will stand as far back from the door as I can, I swear. I swear upon God's bones. Upon the Christ's Holy balls, you pathetic little bastards."

They decided to not believe me so I pissed through the bars. But they did bring me bread and pork and ale and a cup of some poor soul's blood. I devoured it all, praying for the chance to use the strength I would regain.

And then they dragged in Eva.

Rope bound her at the wrist. Her face badly bruised. Both eyes black and her nose broken. She wore no more than her shirt, black with filth and brown with blood. She shivered and when her eyes met mine they were full of a cold fury.

Little John yanked her to behind William's altar and held her there. William and John loomed over Eva though she was not a short woman.

"Shall we try this again, Richard?" William said. "It is my belief that you will try harder to keep this woman alive than you did poor young Tom, who you had already murdered."

"I am sorry," I said to Eva, my face pressed to my bars. "I am sorry that I allowed you be caught up in this."

Her eyes glared from her swollen face but she did not speak.

428

"You seem to believe very strongly in your importance, Richard," William said. "But I would have taken her anyway, even if you had not been swyving her."

William looked across to Little John.

"Now, my lord?" Little John asked, grinning.

"Indeed," William said, glancing to me. "Bring in our latest guest. We would not wish him to miss this."

There was a commotion in the hallway outside the room, coming from behind my cage. Raised voices, stomping feet.

The Archbishop of York strode in. Huge, angry, dressed in his colourful finery as a lord, not an archbishop. His massive belly snug under a blue coat.

Already he was roaring at William to release Eva.

"You fiend," the archbishop shouted. "You black-hearted monster. How dare you do this to me? To me? You summon me as if I am your servant. My men have been seized at the gate and taken away by your damned brutes. How dare you—" He froze. "Eva? Is that my Eva? What is happening here? Good God Almighty, you release her you little shit.

"Ah, Hugh," William clapped his hands together. "I am so glad you could join us."

"You fool," the archbishop said. "You do not know what you have done. Release my girl, right now. And then we shall speak."

"But of course," William said.

He cut Eva's throat.

William was so quick that even I barely saw it. He drew his dagger and slashed through one of the veins on her neck, beside her windpipe.

Eva clapped her bound hands to her neck. Blood welled through her fingers. Her knees buckled but William held her up, grinning at me.

I yelled and rattled the bars. "I will gut you," I shouted. "I will murder every one of your brothers. I will burn Eden to the ground. You will burn in the eternal fires of Hell."

Archbishop Hugh, himself one of William's spawn, moved almost as quickly as William had. But Little John was there to stop him, charging from beside the altar to intercept. John was even taller, even wider than the archbishop was and he grappled the older man until more of William's men could pin him in place. They held the big lord back while he roared and strained to free himself, his eyes bulging and veins standing out on his temples.

Eva stared at me in accusation. Her eyes filled with rage, sadness, and terror, her mouth working as she fought for breath, fought for life.

"Now," William shouted over us. "Richard, perhaps you would be willing to honour this woman with the gift of your blood? We can cut you open again, or you can volunteer your blood freely?"

"Give me a knife," I said, not caring that he was forcing my compliance and that I was giving it to him.

One of William's men was waiting by my cage with a short, slim dagger. Two more of the men, one on either side, pushed their spears through my bars and held them near to my throat.

I sliced the knife through my wrist. It was sharp as a razor and, in my own keenness, I cut too deep.

Blood gushed out in a spurt. I had shed so much blood already in my life but the sight of it made me nauseated. I held my wrist to the channels beneath me. The blood pulsed, pulsed and covered my hand and filled the stone.

"What a good brother you are," William announced. "I very much hope your blood works on this woman. If it does not then I will have no use for you. Perhaps I will keep you for myself, simply to drink from you. Perhaps I will feed you to the pigs."

"It will work," I said to Eva. "Drink from me and live." More of my blood pumped from my wound.

Her knees buckled and she fell. Already her shirt was soaked, glistening and slick from neck to knee. William allowed her to drop to her knees and held her there with the fingers of one hand twisted through her hair.

"No," Eva whispered. William had cut one vein but not her windpipe but I saw, rather than heard her speak the words. "No, please."

"You will die if you do not," I said.

"Eva," the archbishop said, fear and compassion in his voice. "My dear. You will drink and you will become one of us. It is not so bad. Trust me, my dear, it is better than a mortal life."

William's men still held the lord, spears and daggers at the ready. Little John standing at his side.

"Actually," William said, as lightly as if he were discussion the weather. "I have never made a woman before. I am far from certain that she will survive the giving of the gift. Woman is the reason it was taken from mankind in the first instance. We shall discover God's will in her death or her rebirth."

"She will survive," her father said, eyes fixed on her blood as it soaked her shirt.

"Indeed, you will, my dear girl," William said, clapping her on her shoulder. "Listen to your dear old father. Your life with us will not be so bad. You will never carry a child but from what I hear that would not suit a warrior such as yourself. Did you know, Hugh, that she killed three of Little John's men when they took her and the Lady Marian from Tutbury Priory? Three. This woman."

"And she cut Alf's stones off," John said, grinning.

"Indeed she did," William said, smiling down at her. "Their first night as our guests, a couple of the acolytes could not control themselves and let themselves into the ladies' quarters. Your magnificent daughter, Hugh, she took Alf's knife and castrated him. John had to drain the screaming fool to shut him up. Ah, what a brother you will make, girl. Someone get a pail and collect this precious stuff before it has all leaked from her."

While he spoke, I squeezed the blood from my wrist. It filled the channels and flowed down to the bowl.

Eva slumped forward. William allowed her to fall flat onto her face but his men whipped the blood bucket away before she knocked it over. Her head cracked into the stone floor and she lay still, dazed, weak. Dying.

William's men lifted her body and stretched her out upon the table. She was drenched with blood. They bound her to the top at knee, hip and across her chest.

Little John filled the wooden cup with my blood and passed it William, who lifted it over his head.

"Dear God of Eden," William began, his voice filling the

crowded space, the echoes coming close, one upon the other. "The God of the Green. The God of the oak and the vine. The God of the rivers and the earth."

"Just get on with it," the archbishop said. "Spare us your sacrilegious, unholy nonsense."

William's men hissed at the archbishop's contempt for their practices though they were absurd and confused and bordering on pagan. Nothing at all like the holy word of God.

Little John lifted Eva's head and William poured the cup of my blood into her mouth. She coughed and writhed and I was sure she was drowning but William had judged the timing correctly. Eva gulped down most of the first cup and the second.

"Now we wait," William announced. "It is in the hands of the God of the Green."

"If she dies," the archbishop said. "I will have you killed." The big lord turned to me. "And you will die too, you thoughtless great oaf."

"I tried to keep her safe," I said, objecting out of reflex though I knew I had failed miserably.

"I was keeping her safe," the man said. "I was keeping her safe by sending her with you. Do you not understand?"

I did not.

"You have been useful to me," William said, tilting his head to one side as he regarded the archbishop.

"Useful?" the archbishop shook with emotion. "We have helped each other. It has been a fruitful alliance."

"I have given you gifts," William said, studying Hugh. "I have weakened your enemies."

"And I have given you this place," the archbishop said, gesturing at the room around us. "I have allowed you to take Sherwood for your own. You would be scurrying around in the gutter if it were not for me."

"Is that how it is?" William said, pursing his lips. "And here I thought I had welcomed you into our brotherhood when I gave you eternal life? Instead, you have worked against me at every turn. You hold one hand out to me while the other you hold behind your back, holding a dagger."

"Every bargain that we made," Hugh said. "I have fulfilled."

"Is that so?" William said. "Why, then, have you worked so hard to keep my brother Richard away from me?"

The archbishop glanced at me in my cage. "Yes. Very well, I sent him away to the Weald instead of sending him to his death, to you. Do you hear me, Richard? I tried to save you from your brother. When you defied me, I even had you bloody well locked up in that castle to keep you from blundering in here."

"But why?" I asked. "Why would you try to save me?"

Hugh's face twisted. "How can you ask me that? Have I not loved you like a son for these many years? Have I not defended you against your enemies? Why, he asks me. You ungrateful swine."

"But why not tell me?" I asked, astonished. "You could have warned me that this was a trap."

"I tried," he said. "God knows, I tried. I could do no more. If I told you how I was in league with this man, you would have turned on me. You two have this mad desire to slay the other. I sought only to keep you apart. And to keep my wonderful daughter from this monster. He heard about her, somehow, asked

434

me about her. I knew I had to send her far from Sherwood. I had a mad hope that the two of you would run away together for good."

I shook my head, disbelieving what I heard. "But why then did you send that man Little John to be my steward in my absence?"

"I sent no one, you fool," Hugh said. "If I wanted to take your lands I would have done so. No, I meant to leave Ashbury in the hands of your faithful steward but this black-hearted monster sent his blood-guzzling slaves here to wait for your return. It was that man there, not I. No, not I. They call you the Bloody Knight. They should have called you the bloody fool."

I felt winded, as though I had been thrown from a horse. I clutched the bars, my muscles straining as I attempted to prise them apart. The man was right. I was a fool.

William laughed at us. "Your concern for my brother is very touching. Truly, I am almost overcome with your fatherly assistance. Nevertheless, Hugh, you betrayed your word. Where was your love for me, Hugh? Me, who made you into a son of Adam. I became your father. You should have been faithful to me. And you will suffer for your betrayal, oath breaker."

"And you also lied to me," Hugh bellowed.

"Never," William said, feigning that he was offended. "My word is iron."

"A lie of omission, then. You never told me that once you turned me into an immortal, I would father no more children," the archbishop shouted.

William threw his head back and laughed. "How many bastards did you have already? I thought you would be grateful. You could shoot your seed into as many girls as you like, until the end of days, and never be troubled by another unwanted child or its needy mother."

"I love my children," Archbishop Hugh said. "I wanted centuries to father a thousand of them."

William laughed in his face. "My dear Hugh. How can this gift be otherwise? Richard and I were given the gift of eternal life but God took our seed from us. It is the same with everyone that I make. Of course, he takes it away. The only way we can make children now is by making more men like us. You, Hugh, you ask too much of God. And, more to the point, you ask too much of me. You have served your purpose. And now you will die."

"You cannot," Hugh said, struggling with the men holding him. "You need my men. My wealth. You need me to control the new king."

William shrugged and strolled toward Hugh. "I have turned enough of your men that they serve me now. Already they brought me boxes of your gold and silver. As for controlling our new young king, you have failed miserably. William Marshal is the Regent, not you. I have made other arrangements, many of them with members of the Marshal's own family. You have nothing to offer."

"How dare you?" The archbishop's eyes searched the room for allies or a way out. His men were all silent. William's men, now. Still, the man tried to save himself. "You are mad if you think you can find any other lord of my standing willing to do good for you."

William advanced, his dagger in hand. "Now, Hugh, all you are good for is a gallon of blood, a hundred pounds of meat and as much again in offal."

"No—" the big man said but he was held fast and said no more as William sliced through the throat of Archbishop Hugh de Nonant.

Little John and the rest held the big man as he writhed and groaned and shook. William gripped the hair on top of Hugh's head and cut and sawed through the skin, the veins, tendons, windpipe and gullet all the way back to the neck bones, working the blade back and forth with his face twisted in anger.

"This is what happens," William was snarling through gritted teeth. "This is what happens to those who defy me."

The archbishop's cry of defiance was cut off as William's blade sliced through his windpipe, the momentary whistling sound of air escaping from his neck was stoppered by the gushing blood. Hugh's eyes darted about, looking for help. He looked to me but I could not help him. Even had I not been caged, I was not certain I would have moved to help. He had plotted to poison his king, after all. I stared back at him until he squeezed his eyes closed.

William's men scurried forward to collect the stuff as it spurted and fell from the wound that grew wider and wider. Much of it poured into the stone channels in the floor and they collected it from the crater by the altar. After a few moments, Little John and his men threw Hugh's body face down on the floor. His blood continued to flow from him, running into the basin in the floor.

William stepped back, panting not from the effort but from the rage he was feeling. William nodded at me and I thought I was to be next. Instead, they bought a cup of the bishop's blood to me. I did not hesitate. I drank to heal my wrist and to be strong enough to fight my way free whenever the opportunity came.

The archbishop's blood, coming as it did from William, was more powerful than mortal blood. It coursed through me like fire in my veins. I felt like I could bend iron bars with my bare hands. Instead, I sat and focused on controlling my breathing while the strength filled me.

They dragged out the huge body of Hugh. William retired and the men washed much of the remaining blood from the floor.

Then I was alone again. Alone, with guttering candles and the body of Eva upon the slab.

"Please God," I prayed. "I wish I treated your priests better. I am sorry for that. I will try harder if I ever get the chance to. But please do not take Eva. She is a good woman. Well, she is not as bad as many of us. She is a good fighter. Let her wake. Let her wake and remain herself. And let her free me from this cage. Then I will cut off the head of every man in Eden, for you, Lord. Amen."

God rarely listens. Or, perhaps he does, for I have always been lucky. And what is luck, if it is not God either helping you or getting out of your way?

In the end, though, it was not Eva that freed me.

FIFTEEN ~ TREE
OF LIFE

BEFORE THE POWER OF HUGH'S BLOOD faded, I worked to free myself from my cage.

The thing had rattled within its frame when Little John had struck it. I was sure that I could break it free of the timber supports if I thrashed around enough. But that would stir William, from the room beyond, and whatever other guards were close by. If I were to succeed in knocking my cage over then I would simply be in a cage laying on its side.

The one chance I had was in prising open the bolted door. It was half the height of the cage and narrow but almost the full width of one side.

"Hold on to life," I said to Eva. "Do not give up. I will get us out."

I pushed and pulled on the bars of the cage door, heaving and shoving, looking for some weakness.

I could not budge it.

Eva groaned and writhed on the oaken altar. The veins stood out on her temples and forehead. Her fists clenched and her back arched, straining her bonds.

"Do not die," I said. "Please, Eva. Come back to the world, woman, come back."

She thrashed her head left and right and groaned. Her eyelids flickered, opened, closed again.

"Stay with me," I said. "If you live then I will look after you. You will always have a place with me whether you want to share my bed or not. I'll see you right. I'll take care of you."

Eva fell still. Silent.

Was she dead? Her chest did not seem to be moving.

Footsteps approached and I pretended to sleep. My one prayer was that someone would open my door to pass me a bucket or some such. More likely, if a man approached alone I could grab him though the bars and force him to open by threatening his life.

I listened to footsteps shuffling into the cave. The person stopped still in the doorway for a long moment. I expect he was looking at Eva's form, the bloody linen shirt clinging to her cold chest and flat belly in the candlelight.

They approached my cage.

I readied myself. I would never get more than a single attempt at it.

A low voice whispered. "Richard? Richard? By God's eyes, do not be dead, Sir Richard or I will kill you myself."

There, just beyond the bars of my cage door, was Swein. He

440

was cloaked in green and dressed in one of the green hoods that William's men wore.

His face, mostly in shadow, lit up with joy when he saw what must have been my astonished, ecstatic face. I had a hundred questions about how the sneaky little bastard had gotten inside undetected but they could wait.

"Draw back the top and side bolts," I whispered.

He slid them back out of the floor. They both screeched as they ground iron against iron. I cringed, looking at William's door and over Swein's green-clad shoulder at the entrance to the underground room.

"Where is everyone else?" I asked him as I eased myself through the cage door. I straightened, suppressing a mighty sigh of satisfaction as my back cracked.

"They await us beyond the gate and walls," Swein whispered. "We must find Marian and flee before I am discovered. And before they discover the men we stole the clothes from."

"You killed some of William's men?" I whispered.

"Outside the walls of this place," Swein said. "Arrows in the face. You say these men are powerful but I don't know what all the fuss is about."

"Listen," I whispered. "Most of William's men are ordinary. They live in the hope of tasting William's blood and gaining temporary strength. Just like those you killed back in Ashbury and the men whose clothes you now wear. There are a few, though, I am not sure how many who are very strong. Made strong as long as they drink blood, like Tuck. You must not attempt to fight those men."

Swein nodded. "An arrow to the head kills them, too, though?"

"Yes, praise God," I said. "Now, let us go. First, let us take Eva."

"Surely, she is dead?"

I stepped to the massive, thick altar and felt her chest and cheek. "She is bone cold," I said, my own heart racing. "But I think she breathes."

Her neck was thick with blood but I felt underneath the black scab that had formed over the slash through the great vein. The scab flaked away.

Underneath, the skin was whole.

"Oh, God," I whispered. "It worked."

"But where is Marian?" Swein said, his eyes wild and dark inside his hood.

"In there," I said as I untied Eva's bonds. "With William."

Swein stared at the heavy door. "Is it locked?"

"I doubt it," I said. "Give me your sword and I will go inside and kill him."

"What is he doing to her in there?" Swein said, his eyes bulging.

"Give me your sword, quickly." Without waiting for him, I pulled the blade from his scabbard. It was an old thing. Sharp at the edge, though nicked. The iron not particularly hard and it had been straightened so many times I feared it would snap at the first contact with another blade.

"Can you kill him?" Swein asked, mistaking my hesitation for doubt of my own abilities.

"Be ready to take Marian," I said. "And I will carry Eva. What is your plan for escape?"

"Put a sword in your hand and stay behind you," Swein said.

Eva groaned and rolled over toward me. I steadied her before she rolled right off.

"What is happening?" Eva mumbled.

"You are alive," I told her keeping my voice low. "We are escaping Eden. Can you stand?"

She sat on the edge of the thick altar top, swinging her legs off.

"I am thirsty," she muttered, wiping her mouth.

"I will get us both some blood from the first man I kill," I whispered, holding her shoulders. "Which will be William."

Her head snapped up, clutching at her fully healed neck. "They made me one of them." She looked at me, eye to eye, a dozen emotions fighting upon her face.

"No," I said. "Well, yes. But you will not be mad, as they are. You are made from my own blood. Perhaps that will make a difference. And you shall have me to look out for you."

She squeezed my hands upon her shoulders.

"We must hurry," Swein whispered. "Hurry, hurry, speed is the key. We do not have long."

"Eva," I said, "do you feel like you could stand?"

We helped her to her feet. She pinched the front of her shirt away from her body. It was halfway stiff with blood. "I feel like I could kill."

"Good," I said, praying that she would be strong enough to help me rather than weak enough to hinder our escape. "Give me room to move," I warned them both. "But if you can get around us while we fight then you can grab Marian."

443

"Marian is in there?" Eva said, frowning. "Since when has she been?"

Something that William had said came back to me. That an acolyte had tried to rape the ladies in their chamber. I grabbed Eva's arm. "Have you seen her elsewhere?"

She shook me off. "Marian and I were held together, in a chamber of the house above. Until they brought me here. How long have we been here? What day is it?"

Swein and I looked at each other.

"He called to her, as if she was within, when I first arrived," I said. "The evil sod was toying with me. Marian was never in there. That petty, spiteful shit."

"How was she?" Swein whispered, eyes shining in the lamplight. "Was she well treated?"

"I suppose so," Eva said, looking down at herself. "Considering."

"So William is alone in there," I said, staring at the heavy door. "

"Let us go get Marian," Swein said. "You can always come back for William."

"I may never get another chance," I said, my voice low but growing louder in my desperation. "I can go in there and cut off his head while he sleeps."

"If he wakes, though. You two clashing swords will wake this whole place and the rest of us will never get out," Swein said, standing up to me like a man. "Is that what you want?"

"God give me strength," I prayed and I passed Swein's blade back. "Stand aside."

444

Eva and he moved away while I leaned across the huge, bloody, stinking oak altar top. The thing was three feet wide and six feet long. The wood was about three inches thick and the wood was as dense as iron. I heaved it up. It barely shifted. I heaved again, it grinding against the stone supports beneath, juddering loudly.

Swein hissed a warning, frantic that I would make enough noise to wake the dead.

I took a breath, bent my knees and heaved up, lifting with my lower back. The great thing rose with me, with my body along it, one arm on the far edge, the other on the edge near me. I tilted it up, spun it carefully around and waddled over to William's chamber door.

Once, many years before when the lodge had been built, William's room might have been the lord's treasury, or perhaps a dungeon gaol cell for woodland miscreants. Indeed, it was a room able to be secured from entry or exit. The door was thick oak, reinforced with iron bands.

William had removed the oak beam that locked the door from the outside but he had neglected to remove the iron cleats on either side of frame. I eased the altar top into those long iron hooks. I shoved it upright, checked it was secure. The oak altar top covered the door from halfway up, almost to the ceiling.

From the other side, the door rattled.

"Open this door," William commanded from the other side, his voice barely audible through the many inches of solid oak. "Whoever it is, I swear I shall forgive you when you open it up."

"I shall come back for you, William," I said.

He roared and smacked his fits into his door. The altar shook but held.

I shouted through the door, "Perhaps not today, William, but know that I shall come back for you and I shall—"

"Quiet," Swein hissed. "You will wake all of Eden."

On the opposite side of the room to William's chamber, the other door scraped open and I heard a man's voice.

Swein and Eva froze, as surprised people tend to do, staring at the doorway.

Running past Swein, I snatched the sword from his hand, leapt over the stone legs of the altar and closed the distance as the door opened.

Two of William's men pushed their way inside.

Both carried a spear but neither expected to find any trouble. The first got my borrowed blade through his neck. He fell, his bucket and spear clattering as he did so.

The man behind turned to flee but I continued past the first man and slammed into the second, crushing him against the rough stone wall. His spear bounced between the walls of the corridor, rattling loudly.

I stamped on his face and neck and chest until I was sure he would never rise again.

Swein and Eva had good sense enough to come after me, eager to flee. I waited for them, listening along the long corridor for any signs of life.

William pounded on his door from the other side. His blows were massive, like the kicks from a horse, but so was his bloodstained altar top.

It held.

446

"Is it day or night?" I asked Swein as he drew near.

"Should be getting light soon," he said. "Your blade is bent."

The bloodied tip had bent a hand's width from the point. I placed it against the wall and pushed it straight as I could.

"Jocelyn waits beyond the walls?" I asked him. "With horses for all of us?"

Swein nodded. "My men are hidden in the place they fight best," he said. "In the trees."

"Watch the corridor," I said to Swein, handing him the sword.

I picked up the first man by the shoulders. He was one of the ones who had provoked me before.

I drank from the wound I had slashed through his neck. His head flapped back.

After I had a few mouthfuls, I held him out for Eva.

She stared at the blood on his neck and licked her lips.

"Decide now if you wish to live or die," I said to her. "This man is dead. He will never need his blood again. You, on the other hand, must drink in order to live. Drink from him and find such power that you have never known. You will be able to defeat any swordsman, survive deadly wounds. But only if you drink."

William pounded on his chamber door again, shouting words we could not quite make out.

I held the dead man up for Eva. Her lip curling, she bent her neck to the bleeding wound and sucked the blood out. She gagged but kept swallowing.

Eva gulped it down, jerked her head away, eyes shining. "God," she said. "Holy God Almighty." Her chest heaved while she stared at her hands, flexing them open and closed. "Is this how you feel

447

all the time?" Her eyes were wide.

"Someone comes," Swein said from ahead down the corridor.

Eva and I took up a spear each and ran forward to where the corridor turned into a twisting stair. Footsteps and voices came down.

Swein whispered to me. "Sounds like four men? Should we wait here, take them as they come around the bend?"

I could not wait even a moment more to kill the men who had captured me, humiliated me and used me as if I was cattle. Without considering, I ran up past Swein with my spearhead held up and out and I came upon the first man. One of Little John's armoured fellows, as were the three men above and behind him upon the stair.

Their mail had been stolen from better men. Most of it did not fit the wearer and was often rusted, split and then tied bound together with thongs or strips of cloth.

The first man wore no amour on his legs so I slid my spear up into his groin, twisted the head and pulled it out. He shrieked and fell past me, down to where Swein and Eva could finish him.

The next man barely had a moment to flinch before I ran my spear up into his chin. My blade bit into the bone. With surprising swiftness, he grabbed the shaft and attempted to yank it from my grip. Instead, I pulled him down, sending him tumbling by me. The third man had time to draw his sword and he swatted my blade away, slipping inside the reach of the point and thrusting down toward my unarmoured head. I shortened my grip, yanking the spear shaft through my hands until my lead hand was just behind the iron, so I held it almost like a dagger. I slipped aside the sword thrust, charging up the steps, grabbed his sword arm and stuck my own blade through a rent in his mail between shoulder and neck. The spear shaft bounced off the wall and I missed my strike. He drew his own dagger and managed to rake it up my arm before I could thrust into his throat.

The man above had retreated back up the stairs.

I took the sword from the dying man at my feet and charged upward, Swein and Eva behind me.

My fear was that the man would shut us behind some sturdy door but instead, he fled along the corridor up there, shouting for help.

At the top of the stairs, it was daylight. Morning filtering through the holes in the tiled roof of the old, stone built building. It was filled with that acrid stench of old urine, shit and unwashed human bodies.

The corridor had closed doors every few feet along it, four on either side, with one at the far end. The fleeing man banged on the farthest two doors, shouting that those inside should wake up, then kicked open and ran through that far door. It opened to reveal a rectangle of green beyond, lit with the pale blue of a summer dawn.

"Where is Marian?" I called to Eva but already she ran beyond me to the second door on the right. She lifted the bar across the middle of it and bounced it aside.

The two doors at the far end opened, one after the other. One of William's men poked his head out, rubbing his eyes, another came out with a sword already drawn.

"We must hurry," I said and went after Eva who threw open

the door before she rushed inside.

At the far end of the corridor, one of the men shouted back inside his door to the others inside that room.

Swein pushed past me into the room after Eva. I stood in the doorway and peered inside as Eva helped Marian, grabbing her hand and pulling her toward the door. The room was dark and fetid and it reeked of piss.

Marian cried out at Eva's appearance. "What has happened to you? Dear God, Eva, what has happened?"

Eva had fresh blood covering her from nose to neck and old, dried blood caking her from neck to knee.

"I am unharmed. We must run, now," Eva said and yanked her out.

William's men tumbled out into the far end of the hallway until there were seven men stalking toward us along the corridor.

"Stay in there for just a moment longer, my lady," I said to Marian and I checked my stolen blade. It appeared to be a good one. "Swein, Eva, stay with Marian. If I fall, kill as many as you can and run."

William's men filled the far end of the corridor, coming on, two by two next to each other, in four rough rows. They had bunched up, one behind the other, far too close to each other. Bad for them, good for me.

The first two men looked nervous, as well they might.

I sprang forward, slashing at them, shouting. I drove them back toward their fellows. They waved their swords at me and they were fast compared to normal men but they were not practised swordsmen. I lunged low, slid sideways and thrust, gutting the one to the left, who fell to his knees, shrieking and trying to gather up his guts back into his body. I drove my blade into the man to the right. A killing blow for a mortal man, yet he shrugged it off and came back at me, almost taking me by surprise. I had to remember to put them down in a way they could not resist. So I slipped my blade across his throat, slicing his windpipe and neck veins.

The five men still in the fight were brave. Fanatical, even. I was used to fighting in full armour, with a helm and a shield and my inexperience with fighting in no more than an undershirt began to show.

One threw himself upon my blade, ran himself through on it and twisted himself to the side. It caught me by surprise and almost worked but I ripped the blade from him. Still, the man behind him cut me on the forearm, rather badly. I was lucky it was not on my hand or my fingers.

The cut on my arm released even more of my anger. It was like when a bowman is at full draw, with the cord at his cheek, and then he pulls it back even further to beyond his ear.

My sword flashed in the dim light, thrusting through the clothes of the men attacking me. I knew I was shouting as I killed the last few but I could not recall fighting the rest. I cut the last two down in short order, blood spurting from veins I had slashed through. Seven men lay dead or dying in the corridor, groaning, weeping. Blood soaked the floor and those that could move struggled to slurp it up.

"Come, let us flee," I shouted.

"What about the other prisoners?" Swein said, coming out of Marian's gaol, his eyes full of horror.

"There is no time," I said, trying to calm my rage. "William's men will be gathering outside. William could free himself."

"I know some of these men," Swein said, throwing over the beam to the nearest door to him and heaving the door open. "Outlaws like me, taken and locked up. Men who were taken when my father was killed."

Inside that room, it was dark. Two filthy men in rags shuffled out, blinking at the light.

"Come out," Swein shouted. "Hurry, you fools."

"Leave them," I urged Swein. I could hear men moving in the courtyard.

Marian strode up to me. "You must help them, Richard," she said. "It is your duty." She glared at me, hands on her hips. She was filthy. Her hair was matted. She stank like a pig.

"God give me strength," I said. "You sound like Emma."

"Well then," Marian said. "You should most certainly do as I say."

Together, we got all the doors open. While the others helped the stinking blood slaves, prisoners and servants out of their prisons, I picked up one of the men I had slain and I drank from a wound in his wrist.

The prisoners groaned in terror and disgust, edging away from me.

"He is a friend," Swein swore to them. "He is not one of them, he is freeing you."

I ignored them, caring nothing for what those foul peasants thought. I dropped the body into the pooling blood beneath and I looked out the door. Morning was growing brighter. The gate ahead, the gate into Sherwood and freedom, was barred.

William's men stood upon the wall and before the closed gate. The wide, clear path between the gate and my doorway was clear of men but I could hear them rustling in the bushes and trees to either side.

"It will be an ambush," I said to Eva at my shoulder. "I shall fight my way through, draw them out. You and Swein follow, kill any who oppose us." I glanced at Eva. "You should drink some more blood. You will need the strength."

"No," Marian said, hearing me. "No, God. You mean they made you into one of them?"

Eva just shook her head without looking at either of us. "I am strong enough," she said. "And full."

"Suit yourself," I said. "Be sure to move quickly and leave these dying weaklings behind. Some will get away, probably, if we leave the gate open behind us. We cannot carry them."

"Wait," Swein said. "You could draw the Green Men away from the gate. Give the prisoners a chance."

"No," I said. "I am not doing that. I want to live. Look at these men and women here, look at them. You freed them but without horses, they will all be recaptured within a day."

"There are horses," Marian said. "We saw the stable. It is behind this hall, there is a score of horses, perhaps more."

"Set a fire," Swein said. "In the storehouse to the left of this hall. Burn it down. That will give them something to do."

"You and your foolish stratagems," I said to Swein, shaking my head, and I glared at Marian for good measure, for she was almost as bad as he. "I go for the gate, you follow as soon as it is open. Get to the horses and ride as hard as you can. Go north, then west. We will raise more forces, come back in a week or two and destroy this place."

Without waiting, I charged out into the courtyard.

There were men there. Men in green, perhaps a score. Some were armoured in mail shirts or coifs. Many had open-faced helmets. All were armed.

I felt naked without my armour. Without a helm. Without even a gambeson. It was terrifying.

All I could do was put my chin to my chest, hunch my shoulders and run through them. Without the armour to weigh me down, I did, at least, move with a speed that astonished even myself. The men in green leapt aside from me, shouting warnings at each other.

Men upon the wall by the gateway shot their bows at me from less than twenty yards but I ran so fast they had little hope of hitting me. An arrow bounced from the pathway into my legs, missing me but almost tripping me. I took the wooden steps up to the wall in two strides, leaping up with my sword up and cutting down the three bowmen at the top.

The men who had scattered at my charge now moved back to the courtyard, shouting at me and each other, gathering their courage. I leapt down from the wall, put a shoulder to the timber and heaved up the great beam out of the cleats across the double door gate. My back itched, so sure was I that I would catch an arrow, a bolt or a spear while my back was turned. I gave half of the gate a mighty heave and it swung open.

I span about in time to parry a wild blow and split the fellow's skull down to the nose. His friend went down with the very top of his skull sliced off by a half-pulled backhand blow.

I wished that I could retain such strength as that at all times. No wonder William and his men had built a blood farm. It was intoxicating stuff. A small part of me dreamed of a time when I could drink blood every day, for the rest of eternity and fight back whole armies with my bare hands.

But more men were coming. I edged away from the gate, my back to the timber wall. They moved to follow me but more stayed back amongst the vines in full leaf. I had to get them away from the gate so Swein and Eva had a chance. "You cowards," I shouted. "Kill me. Capture me. The Green Knight will be ever grateful to you."

That brought a few toward me. A horse whinnied from behind the hall, beyond the big timber storehouse.

"I am going to slaughter your horses," I said.

A few more came for me.

"I have William's treasure," I cried. "I am making off with his riches."

Many more moved to cut me off so I ran along the path away from the gate further into the compound, I ran beside the wall, past the storehouse toward the stables.

Two men twisted out from behind the wall of the storehouse. I put them down, injured but it took a few moments and the men chasing me were almost upon me.

I checked my run, span and swung my sword in a wide arc, screaming like a madman. The three closest to me jumped back, scattering from me.

I turned and ran to the stable. It was huge, built to house a lord's hunting parties. Stone at the foundation and lower wall with a long timber roof, open on the sides. It was packed with horses. The grooms were already running away when I shouted at them to move, to get away or die. I ran into the central isle. It was dark inside. The horses and ponies were scared, shying away and tossing their heads. I kicked open as many stalls as I could as I moved down the stable building. My pursuers shouted at each other to surround the building and as I opened the stalls, the men gathered at either end of the long structure. When I had run in, I had conceived that the horses might bolt, throwing Eden's men into more disorder, perhaps making a herd of panicking horses that we could flee amongst. But of course, the horses were afraid to leave their pens.

Instead of fighting my way through the men cautiously edging into each end of the stable, I pushed past a big stallion, going for the open side of the stable. It had the short back and powerful rump of a charger and I was tempted to leap upon its back, or push it into the aisle and slice its rump into bolting through the men. Instead, I shoved the fine beast aside and clambered out over the outside wall of the pen.

On the other side, I took a breath while the men came to cut me off again. I hoped I had already caused enough disruption for Swein and Eva to fight their way through to the open gate. I prayed that Jocelyn and Anselm were ready with mounts and that the archers could cover our escape just as they had done in the raids on Dover.

I charged the men closest to me. These fellows were well rested and prepared for me. But I was becoming tired and I was slashed in the arm and a blade slashed a glancing blow along my skull over my ear. I killed or put down four men and ran along the path back toward the gate. William's men were following but avoiding contact, fearing me now, perhaps, more than the Lord of Eden's ire.

I rounded the storehouse, into the courtyard by the gate, and ran into a cacophony of shouting and the clash of weapons.

The prisoners, William's blood slaves, were streaming from the hall. The ones who could move faster than a walking pace were already out of the gate. Others were supporting each other, limping, wincing at the light of the dawn and from the effort of walking.

Eva stood by the open gate, laying about her with her sword at a group of green-clad soldiers by the stairs. She was magnificent. Always, she had been fast and skilful but now she was strong and relentless and even faster than before. Three dead men were at her feet and three more circled, probing her defences.

Swein, however, was wheeling backwards from two men parrying and ducking, his sword bent. He was bleeding, moving slowly, breathing heavily. For all his gifts, he was no swordsman and was fighting William's monsters. It was a wonder he yet lived.

Just by the doorway to the hall, Marian helped an old man and a couple of broken fellows out into the air, concern for them all over her face, though she herself was filthy and struggling. I cursed her stupidity. I cursed her compassion that was going to get her killed, after all that we had done.

More of William's men came from deeper within Eden, from

the far side of the courtyard and from around the sides of the hall, to shove the blood slaves back toward their gaol. One of William's brutes punched two prisoners to the ground and went after more. Another cracked a stick into the side of a young woman's head and pulled her to the ground by the hair. He was set upon by the woman's friends who he threw down as if they were children.

The men pursuing me gathered by the storehouse at my back, arguing with each other about how best to attack me.

I decided to save Swein first, then Eva and then Marian.

"Sir Richard!" Little John strode around the far corner of the hall, crashing through the vines and fruit trees.

The man had somehow found mail and helm to fit his giant frame and his monstrous head and he had a sword drawn. Though the mail was tight across his belly and it was split on the inside of his arms and tied together, and it was short at the wrist. The helm was an old fashioned one with an open face and a nose piece but he wore a mail coif underneath to protect his head and neck.

Little John was a huge man, filled with rage and the strength of William's gift but he was not a knight. He was a bailiff, used to breaking the heads of commoners. I was tired but I thought I could take him.

With him were three men dressed in mail that fit them perfectly and all three held shields painted with the same red and white stripes. Those men were trained fighters, presumably come over from some lord or mercenary company and though they looked like children beside Little John, they were just as dangerous as he.

John pointed his sword at my face as he strode toward me.

"Leave the blood slaves," John shouted. "They will not get far. Kill that one there and the rest will fall."

He smashed his way through the prisoners, knocking down and stomping on a man and woman who had been too slow to move aside. Others scattered from him, falling down from fear and in their haste to get away from him.

There was no time to fight him. I could not kill every man in Eden. Even if I fought John and his men, it would leave at least a score for me to kill or drive off, perhaps twice that many.

The altar table would not hold William for long and his men could have already freed him even if he was unable to break through alone. I glanced at the hall doorway, by Marian, and imagined William suddenly appearing there.

I considered fleeing into the storehouse and setting a fire as some sort of distraction, as Swein had suggested. I wondered if I could flee through the gate and draw Little John away from the prisoners out to where the archers could take them. Backing away from John's approach, I searched for stratagems, for some clever trick of the kind that Swein liked.

But Swein fell. A cut sliced him upon the arm and then another and he cried out and fell, fighting as he went down.

The red rage came upon me and I decided to just kill them all.

John's soldiers spread out as they approached. The men who had pursued me from the stable spread out behind me, near the storehouse.

The prisoners fled as best they could. I willed them to run while I fought.

I chose the soldier on the farthest right and, feinting left, I charged him. Like a good knight, he braced behind his shield so I crashed into it with my shoulder. It hurt, badly but I knocked him down and while he was flailing, I trod on his sword hand and stabbed the point of my blade into his armoured neck. It may not have split the rings of mail there but I leaned on the pommel as I drove it down, crushing his windpipe.

Little John charged me like a bull and I had to leap over the fallen man and dance away like a coward, lest I be felled myself. A thicket of berry bushes blocked my way behind me but I leapt through a raspberry bush, hacking and tearing through the tangle. I found two of William's men on the far side, shocked by my sudden appearance. I cut almost all the way through the neck of the first man and the second I speared through the lower back as he turned to flee, all the while I kept moving.

Two of John's soldiers hacked their way toward me through the bushes but the idiots got themselves and their shields caught on the tangled branches. The nearest man looked down at himself to see where he was snarled up. I hacked my sword down on the crown of his helm as if I was splitting logs. The metal on metal sound clanged and he went down as if he was a candle that had been snuffed out. But my sword broke, right at the cross guard. I stared at the handle like an idiot though I had known for a long time that using my full strength in a fight was often a bad idea.

The other man-at-arms dragged himself through the bushes and aimed a clumsy strike at my head. I raised my hand to block it. Only at the last moment did I realise that my sword was nothing more than a handle. I ducked and the blade cut no more than the air an inch above my head.

Little John, unseen beyond the dense thicket, roared at his men to kill me and to feast upon my corpse

I dropped my ruined weapon, grabbed the man-at-arm's sword arm and snatched his sword from his mailed hand. The man thumped me with his shield but it was no more than irritation and, with my bare left hand, I guided the point of my blade into the eye slit of his helm and shoved it in. He screamed and jerked back, at the very least blind on one side and hopefully dying.

More men were crowding into the overgrown thicket of mulberry and gooseberry. I hacked my way free, coming out beside the storehouse.

One of William's men turned to shout that he had found me and I cut his head from his body while he was still shouting. It was one of those rare times where the body of the beheaded man does not yet know it is dead and the man, without a head, stood upright, hands out to balance itself. The body took a full step forward even while its head rolled away from it. I am sure it fell soon after but I did not see how many steps it took. For I turned to defend myself from the great beast that charged me.

Little John, his face contorted in rage, swung his sword overarm at the top of my head.

I was tired. No mortal man, no matter how much he trains, can keep up intense combat without periods of rest. And even I was breathing heavily, sucking down air like a drowning man. I had cuts all over my body, some of them bad and one on the side of my skull that I was sure would be ugly. My blood leaked out all over. I was desperately thirsty, for water and blood.

I got my sword up to deflect the strike. And I moved aside to get out from under that wild, brutal blow.

But I was slow and my arm was weak. Little John's blade knocked mine aside. His sword missed my head but cut into my body, smashing my collarbone and driving me to my knees.

A strike that like, with that kind of force, while it might not sever a vital vein or organ, can be enough to kill a man outright. The shock of the blow will travel through your bones, through the centre of your body, jar your brain inside your skull. The power of it can shut off the flow of your life like twisting a tap.

I knew it was bad. Looking up at his red, furious face as he yanked the sword out of my body, I could see just how he would hack it back down into my neck the second time. It was curious how I had time to think. I had time to rue being killed by an untrained brute after having defeated so many skilled knights in my life. A bailiff, of all people, a man who wielded a blade with all the finesse of a butcher. His grip was all wrong. His edge alignment was appalling.

And yet I could not move. I was done. Defeated.

John dropped his sword and stiffened. His face twisted and he jerked and clutched his chest. He twisted and fell to the side, his mouth opening and closing, trying to see behind him. He staggered a few steps, wailing like a skewered boar and he crashed to his side in a clatter of iron and bone.

It was Eva. She had run him through the arse with one blade, striking up beneath the hauberk that was far too short for him. Then she had seen a long rent in the side of his mail and stabbed her second blade up under his ribcage and into his chest. The hilts of her blades stuck out of his arse and his ribs.

She helped me up. The poor woman was covered in blood from head to toe, shivering in her undershirt and bare legs. She shook from exhaustion and excitation.

"Drink some blood," she snarled in my face and she snatched up John's dropped blade. She stood guard over me while I staggered to a headless body next to us.

William's men — seeing John fall, seeing Eva's power, and me rising — retreated from us.

I sucked a mouthful of spurting blood from one of the big veins of the body near me, lifting it with my right arm. My left shoulder was barely attached to my body. A piece of long, tattered skin found its way into my mouth and I almost vomited it back up. But I kept drinking. I needed it, all I could get. Even then, I felt like I was dying.

The scream from the courtyard was chilling. I dropped the body and with Eva's help, ran round the bushes into the space between the gate and the hall.

The prisoners had mostly all escaped from the hall. Some lay dead, others were being held or beaten by William's men.

But in the centre was the man himself.

The Green Knight, the Lord of Eden. My brother. William.

His eyes were wild, he was angrier than I had ever seen him. His fists were bloodied and swollen. His mouth and jaw were red with fresh blood.

There were dead all about him.

He held Marian by the hair.

"Come here," William snarled at an old man, who limped

over to William, tears running down his face. "Here, Geoffrey."

"Please, not my daughter, please," the old said.

It was Sir Geoffrey of Norton. Aged, thin, his hair almost gone and what remained was white and brittle. But it was he. A man I had drunk with, fought with when we were young. I was astonished that Marian's father yet lived. He and his soldiers had been ambushed so long before that no man in his right mind had believed him so. Yet there he was, begging for Marian's life.

Of course, that was why Marian had dawdled so long. That was why she had been helping a decrepit prisoner instead of fleeing for her life. She had found her father, finally, against all hope.

There was movement among the fallen. Swein crawled through the bodies of soldier and slave alike toward William. But he was ten yards away and heading for nowhere but the grave. The lad was drenched in blood, pale and moving far too slow. Even if he reached William, there was nothing he could do.

Eva steeled herself to attack but she could barely hold herself upright. Her teeth were chattering in her head. I was leaning on her but she was also holding to me.

The blood I had drunk was working in me but still my left side was useless. The blow had cleaved through me deeply and there was no way I could use my left arm. I could not even feel it, it hung by my side like a leg of lamb on a butcher's hook. I needed more blood, more time.

"You shall watch what happens to those who defy the Lord of Eden," William shouted in Marian's ear. Still holding on to her hair, he stepped forward and ran his sword through her father's throat.

Sir Geoffrey jerked as the blade gouged out his neck and the old men fell.

Marian screamed as William threw her upon her father's body.

"Do you see?" William shouted at her then he addressed his men. "Take all their heads and we shall stick them upon the walls of Nottingham Castle. We will show England what it means to be the sons of Adam. John, where are you, you great fool?"

"Brother," I shouted. "Little John is dead."

His head snapped round to me.

"And," I continued. "Now it is your turn."

I finished in a fit of coughing. Blood spattered from my mouth. My wounds were greater than I had thought.

"Brother?" William said. "You are no brother of mine. I would have given you a place in our new world. Instead, you wreak this pointless havoc. What a waste."

He grabbed up Marian again, forced her to her knees and held his sword across the back of her neck. She knelt among the bodies of men that William had killed to reach her and her father.

Eva stalked forward and I took a step with her but my legs gave way. I needed blood.

"Stop," William said. "Eva, my dear, you are one of us, now. And if you take another step, I shall remove your friend's head. Richard, I will very much enjoy peeling off chunks of your flesh. I wonder how long you could live without skin. We shall find out together."

Eva turned to me, looking over her shoulder. "Drink my blood," she whispered. "Then kill him."

I shook my head. She was shaking all over. To take her blood would surely kill her and William would kill Marian anyway before I could reach her.

William's men gathered, their bravery regained.

"Return all the escaped blood slaves to their pens," William commanded and they moved to obey. "Close the gates, and then form groups to round up the ones in the wood."

From nearby, bowstrings twanged, the air split to the whooshing sound of iron in flight. Arrows smacked and thudded into William's men. A dozen. One after the other. Thrashing and cracking, splitting flesh. A half dozen men fell, others scattered away from the gateway and the wall.

William shouted, pointed at the wall of Eden.

Swein's archers had scaled that wall from the outside and shot down into William's men. After that first volley, they loosed another, and another, each man shooting as fast as he could. The wet thud of iron splitting clothes and skin and flesh sounded, again and again.

From the open gateway, a group of four archers ran forward, drew back their bows and shot as one, straight across the courtyard toward William.

My shout of warning got no further than a strangled cry as my own blood filled my throat. I wanted to warn them that they would hit Marian.

Four arrows plunged into his chest, knocking him back and down.

At once, Marian crawled away to her father.

Eva turned to me, a triumphant smile on her bloodied face.

466

William could never be killed by arrows, I tried to tell her but all that came out was blood.

Jocelyn rode through the gate on his magnificent bay courser, the brown coat shimmering. Jocelyn was fully armoured, the long shield covering his left side, his lance in hand.

William leapt up, ripping the arrows from his chest, spurts of blood and lumps of flesh coming with them. He lifted one of the bodies at his feet as if it were a leg of lamb, bent his head to it and drank.

More arrows thumped into William's men. Those who could move fled for shelter. Those felled by the arrows suffered more shafts shot into them.

William snatched up a shield and stalked toward Marian. I supposed he knew that his best chance of escape lay in taking her hostage, using her as another shield while he rode for freedom.

I struggled to my feet and lurched toward him. I was in no state to run and I knew William would reach Marian before I could get to her.

Jocelyn knew it too. As soon as the arrows hit he had raked his spurs back and his courser leapt forward. It was a magnificent charge to behold from across the courtyard. The horse was well trained and perfectly attuned to the rider. Jocelyn's form was faultless, his lance point under the finest control. Beast and man charging as a single entity, existing purely as a means to drive an iron point into a small target with the greatest possible force.

William stopped before he reached Marian. At first, he was shocked. But amusement spread across William's lips as he turned to Jocelyn's charge.

I shouted a warning but before the blood was out of my mouth, William had leapt to the side, raised his shield to deflect the lance and swung his sword low at the horse's legs.

Although he was a mere mortal and could not match William's speed, Jocelyn had anticipated just such an evasion and had already moved the tip of his lance to where he expected William to be.

The lance caught the Lord of Eden low in the chest. It spitted him through, knocking William down as if a giant had swatted him, the iron point driving right through the skin, the bone and out the other side, the ash shaft pushing through and through William's body.

William, though, contorted with rage and twisted as he fell. The shaft knocked Jocelyn from the saddle. Jocelyn fell, hard and William snapped the lance shaft at arm's length, then pushed the remainder through his body, reaching back to draw the final splintered part out.

Jocelyn rolled to his feet, dazed and placed himself between Marian and William, drawing his sword.

I staggered toward William as he slashed the throat of Jocelyn's beautiful horse and shoved it aside. William darted forward, smashed Jocelyn's sword thrust aside with his bare arm and picked up Jocelyn in his armour by the throat, wrapping both hands around his neck.

I screamed, blood spraying from my mouth, as William snapped Jocelyn's neck.

He tossed Jocelyn's body aside like a ragdoll just as I reached them. Thrusting at full stretch, I ran William through the side of the body and William jerked away, blood pouring from his chest and his side. The weight of his body slid off my blade and I stalked after him. William was afraid. He backed away across the courtyard, bent over his wounds. Arrows thumped down around us and I was aware that I was between the archers and William, blocking their shots but I meant to kill him myself. I was going to peel off his skin. I was going to make him suffer. I would take his eyes. I wished I could tell him but I could not speak. My vision faded and I knew I had to catch him before I succumbed.

Shouting behind me. I glanced over my shoulder in time to see Little John, lumbering forward like a dying bull, hack Eva down as if she was not there, his sword cutting into the side of her head. She had her sword up to block the blow but his strength and fury were too much and she fell. Her body hit the cobbles hard. I prayed she would hold on to life until I could reach her.

John, the monster that he was, had recovered from Eva's fatal blow. Someone had drawn the blade from him and the giant was coming to kill us all.

I turned back for William, reeling, unsteady on my feet. A horse charged right by me in a clatter of hooves and a roar of anger from the rider.

Anselm, defending Marian from John, rode his sorrel rouncey at the giant. Dear, brave Anselm sat perfectly in his saddle and held his sword straight, in line with his arm, to pierce the man's huge head. But Little John roared, moved like lightning and smashed his sword into the rouncey's face before Anselm's point could reach him. The beast reared, throwing Anselm down onto the cobbles. His horse trod on him, crushing his chest and falling on him, legs kicking.

Little John stomped past Anselm and lumbered toward me, his blade high over his head, arrows sticking out all over his body, his face and neck covered in the blood he had drunk to heal his wounds. He was roaring with fury, spitting curses in a shower of blood.

I charged him. Using everything I had left, I stabbed my blade straight through the rusty mail at his chest, snapping the rings and breaking my sword blade in his heart. He fell to one knee and I smashed his face into pulp with my bare hands, breaking my knuckles, lacerating my skin. I ripped off Little John's helm, tore up a loose cobblestone and caved his skull in until his head was tatters and shards and a quivering liquid mass.

"William," I said, dragging myself to my feet. "Where is William?"

My injuries caught up with me at that moment and the ground rose up to crash into my face. The world faded into darkness.

It was Marian who saved us. Despite losing her father and almost losing her own life, despite the horrors of the carnage around her, she knew what to do. She was a sharp young woman and knew from travelling with Tuck, from the rumours about me and of course, Swein had told her about my drinking of blood. She knew well enough what I and her friend needed. God bless Lady Marian, for she cajoled the archers to give us blood from the men I had slain. Those poor archers later told me how they held a severed arm over my gaping mouth and squeezed the blood into me. It was only a few moments after that I came back to myself.

"Where is William?" I was saying the words before I was fully conscious. Marian had already left me to see to the other wounded.

"He ran, Sir Richard," an archer said, his face grim. "Don't worry, sir, we'll track him for you. Here, drink a bit more of this blood, my lord. Tom's getting you a fresh leg to drink from."

Eden was a bloody mess. The survivors were dazed and those that could continued to flee from the carnage out into the wood where they gathered together for safety.

"Jocelyn," I cried, recalling the horror of his charge. The archers helped me over to my man.

Jocelyn lay on his back in the centre of the courtyard. I gently pulled Marian aside from him. I removed his helm to give him my blood.

His eyes were already unseeing, his skin growing cold, his neck twisted unnaturally. I dripped my blood into his mouth anyway and reached under his coif to massage his throat. He was too far gone to swallow. He was beyond saving.

I sat back. I knew I should have felt anger at William and at myself but all I felt was a great sadness. Tears flowed down my face but I felt numb, as I usually did. The feeling was too great to be felt until later when the weight of his death truly hurt me. For months and even years after, I would turn to an empty room and begin to address him only to remember that he had fallen there in Eden. He had been my son, my sworn knight and my closest friend.

"I am sorry," I said to his lifeless eyes. "I am so sorry, son."

He had given his life to protect Marian and so doing had saved the rest of us, too. Marian threw herself upon his chest and wept, telling him he was a true knight. The truest, bravest knight who ever lived. He would have liked that.

I left Marian weeping for Jocelyn and went to find the others.

Swein lived. Though the young man was wounded, the cuts were not deep and two of his archers dragged him into a sitting upright and got a cup of ale into him.

"Will I lose my arm?" he asked, his face grey. "Please, I need my arm. I have to draw a bow. I have to."

"I suppose you are right," I said. "You are no good with the sword. Drink my blood, heal yourself."

He did not want any part of it but Swein wanted to live even more. He was young and full of life and he was unwilling to trade his future for his principles, such as they were.

Swein drank and healed completely.

Next, I ran to Eva. The poor woman had been hacked down with such force that her skull was cracked front to back along one side. Her hair was hacked off on one side, the remains stuck to the scalp by the shining dark ichor. I lifted her up from the blood-drenched cobbles. Her skin was white where it was not covered in blood. Yet she breathed. Her eyes flickered when I called her name and tilted her head. Faithful Swein brought blood from the fallen and I poured it into Eva's mouth. She coughed and swallowed it down. She fought her way back from death once more.

"What happened?" She coughed and grasped me, her fingers like iron.

I was relieved she did not remember the blow that had felled her. Recalling one death is bad enough. Near to us across the courtyard, Swein and Marian called for my help.

"Recover your strength," I urged Eva. "I must see to Anselm."

A pair of Wealden archers rolled the dead horse off Anselm's body and dragged him out from under it. They called me over, weeping in desperation.

"Please save him," Marian said, wiping her tears and many others pleaded for him, also.

The young squire struggled for breath through his crushed chest. But before he took his last breath, I trickled my blood into his mouth.

Like Swein, Anselm did not want it and he squeezed his lips shut.

"This will heal you," I said to him. "It will not change you into one of them."

Sadly, I was not entirely correct about that. I was giving out my blood left and right, thinking simply to save my friends and sworn men. But I had no thought of the consequences that ingesting my blood might have. A seemingly permanent side effect that I did not discover until later.

But in the courtyard that day, Anselm recovered from his grievous wounds instead of succumbing to them.

Everyone recovered but poor Jocelyn. I would have his body taken back to Ashbury to be buried. He would have made a good lord, I think and a good husband. But it was not to be.

While the Wealden archers under Swein's command hunted down the surviving sons of Eden, I found myself a new sword, a fresh horse and began the hunt for William de Ferrers.

The Lord of Eden had fled while Little John had attacked. Most of William's men were tracked and killed by Swein's remaining archers within the first day but William had slithered away into the wood like a worm. The Wealden archers tracked his trail too but he had melted into Sherwood.

Still, I followed. I searched. I scoured the wood and the hills. I kicked my way through barns and outbuildings. We searched the fens and marshes of the east. Some archers I sent south, others west while I went north to the Humber. After two weeks I had to admit that I had failed once more.

William was truly gone.

SIXTEEN ~ CAST OUT

"WE CHASED HIM FOR DAYS. I sent men in every direction. Your son, Anselm, was of great help as he can read the signs and tracks of men very well. I exhausted a number of horses chasing word of him. God bless those Wealden archers and the rest of their efforts. But every trail led nowhere. Then, many days after the scouring of Eden, there was a series of bloody murders in Grimsby. There was no doubt who had done them, as the bodies were rent at the neck and a couple of women went missing. By the time I arrived there, William was gone. Some said they recognised my description of William in a man who had been seen in the town but no one knew what ship he had boarded. So I fear it is beyond doubt that he has fled the country by now," I said. "From Grimsby, he could have taken any number of ships into the North Sea. He could be in France, Frisia or Denmark and from there he can go anywhere in Christendom. And beyond."

"That is a terrible shame," the Regent of England, William the Marshal said to me. "After all that you went through, to lose him at the last moment. A terrible shame. But you must not blame yourself, Richard. That man is a snake and a coward and he crawls upon his belly back to some hole instead of dying like a man. No, do not blame yourself."

It was the end of September 1217 and two months since we had destroyed Eden. We sat together, alone, in a small day room of the royal castle of Dover. The chamber and the castle belonged to King Henry. But since the king was yet a small boy, he was not in attendance. We sat by a narrow window overlooking the sea. Outside, the gulls cried their endless cries, wheeling and battling through the sky. The cold wind blowing through the window tasted of salt spray and reminded me of the battle I had fought outside. There were few remains of the ships I had burnt but still there were charred timbers here and there on the shingle. It felt good to remember fighting with Jocelyn at my side.

"I will find him," I said. "I have sworn it so many times that it may sound meaningless but I will find him, my lord and I will ensure he pays for his countless crimes." My shame at allowing him to escape was almost overwhelming. If only I had known then how long it would take for me to fulfil my oath.

"Of course," the Regent, William Marshal said, nodding to emphasise his sincerity. "Well done to you, nevertheless. You scoured him out of Sherwood. But, the Archbishop of York's tragic death at his hands leaves the kingdom with a chance to heal the wounds caused by the past few years."

The Marshal looked at me carefully, judging whether I had killed the archbishop, as I had agreed to do. William had killed him but I was willing to take the credit if it meant gaining a few more of the Marshal's favours. I had family and friends who had to be rewarded for their loyalty.

"I am glad to hear it and I sincerely hope that with his death, you can bring peace to the kingdom," I said to the Regent. "The whole kingdom, that is, including the men of the king's forests."

"Good God, not you, too," he said, scowling. "My son has been nagging me about the king's forests without let up. Penalties too harsh and rights not granted and officials corrupted. What have you done to him, infesting him with this absurd concern for the welfare of the residents of the forests?"

"I care nothing for those residents," I said, which was not at all true. "But you should know, my lord, how close to disorder the forests are. The penalties for the smallest of crimes—"

"Yes, yes," the Regent said, waving his hand at me. A tiny gesture but full of his almost total authority. "I have heard it all a dozen times, from Anselm and from a score of other men. Do not fret, we will issue a charter to remake some of the laws. Enough to keep the common men quiet and happy. And your friend Roger de Lacy will retire to his estates and keep out of everyone's business for the rest of his life if he knows what is good for him. I hear his wounds were so grave that he will likely be bedridden until the end of his days, which is probably what he deserves. I have given the post of Sheriff of Nottinghamshire to Geoffrey of Monmouth. A noble lad, if somewhat arrogant. My hope is that a position of genuine authority will be the making of him. The chief bailiff is Sir Guy of Gisbourne, who has agreed to remain. It will be beneficial for Geoffrey to have an experienced man who knows the land and the people."

"That is good," I said but of course, I did not mean it. Geoffrey was a petty, vile little tyrant and I felt sorry for the common people of that fine country. "When does the French fleet sail?" I asked. "They look ready to go."

The Marshal's voice, always steady, rose in anger as he spoke. "They bloody better well sail tomorrow or I shall burn the lot of them. Louis, Prince of France has sailed already, tail between his royal legs." William Marshal allowed himself a small smile. He looked old, thinner even than the last time I had seen him, but still he had a core of steel. "Had to pay the little shit ten thousand marks to get him to sign the treaty saying he had never been the king of England."

"Ten thousand marks," I said, whistling.

"I know," the Marshal said, grimacing. "But it was worth the price to be sure he can mount no objections and will not pursue any claim to Henry's throne. Not to the Pope or to his father or anyone. Henry will be the king of England. And none shall challenge him."

"I am sure that with you to guide him," I said, "Henry will make a fine king."

He waved that way as flattery. "If you would stay in England," William the Marshal said. "I would find a duty for you. Not simply instructing the king with sword and lance but with a proper place in court. He is a bright young fellow but he is rather godly. Already, the priests gather and whisper soft, holy words into his ear. I admit, I am afraid that when I am gone they will have him building churches rather than castles and raising cathedrals over armies. The boy needs soldiers around him to harden him into a man of action instead of a man of God."

"You honour me, my lord. I wish you knew how much it meant to hear you offer me such a thing. But I must find William," I said. "And cut out his heart." My own heart ached that it was not so.

"I understand," William Marshal said though he seemed a little irritated. Most men did not say no to the Marshal. "I am sure you will do him the justice due to him."

"A thousand deaths are not enough for William de Ferrers," I said, unable to keep the emotion from my voice.

"No, indeed," the Marshal said, solemnly. "But one will do, will it not?"

We shared a cup of wine and I was shown the door.

"And I must thank you," the Marshal said, grasping my shoulder before I left. His grip was like iron. "For leaving Ashbury to my son."

"Anselm earned it," I said. "And he will make a very fine lord and a good knight. It is not my place to say so but you should be proud of him."

"Be sure that you never tell him this," the Marshal said, lowering his voice. "But Anselm is my favourite."

∞

The Charter of the Forest was first issued by William Marshal in the young King Henry's name on 6 November 1217 and again in 1225. Amongst the articles rolling back the extent of the afforested areas, limiting the powers of the foresters and verderers were declarations I was certain had come from Anselm's discussions with his father, based on the injustices experienced by Swein.

There was an article granting that every free man can conduct his pigs through the king's wood freely and without impediment. And if the pigs of any free man shall spend one night in the forest, he should not be so prosecuted that he loses anything of his own.

Another article removed the punishments of death or the loss of limb for anyone taking venison. Finally, an acknowledgement in law that the life of a common man was worth more than the price of a deer.

And, finally, there was a general pardon for any man who had been outlawed for a forest offence. The king commanded through the charter that they should be released from their outlawry without legal proceedings after swearing that they will not do wrong in the future in respect of the forest.

So, Swein would be a free man once more.

The Charter of the Forest was drafted as a companion document to the reissued, rewritten Articles of the Barons. To differentiate the lesser Charter of the Forest from the other, the document dealing with the relationship between the barons and the crown was referred to as the Great Charter or Magna Carta.

The Marshal died a few years later, after seeing that his work was finally done. He had guided England through the greatest crises it had ever known. He had secured the succession and surrounded Henry with fine men.

Anselm was the fifth son. What was remarkable was that he did inherit his father's title in time. Every one of his elder brothers inherited the title in turn and then died without producing an heir. Poor Anselm himself died, aged forty-five and left no heirs of his own. The great estates of the Earl of Pembroke were divided amongst Anselm's four sisters.

The extinction of the male line is remarkable. I often wondered just how far William de Ferrers had seduced the lords of England. William Marshal's eldest son had been with the rebel barons before being welcomed back by his father. Was he one of the sons of Eden even then? That would explain why the young Marshal had freed me from the dungeon of Newark Castle. Had his Lord of Eden commanded him, so that I might run into Sherwood to be captured?

Perhaps the eldest of the brothers had brought his siblings over to Eden to be turned. Only Anselm remained beyond his grasp. And I had fed Anselm with my own blood, enough to bring him back to life. Had I saved the young man merely to condemn him to a life without the joy of children? Still, he died in his own bed with his dear wife at his side. Not a bad way to go.

But it was later when I understood these things clearly and by then it was already long past. We must accept what we cannot change, even if we were entirely at fault.

Despite the collapse of the Marshal family, King Henry ruled England for an astonishing fifty-six years. His reign was not necessarily a very successful or happy one. He fought his own wars against a new generation of rebel barons, including Richard Marshal. I was not in England for any of it, or else I would have happily slaughtered those selfish nobles. England would only be beaten into submission by Henry's son, Edward Longshanks, the Hammer of the Scots who was crowned in 1274.

But back in late 1217, I said my final farewell to the Marshal in Dover. Then Eva and I rode for the Weald.

We made it just in time.

∞

My dear Emma and William of Cassingham married on the steps of the parish church in Cassingham. Emma wore a loose dress so that her swollen belly did not show too much. But everyone there, including Cassingham's priest, was already so in love with her that they felt nothing but joy for the husband and wife.

So many people came to celebrate their union, I was astonished, although I should not have been. Cassingham was by then a living hero to the Kentish folk. He had protected them from the predatory French and everyone wished him well. And Emma was the kind of person that decent people loved. They flocked around her, every face grinning and winking and wishing them well. That was a kind of love and joy that was beyond me by then and, truth be told, probably always had been.

After the short ceremony on the steps of the church, there was a great feast in the village. Swein and Marian had both travelled to the Weald with Eva and me, for the marriage and also so that

Swein could accept his pardon and swear allegiance to the new king.

Swein and Marian would return north, to Sherwood, right after Emma's marriage and get there in time for winter. That celebration was the last time I saw either of them. We stood in the centre of the village, drinking ale and eating with gusto.

"The Marshal has awarded you some fine land in Sherwood," I said to Swein. "Now you have sworn allegiance to young King Henry, I suspect you will be returning there for good? Settling down?"

"Someone has to look after the good folk who live in the wood," Marian said, a twinkle in her eye. "And that will be me and Robin."

"Who in the name of God is Robin?" I asked Marian.

Swein rubbed the back of his neck and scuffed his shoes. "There was a man called Swein, up in Barnsdale where I'm from. He was a bit of a hero of mine. But Robert is my real name," Swein said. "My dad and my friends always called me Robin." He shrugged.

Marian looked at him with deep affection in her eyes. I remember thinking that it would be difficult for her to marry him, an outlaw commoner, but hoping that they would be happy in whatever way they could. Of course, they did marry. Who knows, perhaps they already had.

"You do not look like a Robert," I said, looking up and down his lanky frame. "Or a Robin. A heron maybe. Or a stork."

As it turned out, the man who once called himself Swein went back to Sherwood and that small band of Wealden archers went with him to take up their own lands they had been awarded by a grateful Crown. Sherwood had been badly depopulated by William's activities and the decent farmland was crying out for quality men to work the land again.

I have no doubt that Swein - Robin — meant to be a good farmer and to live a dutiful life within the law. However, within a few years, he was an outlaw again. Not only that, he became the leader of the outlaws of Sherwood and they fought to keep the new Sheriff of Nottingham in check. Luckily, he had that core of Wealden archers who became Sherwood freemen, to help him.

Geoffrey of Monmouth would turn out to be a deeply unpleasant, spiteful character. Of course, once he saw her beauty, Geoffrey became infatuated with Marian and he abused his position as sheriff trying to take her for himself.

Robin's love of disguises and stratagems came in handy over the years as he and his men looked to combat the corruption of the new sheriff and his men. Despite the sheriff's best efforts, nothing could separate Robin and Marian. He was another soul I had saved with my blood who never fathered a child. Despite that, I am happy that their life and adventures have grown into legend. Most of all I am well pleased that they found each other.

∞

"It gives me joy beyond measure to see you smiling and big with child," I said to Emma before I left England. "And I am so sorry that I could not protect Jocelyn. He would have been so proud of you."

Two days after her wedding, we sat close together on a bench at the top table in her new home, a large country house with a good hall and many chambers off either end of it. The fires burned hot, driving out the moisture of autumn. The servants brought Emma a steady supply of warm wine and morsels to eat. It was clear they were devoted to her, as were the other wives and older women of the village who sat in the hall, working and gossiping and throwing smiles her way. I was glad she would have women around her once again, especially once she began her lying in before the birth.

"I know you are sorry about Jocelyn," Emma said and reached up to rub her hand on my cheek just as she had done when she was a tiny girl, sitting in my lap in the Holy Land. "My heart breaks a hundred times a day when I think of him. I wish that he could share in my happiness. But he died a knight. You say he died saving Marian's life? He dreamed of such a death, ever since he was a boy. A death like in the songs. But still, my heart breaks. I think he would have made Marian a good husband."

I was not certain that the young lady would have taken Jocelyn even had he lived but I said no such thing to Emma and simply nodded.

"William the Marshal will see that Cassingham gets an annual payment every year for the rest of his life," I said. "And he has granted you both land and the rights to cut and sell wood in London. You will both do very well and so will your children."

"I swear that I do not mind you have left Ashbury to Anselm rather than to me," Emma said, smiling. "Still, I wish you would stay in England. Let William go. Do not waste any more of your life chasing after him."

"He has killed so many people that I love," I said. "I must pursue him, even to the ends of the Earth. And I cannot live in England any longer. For years already, they have been whispering about my eternal youth. I hid away as much as I could but how long can I live as Richard of Ashbury before I am driven out? In ten years, I will be almost sixty. What about ten years after that? And all the while, I will look like this. At least by leaving now, it can be in a manner of my own choosing rather than being hounded out by an angry crowd that believes I am in league with Satan. And I am not made for this land, I do not deserve to stay. I am not a good man, I know that now. I am a killer. I tortured a man, prolonged his wretched life and I did not feel guilty for it. I bring death to my enemies but also I bring my curse down upon those around me. I cannot fight it. I must go away. The Holy Land is the only way. I can move from place to place, selling my lance and sword. It is not a bad life. Bloody, perhaps. But better suited to my kind of evil."

"You are a good man," Emma said, firmly. "You are. I know it, even if you do not. Do not submit to the thought that you are the same as that corrupted lunatic."

"We have the same blood," I said.

"You think that is what makes a man or a woman good or evil?" Emma said, growing angry. "You are not a perfect knight from a ballad, Richard but you fight for the right things. You try, at least. You saved so many of those people in Sherwood. All those prisoners, I heard there were dozens. Just as you saved Jocelyn and me when we were children. You burned yourself almost to death in rescuing us. Would you have done such a thing if you were evil?"

"You were too young to remember," I said, certain that she knew of the fire from Jocelyn.

She fixed me with her beautiful eyes. "I remember everything."

"I pray that is not true," I said, recalling the horrors of that cavern.

"I remember being certain that we would never get out of that cage," Emma said, her eyes looking through me. "I remember the people screaming and the smoke. Jocelyn held me, sheltered me from the flames. He said to me, over and over, to close my eyes and that all would be well soon enough." She took a deep breath. "And then there you were. My father. You used your body to hold back the flames so we could get out. I remember your skin turning black and cracking. But still, as soon as I saw you I knew you would save me. And you did."

I had saved her by giving her some of my blood. Never had I considered that my blood might have been the reason she had brought forth her previous children before their time. Even the fact that she had ever conceived a child at all seemed counter to William's assertions about infertility. But perhaps it was because she had been so young when she drank that she had overcome it. Obviously, I said nothing whatsoever about this to her at the time, while she was great with child. I prayed that she would bear the child to term.

I took a deep breath. "I had no idea that you remembered anything of it at all. You were so young. I thought you would not remember me at all. And then I abandoned you."

"And it was years before I forgave you for that. But even then, we never doubted that you would welcome us when we came to your door. You never once begrudged us anything. You bought Jocelyn finer horses and armour than you had yourself. You welcomed into your hall men and women that you despised so that I might have the proper company." She laughed. "You are not an evil man. A fool for women, perhaps."

I took her hands. "I always hesitate to call you daughter. But if you were truly mine, I could not be prouder of you. Nor could I be happier."

"You are my father," Emma said, smiling her lovely smile. "In every way that matters. And you always will be."

Kinder words were never spoken and I remember them fondly. On dark, bitter nights over the centuries, I have recalled them and they have made me warm. For all I have done wrong and all I have lost, at least I did some things right.

Before I left, I took William of Cassingham aside. "I like you, William. I always have. But if you treat her and her children with anything other than profound respect then I shall return to England and cut out your heart, do you understand me?"

He looked very grave, swallowing but he looked back across the hall at his new wife before he answered. "Once, I loved fighting. I wanted to win a knighthood and be a great man. Now, all I want to do is make her happy."

I never saw Emma again. But I do know that she lived a long, good life with Cassingham and three healthy children, taking care of her own family and of the people of the Weald. It is my belief that she lived the life that she wanted and that she deserved.

488

∞

And so it was that I left England once more. I left behind my land. And my name.

I left with Eva. When she drank my blood after being drained of her own, she had become immortal, like me. The difference was that she had to drink blood every few days or she would grow weak, get sick and die.

After Sherwood, she had taken days to accept her fate while we hunted William. She never spoke very much and I fretted about what she would do. At times, she was angry and I knew not to speak to her. Other times, usually in the dark of the night, she would become disheartened and sit curled up into herself. I never knew whether she would welcome my embrace or angrily punch me away. I blamed myself for what happened to her, for leaving her at the priory was an inexcusable blunder.

At the time, I had convinced myself I was protecting her and Marian but really I wanted the women out of the way while I waged my war. Eva could have fought beside me on the walls of Lincoln and been safer than she had been at the priory but for all she had shown her ability, she was a woman and I had put her away. She had warned me, I had ignored her and she was the one who had paid the price.

I remembered how it felt to die. I remembered the fear and anguish that resounded after waking again like an echo in an empty hall. I remembered that the horror of it faded in time, like all things. So I gave her time. Whenever she would allow it, we slept entwined and I wrapped her in my arms through the darkness.

Eva had left the land of the living and dying. The consolation was her enormous strength and speed. And, I think, that at least I would be beside her.

Before heading south from Derbyshire that last time, we stopped off at Tutbury Priory in the dead of night.

I banged on the door of the prior's house. It took the young man a long time to answer, it being between matins and lauds. I knocked quietly but insistently.

He was muttering under his breath when he yanked the door open.

"This had better be—" Prior Simon started. He froze, dropped his candle and attempted to slam the door on me.

I placed my foot in the door. "My dear prior," I said into the shadows. "You sold out the innocent young women left in your care, do you recall?"

"I had to," he said, backing away. "They forced me to do it."

I pushed the door open, stepping inside, into the light cast by a single candle lit on the prior's bedside. "They paid you."

"It is my duty to do what is best for the priory," Prior Simon said, then gasped as Eva stepped into the room behind me with her dagger drawn.

"I will kill him," I said over my shoulder. "Then you drink his blood."

"No," Eva said, pushing past me. "I will kill him, too."

The prior's scream was cut off before he could utter it. We

490

filled his robes with rocks and slid his drained corpse into the fishpond and we watched his body plopping beneath the black waters.

"The monks are waking for prayers," I whispered to Eva and we rode south for the Weald. She wiped the blood from her chin and nodded.

After Emma and Cassingham's marriage, we went to Dover to catch a boat to Calais before the autumn storms ruined the short passage.

"I have to drink blood," Eva said to me while we waited on the cliffs of Dover looking down at the fishing boats bobbing far below beyond the beach. The thriving town was behind us. Down on the beaches, it thronged with fishermen and traders.

"You do," I said to Eva, standing close to her.

"I must drink blood every day or two in order to stay strong. Or I will become ill like that creature Tuck, ashen and green of skin and raving mad. So, in order for me to live, others must die. I know what you have said, that some men deserve death. I do not disagree. But there are not enough of them to keep me alive."

The sky was clear and light blue though the wind was growing colder every day. Though it was yet daytime, the crescent of the moon hung above the massive walls of the unconquered castle, higher up the cliffs to the north.

"You have never been to the Holy Land," I said, facing south. "You have not seen the rest of the world. Everywhere on this Earth, there is war. And anywhere there is war will be blood enough for the both of us. And whenever there is not, you will drink my blood," I said, looking out at the choppy waters of the

English Channel. "You can drink from me every day if you prefer. No one has to die for you to get blood."

She scoffed. "So you wish me to be as dependent upon you as a baby is on its mother."

She spoke half in jest yet the word fell heavy upon us. She had died, my blood had brought her back but she would never now create life from her womb. Eva was the first vampire that I ever created with my own blood. She would not be the last. Just as my seed was barren, all vampires that William and I made over the centuries were infertile. William had told us the truth, in that at least. Years later we discussed our first months together. Eva said she had half hoped we would have a child from our many couplings. It was never to be but already, in Dover that day, we were accepting of it. In fact, it drove us together even more because we thought that we would have no one in our lives but ourselves. We were wrong about that.

"I swear, Eva," I said to her on the white cliffs. "I swear that I will stand by you. Through all of this. Through whatever it is that we face out there in the world."

"We are leaving the land of the living," she said, reaching out to take my hand. "Destined to live on, ageless, undying. But never truly part of the world."

"Don't be ridiculous, woman," I said. "Our life is going to be full of wonder and beauty. And plenty of fighting."

"Is this some sort of marriage vow?" she asked, looking up at me.

"Yes," I said, squeezing her hand. "If you will have me." I held my breath. People said that I gave little away of my true thoughts and feelings but Eva was so much more difficult to read than I was, I am sure. Especially then.

Eva nodded, almost to herself. "Do we not require witnesses?"

"Who would we have to witness our union?" I said, smiling. "We are leaving England, so why would we need them? And anyway, whoever they are, we will outlive them. The only witnesses worthy of us are the sky and the sea and the moon above us."

"Well," Eva said, smiling, finally. Her face came to life. "Alright, then."

We sailed for France. We travelled to Italy, to Cyprus, to Outremer where the last Crusader kingdoms held on to their lands. We travelled to Constantinople and then back to Italy and France. We went to Spain and spent many years living in that fine land, fighting in the endless struggles amongst the Spanish kingdoms and against the remaining Moors.

We fought for one lord or another in many battles. I earned my keep as a guard for many a merchant. Sometimes Eva disguised herself as a man. When she could, she fought openly as a woman, though often that was difficult. Other times she had to put up with posing as an ordinary wife. We had to run from a number of towns and mercenary camps.

To obtain blood for us both, we killed men who deserved to die. Criminals, mainly and we fed well while punishing the guilty wherever we went. For a while, we kept a tavern in Acre and even tried farming, growing fruit and felling trees. We always went back to what we knew best, for I knew by then that I was not truly a good man. I was not a true knight. Killing and torture and blood by the bucket load were entirely my nature. But I tried at least to always be good to my woman. A sword in my hand by day, Eva in my bed at night and a belly full of blood as often as I could get it. And so we were contented.

Always, though, I knew that I would find William again somewhere, someday. It was many years later and the place was farther east than I had ever travelled before, to the grandest and most civilised city in the world. A centre of learning and culture the likes of which the world had never seen. The citizens were the most literate, the most highly educated, most cultured on earth. A city that was both a crossroads and destination for trade between China and Syria, Russia and Arabia. East and West. The greatest city of the age, Baghdad.

Amongst the beauty and riches, I encountered William once more. But he was fighting with the most terrifying warriors and agents of destruction the world has ever known. William had finally encountered an entire people whose love of mayhem and murder rivalled his own.

The Mongols.

AUTHOR'S NOTE

Richard's story continues in Vampire Khan the Immortal Knight Chronicles Book 3.

If you enjoyed Vampire Outlaw please leave a review online! Even a couple of lines saying what you like about the story would be an enormous help and mean the book is more visible to new readers.

You can find out more and get in touch with me at dandavisauthor.com

BOOKS BY DAN DAVIS

The GALACTIC ARENA Series
Science fiction

Inhuman Contact
Onca's Duty
Orb Station Zero
Earth Colony Sentinel

The IMMORTAL KNIGHT Chronicles
Historical Fiction - with Vampires

Vampire Crusader
Vampire Outlaw

GUNPOWDER & ALCHEMY
Flintlock Fantasy

White Wind Rising
Dark Water Breaking
Green Earth Shaking

For a complete and up-to-date list of Dan's available books,
visit: **http://dandavisauthor.com/books/**